The Legends of Valoria

The Last Paladin of Highmoore: Enhanced

By J.A. Bullen

To my Ash Rose, Mumma K, and those who have helped me keep the way. A special thanks to my fellow travelers, who keep my journey going.

Contents

Prelude

"You do not understand. I must leave in order to learn what it is these visions of mine entail. If I am right, then, the Destroyer is trying to return," the young, petite woman spoke urgently, her auburn hair pulled into a tight bun behind her head. Her voice echoed off from the walls of the marble chamber in which she stood.

"Talia, I have already told you, it is simply too dangerous for you to leave while the Forsaken are about." The blonde haired woman spoke through the hooded veil of her long black robes, her mysteriously blue eyes illuminating beneath the shadow.

"High priestess Angelica, I am telling you, I have not another choice. I need to learn what mine visions mean. If there is any chance that the Destroyer is returning, we must make any sacrifice to ensure that he cannot." Talia spoke firmly while feverishly whirling her fingers, trying to fasten her light grey cloak around her shoulders.

"Talia, I am not about to repeat myself again! You are simply too valuable for us to risk. The last priestess to be blessed with Aneira's sight died centuries ago. We must use your abilities for their true purpose, the return of Aneira." A large man with a thick black beard, armor gleaming gold, red and silver stepped forward and stood next to Talia.

"Mistress Angelica, I will travel to the shrines with Mistress Talia and ensure that no harm befalls her. I swear it on my very life." Angelica and Talia both grew quite stiff and uncomfortable.

"Sir Marec, will you make the blood oath? Will you swear upon your life and your very soul that you will protect Talia from any dangers that she may face?" Marec cleared his throat and straightened before responding. Talia shook her head interrupting Marec.

"Please Sir Marec, you do not have to do this. If anything were to happen to me then you would die."

"I am aware of the penalty for breaking a blood oath, though I am willing to go through with it nonetheless." Marec nodded his head, his stern expression unchanged. The black robed woman looked at Marec and nodded her head.

"Do this and I shalt not impede your path. However, I demand your return well before the eclipse. It is imperative that you be here in order to fulfill your true mission."

"I, Marec Kaldur, paladin of Aneira, swear on my life to protect the priestess Talia Degracia from danger." Marec continued with a sacred ritual that required him to make a small incision on the palm of his hand. A crack of thunder sounded off in the distance as Marec's blood began to glow brightly. After he was finished, Angelica contemplated in silence for a moment.

"Very well, Sir Marec, you are to escort Talia to the other shrines and help her decipher her visions."

"It shall be done, mistress." Marec clapped his hand to his chest while dropping to a knee.

"Thank you High Priestess Angelica." Talia graciously thanked the elder, black-robed woman. Talia and Marec left the grand temple of Aneira without further notice in order to begin their voyage to journey to the other shrines.

The Aneiran shrines, centers of religious salvation which are scattered throughout the continent, pay homage to the goddess Aneira, matron goddess of Valascaana and Highmooria. The Grand Aneiran Cathedral protects their principles, beliefs and traditions. This focal point of Aneira's power lies in Valascaana. It was once believed that the true shrine of Aneira, the original goddess spire, lie somewhere far to the west. The true spire was said to be surrounded by high mountains on all sides, only being accessible to the most worthy and capable of Aneira's children and was even rumored to house her throne. Despite the rumors, none have ever found the true spire of the goddess. Pilgrims from all across the continent flood to the gates of the goddess spire that rests within the Grand Aneiran Cathedral in Valascaana.

This imitation spire of the goddess, though not the original, still serves as a wonder of the world. The structure of the spire, rivals all other constructs on the Exodon, with its sky piercing height. From a distance, it is nearly impossible for travelers to see the highest floors of the tower, without peering through the veil of clouds.

It is not only the sheer size of the spire, which marvels the people but the interior as well. Carved from ancient stone, with a lost technique from ancient age, the entire interior of the spire appears to be made of marble stone. Endless, spiraling stairways, wrap the interior of the spire, which is connected to the Grand Cathedral. It is once you have reached the top of the spire that you come upon the true wonder of the spire, the oculus. Though none understand its purpose, or when it was created, the oculus when opened, allows the clearest view into the heavens, making it a well sought after destination.

Valascaana, as a whole, is a rich and relatively level country, filled with woodlands and plains. Traditional roads and caravan trails, allow for transportation of goods between the heavily populated cities of the nation. The capitol city, Valascaa, is a densely populated city. It is filled with rich heritage and residing upon the westernmost peninsula, is the largest port in the country.

Due to this, large assemblies of caravans often line the streets, transporting goods from the port to the other towns, cities and villages in the area. Most prominently; Roak and Kroas, in the north, Ternia to the east and the Grand Shrine to the south. Traveling diplomats, from across the ocean, also call upon Valascaa to serve as their home, when abroad.

Towards its southern borders, lie vast lengths of rolling hilltops, which eventually lead to the Grand Shrine, housing the Grand Cathedral, and to the ocean. The Grand Shrine, essentially a city of its own, houses much of the Aneiran order. Though most of its activities, happen upon the cathedral grounds, a small village does stretch out from it. Tall, stonewalls defend the shrine, and in the heart of the cathedral, lies the goddess spire.

To the far north, past the cities of Roak and Kroas, hidden from the world, lies the Vestigian Circle, a mountain range to the north, where proud cities were once carved into the mountain faces. Though the cities have been cut off from the rest of the world, it is here that Valascaana's main territorial enemy, the beastmen, hail from.

Looking upon the map of the Exodon, you will find Valascaana, resting on the western edge, while its sister, Highmooria, resides between it and the lands of the Forsaken, the Scar. Highmooria was once a rich, fertile land of endless forests, filled with natural wonders. It truly was a place of magic and miracles, most fairy tales in the land having been inspired by ventures into the Highmoorian forests.

Beyond the forests, other phenomena existed, one being Ariadne's Wood, a place where the great Nymph, Ariadne, created a safe haven for all creatures loved by Aneira. At the heart of her sanctuary, another shrine to Aneira, was built beneath the earth. Scholars believed that the shrine had been built by an unknown race of peoples but no record existed to prove such a claim.

Beyond Ariadne's wood, lies the heart of Highmooria, the capital city of Highmoore. The capitol city, crowned, the jewel of the Exodon, was surrounded by a number of high stonewalls, each housing massive fields for farming and even an entire city within. In the centermost wall, the magnificent Castle Highmoore rested proudly, the former seat of power in the Exodon. Beyond the walls of Highmoore, several cities, had chained together, to be close to the jewel. Now, no one, since its fall, has ventured through the mountain passes connecting Valascaana and Highmooria and returned to report upon its state.

The three lands of the Exodon, Valascaana, Highmooria and the Scar, were once one, in the time of Aneira but were soon separated amidst the chaos of a great war by an ancient evil, the god Daemon.

With Aneira's guidance, the lands of Valascaana and Highmooria defeated the forces of the evil god and struck a terrible blow to the land now known as the Scar. The Scar, once a rich country surrounded by beautiful mountain tops, grew tainted and barren Now, it holds nothing but deserts and wastelands populated by the descendants of the once mighty army, now the Forsaken, those banished and untouched by Aneira's love.

Over the millennia, the Forsaken have risen up time and time again but with each generation of Forsaken, legions of united Valascaans and Highmoorians have risen up to strike them down. The mightiest of the paladins, the fabled Sidonis was the last great paladin to face the Forsaken on the battlefield. His name became the legend that young men aspire to become. It was he, who founded both the Valorian knights of the capital city of Valascaa and the Aneiran paladins of the Highmoorian capital, Highmoore.

Two centuries later, the Imperial council, having long since lost the royal line that once governed them, rules Valascaana. Highmooria, which continued their sacred duty of defending the border to the Scar was lost eleven years ago to the last great tide of Forsaken who have all but disappeared. Now, the refugees of Highmooria reside within Valascaana, led by the Imperial council, have nearly lost their former heritage.

Deamon's forces quelled, the light of Aneira has spread to touch all corners of the Exodon. The children of Aneira sleep soundly in their beds for the darkness of their nightmares ceases to exist in the waking world, or so it is told.

Chapter 1 - The Burden of Youth

"*BOOM*," thunder roared in the distance preceded by the blinding flash of lightning. A young boy wanders out into the engulfing darkness of the night rubbing his white linen covered arms. He wore a green tunic and tan breeches but still the night air nipped at his small frame. He looks up to see the bursts of light raking across the sky.

"Rayne," the boy called for his younger sister while hiding under the small section of roof.

"*BOOM*," thunder crackled, preceded by a streak of lightning as it seared the sky only a second before. A thick curtain of bone piercing chill began to fall from the dark veil. Cursing the weather, the small, brown haired, green-eyed boy stepped out from under the wooden shield and shivered violently.

"Rayne!" He called again, taking another step forward and stopping suddenly at a particularly violent boom. The boy quickly reached up to shield his eyes from the lightning and after several seconds lowered his hand when it never came.

He looked up as the next flash of lightning, "*BOOM*," followed and another blasted sounds from the level of the ground. Staring into the uninterrupted darkness, he heard the sounds of screaming villagers.

"Rayne!" He yelled out again as he resumed his flight and searched for his sister.

"Alec!" He turned and ran in the direction of his sister's voice. His eyes gazed across the burning village, of large Highmoorian houses, their cores and rooftops ablaze with the dancing tongues of incendiary death. Alec ran around the corner passing the last house leading to the courtyard and stopped; his heart racing. Fire streaked across the opposite side of the road, people fleeing from the direction that he is headed. From between the overlapping walls of flame, he spied a group of men fighting, the sounds of their blades clashing drowned out by the roar of both flame and beasts.

Alec turned to his left as he saw a golden armored man, fleeing from the battle, two robed women in tow, one fully grown the other a child such as he. The girl turned and for a moment, their eyes met. Alec watched as the green eyes of the young woman turned back away from him and the three disappeared.

"Alec! Help!" The cry had become much more desperate than it had been previously.

"Rayne!" The boy dived through a wall of flame with no regard to his own safety and patted an ember out of his sleeve as he rushed forward. One armored man, bright with silver and red, noticed Alec's flight toward danger and tackled him.

"No, boy you cannot go that way, the Forsaken have marched on your village. Quickly, you must hide." Alec flailed and kicked against the man but lacked the strength to throw the man off from him.

"My sister, Rayne, I have to save her." Alec clawed in the direction he had been running.

"ALEC!!" This time, the soldier heard and released the boy who quickly squirmed to his feet and dashed alongside the soldier. They ran towards the sound of Rayne's voice, dipping and ducking between buildings in an attempt to conquer the labyrinth of flame that had descended around them. Three black-garbed men with masks and hooked swords marched in the way, blocking Alec and the soldier.

"Boy, draw that shield and protect yourself." The soldier tipped his head toward the body of one of his fallen comrades. Alec rushed toward the unmoving silver-armored man and grasping the shield received a good look at the insignia on the man's cape. It was a golden lion on its hind legs against a sea of red.

He pried the shield from the dead man's hands as the soldier raised his own sword ready to strike. With little hesitation, the three masked men rushed forward swinging at the knight who knocked away the blows with his shield and smote one of the men with a mighty blow of his sword. As the masked man fell to the ground, floating within the wind as if made of dust, his companions closed in on the knight and swung from either side. The knight did his best, fending off one blow but was sliced in his left shoulder by the other.

The knight grimaced as his shield fell from his crippled arm as he swung at his adversary who stumbled backward and fell. Alec clubbed the creature several times with his shield as the knight slew the third. Trying to catch their breath, the victors looked to one another and nodded when another cry rang out.

"Alec, help me!" Both the boy and the man ran between the flaming buildings around them and stopped.

"Aneira help us." The man shook as they came within only a few paces from another of the Forsaken and one of their pets, a massive black bear. This one, in particular, was much larger than any Alec had seen in the woods. The bear wore little armor, only on its body, legs with a spike collar around its throat, though the additions were highly unnecessary. The beast was at least twelve feet long with massive shoulders atop its even larger arms. Opposite of the bear, sat little black haired, freckle faced Rayne cowering beneath a wagon, clutching her most prized possession to her chest; a large speckled egg, she had found only a couple weeks prior.

The bear growled ferociously as it tugged against the chained lead bound around its neck, its handler keeping an unnaturally powerful grip on its pet. Rayne looked over, saw Alec beyond the bear, reached out to him, and mouthed the words, "save me." The beast master turned his hooded head toward Alec and the knight, revealing the metallic face partially concealed underneath. A hollow echo emanated from behind the mask, raised one hand to point at the two, and spoke in a foreign tongue that rang with the sound of scraping metal. The bear turned its head, as with a flick of the man's wrist, it was freed to barrel towards Alec and the knight.

Alec dove to the side and began to run to his sister. The knight spun outward in a half circle and with as much strength as possible brought his sword down over his head slicing into the shoulder of the bear. The bear fell onto the knight crushing him in the process.

Alec made his way to his sister as the metal-faced man stepped in his way. Alec lashed out at the man with his shield but was struck backward several steps when the man kicked the shield back into his chest. His lungs burning, Alec gasped for air as he reached his hands out to pick himself off from the ground and noticed the knight's sword. Placing both of his hands on the leather grip, he raised the sword to his side and bore down on his enemy as the beast behind him began to stir.

Alec cringed as the sound of the grinding laugh assaulted his ears and he turned his attention to the hairy monstrosity behind him. With a tip of its head, the beast let out a deafening roar and swiped a massive paw toward Alec. He barely stepped away to avoid the blow. Alec swung the sword at the mighty man who batted the blow away with a metal gauntlet as he stepped backward laughing. Alec prepared for another strike, while motioning for his sister to come out from under the wagon and carefully walk behind as he strained against the combined weight of sword and shield. As Rayne ran behind the protection of her brother, the small boy affirmed himself and took a stronger stance.

"Rayne run, get far away from here." He stood ready to do anything necessary to see his sister to safety. Rayne began to run when the armored man quickly threw out one hand and with an invisible pulse, shattered the building beside them, which crumbled to the ground and barred their path. Alec and Rayne trembled as the metal faced man laughed in his raspy foreign tongue. The bear pawed the ground angrily, pulling against its master's inhuman grip. Alec gripped the sword tightly as he felt an unknown power surge in his veins. His sword felt lighter, his body felt lissome, his limbs, powerful. He focused in as his vision narrowed and the world around him seemed to slow into a lulled daze.

Again, the bear roared as it stepped forward and glared at Alec for a moment before charging again. At his command, Rayne ran to the side as Alec stood his ground until the very last moment when he dropped to one side, turning enough to whip the sword across his chest. The sword panged loudly against the bear's skull and flew from Alec's hand as the beast roared in agony and batted at the long jagged gash Alec had cleaved stretching from the bear's jaw over its eye and across its skull where one of its ears was now missing.

Alec steadied himself and ran for his sword just as the bear turned and raked a mighty paw against Alec's chest and shield, sending it and Alec through the air. Alec hit a wall and lay on one side unable to move, a thick stream of crimson gore flowing from his chest. Blind on one side the bear swayed back and forth as its master tried to calm it. Alec placed his hands beneath and cried out in agony as the ruined flesh continued to rip and tear as he struggled against its handicap. He managed to place one leg beneath himself and called for his sister to run. Turning its head to one side the bear roared and charged at the only other soul within its field of vision. The little girl placed her hands in front of her attempting to shield herself.

Alec shot upright in his bed as the shrill scream of his baby sister, shattered his skull and tore out his heart. Sweat poured from his brow, looking down to his trembling hands and to the raked scar that ran down across his torso from the right side of his chest.

"Rayne," he whispered as he lowered his head into his hands and pulled at his hair as he rocked for a moment. His heart still pounding, he regained his composure and looked up from his lap across the room to his sister's keepsake; the egg that she had loved and treasured.

A light knock banged on Alec's door as he stared off into space, haunted by his moment of failure. The knock rang out again followed by the call of a young woman, which remained unnoticed by Alec. A third set of knocks echoed off from the walls.

"Alec, it's Eliza, I'm coming in." the young woman opened the door and walked in with one hand over her eyes.

"Alec put some clothes on we have to get moving. We have to get ready for today's lessons and prepare for the knight's trials." Alec slowly turned his head toward his friend. Eliza had long brown hair, green eyes, tanned skin and elegant features that would render her irresistible to any man though to Alec, she was more of a sister.

"I'm decent Eliza, come in and close the door please." Eliza did so without removing her hand from in front of her eyes and spoke again in her demanding tone.

"Well, if you are dressed then why are you not ready yet?" She finally removed her hand and saw the grave look on Alec's face and the sweat that decorated his brow and bare chest. Taking a more nurturing tone, Eliza sat on the bed and sweeping her long brown hair from out of her face placed her hands on Alec's right forearm.

"Was it the dream again?" Alec did not have to respond, Eliza had been Alec's closest friend for almost eleven years now, ever since the night when her father saved him from the Forsaken and had brought him to live with them. She and Alec were the same age and had grown a very strong sibling bond, often being mistaken for twins by other townsfolk. Even though they shared the same eye and hair color, little other resemblance remained. Placing one hand on Alec's back, she gently traced her palm across his shoulders in an attempt to slow his breathing and racing heart.

After a few moments, Alec calmed down and turned his head toward Eliza, who looked down to Alec's left hand, which still lay upon his chest.

"Your scar, does it still hurt?" Alec nodded his head. Eliza tried to suppress the worried expression that began to creep across her face.

"Alec, the healers told you that the pain must exist within your heart, with the exception of your scar, no physical damage remains." Alec looked Eliza in the eye and she caught a glimpse of the infinitely burning guilt searing within his heart. That night when the rest of the knights arrived, it had nearly been too late. Rayne was already gone, taken by the enemy, and the only reason Alec had not died with her was due to the arrival of Eliza's father. Somehow, the devil that was to claim him had vanished.

Alec's situation was so dire they had not even had the time to collect his sister's body. Thus, he had never been able to bury her. Eliza had been small then but she remembered the grave expressions that the men bore once they finally arrived home. They all seemed haunted as if madness had claimed them and despite the many times that Eliza had tried, she could never seem to steal an answer from any of the survivors.

Even her father, the knights' commander of Valascaana seemed to age well beyond his years whenever the subject was mentioned. Alec and she had on many occasions attempted to acquire records of that night but much with everything else, little record of Highmooria remained, especially of that night.

"Alec, I know you have heard me say this a thousand times and I am sorry that you lost your sister but there was nothing you could have done. Not even Father's knights were able to bring down that beast and its master. What could you have possibly hoped to achieve?" Alec did not answer. Eliza knew that no matter how much pain Alec suffered from that night he would never admit it. She had come to admire his strength but could not help but ache inside at the soul crushing anguish that she knew plagued his mind and poisoned his spirit.

"Come on Alec, please get ready and come to the sparring grounds. Will you please do that for me?" Alec looked at Eliza and knew that despite her kindness, he would rue the day he disappointed her.

"Let me wash my face." He rose from his bed and walked to the washbasin, filling it as Eliza began to close his door.

"I'll be waiting just outside, take as much time as you need Alec." She said and the door closed behind her with a gentle click. Alec slowly rose from his bed and lazily dropped to the floor to begin warming his body and muscles. He began to rapidly press out a number of pushups until his arms began to grow unsteady then he rolled to his back and began to exercise his abdominal muscles.

When he was finished, Alec rose, walked to the washbasin and began splashing the water against his face. He looked up at himself in the reflective surface of the water. He had spent most of his life since that night, attempting to press his body further and grow stronger so that he would never fail to save someone again. His body had grown and his muscles had become hard, firm and yet he still knew that he was not strong enough.

Alec turned his attention towards his wardrobe. Typically, it was customary of the Valascaan knight cadets to wear their uniform armor and tunics. They were blue, silver and white, bearing the crest of Valascaa, a white lion atop a shield before a sea of red. In Alec's case, however, he was Highmoorian and as such, was expected to wear garments and emblems that were representative of his nation.

This was an act to distinguish him from his peers to help show the worth of the Highmoorians and to give the council and the knights clearance, should he fail to become all they hoped. Alec thought of the countless people relying on him in the Highmoorian sector and swallowed his anger. He reached into his wardrobe and grabbed a red Highmoorian tunic.

Only a short few minutes later, Alec emerged from his room freshly washed, his sword and scabbard belted around his waist a red tunic with the crest of the old order. Now a revered symbol of the Valorian knights, it was a mythical creature with the head and wings of a hawk but with the body of a fierce lion. The symbol remained sacred. However, the Valorian knights were now titled the Valascaan knights. Alec had heard that once upon a time, the knights spread throughout the world and a great alliance was forged. The knights were a global force for good trying to stave back the taint of the Forsaken. Now, little was known of the outside world and former alliances no longer existed.

Alec squinted his eyes slightly, as the bright, morning sun assaulted them. He slowly opened them as they adjusted and looked around the marketplace district, just outside of the nobles' quarter, where he lived. The streets smelt of fresh food, lumber and other trade goods, accompanied by the ever so slight smell of manure, from the caravan horses. He saw the busy streets and the excited looks upon the peoples' faces, and yet, he saw the destitute, off in the corners, living off from the scraps of the prosperous, as well. Eliza turned to see that Alec had come outside and smiled at him.

"You wear the old insignia well. One day you may yet wear the Lion Hawk crest into battle provided you are accepted into the order of Sidonis. Perhaps then you could move into the noble's district with the rest of us." Eliza said.

Alec knew full well that he would never be accepted by the people. In their eyes, his common blood would be a stain upon their proud city. "Commoners" would never been deemed worthy in any way.

"You and I both know that the paladin order has not been the same since the fall of Highmoore."

"Perhaps you could be the one to bring back their glory."

"I think that you should both focus on being knighted first." The duo turned to the source of the voice to see the well built, fair-haired man if front of them.

"I would not worry about us Zelus, you should be more concerned that you do not embarrass yourself again as you did last time." Alec grinned as his rival's face twitched showing that he had struck a nerve.

"You only got lucky last time." The man glared at Alec with bright blue eyes his blonde hair shining in the sunlight.

"Lucky," Eliza laughed after saying it aloud. "You call it luck that Alec humiliated you the last time you challenged him?" Zelus grimaced, his pride beaten and bruised.

"If my sword belt had not been so loose, I would not have lost my footing and I would have easily overcome you." Alec and Eliza both laughed at Zelus' futile plight before Alec responded.

"Zelus, if you are feeling so confident, then challenge me to a rematch. I would gladly burn off some steam by reuniting your face with the floor." Zelus' cheeks began to glow a deep shade of red just before he excused himself and walked away from Eliza and Alec with only one last sneer.

"What do you think his problem is anyway?" Eliza turned to Alec who shook his head before he led the way toward the training grounds. As they rounded a final corner, they passed a massive marble statue of Sidonis, the paladin, who founded the Valorian knights. Alec paused and looked up into the strong, bold face of the statue and sank deep into wonderment.

Chapter 2 - Training Day

Valascaa, a rich and fertile land, is the only remaining capital upon the Exodon, the exiles continent. Its solid stone roads ran rich with history, the city having been rebuilt long ago after a long war. Centuries later, the city still stands as a sanctuary to those graced by Aneira's love. Once, two other powers existed, Highmooria and the long lost country that has now become the Scar.

No one remembers what the Scar was once called but it is said that it was once a cradle of life, lush and green. With the refugees of Highmooria now dwelling within Valascaana, the capital city of Valascaa had become rather overpopulated. Outside of its inner wall, lie the expanded common district, where mass numbers of the under privileged live.

For some Highmoorians, such as Alec, they were given the opportunity to mingle with others within the noble's district as a sort of social experiment proposed by the Imperial council and it was these chosen individuals who were ostracized the most severely. As much as they might try, and as much as they might endure and overcome, it was to their extreme disadvantage to allow anyone know of their heritage. The nobles of Highmooria of course were welcomed into Valascaa with open arms, though given the rights of second class nobles. Their numbers however, now only consisted of the elderly. All of their heirs lost in the fall.

With himself as an exception, the majority of the Highmoorian lower class, lived in the run down northern sector, which had previously been inhabited by the dredges of the city. Banding together, the new residents had made the best of it and were able to enjoy their lives in minimal comfort. For the few children that had been born after the fall, an orphanage had been set up at the heart of the district. Alec often frequented the district to play with the children who had never once seen the place of their birth.

There were others however, who had been welcomed in by nobles and allowed residence in some of their less luxurious homes, as was the case with Alec. The family of his best friend Eliza took him in and it was thanks to them that he was admitted into the knight's college as the council's latest social experiment. Should he prove himself a strong, noble and dependable knight then his people would be given a chance to join their ranks and finally, after eleven years earn their place among the people.

Alec stood within the center of the training grounds, which lie within the noble's district of Valascaa. The knight's college sat towards the back off to the western side of the district, enveloped on all sides by walls. To the south lie a residential area, to the north by the Valascaan cathedral and the labyrinth, a strange illusionary place which served as the final test of worthiness for the knights.

To the east of the college, one could see the palace, though for some time now, the throne had sat empty and instead Valascaa turned to its Imperial council for guidance and leadership.

Alec stood staring off into space within the middle of the training grounds as another of the knight squires launched blow upon blow unto Alec's shield. Alec continued to block the blows with little attention to his opponent until Eliza snapped him back to reality with an angry yell.

"Alec what are you doing, you idiot? Quit wasting everyone's time and fight back." Alec startled looked around in time to see another blow veering toward his ribs. With a quick parry, Alec caught the blade with the hilt of his sword and with a simple twist and flick of his wrist sent the blade flying through the air. Before the blade had touched the ground, Alec began to walk from the dueling circle, leaving his opponent bewildered. As Alec passed through the crowd of onlookers, Eliza reached out and touched Alec's shoulder, mouthing the words. "What is wrong?" Alec shook his head and shrugged before waiting for the next contender.

"Alec, good form but you need to pay more attention," Keagen, the knight's second in command chided. "I want you to run another round." Alec dropped his head slightly as he walked forward, catching the eye of Mariah Aetrian, a friend from his days in Highmoore. Unlike him, Mariah hailed from a Valascaan noble family, her father having married a Highmoorian woman. As such, after the fall, Mariah returned to the estate of her aunt and uncle. Having lost both of her parents during the fall, she was raised as an Aetrian and had disregarded her heritage as a Highmoorian.

"As Alec entered the ring once more, his opponent, another cadet one year older charged at him. Alec held his shield up to cover his chest as his adversary slashed. Alec tipped his shield and propelled the sword away from his body with little effort as he stepped forward and twisted his body. Alec's change in momentum atop of his opponent throwing himself off balance allowed Alec to easily press into him as he lazily tapped him on the ribs.

"Much better, Alec! The battlefield is no place to grow complacent" Keagen spoke as Alec again turned his back and walked from the circle, everyone's' eyes upon him once more. After depositing his shield on the weapon rack, Alec pressed pass the onlookers and assumed stance behind the group where he folded his arms and leaned against the wall. Eliza, wanting to duel next, walked into the dueling circle.

Searching the weapon rack Eliza pulled from it a scimitar, curved blades being her preferred melee weapons. She was one of the few women who had chosen to contend for the knights but as each of them had proven their battle prowess against their fellow students, no special quarter was granted and her opponent was a much larger, male candidate.

At the command to start, the man lifted his sword above his head and swung at Eliza. Eliza the creature of grace that she was sidestepped the blow with little effort and the man's blade struck the ground causing him to stumble forward.

With a laugh, Eliza readied herself as the man swung his weapon again, this time with more promising skill.

Opposed to attempting to parry the blow, Eliza simply back stepped and swiped her scimitar across the blade, propelling her opponent's claymore forward unbalancing the man where she simply tapped him on either shoulder and quite simply announced, "dead."

The man, feeling ashamed, walked away from the circle his head hanging low. Eliza approached Alec, who was otherwise, involved staring at the statue of Sidonis across the courtyard. He was studying the strong masculine features of the fabled paladin. He was tall and noble, a lightly filled out and dark beard which ran from ear to ear. His body was broad and muscular, the icon for what young men aspired to become.

"You didn't even wait to see how I performed?" Eliza asked annoyed. Without taking his eyes away from the statue, Alec answered in a seemingly bored monotone.

"I knew the outcome before I knew who your opponent was Eliza. There are few who can compete with you." Eliza smiled accepting the compliment as Zelus approached from behind.

"Alec, I challenge you to a duel of blades, do you accept or do you cower?" Alec gripped his right hand tightly causing the knuckles to pop and a smug grin to cross his face.

"I was hoping for some entertainment. I accept, unless your senses have returned and you wish to repeal the challenge?" Zelus smiled as well, pulling his weapon from its sheath and waving it through a few mock slashes before walking towards the center of the dueling circle. Eliza looked to Alec for a moment and shook her head in disbelief.

"You know I swear you two are perfect for one another." She giggled as Alec's expression changed from excitement to horror. "Alec, after the two of you are finished how about you and I walk over to the archery range, I would greatly enjoy the opportunity to work on my bow arm today I think."

"As if you needed the work, Eliza. You were practically born with a bow in hand."

"Regardless of what talents we possess, an accomplished warrior never lets their skill diminish, lest they be caught off guard and raw talent fails them."

"Your dad?" She smiled at Alec's guess.

"My mother." She triumphantly clarified. "My father may be the knight's commander but my abilities come from my mother's side of the family." Her smile persisted as Alec drew his sword and matching Zelus' approach grabbed a buckler and stared at his rival.

"Are you ready to lose?" Zelus taunted Alec as his friends smirked and laughed at Alec from outside of the ring. Alec eyed Zelus' entourage and smiled as each of them averted a direct gaze from him. Zelus was noble born, his mother died when he was young and his father was gone overseas tending to personal matters of the council, serving as an ambassador to a friendly country far to the west. It was Zelus who was the favorite among the cadets and though Alec suspected that he was indeed Zelus' only friend, he had managed to gain quite a few followers eager to ride his coattails. Alec turned his eyes back to Zelus and began to taunt him.

"Unless you awoke this morning an accomplished swordsman, then I think that your pride is sorely overdrawn." Alec raised his shield to his chest so that his neck and torso were protected and slid the tip of his sword over the top of the buckler.

"I am twice the swordsman that you are."

"Even with all of your lackeys to aid you, you are not nearly enough the swordsman."

Zelus was the first to strike, roaring out as he brought his sword down at an angle in an attempt to knock away Alec's shield. Alec retaliated by tipping his shield against the blow deflecting the weapon and countering with a thrust, which Zelus blocked with his shield.

"Come on Alec, wipe that smirk off Zelus' face." Eliza cheered jumping up and down excitedly. Alec paid little attention to the spectators but saw that Eliza, Mariah and several of the other cadets his age had swarmed around to see who would be the winner. Everyone was eager to see just who the best of the elite was.

"You can do it Zelus, you have been practicing night and day for this." Alec raised an eyebrow. It had not occurred to him that Zelus had been putting time outside of their duels in preparation for their fights. Alec smiled, hopeful that Zelus would be a more competent match for him.

The two of them let into one another, their blades dancing in a manic exchange of blows, blocks and ripostes, until their shields began to crumble and their arms grew weary. Sweat poured from their brows as they continued their plight. They both smiled at one another, as they bounded back and forth neither one gaining a decent enough advantage over the other to finish the fight. A commotion stirred from behind them as they fought but neither paid attention to their onlookers walking away as their swords began to chip and crack.

"I said fall into attention!" These were the only words that Alec and Zelus heard before a massive set of hands captured both of their blades and propelled the two of them through the air where they landed hard on their backs. Gasping for air Alec rose to a seated position and saw The Lion standing where they had just been.

"Yes, sir," the two of them yelled in unison as they scrambled to their feet and fell into formation with their fellow cadets, many of which were attempting to hold back a violent stream of snickers. The Lion stood upright his hands behind his back and looked at his recruits with a stony face. He was a man of above average stature, with the arms, shoulders and chest of a titan. He had dark brown hair, identical to Eliza's and green eyes. His beard was thick and dark, as well, which made him appear much more deceptively menacing than he was. In this case the look he gave Alec and Zelus, was already especially menacing and so his scowl looked as though it were filled with the promise of death.

"Good, that is better. I have come before you today, to inform you that the council has decided to test all of your abilities within a fortnight's time to determine who among you has proven their worth and is ready to be granted the title of Valascaan knight." Eying the candidates ever so carefully his gaze stopped upon Alec, Zelus and Eliza. Alec and Zelus cringed slightly and did their best to find a way to appear even more at attention.

"I would like to see the three of you in the commander's quarters after you have finished today's training." The three of them saluted and confirmed that they would indeed be there.

"Good, cadets fall out." All those that were at attention funneled out to various different places where they continued their studies of combat. Just before departing, Mariah stopped before Alec and nodded her head.

"You performed marvelously today, Sir Alec." She spoke as she passed by. After thanking her, Alec turned to Eliza.

"Your dad seemed to be in a worse mood than usual. What do you think the matter is?"

"I have not the slightest idea. I am worried, however he wants us to come by later this evening let us not worry about it until then. For now how about we go work on our skill with the bow?" Alec let out a slight sigh.

"You know that you are going to win. I may be the better swordsman but you have me bested with a bow."

"You are only the better swordsman, because I'm a swords woman. For all you know I could exceed your abilities in all of the combat disciplines." Looking to Eliza, he noticed her wink after her taunt.

"Hey now, there is no need for that. You stick to what you do best and I will stick to what I do best." She clapped her hand on his shoulder as she led him onward.

"Well then we will just have to find something that you are good at." She smiled as they walked towards the archery range.

Chapter 3 - The Priestess' First Steps

Talia searched her surroundings with unease as she walked the road leading away from the grand shrine, everything around her foreign and exotic. The roads exited the grand shrine from the south, east and west then wrapped around the shrine in its entirety.

They had opted to take the west road leading towards a small outpost town in order to gather provisions. As they left the shrine, Talia looked out to the sight of endless green hills and plains that ran to the horizon. She marveled at them for some time, as it had been the first time in over a decade that she had seen a view that did not contain the sight of the wall surrounding the grand shrine.

She took in a deep breath smelling a delicate hint of salt and remembered that very near to them was the ocean. She felt the cool spring breeze blow through her hair, her cloak flapping in the wind. She clutched it closer to her body securing its warmth, as Marec approached from behind her.

"It has been sometime since milady has been outside the walls of Aneira's sanctuary. My how things must be overwhelming." Talia turned to Marec her solemn pained expression, always marring her beauty, bore into him.

"It is rather a relief to be outside of the walls able to walk about and feel the wind nip at my cheeks. I have not been outside the walls much since the disaster when it was discovered I might possess Aneira's power of foresight and when they learned of it, I was cursed to a life of tragedy and imprisonment."

"Surely milady being able to foretell misfortune cannot be too great a curse." Talia turned back to Marec and he immediately sensed the error in his words.

"I was forced to predict the inevitable deaths of both my parents and my entire village and mourned their demise long before they were gone from this world, even now Marec if fate deemed it, I would know of your final hour and would have to bear the burden of the knowledge long before we were forced to depart. Surely, you do not believe that you would be of sound mind, knowing the fate of everyone you grew close to. Would you wish for me to search your fate?" Marec dropped to a knee and bowed his head addressing Talia as royalty.

"I am sorry milady, I had not considered the full weight and depths of your pain. Please forgive me?" Talia placed a gloved hand on Marec's shoulder.

"You are forgiven, my friend. It is not my intention to chide you, merely to continue on our way to the first shrine of Aneira."

"I thank you for your forgiveness. In regards to your offer, I must humbly decline. No one should know how they are meant to leave this world before it is their time. It makes people forget how to live, which is by far, worse than death." Talia nodded her head as she allowed the comment to sink in.

Since she was young, Talia had been given glimpses into the future. Glimpses that told her of the final days of those around her. It had been such a vision that had eventually led, to her being transported behind the high walls of Highmooria, though her parents had not survived the journey. Talia shook herself free of the thought and asked a question, which had been bothering her.

"How far away do you imagine we are to travel?" She asked Marec.

"Well milady, our first priority should be to head down to the stables and secure a couple of horses for ourselves so as to make our journey progress all the faster. I do not wish to tarry about when the matter of your safety is at hand. Surely, you understand the weight of my responsibility to protect milady?"

"Marec, if you please, refer to me as Talia for I fear that your sense of formality may expose us to more attention than we desire. As for your burden, I truly wish that you had not made the blood oath for my sake." Marec held out his hand to stop her.

"Please milady, you do me a most unfit service to imply that my life be of comparable value as yours. I have sworn my oath not for just your sake but for mine own and for the sake of all blessed by Aneira's love. To do anything less would have been to forsake my duty and name me among the unhonored dead." Talia took in a deep breath and deeming the venture fruitless, stared off into the distance for a time. Marec rose to his feet, eased forward and stood beside his charge.

"Are you certain that it is you that must undergo this ordeal? Why not leave the task to myself or one of the other warriors? Any one of us would lay down our lives for your sake!"

"And that Marec is exactly what I do not want. Only I will be able to learn the purpose of these visions but I must seek consort amongst the sages and pray to the statues of Aneira. The nymphs have grown silent; none have made contact save Aurora, whom stills ferries the deceased. I must know why I receive these whispers and for that, I must seek out the shrines. Only then, will the answers become clear to me and I will learn of what is in store for us." Marec remained silent for several moments, as did Talia. They continued their trek towards the village for nearly an hour and not one word was spoken. Finally, they came upon the tall wooden wall that served to keep out any unwanted visitors. The gates were open at this time of day as many travelers came in and out on their way to and from various places, from the grand shrine, to the capitol and anywhere else that people may have need to travel to.

They continued their stride through the village as Talia looked about from side to side, paying notice to the many different food stalls. She could see a large variety of fruits and herbs that she recognized and many other things that she did not. It had been made clear to her that she was not allowed to enter the kitchens of the grand shrine and so many of the raw materials that she saw before her were alien.

The few places Talia had been granted access to; her private room, the library, sanctuary and bath house, all under supervision. Her newfound freedom began to sink in deeper as nearly everything she bore witness to, proved to be a first experience for her. She was glad to have Marec by her side for this as well, fearful of the overwhelming number of things she was soon to face.

She thought to herself about how different life would be on the outside and she was eager to embrace it. Ever since she was a child, she had been doted and waited on every moment of her life. She could not help but feel that the change in pace would prove most exhilarating. They carried on towards the heart of the town until Marec addressed the stable master and requested two horses, after Talia refused to ride about within the confines of a carriage.

Talia turned away from the men as they discussed business and continued examining the small town. The town was not much to look at in comparison to the grand shrine, but it was everything that she so longed for in life. This life, the one that the people here lived was simple, quiet. She could not even fathom how much she would love simply to be able to live, as she wanted. As she continued to think about the freedom she longed for, she remembered her duty to these people and the overwhelming responsibility that came along with it.

As Marec continued to bargain with the merchant, Talia walked over to a nearby fountain where she sat along its stone border and looked upon the water. Reaching out, she danced her finger across the surface of the water distorting her own reflection until something presented itself within the ripples. Pulling her finger away, she stared intently at what she saw. The image she bore down upon was so heavily distorted the most that she could make out was wavy brown hair and what she could guess were piercing emerald green eyes, resting on a handsome face. She saw before her the literal man of her dreams. She had been having visions of the same boy for nearly a year and it was with him that her dreams lit up her heart. She only hoped that one day she could meet this boy, the beautiful boy with the emerald green eyes that matched her own.

She neared closer to the surface as the water settled more, when the sound of Marec's voice broke her concentration. Startled, she looked away for only a second and when she turned back, the man's face had vanished.

"Yes, Marec?" she spoke to him trying not to allow irritation to accompany her voice.

"I am sorry milady. Have I disturbed you?"

"No Marec, of course not. Please do not refer to me as milady any longer."

"Of course, my apologies, it will take some getting used to milady." Talia closed her eyes and accepted that Marec would try. The mare that Marec presented to Talia was indeed beautiful. She was a chestnut horse with white on her flanks and up the middle of her snout. The horse looked at her with her large watery eyes and sniffed her hand as she held it out to her.

"What is her name?" She looked to Marec as she accepted the reins.

"The man named her Windsong. He says that she is a fine mare and that she will serve you well." Talia began to climb onto Windsong as Marec, to her irritation insisted on aiding her. After Marec mounted his steed, a red stallion by the name of Rinak, named after an old warhorse, he and Talia turned their horses and steered them through the town where they would gather supplies and then truly head out on their voyage.

Chapter 4 - The Chosen Cadets

"Come on Alec, she is beating you." The crowd jeered as Eliza sank another arrow into the deep red center of the bulls-eye. The archery range was located near the dueling grounds and had been a quick walk for them. Several other cadets were practicing not far from them as Alec and Eliza were locked in competition.

"That makes four more than you Alec. Your shot," she smiled as she turned on a heel and pranced away from the target. Alec approached, taking up stance where Eliza had just walked away from and knocked an arrow. Alec stared at his target as he raised the bow and pulled the string tight. The center of the bulls-eye grew in his gaze as he focused upon it. He drew in a deep breath and readied his release.

An image of a woman flashed before his eyes, clouding his vision. He stared into her beautiful emerald eyes, distracting his mind. She turned to him and smiled, making him forget to breath.

"Alec!" He jumped, startled from the sudden outburst and his arrow struck the outer ring of the target. The spectators laughed as Eliza raised her arms into the air in triumph. Alec stood staring off into space as everyone congratulated Eliza. Eliza turned from her entourage and eyed Alec suspiciously for a moment.

"Hey, everyone, get back to training. We will catch up in a minute." Eliza turned back and walked towards Alec.

"Ha ha, look at him, dumbstruck because he lost, how sad." A random spectator uttered a last remark as they walked away.

"Alec, what is the matter?" Eliza placed her hand on his shoulder. "Are you alright?" Alec just shook his head for a moment before looking at Eliza.

"Just confused or daydreaming I guess." He finally averted his gaze from the target and walked forward, to begin retrieving their arrows. Placing her hand over his much larger hand, Eliza tried to pull Alec's attention back.

"Was it her again? Did you see that woman again?" Concern poured from Eliza's voice. Alec nodded.

"In the middle of the day? I thought you said that you only saw her in your dreams?"

"That's the trouble Eliza. It is not just in my dreams anymore. I am seeing her during the day now, while I am awake and walking around. I do not know what is going on."

"Well, how about we take you to go and see the medic?" Alec looked at her with a look of surprise.

"I am not sick Eliza. I do not think that a trip to the medical station is going to help me." He turned his gaze toward the city walls before turning back toward the post, removed his final arrows and walked away. He looked around, seeing the other cadets, practicing themselves as Eliza accepted her arrows from Alec.

"Alec, are you sure that you are going to be alright?"

"Come on Eliza, your dad is waiting for us." Eliza attempted to vent her frustration and followed Alec.

"Ah, Zelus, Alec and Eliza I was wondering when the three of you would stop by. I take it that you are already aware of the purpose for our meeting?" The tall, broad shouldered man stood at ease, looking out the window that loomed over the training ground.

"Yes commander," the three of them spoke in unison.

"No need to be so formal at the moment. Eliza, congratulations on yet another victory on the archery range. Alec, you need to work on your discipline." Eliza and Zelus turned, smirking at Alec who squinted slightly and let out a slow breath.

"The reason that I have brought the three of you together is to inform you that tomorrow morning, you will finally be undergoing your knights' trials." All three cadets smiled this time.

"You will meet at the proving ground, at first light tomorrow. Now, please take the rest of the day to prepare for your trials." The three of them left the room, Eliza glancing back over her shoulder at her father as she passed through the doorway.

"What is your plan for tomorrow?" Zelus asked Alec and Eliza as they walked through the courtyard.

"What do you mean?" Eliza asked.

"Well, we are likely to be in the same group as the trials are set to be overcome by a team. I was just wondering what the two of you had planned?" Again, Eliza answered.

"We will just have to go in there, watch each other's backs and forge on through anything that comes our way. What other plan do we need besides that?" Alec smiled as Zelus looked to her with an oddly concerned expression.

"What is the matter Zelus, you hoping Eliza will protect you?" Zelus looked away not ashamed but embarrassed by his true reasons, Eliza however, turned on

Alec.

"See this is the problem with you two, always after one another trying to rouse the other into a confrontation. Zelus, we will see you in the morning and decide what to do then, alright?"

"Fine, I will see the two of you in the morning." Zelus stormed off and Eliza let into Alec once more.

"What is your problem with him anyway? Sure he is weird and overly energetic but what has he done to you, to make you hate him so?"

"I do not hate him Eliza. And after that, I do not see where it matters." They had reached Alec's quarters by then. Alec opened the door to his house and walked inside, setting his things on the table. He sat across the room from his window and stared intently at Rayne's egg. Eliza walked forward, sat next to him and stared at the large white and brown speckled egg.

"You will do a fantastic job tomorrow, Alec. You have trained harder than anyone else, in the cadets has. You are not about to fail tomorrow."

"I am not worried about failing the trials. I am fine Eliza," he flashed a smile that could have fooled anyone else. With a soft sigh, Eliza shook her head and placed a gentle hand upon the egg, which felt warm to the touch.

"May you not be so burdened, little one." She walked away with a wave and closed the door behind her. Alec sat in silence for several moments before he too, approached the egg and placed both hands on it. As it always did, the egg was warm within his hands and pulsed, the heart of the creature within beating strongly. Alec smiled as he recalled the day that his sister had found the egg, while out in the woods one day.

"Rayne, where are you?" The seven-year-old Alec searched about for his five-year-old sister.

"Rayne, come on. Where are you? Seriously, it is time to go back. Grandmother is going to be worried" Alec called for his sister once more when he heard a rustling in the bushes and his tiny sister appeared straining to carry an enormous oval half her size.

"Rayne what is that? Put it back." A wide, foul tempered look crept across her face and she began to fuss.

"No, I am going to keep it. It is my baby." She yelled at Alec and clutched her possession tightly.

"Rayne, come on. Do you not think someone or something is going to come looking for it?"

"No, it was just sitting by itself. I found it while I was picking flowers for Gram and I am going to keep it." Again his sister took a more ferocious stance, gripped her treasure tighter and attempted to move around Alec who remained in her way. With a deep sigh Alec gave in to his little sister's stubborn behavior.

"Fine, you can take it back to the village. We will see if Grandma knows what it is, but will you at least let me carry it?" He smiled at the end of his question seeing his sister's entire body quivering from the strain of holding the egg.

"Okay," she handed the egg over to Alec who was shocked by its weight, but still easily managed it and made sure that his sister led the way back to the village.

"So, what do you think this is?" he asked her on their way back.

"It is an egg silly, can you not feel the baby inside?" Alec stopped for a moment and realized that she was right. He could not think of anything else that it could be.

"Well then, when it hatches what are you going to name it?"

"Oswald." His sister blurted out as if she had spent several long hours in deep contemplation.

"Oswald? What if it is a girl?"

"The baby's name is Oswald! Or Oz!" Rayne answered. Alec thought to himself for a moment, shook his head and smiled letting the moment pass as he and his sister came to the entrance to their village.

Alec's eyes focused on the present as he continued to stare at the egg in front of him. He swiftly reached up and wiped away the single tear that sparkled in his eye and turned away from the egg and walked outside. Though nighttime had not yet arrived, the air had begun to grow brisk. Alec took in a deep breath of the spring air and exhaled.

As he looked up to the walls of the city, he saw that the evening beacon had already been lit, as it had each and every evening since he had been brought to Valascaana. As he walked, many acknowledged his passing with a simple nod. Alec walked to the academy grounds and stared at the many statues that were scattered about.

He knelt down before the statue of Sidonis and imagined to himself, how the legendary man must have been in life. He recalled the few stories he could remember from his grandmother, of Sidonis, Aneira and her Nymphs. He could recall a number of different Nymphs from the stories. Some were guardians of nature, while others existed to serve as messengers of the holy mother.

Still others existed, which he was less familiar with. Those who had served to aid the paladins, in their training and their mission. There were others still, who served as muses to inspire music, art and culture. Of all of his grandmother's stories, he could still only recall the name of one Nymph, their leader, Aurora.

Alec rose from his kneeling position and walked on towards the temple grounds. As he walked, he noticed as the night guard began lighting the evening torches. He continued his solitary walk as he saw the lights of the temple, still lit in the distance. Alec walked towards the light and smiled as the head priestess, Mayella, greeted him. She was a short, petite woman in her later years. She had grey hair and a warm, kind smile.

"Good evening, young Alec. What brings you our way at such a late hour?" Alec was unsure himself and was lost for a cohesive response.

"I suppose that I just was not ready to turn in. I thought that I might enjoy the evening air and clear my head." Mayella smiled.

"Then by all means, come inside for a spell. You are always welcome in the home of the holy mother." Alec looked around curiously, looking to see if there were any of the noble class about. Mayella sensing what Alec was looking for, placed a gentle hand on his shoulder.

"None in here except the other priestesses, the lady Kaldur and the presence of the holy mother." Alec nodded his head as he allowed Mayella to guide him inside. Alec had not spent much time within the temple, as the nobles of the city often frequented the site and were yet unpleasant to him.

He looked up at the high walls and to the stained glass depictions of the holy mother, the Nymphs and Sidonis. As he walked further within, he saw Kristiana kneeling up ahead before the grand altar, head down in prayer.

"I beg of thee, oh holy mother, please allow her to find rest." Kristiana looked up at the statue of Aneira and kissed her closed hand before touching the space just below the goddess' feet. Kristiana stood and brushed out the wrinkles in her purple dress and smiled at Alec and Mayella.

"My, my, Alec. It is a most pleasant surprise to see you here of all places, even at such an hour. What has brought you here today?" Still at a loss of an answer, he hesitated only for Mayella to answer.

"I feel that our young friend has been stricken by the illustrious call of his destiny approaching. He has long since reached the end of his childhood years and has now come upon the eve of his proving. Tis a most confusing time, for any youth."

"I remember well, high priestess Mayella. However, I believe that young Alec shall have naught to worry. You will perform most admirably tomorrow, as always." She smiled at him as Alec saw bookshelves to his left, covered with a massive number of literary secrets. Mayella turned her head to see what Alec was looking at and smiled.

"You are more than welcome to look, Alec. Pleases me to see a youth that still values reading."

"Thank you, if you please excuse me." Alec spoke as he walked over to the bookshelves and began to look upon the various titles. There were numerous books, which contained information on the history of Valascaana, scriptures of Aneira and various other subjects, which held no bearing for Alec.

"Having a difficult time deciding?" Mayella asked. Alec looked back at her and smiled.

"I have read many of these. I am just not sure that I was in the mood for reading is all." Mayella smiled once more.

"Perhaps on your next visit, I shall show you my library. Mayhaps there is something there which you have not yet feasted your mind upon."

"Thank you, lady Mayella. Good evening, lady Mayella, lady Kaldur." They all bowed their heads to one another as Alec left.

Once back outside, Alec again took of the cool evening air and continued his walk around the capitol. He thought to himself of the woman he continued to see in his dreams and wondered if perhaps after tomorrow, he would be on his way to finding her. As he looked out to the high walls of the city he remembered everything, which rode on him tomorrow. Alec took one last deep breath before heading back towards his home.

Back within the confines of his home, he laid out his things for the following morning. He turned back, said goodnight to the egg and went to his bed to rest for the coming day. As Alec's eyes closed and he readied himself to fall sleep, he failed to notice that the egg across the room for the first time in eleven years began to stir.

Chapter 5 - Troubles Along the Road

"Hurry ma'am, we must get behind cover before we are spotted." Marec pulled the reins of both horses urgently trying to hide them behind a couple of boulders that lay off from the main road. Talia quickly dismounted her steed and crouched low behind some bushy vegetation that was common along the mountainous terrain.

"Who are they Marec?" Marec dared not take his eyes off from the band of black cloaked figures that marched down the road.

"Those are the Forsaken, but what they are doing this far into the country is beyond me. It is even stranger, yet that so few are along the road. Normally, they would not dare come this far into Aneiran lands unless they were part of an invading war band." Talia tried to shift so that she could better see the mysterious wanderers.

"They do not look so imposing to me Marec. Why then do we hide amongst these bushes as if we were but common thieves?"

"Mistress!" Marec barked. "You do not know the ferocity with which the Forsaken bring death to the battlefield." Talia continued to watch the five as they neared them and marched past. She could see more clearly, there were four large armored men marching with a much smaller, cloaked Forsaken, which might have been a child. The four that wore armor, stood behind the smaller one as they walked down the road. Beneath their hoods, Talia could make out the black horned armor and metal faces.

"Are you saying that the mere five of them would be a threat to a paladin of Sidonis?"

"No, my lady, it is not that, it is merely how many more that could appear if these came up missing. Worse, if one reported that we had been spotted. Even if they do not know of who you are, we must keep you concealed. If there was a spell caster among them, then things could prove all the more perilous." Talia focused intently on the five before them and felt a slight hum, emanating off from the smallest.

"There is one among them, who possesses the ability to channel spells. I detect their energy is not quite the same as the others. Perhaps it is similar to mine." Talia spoke as the smallest of the Forsaken turned its head up towards them. Marec and Talia quickly ducked down behind cover as the armored Forsaken turned their attention as well.

"Your benevolent sight never ceases to amaze me, my lady." He spoke from behind cover and waited, peering through a tiny gap in the bush. He watched as the smallest of the Forsaken turned its head away, as did the others. After a moment, the paladin bowed his head and glanced back to be sure that the Forsaken were gone. "Aneira favors us. They have left and on a different route than ours."

"Good, then would it be alright for us to get out of the dirt now?"

"Yes, of course, my lady. Please forgive me."

"Marec, please stop referring to me as 'my lady'. You told me you would desist."

"I agreed to no such thing, only to address you slightly less formally whilst among the common people and, as only you and I are here, "my lady," it is again." Talia sighed in frustration but did not further press the issue. She had accepted being pampered, spoiled and awed at as the first to be gifted with Aneira's sight in over two centuries but never had she enjoyed the experience, longing for a more simple life. She sighed again, knowing that such things were not for her. She continued to ride on for several hours before stopping at an outpost to rest, as the sun dipped down beyond the mountain veil.

As they entered the outpost, a guard stopped them and asked for their names and intentions. Along the way Marec had concocted a story, his name was Farus, he and his daughter Relina were traveling and were hoping to rest the night at the outpost on their way to Ternia. After hours of recitation, Marec and Talia were able to explain their story to the guardsmen with such conviction he finally warranted for them to enter the city. The gates swung shut behind them causing the horses to nicker slightly. Talia and Marec ventured into the local inn and Talia took a seat at the table as Marec spoke to the innkeeper in order to secure a room for the night.

"Anything I can get for you darling?" Talia looked up to see the waitress standing in front of her waiting for a response. The woman was older than Talia, but not significantly. She was tall and had long brown hair. She spoke with a strange accent that Talia had listened to many of the townspeople speak in. She stood in front of Talia with her hands on her hips, yet a friendly smile on her face.

"Umm, I uh, no thank you." Talia attempted to hide her face as the waitress bore into her with a wide smile.

"Don't worry about money hon', I'll at least bring you some water." The waitress returned only a short few moments later with a glass of water and a plate of bread and cheese as well. Talia attempted to refuse the plate, but the waitress insisted that Talia looked as if she were hungry and that she wasn't to worry about it. Grateful for the act of kindness, Talia nibbled at the food in front of her, watching intently as Marec spoke with the innkeeper. As she watched the two men laugh merrily, she could hear the slightest of whispers from somewhere around her.

Talia searched all around her, but could see no one speaking to her. Shifting in her chair to be sure no one was behind her and still she could hear whispers. Hoping that she had not drawn much attention to herself, she slowly faced forward and placed her hands in front of her on the table. She tried to instead, focus on the whispers. She looked down at her soft tiny hands and saw an image within the water glass before her.

Awed, she leaned her head forward trying to look as though she were tired and not taking an invested interest to the glass that sat before her. She watched the images flicker back and forth and could still hear a young man and a woman speaking. She watched intently and recognized the soft wavy brown hair and piercing green eyes. This time she caught a glimpse of the man, and as always, found him to be quite handsome. Indeed, the butterflies in her stomach started fluttering about. As she continued to admire the image before her, she could not help but notice the great deal of pain behind his eyes that greatly resembled hers. She tried to catch a glance at the woman that he was speaking to, but instead caught something much more interesting. She noticed the two words in their conversation that summed up everything that was concerning her; "Lion Hawk".

Chapter 6 - The Lion Hawk

Alec stirred in his sleep to a strange, low-pitched rumbling that vibrated his chest. He shifted to his side in an attempt to ignore the noise, but the rumbling grew louder and this time he felt a warm pressure on his chest along with the vibration. Alec lazily opened a single eye and strained to look down at what was upon his chest. It was hard to make out in the dull light, but what shape he could make seemed to be that of a cat's paw.

"Weird, I did not know I had a cat." He murmured sheepishly to himself as the eye he had opened, closed and he began to drift back to sleep. He lay there for a moment with no idea as to what was going on about him.

"*Mweerp reep reep.*" The odd noise with the brushing against his cheek was enough to cause Alec to bolt upright; frightening whatever it was that had been next to him. He caught a glimpse of a tail flitting through the air as the creature leapt under the bed. Alec quickly jumped to the other side of the bed, drawing his sword and lit the lamp by his bedside. Lowering the glowing orb to the floor, Alec readied his sword to thrust as he crouched down to peek at the creature.

At first, he saw nothing of note, just darkness but as he pushed the lamp forward, the veil of darkness shifted and he could make out the slightest sign of feathers. He pushed the lamp just a little bit closer and confirmed his footing before reaching out to prod the creature.

"*Mweerp mreep kreep.*" He could hear the creature chattering at him. He tried to get a better glimpse of it but sensing no malicious intent, he began to speak to the small bedtime intruder softly.

"Hey little guy, let me get a look at you." As if understanding, one of the feathery arms moved revealing the shoulder joint of a wing and a pair of hind legs. A tail belonging to a large cat also appeared. Alec leaned his head to the side and saw the head and neck of a baby hawk peer out at him.

"*Mreep?*" The creature chirped at him again and Alec felt as if immediately that the creature was his to protect. He lowered his sword and instead reached out a hand toward the creature. He touched the tip of his fingers onto the flank of the baby and scratched gently across the fur. The rumbling sound from before started up again and this time he recognized it as a purring sound similar to that of a cat. He smiled as he stroked the creature's flank some more. The purring intensified and the baby brushed its head against his arm as he did so.

Alec examined the griffet carefully; its large intelligent brown eyes, its white and brown head and white feathered neck gave way to its tan fur. Between its shoulders sprouted two large jointed wings filled with bright brown, gold and white threaded feathers. Alec followed the baby's body down to its front and back paws, seeing that all four were massive for the size of the baby. They resembled those of a jungle cat. Alec followed the rest of the body down towards the tail, which ended in a whip like a lion.

Withdrawing from the bed, Alec backed away slightly and motioned for the baby to come out from underneath his cot. The creature followed the motion of his hand and eventually he had coaxed it into leaving the underside of the bed entirely. Alec sat down and the babe jumped onto the bed and lay next to him with its head and paws resting on his lap. Alec gently stroked the creature and scratched it along its neck. Instantly, he felt overwhelmingly drawn to the creature as if it were his own child.

He sat in silence for a moment and looked down to the creature, which looked back to him with a fierce intensity within its large brown eyes.

"I need you to stay here for a moment and be good, alright?"

"*Brrrr reep breep.*" The Lion Hawk responded.

"I'm going to go and get you some food, alright?" The baby purred at the sound of that. Alec rose and headed toward the door and the Lion Hawk hopped down and began to follow him. On all fours the griffet's body stood just below Alec's knee and it was almost as long as a full grown house cat. Its wings, when outstretched, were not yet much larger than a couple of feet in length. He knew that they were bound to grow much larger. Alec guessed from its size that it weighed near twenty to twenty five pounds at least. He began to prop open the door and the baby nearly pushed its way out before Alec could stop it.

"I need you to stay here little one, I promise that I will be right back." The Lion Hawk looked at him with sadness in its eyes, breaking Alec's heart as he exited and began to close the door behind him. Realization pounded down onto him as he walked down the street and leaned his back against a wall. He ran his trembling hands through his hair and began to dwell upon the sudden change in his situation. He was soon to undergo his trials and he knew not the outcome of them. He had never imagined that Rayne's egg would hatch and when it had he had thought that it would be after he had already been knighted.

"What do I do? Will they let me keep him?" He looked back to the door of his home and continued on his way toward the kitchen. An overwhelming sense of loss and yearning pierced his heart and burned in his veins at the thought of losing his sister's Lion Hawk, his Lion Hawk. He managed to grab a small amount of meat and some milk from the kitchen. He only knew of one solution to his problem, so he took a slight detour and gently knocked on the door in front of him. There was no answer from the other side and he could not afford to be any louder. He searched all around him for signs of any onlookers. When he was certain that it was safe, he gently twisted the door handle and found it to be already unlocked. He pushed the door open, and Alec entered the home. Being careful to creep through, Alec walked across the house and crept up the stairs. He stopped in front of Eliza's room and gently cracked open the door.

"Eliza." Alec whispered into the darkness of the room. He peered in a bit more and whispered her name again, only slightly louder, but still she did not answer. Stepping fully into the room he closed the door behind him and crept up to the bed. He could see Eliza's silhouette from where he stood and slowly he reached out and touched her shoulder.

"Eliza…"

"Hyaah." Alec jumped backwards as a sword whipped through the air passing just to his side as he dove to the floor. With a flick of the covers, a blanket flew over top of him and he struggled to free himself from under it as he called out her name again.

"Alec?" She held her sword above him, her weapon poised in a killing strike. Lowering the sword, she pulled the last length of covers off from Alec's head.

"Alec what are you doing here?" Alec looked up and, noticing that Eliza's nightgown was not on her body, quickly diverted his gaze.

"Eliza, here you may want this?" He held the blanket out to her. Realizing her lack of modesty, she quickly snatched it and covered herself. Her cheeks burning from her accidental display she attempted to seriously ask her question again, while trying to hide her humiliation.

"Eliza, I need you to get dressed and come to my place." She looked at him with a reluctant stare.

"Alec it is the middle of the night, if you have found some new way to test your body can it wait until later? Our trials are in the morning and we both need our rest. I will come over in the morning before we leave for the trials. Good night, Alec."

"Eliza, it is not some training regimen, it is the egg." Eliza spun on her heel and kneeled down so that her face was level with his.

"The egg, has something happened to it? Was it stolen?"

"No, Eliza it hatched." Her eyes opened wide and the corners of her cheeks turned in producing a wide smile.

"Wait outside. I will put some clothes on."

Alec had barely closed the door when Eliza came out after him, her hair a tangled mess, her clothes hastily pulled on over her nightgown. Alec was foolish enough to comment on her hair and she slugged him in the shoulder, hard enough to cause the muscle to cramp. He smiled at her as he rubbed the muscle and she glared at him with the ferocity of a cornered animal.

"I only look like this, because you made it apparent that the situation was urgent that is all."

"Are you sure it is not because you want to see the baby?" Eliza did not look at him, but answered after a brief pause.

"Perhaps." By that time they had arrived at Alec's door. Alec reached out and turned the handle and peered inside to ensure that the baby would not rush out.

"Little one, where are you?" He spoke into the darkness as he and Eliza entered the room. They walked into the pitch black, the only sound other than their own steps was a quiet clicking. Eliza closed the door behind her as Alec crept towards the bed stand and lit the lamp.

"Where is he Alec?" Eliza looked around the room but saw nothing.

"I hope that he didn't get out." He hurried over to the window and looked outside for any sign that the Lion Hawk had left.

"*GGGrreeeooowww!*" Alec and Eliza searched around some more as the growling continued.

"What in the world?" Eliza turned her face upward toward the source of the noise and eyed the Lion Hawk roosting on a beam. Before she could do more than let out a terrified yelp, the baby had pounced and pinned her, its paws pressing her to the floor its beady eyes staring into hers.

"Alec, help." She trembled as the creature continued to growl at her, its fur and feathers ruffling.

"Hey, come on. Get off from her." Alec grew stern and tried to sound as commanding as he could.

"*Brrrrrr*," the baby cooed as it shied away from Eliza with its head tucked down under its wing, after being scolded. Eliza rose to her feet as the hatchling backed further away into the corner of the room.

"Oh, I think that you scared him, Alec." Alec stepped toward the Lion Hawk, which pressed its side against the wall and looked at the floor.

"Hey it is fine, I am not mad, alright?" The baby turned its head so that one eye was on Alec as he reached out and began to pet it. A deep rumbling sound echoed through the room as the baby began to purr. Eliza stepped forward and the creature let out a slight squawk as if afraid of her.

"Oh, it is alright little guy. Come here, come on. It is alright." Eliza stepped forward with her hand held out in front of her. "Alec can you please hand me the piece of meat?" She reached back with her other hand and Alec did as she asked. Eliza held out the meat ahead of her and looked at the griffet with wide eyes.

"Come on baby, come here." They stared at one another for several seconds before the hatchling reached out, gripped the meat within its beak and began to eat.

"There you go, good boy." Eliza whispered to him as she began to stroke his head, which prompted the babe to purr again.

"What if it is a girl?" Alec asked her, which Eliza turned to him with an almost dumbfounded smirk on her face.

"Are you blind Alec or do you fail to recognize anything you two might have in common?" She tipped back from her seated position, motioned forward with both hands to the baby's underside as if presenting the sex to him.

"He is a good boy, isn't he?" They both smiled as the baby let out a satisfied snort as it tore away at the meat. Eliza joined Alec, sitting on the bed watching the baby with intent eyes.

"What are you going to name him?" She took her eyes away from the griffet and waited for his response.

"Oz." Alec said without hesitation.

"Oz?" Eliza repeated.

"That is the name my sister gave him when she found his egg."

"I suppose Oz it is then." She reached out her hand and smiled as the baby finished eating. He looked at her and allowed her to stroke his head as he purred and rubbed his neck across her thigh.

"Do you think that your father will let me keep him? I do not know as though I could bear losing him. I do not understand, but I just feel as though he is connected to me. It is hard to explain." Alec tried to explain. Eliza looked at him curiously and patted his hand.

"Let me talk to my mother first. If anyone could convince my father to overlook a few things, it is her." Eliza said.

"Do you think that she could honestly convince him?" Eliza laughed at Alec before answering.

"My father may be the Lion of Valoria, but it is my mother who guides his hand. Without her, my father would never have consented to letting me become a knight. I would surely have become some homely noble, confined to my chambers ordering servants about."

"Eliza, I cannot imagine you ever sitting about, a knight cadet or not." Alec teased. Eliza looked at him and slugged him in the shoulder again.

"But you could see me growing homely, thanks." They exchanged a laugh for a moment until Eliza stood, causing Oz to let out a growl of discontent.

"I am sorry baby boy, I have to go back home, Alec and I have a test tomorrow and we need our rest." She turned to Alec and nodded. "I will see you in the morning. Do not worry, I will talk to my mother before the trials."

"Thank you Eliza, I greatly appreciate it." Alec said. Eliza opened the door and Oz began to follow.

"Oz stay, I will come see you tomorrow, alright?"

"Bree?" the Lion hawk looked at her with wide sad eyes.

"You are cute, but I cannot stay, I will see you tomorrow." Eliza quickly stepped out and shut the door behind her so that she could not be further compelled to stay. Alone, Alec turned and looked at the baby in front of him.

"So Oz?" The lion hawk perked up acknowledging the name and Alec smiled.

"Jump up on the bed. We need to get our rest. We have a long day ahead of us tomorrow." Oz hopped up on the bed next to Alec and the two fell asleep.

Chapter 7 - Final Preparations

Only a short few hours later, Alec's eyes flitted open as the light crept through the window from the morning sun. He tried to rub the sleep out of his eyes, but to no avail. He turned his head to the side and his gaze met the Lion Hawk's.

"*Brrreep beep.*" Oz rubbed his head against Alec's chest as Alec stroked the baby's back.

"I have to get up buddy. I have to get ready for my trials." Oz struggled to keep Alec from rising from the bed, but little by little, he made his way off from the bed and began to perform his morning warm up. As Alec began, Oz watched intently, bobbing his body up and down in sync with Alec. Once Alec rolled onto his back, Oz jumped off from the bed and laid on his back on the floor.

As Alec began bringing his torso to his knees, Oz curled himself into a ball and swatted at his tail each time. After he was finished, Alec rose from the floor and filling his washbasin began to wash his face and his body. Then he attempted to get dressed. As Alec began to pull his shirt over his head, the griffet reached out with a paw and swiped it from out of his hands.

"Alright, now give that back." Alec laughed as he tried to wrestle his shirt back from the Lion Hawk. There was a soft knock at the door followed by Eliza's head peeking in.

"Alec are you…oh, my never mind." The door quickly closed.

"Eliza it is fine, just having trouble with my shirt." The door opened again and Eliza laughed seeing Alec without a shirt, which was in Oz's beak.

"Oh my, I see that you do have a problem." She walked towards the bed slowly, followed by Eliza's mother, Kristiana. She was slightly shorter than Eliza with blonde hair, but her stature was of little consequence next to her commanding presence. She was without a doubt, a creature of beauty and grace, while all the same an accomplished warrior by her own right. As she entered the room her bright blue eyes quickly examined every intimate detail of the room and then rested upon Oz.

Alec froze, he was afraid of what Kristiana might say or, even worse, what she might do. Alec stopped fighting for his shirt and instead stood at attention and awaited her judgment. She swiftly walked across the room, the sound of her boots leaving only a faint tap with each step. She stopped next to Eliza and, looking over to Alec, smiled.

"You may stand at ease Alec, I am not here on formal business, relax." Alec let the tension in his shoulders go, but did not release his gaze on her.

"I assume that you have named him?" She motioned toward the Lion Hawk. Alec nodded his head before answering.

"His name is Oz." Alec began. "It is the name that my sister gave him, while he was still an egg." Again, Kristiana's attention was fixed on the hatchling, who continued to wrangle Alec's shirt within his beak, as if it were quarry he had recently captured. She reached her hand out, holding it in place in front of the baby and waited. He looked up and held out his beak and allowed Kristiana to begin petting him. As she did so she quickly pulled the shirt from out of his mouth and tossed it to Alec.

"Go get ready Alec, you and Eliza have a busy day today." She sat atop Alec's bed and began to stroke Oz's neck. Alec did not budge, he stood trembling fearing for the fate of his precious griffet. Without turning her head, Kristiana spoke with Alec.

"Alec, if you are worried about Oz, do not worry. He will be here when you get back. Far be it from myself or my husband to separate a precious creature as rare as the lion hawk from its empathy partner." Alec was relieved, yet confused at the same time. Eliza even looked up at her, bewildered.

"Empathy partner?"

"You have not noticed it yet? Surely you feel as though this creature represents your entire being as if he were your own child? I will explain more of it at a more opportune time, but the two of you must be off." Alec looked back at his newborn infant and longed to stay. He took one last look at Kristiana who waved for him to leave the room. Eliza smiled, grabbed Alec's sleeve, dragged him from the room, and shut the door as Kristiana continued to speak lovingly to the baby lion hawk.

As they walked the street leading down to the courtyard, Eliza turned to Alec.

"What's the matter? Are you alright?" She grabbed Alec by his shoulders and forced him to look at her. He looked into her eyes, smiled and tried to understand the burning ache within his heart.

"Yeah Eliza, I'm fine." Eliza looked at him and frowned.

"You're a terrible liar, you know." She told him. Alec smiled again ignoring the new emotional sensation that continued to pound away at his core.

"Alright, are you sure that you are ready for this? I mean if we fail...?" He looked back to Eliza who looked at him angrily.

"Don't even try to make me sweat this Alec. I have been ready for this moment my entire life. I will not have you giving me a case of the willies now." As if on cue, Zelus approached and cut off Alec's teasing.

"Good morning Eliza, Alec." He said, pressing himself between them. "It looks like we will be fighting live monsters as part of our trial."

"What do you mean, Zelus? Surely father wouldn't have approved of such a thing?"

"I know Eliza, that's because he didn't. The council must have intervened. I saw the cages come through the west gate only just a short few hours ago." Eliza raged at the nerve of council.

"Father must be absolutely furious. He has kept this city free from invading beasts for almost twenty years now. His fearlessness in guarding the north wall against invading beast masters of the Wolds is what earned him his status as captain."

"Believe me Eliza, he was mad with rage, but it is beyond him now. We are to fight live monsters as part of our trials." Alec spoke up this time excited yet wary of the impending danger.

"Zelus, where did you see them, taking these monsters?" Alec looked to Zelus, who took a moment to answer. When he did, he cleared his throat and then changed tone to one more of concern.

"They have taken the monsters onto the courtyard just outside the inner wall." This surprised both Eliza and Alec.

"Why would they have done such a thing?"

"I do not know. I suppose to give a good show to the nobles and townspeople, but at least your father and his knights will be on standby to ensure that none of the creatures get into the village."

"Father will not be in any sort of sociable mood I'm afraid. Perhaps, we should wait to tell him until a later date." Eliza said, looking at Alec with a degree of worry, apparent in her eyes. Alec nodded not wanting to elude anything further to Zelus, who thankfully did not try to press for further information.

"Well at any rate, I think that it is obvious that we will have to take a different approach in dealing with these beasts than if we were running drills." Alec and Eliza agreed and continued on their walk. As they neared the courtyard, they began to notice other cadets forming around the gates trying to view the ongoing commotion. They arrived amongst the crowd and took a glimpse at the beasts they were to be thrown against.

"Alec, lift me up. I want to get a better look of what we're up against." Alec frowned and took a knee allowing for Eliza to climb onto his back. Planting his feet firmly, he lifted her into the air allowing her to glimpse over the tops of everyone's heads.

"I see a lot saber wolves, some feral cats and oh my.." Alec looked up at her and saw the shock on her face. Zelus shifted about impatiently and then looked at Eliza as well.

"What is it, Eliza what do you see?" Eliza just looked to Alec with a look of horror. Before she had the opportunity to answer, a powerful roar shook the windows and caused the cadets to shudder with fear. A number of screams from the other side announced a large collaboration of spectators that were out of sight.

"My word what was that?" Zelus looked around at the various grim expressions of all those around him. Alec's heart stopped when he heard the all too familiar roar and all of his memories returned to him. He griped the hilt of his sword angrily.

"That's the sound of a great bear, a Valdurn as the people here refer to them." Zelus' eyes widened at the sound of the name.

"A Valdurn? Has the council gone mad? What could they possibly be thinking to bring a Valdurn here?" As if things could not have been worse, more roars echoed out, each from a different location. Alec angrily punched the wall in front of him, causing Eliza to shake in her roost.

"How dare they bring such dangerous beasts into the city? Is the council trying to get us all killed?" All of these comments were among many of the frightened remarks that rang out from the other cadets. Eliza and Zelus looked worriedly at Alec as he lowered his hand, a small trickle of blood running down his torn skin and dripping onto the road.

"Alec, are you going to be alright?" This time the question came from Zelus who placed his hand on Alec's arm next to Eliza's thigh. Alec nodded and dropped to a knee again allowing Eliza to hop down from off of his back. He paid little attention to Eliza looking at his hand, but instead turned his angry gaze from the Valdurn toward the balcony of the palace where he noticed figures off in the distance that could only belong to the council members.

"Those pampered bastards want to test the strength of our mettle. Then, by all means, let's slay some monsters." Gripping his fists into iron hard balls, Alec began to march forward pushing his way through the crowd. Cadets stepped out of his way at the sight of his fury, unsure of whether to fear him or the monsters.

"This is unacceptable. Why have you brought these beasts to our home? The knight's trials are already enduring, but now they are being made just plain dangerous. Are your masters hoping to kill off my knights?" The Lion tore away at the guards that stood cowering before him.

"We are sorry for the inconvenience, sir, but it is the council's wishes that any who desire to become knights are well suited for the dangers ahead. The council plan to use the knights in a more practical fashion and we need warriors who are suited to travel through the countryside."

"That is no excuse to bring the beasts here where our villagers will be placed in danger."

"Sir, again if I may, have faith in those that have deemed this necessary. You and your knights will be on guard in case any beasts escape the boundaries, and if I may, is not your daughter amongst the recruits. Have you no faith in the poor girl that you must try and stop her first step toward glory and valor." The Lion made clear his feelings as he lunged forward and with a mighty fist, hammered in the faceguard of the man's helmet with an ugly metal upon metal clanging. The other guards rushed to aid their fallen comrade to regain his feet as he attempted to shake off the daze and confused state.

"You will be reprimanded for this, sir. The council will not stand for this outrage."

"Then bring them and they will learn how I earned my namesake." He growled at them angrily as they cowered away. Eliza, Alec and Zelus all approached him cautiously.

"Father, please calm down, we need you at your best to defend the townspeople. Alec, Zelus and I will be fine, I promise." Eliza's father looked down to her and held out his arms and hugged her.

"Eliza, you are my only child. If your mother hadn't forced my hand, then you would have never entered the knights academy."

"Luckily for me then, mother is just as tough and unwavering as my father." She smiled at him as his expression became less concerned and more annoyed.

"I will worry about the townsfolk. You all be careful and do not forget what I have taught you. Strength and valor will guide you, your courage arm you, and may Aneira and Sidonis watch over you."

"Don't worry father, I'll protect both of them for you." She smiled as Alec and Zelus gave her a disapproving look. The Lion straightened himself, placed his hands behind his back and spoke in his usual commanding voice.

"Alright then, you three go get in line with the rest of the cadets or, do you want me to fail you now." The trio walked away smiling as they joined the line with the other few cadets who were undergoing trial that same day. There, the three of them stood as the Lion and a few of the other senior knights paced back and forth explaining to them what was to be their mission.

"First off, this year's trial will take place within the Valorian maze as it has each and every year. A few of you have, without a doubt, broken our rules and have already been within the maze." Alec and Eliza tried their very best to withhold their smiles while Zelus shifted uncomfortably and attempted to silently clear his throat as the senior knight continued.

"With that being said, the maze never remains the same. It was created eons ago when Aneira first made the world. Sidonis, the founder of our order, came upon this place in his search of a home for our order, and it was he who was the first knight to be tested within. He chose this site because the maze is alive with old magic that will peer into the souls of those it tests and it will deem which of those are worthy." The senior knight concluded his story and stepped aside allowing the Lion to step forward.

"There are five of you that stand before me today. When you joined our ranks, there were many more. While I am displeased that more have not managed to arrive on this day as quickly as you and that others never will, I do say that I am most proud of you five for reaching this day. As with all of my cadets who I select for these trials, I have the utmost faith that you will make it to the other side and be named knights. However those," he paused for a moment, "our esteemed ruling party, the council, has deemed it necessary that you also encounter live beasts. It is therefore allowed that you carry full protective equipment and the weapons of your choosing." The Lion motioned his hand towards a nearby weapons rack and then continued on to his speech.

"The five of you will be working together as a team. Fortunately for you, there are five of you. Five members gives you a full squad and you will need to perform as such in order to make it through this trial successfully. Now go, prove yourselves to Sidonis and become knights, protectors of all those under Aneira's love." The Lion stopped and looked at Eliza for a moment and then turned his head and walked away. As he walked away, the senior knights approached and coaxed the cadets toward the weapon racks where they armed themselves. Zelus grabbed a simple sword and shield and a six-inch knife to hang on his side. Eliza grabbed two long daggers that she placed in scabbards hanging on either hip and a bow and quiver full of arrows.

"Alec, aren't you going to grab something?" Alec turned and looked at his fellow cadet Dominic who was grabbing a tower shield and halberd. The fifth member of their squad, Dominic's younger brother Nilus, grabbed a bow. Alec looked down to the sword that he carried with him. And looked to the weapons rack.

"I think that a shield and knife would suit me just fine." He reached out and grabbed a kite shield and a long hunting knife. Zelus smiled at Alec's choice as they all turned their attention towards the labyrinth. High above the labyrinth floated a magnificent liquid orb, named the eye of Aneira. Alec admired the eye and knew that its magic would allow for any of those outside to watch the ongoing chaos free from harm's way.

"Would you do the honors and take lead Alec?" His attention was quickly directed away by Eliza who had called to him several times.

Alec looked around to the group, and after the only protest came from a quickly quieted Zelus, he smiled, nodded his head and led the group into the labyrinth. They stopped before the massive hedges that led within the tall iron gates looming high overhead. The gates, as if sensing their arrival, swung open to greet them. Alec looked to his team and confident in both their abilities and their eagerness walked inside.

Chapter 8 – A Moment's Distraction

"Are you certain, miss? Are you certain that you saw a Lion Hawk?" Within the safety of the room that Marec had reserved, Talia had begun to relay what she had seen within the reflection.

"A brown-haired, green-eyed man, who found a Lion Hawk, by Aneira. That is indeed news, but how do we know that? Forgive me mistress, but how do we know that this was a vision and not weariness?" Talia pressed her fingers to either side of the bridge of her nose and massaged the edges of her gleaming eyes.

"This was no clear vision, true, but I assure you Marec, that this was not mere exhaustion. I have seen him on more than one occasion, and I know that I must find this boy, of that much I am certain. Aneira is guiding me, showing me glimpses of him so that I may recognize him when the time comes for the two of us to meet." Marec eyed Talia carefully.

"Milady? Do you have feelings for this boy?" Talia blushed intensely and found her tongue tied as a hard lump formed in her throat. She paused for a moment without answering. Marec sat on the floor, placing his back to the wall and tilting his head back to think.

"What is it that your highness wishes? Do we divert course in search of this boy or do we continue on?"

"No, Marec, we must continue on toward the shrine at Roak. There, I may complete the first stage of my pilgrimage and hope to obtain more insight on my visions."

"Very well, ma'am. Then by all means, please get some rest and we shall continue on in the early morning." Talia nodded as she sat down on the bed across the room and then looked to Marec.

"Marec, will you at least attempt to get some rest tonight?" Marec's back straightened, his head held high.

"I shall remain as I always have, vigilant." Talia frowned as she placed her head onto the pillow.

"Just promise that you will sleep for a little while." Marec smiled as she drifted off to sleep and he rose and moved the chair in front of the door where he placed his sword across his lap and waited.

Morning arrived and Marec awoke abruptly as his sword attempted to dip from his lap to the floor.

"Blast!" Marec stumbled out of his chair and searched about the room for

Talia but saw no sign of her. Quickly, he dashed into the hallway and began calling out her alias.

"Sir, is there something the matter?" The innkeeper stepped forward from out of the back of the main room. Marec turned swiftly and stared at the man for a moment.

"Yes. Have by any chance you seen my daughter? I awoke this morning and she was not here."

"Aye, she came down this morn and had some breakfast, then went outside." Marec, with a nod of his head, thanked the man as he quickly exited the Inn and renewed his frantic search. He hadn't run far when his eyes came upon a very merry Talia in the grass playing with a group of children. Marec smiled as he watched her and the children laughing as they chased one another around in a circle yelling back and forth. Talia looked up and saw Marec, whose smile instantly dissipated.

"You didn't sleep for as long as I hoped you would." Talia frowned as she spoke the words. Marec looked her in the eye as he looked around to the children who were waiting for her to come back and play with them.

"Mistress?"

"I know Marec, we must be off. If you give me but just a moment, I shall be ready."

"Aye, I will ready the horses." Marec turned and walked toward the stables while Talia explained to the children that she must be off. Marec returned only a few short seconds later with the two roan horses and helping Talia onto her horse, mounted his own and they rode off toward Ternia. As they rode, Marec looked over to Talia and was sorry to see the joyous look upon her face had long since drifted away and was left with the usual sadness that always bored from out of her eyes.

"Mistress"

"It is alright, Marec. I have a duty to all the people of Valoria. I cannot afford to be selfish and waste time idly sitting about while so many still suffer and the Forsaken march within our lands."

"Your highness is most eloquent in her speech per usual." Marec nodded humbly and spoke little but for the very few unsuccessful attempts to break his charge's sorrow.

Chapter 9 – The Trials

"What's the plan, Alec?" Eliza asked. Alec searched their surroundings. There were three passageways before them plus the one they had just come through. He straightened his back and looked around to his companions. Dominic and Nilus both stood tall and proud, slight scratches adorning their armor from the multiple scuffles they had encountered thus far. Eliza's hair was pulled back in a bun, to keep it from snagging again, on the whipping vines and branches they would encounter. She had one long scratch on her right bracer from a sabre wolf that had gotten past Dominic. Alec looked at Zelus who had a long stripe of blood across his face from a trap that they hadn't seen in time.

Alec looked down to his own hands. His left hand was bloody from the slice on his forearm he had received trying to help Zelus keep the trap from striking Eliza. Returning his attention to the three paths before him, he carefully studied each possible option.

"Nilus, I need you to plant an arrow into the ground in front of the right path." Nilus nodded and did as he was asked.

"That is the path that we will follow. If we wind around again, then we will know which path to follow." Zelus stepped forward and placed a hand on Alec's shoulder.

"What if there is another trap?" Alec turned his attention toward Dominic.

"May I borrow your shield, Dom?"

"Alec, you're hurt already I would gladly take, your place," said Dominic. Alec smiled.

"No need Dominic. Please hand me your shield. I need you all to stay between ten…maybe fifteen paces behind me and wait around the corner, just in case."

"Alec, are you sure? If you take a heavy hit, your arm may not be able to hold back the blow in that condition." Eliza spoke as he began to walk forward. Alec turned around and smirked again.

"I can manage this." He stepped forward and began to walk around the corner when he noticed another trip wire. Throwing up his hand, he motioned for everyone in the troop to stop.

"What do you think it goes to, Alec?" Eliza asked him as she leaned her head around the corner to see why they had halted.

"I am not sure but…" Alec lowered into a crouching position and stepped back a few paces.

"Alec, please do not tell me that you're about to..." Alec reached out with his sword and tapped the wire, the resulting "snap" interrupting Eliza. Everyone jumped backward a few steps as a large volley of ball tipped arrows shot back and forth only a few feet ahead of Alec.

After the volley subsided, Alec stepped forward cautiously and noticed several paces down that the path grew obscured by a medley of thorny vines. Alec turned his head back toward Eliza and frowned.

"Eliza, you are not about to enjoy this." He turned and with his head motioned towards the obstruction. Eliza's jaw opened wide, closed and then opened again before she let out an annoyed sigh. Alec and Zelus pulled their swords and began to hack away at the vines, clearing out a path for them to follow.

"Grrr!" Eliza snapped around to peer behind them, but saw nothing. She turned her head and saw that Dominic and Nilus had both also turned their heads. They heard the growl once and twice more and continued to fixate their gaze in every direction, until they heard a high-pitched whimper followed by a broken silence interspersed with the sounds of crunching bones.

"You hear that too?" They both nodded and continued to search around for the source of the noise. Eliza glanced over her shoulder briefly to watch Alec and Zelus' progress. She began to turn her head back when she noticed the tops of the hedges rustling.

"Um, boys?" She nervously called to Alec and Zelus, who continued to hack away at the greenery. The hedges rustled some more and as the duo continued their assault, Eliza saw the source of the rustling.

"Everybody run!" She yelled as Dominic and Nilus joined her barreling past Alec and Zelus, risking the vines. Alec and Zelus looked at each other as they heard the rustling noise and watched as the hedges came alive and took monstrous form. The creature stood ten feet tall, with tendrils of whipping vine, and a gaping mouth filled with thorny teeth. Alec and Zelus looked to one another and they too ran for their lives after their comrades.

As they ran, Alec looked forward trying to keep up with Eliza while keeping an eye out for any more tripwires. Eliza was running at full throttle, Dominic and Nilus trying desperately to keep up with her. As they ran, they accidentally tripped a few of the traps. Alec did his best to attempt to eschew the springing vines and volleying hammer arrows. His shield arm was growing numb and his ears were growing deaf as his shield rang and rattled.

Alec turned his head and watched as the treant burst through the wall of vines with an angry cry that sounded of a deep throated war drum booming through a hollow wooden tube. It whipped and lashed its vine arms sadistically as Alec rolled his eyes forward again, glancing pass Zelus who was headed straight for a trap.

"Zelus shield up!" Alec yelled. Zelus looked at Alec and then raised his shield just in time to block a branch that whipped across at his eye level. Zelus ducked beneath as he continued to run.

"Watch where you are running!" Alec yelled up to the leaders of the pack. Eliza, Dom and Nilus must have heard as they began to slow their pace slightly, though not enough to allow for Alec and Zelus to easily catch up with them. Alec peered over his shoulder as the gardener's worst nightmare neared them. Alec leaned his forward and increased his pace propelling himself far ahead of Zelus as he continued to leap hurdles and bound over pitfalls.

A series of large branches swung out at him, the spring loaded contraptions supporting them having been triggered by the massive hedge from hell. Alec leaped over one, jumped to the side and slid beneath another. As he did so he noticed Nilus' arrow sticking out of the ground to his left.

"Everybody this way!" Alec called as he spun on his heel and bolted to his left. Zelus followed him as everyone else turned and seeing that they had passed their pathfinder, all turned and followed Alec and Zelus. The treant roared with rage as all of the traps, which all the cadets, had managed to avoid, ensnared it.

The five of them all proceeded to carry on their maddeningly frenzied pace until Alec watched as the hedges began to recede and give way to an ancient marble building. Sensing that they were no longer in danger of becoming compost, Alec slowed his pace and attempted to catch his breath whilst walking forward. He stopped just before a large set of stone stairs and turned back towards his fellow cadets.

"We are almost there." His four companions followed him at a distance. Alec reached the top of the stairs, which led to a large heavy portcullis. Alec motioned for his squad to assist him. After relinquishing Dominic's shield, they tested their combined might against the door, but were unable to so much as break the seal of earth at the gates close. Searching around, Eliza noticed a small alcove above.

"Alec look." She pointed at the small ledge above the vine covered wall.

"Dominic, if you please, give me a boost. I can try to open it from the inside." Dominic looked to Alec for his thoughts, but it was Zelus who answered.

"No Eliza, we need to stick together. We cannot afford to lose a member of our squad. What if the animals got in there?"

"Zelus, please, if we cannot get inside the building, however, do you think that the animals managed?" Alec looked to Zelus and then to Eliza.

"No Eliza, Zelus is right. This portcullis was not here before when the three of us came last time. This maze is meant to test the worth of Valascaa's knights. It would not act out against the beasts within. Nilus, you are the only other one that may fit through there. Would you please accompany her?" Eliza snuffed at the thought.

"I do not need a babysitter. Alec, I will do quite alright on my own."

"Eliza, I would never be so bold as to doubt you, but this is an immensely heavy door and it is going to take at least two people to open it." Again, Eliza snuffed at the idea, but inclined her head in the slightest of nods all the same.

"Zelus, Dom?" Alec looked over to the man, his arms still crossing his chest and Dominic who both stepped forward and began to help Nilus and Eliza up onto the ledge. The three remaining men waited for several minutes when the gate began to clank and then slowly rise.

"Eliza? Nilus?" Alec called as he and his men entered the large corridor.

"Here Alec." The two archers called back as Nilus lowered himself to the ground through a series of nimble acrobatics ending in him sliding down the side of a marble column. Eliza remained a story above the others looking around.

"Eliza, what's the matter?" Nilus waved at Eliza and began to whisper.

"Before we found the crank to open the portcullis, we heard some more of those sabre wolves. Eliza and I agreed that it would be wisest for one of us to remain on high to fend off anything that might try and take us by surprise." Alec looked up at Eliza as she crouch-walked, an arrow already nocked, another between her teeth ready for a second quick shot, and her quiver belted low over her opposite shoulder in case they found serious trouble. Alec nodded to her as he silently motioned for his men to move forward.

They walked through one stone room after another, each with its own cathedral ceiling filled with various floors and beams Eliza used to bound back and forth above them keeping careful watch.

"What is it that we are looking for exactly?" Dom whispered to Alec.

"Well Zelus feel free to object if you need, but I can only imagine that we have to reach the fountain, where the shrine of Aneira rests. It was there that Sidonis was tested and there that he prayed to Aneira to grant him her wisdom."

"No Alec, I agree with you. If our goal is to be branded knights of Aneira there can be no other destination." They continued to march forward when they heard a low echoing growl. Alec held out his hand to signal the halt. He raised his sword and readied his shield as an arrow shot past him followed by a yowl as a sabre wolf rounded the corner and fell dead, Eliza's arrow sticking out from within its rib cage.

Alec could not see Eliza's shadow concealed face up above, but he knew full well the smug grin that she was bearing.

"At least we know what she'll be boasting about on the walk back." They continued to sneak forward the whole while wondering what manner of beasts still awaited them. They entered into another large room and Alec could make out the faint sound of falling water.

"We are rather close now. I can hear the fountain." He looked around for a moment and saw an opening.

"My guess is through that door." Zelus pointed as he stepped forward. Alec looked in the direction and noticed the trip wire only just too late. Before Alec could call out to stop him, the wire snapped and Zelus was flung across the room and the sound of several iron grates opening filled the room with a horrible grinding.

"Zelus are you alright?" Alec asked. Zelus did not move, though Alec's attention was seized as Eliza called out.

"Alec, there are too many of them up here!" Alec looked up and then turned back to Zelus.

"Dominic, check on Zelus, Nilus cover fire, I'm going to help Eliza." He began to run for Eliza, climbing on anything he could get a handle on. Nilus turned to Alec and tried to stop him.

"But Alec, wait, we need to stick together." But Alec was in no state to listen to warnings. His blood was coursing with adrenaline, his heart was pounding so aggressively it threatened to burst from his chest. He managed to reach up to a ledge just below Eliza who was attempting to make her way down from above. She ran quickly, shooting an arrow or two behind her slowing the wolves, but not halting the dozens of beasts that swarmed her. She cried out in pain as she tripped a wire and a heavy gate swung forward and struck her several feet back. She stumbled trying to catch her breath as the first of the wolves was upon her.

"Eliza!" Alec yelled as she stumbled backward holding the gash running across her torso. Alec continued his climb and managed his way up to the ledge where he struck out at two of the wolves and began to drag Eliza away who as she groaned painfully. The wolves growled fiercely at them as Alec looked for a way out. He looked from side to side in search of his solution and then looked to Eliza.

"Alec, we are going to have to jump down." Alec turned his head from her as he bashed one of the wolves aside with his shield.

"Are you sure that you can manage?" Eliza nodded her head. Alec did his best to lift her up, supporting her weight with his shoulder as he continued to hold back the wolves. Eliza limped as he walked toward the edge of the walkway and looked over the gap towards the next several feet below. Eliza looked him in the eye and nodded her head. Alec braced her torso to save it from the shock and they jumped.

They struck the cold stone and Alec's legs buckled from Eliza's added weight. He tipped backwards and fell to his backside as he caught Eliza on his lap. He looked up as the sabre wolves began to jump after him. He pressed her back up against the wall as she drew her bow and laid her quiver across her lap.

"Ahh!" Alec cried out in pain as one of the wolves landed upon his back and sunk its teeth deep in his shoulder. Alec reached back and grabbed the wolf by its mane and attempted to throw it off.

"Alec, turn around!" Alec did as he was told, and his eyes were filled with the sight of half a dozen wolves that had managed to make the jump, several others having fell to their deaths below. The wolf on Alec's back loosened its grip as Eliza shot it in the head with an arrow. Alec threw the beast off from his back, and pulled his sword and shield to defend himself. He slashed out at several more of the beasts as he continued to shield Eliza with his body.

"Alec, look a staircase!" He turned his head toward the direction that Eliza pointed. He threw his shield onto his back as he walked back and lifted Eliza onto her feet. He looked her in the eye and saw that she was having difficulty staying awake.

"Alec, Eliza hurry!" Alec was relieved to hear Zelus call out, but concerned from the sound of panic. Alec continued to pull Eliza as the sabre wolves growled, but fortunately backed down. Alec did his best to keep Eliza conscious as they scaled the staircase leading down near the room where he had left the others.

"Zelus, Eliza's hurt, but she's going to be alright."

"Alec, watch out!" The warning came far too late. Alec was blinded for what seemed to be several hours as he felt his body fly through the air where he crashed onto the floor and continued to slide for a distance. He groaned as he attempted to steady his shaking knees when he heard the colossal roar of a Valdurn.

The hot flowing blood in his veins iced over as he searched about and saw splotches of blood on the floor and his sword and shield nowhere in sight. Worse of all, he could not see where Eliza had fallen. Alec stumbled forward just as Zelus rose to his feet. Alec looked past Zelus and saw Dominic and Nilus stir unconscious and wounded, but alive.

"Alec, are you alright, where is Eliza?" Alec shook his head and looked into the room where he could hear the Valdurn's snarl. They both drew the same conclusion and continued forward as Alec pulled out his hunting knife and Zelus drew his sword. As Alec entered the room, a horrifying vision from his nightmares flashed before his eyes. He could see Eliza trying to crawl away from the massive Valdurn that stood between them.

The memories of his haunted past tearing his heart from his chest, Alec dashed toward the beast and sank his hunting knife into the creature's side. His knife sank deep and the monster roared out in agonizing pain, but Alec's blade was far too short to drive deep enough to pierce any vital organs. With a powerful heave, the Valdurn reached back and slammed Alec to the floor, where he landed painfully on his side. He spat out a trickle of blood as he struggled to his feet. He fell back to the floor and he looked to his right arm that hung at the wrong angle.

Zelus had followed Alec in his charge, but was swept away by the back of the bear's boulder-sized palm. Zelus hit the wall, dropping his sword but failed to rise again. Alec finally rose to his feet and ran for the sword. With his left arm outstretched but missed the hilt as he narrowly dodged the swipe of the Valdurn's arm. He rolled painfully but managed to land on his feet as Dominic entered the room.

"Dom, grab Eliza." Dominic looked over to Eliza who was still slumped in the corner, threw his halberd over to Alec as best he could. The Valdurn reared its head at Dominic and roared. Dominic bolted out of reach of the raking paw and stood blocking Eliza as the Valdurn charged. Alec grabbed the handle of the halberd with his left hand and ran toward the Valdurn's flank Dominic planted his mighty tower shield into the ground in front of the Valdurn and placed his massive body against it.

The first strike knocked against Dominic's shield, which slid and buckled slightly but the powerful man remained in place before Eliza. Before a second blow could be made Dominic thrust back with all of his might, forcing the bear back several paces and onto its hind legs where Alec cut heavily into its back, the weight of the halberd throwing him off balance at the same time. The Valdurn's pained cry shook the walls as the full force of its weight came tumbling down upon Dominic, toppling the mighty man.

The beast's terrible cry of pain continued as it reared its ugly head onto Eliza. Again, the traumatic memory of his sister's death rained down upon him as the bear rose onto its hind legs and roared, ready to charge. Alec, filled with strength, lost the sensation of pain as his body felt inexplicably empowered, lifted the halberd into the air and ran to intercept. The Valdurn wasn't even a few seconds from Eliza when Alec jumped forward and slid across the ground planting the end of the halberd into the ground and pointed the tip toward the Valdurn's breast. Alec's cry of fury matched the dying cry of the Valdurn as the beast plunged forward and fell upon him.

The weight of the Valdurn pressed the air out of Alec's lungs and he began to lose consciousness. Curtains of black began to roll over the corners of Alec's vision and he again saw glimpses of the auburn hair, green-eyed woman from his dreams. He could see worry and sadness in her eyes even amidst the brightness of her eyes and her heart-stopping smile. He smiled, while clutching his side, which was bleeding heavily. He feared that he might never have the opportunity to meet her.

Chapter 10 – The Morning After

"That is absolutely outrageous. I will not stand by this decision!" The Lion roared out with rage as he yelled at the high council over their recent decision. The magnitude of his voice reached up to the high stained glass ceiling and echoed off from the walls of the brilliantly lit chamber, gleaming with royal red and imperial gold. The council, up high on their platform, continued to look down upon the Lion with disdain in their eyes.

"On what grounds do you challenge our decision? Your cadets undertook the trials and failed. They made a mockery of your knight's college, while all viewed the events on Aneira's eye. How is it that we are to admit these failed cadets into your ranks, proving that the knights have truly become spineless and weak." The Lion boomed again, at the long list of insults the speaker of the council unleashed.

"Never have we allowed, nor even dared to pit our cadets against legions of monsters, during their knights' trials. First you force them to undertake such a task and now, even after they reached the center of the maze, you have the audacity to deny them their sacred rite?" the speaker smiled a malicious smile and he clapped his hands slowly before answering.

"I believe that your case is not without its merit. We will be more willing to discuss these most unfortunate circumstances at a later date knight commander. However I would implore you to take better care when choosing the manner in which you speak to us. It has been expected for some time that the Highmoorian would fail, his attendance after all was never more than a simple test to prove the worth of the filthy wretches that inhabit our glorious city. Never forget that so long as the throne remains empty that we the council are the rule of law and it is our choice not yours as to who will protect our citizens." With the wave of his hand the speaker dismissed the lion who stormed angrily from the room followed by his second in command Keagen.

"Who do they think they are? Claiming the people of this city theirs. Blasphemy!" Keagen raged on his tangent until finally the Lion stopped him.

"No good will come of attacking their loyalty to Aneira, not while the walls remain ever aware of whispers within their halls." Keagen looked about cautiously as they continued to walk down the hallway. The Lion was still clutching his fists angrily. He knew full well that Alec's "failure" as they had deemed it, would prove cause for them to impede anyone of Highmoorian or common blood from attempting to earn their place among the people.

"So what do you suppose will happen to your golden boy, now?" The Lion shook his head and sighed.

"I do not know. The poor boy deserves a break. There are few who know or can even understand what he has been through. Perhaps, they will see reason once you know who steps in. They tend to be more receptive to her."

"You are going to sick the Lady Kaldur on them then?" Keagen asked.

"Alec is as much a son to us as Eliza is our daughter. They will be swayed to think the matter over more carefully."

"I do admire her." Keagen smiled as they walked.

The auburn haired woman walked gracefully across a field of wildflowers, slowly climbing a hill. Alec watched as she reached the summit and sat upon the bow of an Aneiran blossom and looked out over to the sea as the bright blue flower petals fell with the wind and landed into the setting sun reflected off from the surface of the water. He could smell salt in the air, and though it smelt of Valascaa, he knew that without a doubt that he had been taken somewhere far away. The tree resembled a weeping willow, yet the whipping vines were covered in an array of sapphire blossoms. The woman looked back to him and smiled, her radiant green eyes shone into him and he felt his spirit glow.

"Alec." The woman smiled again, and Alec walked towards her.

"Alec, wake up." He walked closer to the woman who wrapped her arms around him.

"I am awake. I'm right here with you." He leaned forward and kissed the girl.

"*SMACK!*" Alec's eyes shot wide open as he nearly jumped out of his bed in shock. Suddenly filled with pain which coursed through his entire body he slowly sank back down into the bed his hand held close to his side.

"Eliza, why did you have to wake him up that way? You've caused him to reopen his stitches." Kristiana was leaning over him, tending to his right side before his vision cleared. When it did, he looked from her to Eliza who was wiping her face and bore a horrified expression. Suddenly, Alec's eyes shot wide open as he realized what had happened.

"Aw, sick, oh by Aneira that's disgusting." Alec began to wipe his own face as Eliza came after him again. Eliza's eyes alight with an impassioned fury, which she bore down upon Alec with a most violent roar.

"Oh, so now I am gross. I should slap you again, you jerk. First you cram your tongue down MY THROAT like some sort of beast regurgitating to its infants and now you have the audacity to call ME gross." Eliza raised her hand to slap him again when Kristiana interrupted.

"Oh, Eliza, do not be so dramatic. By the looks of things, he must have enjoyed it a lot." Both Alec and Eliza looked down at the same time towards, but not quite halfway, to, Alec's feet and cried out again in horror.

"Alec, how could you? Is this because of the other night? Oh by Aneira's nymphs, this is worse than the Valdurn, I feel so disgusted. I think I am going to throw up." Eliza turned her back to Alec who was still trying to burn the experience from his mind all the while Kristiana laughed maliciously. Kristiana attempted her best to speak to the two of them between bursts of laughter, but eventually managed to take a deep breath and squeezed out a simple sentence.

"Alec, please dear, you need to lie back so that I may reseal your wounds." Alec did as he was told, lying back on the bed, still horrified by what had just transgressed, but noticing the absence of his Lion Hawk, quickly forgot the incident. He looked Kristiana in the eye and placed his hand over hers.

"Where's Oz?" Krisitana looked him in the eye, a very grave, solemn expression on her face.

"Alec, I spoke with my husband about your Lion Hawk and he was most displeased with the situation. I'm afraid that he is unwilling to allow you to keep him here." Alec's heart sank, despair filled every fiber of his being. He sat up straight and placed his balled fists on the bed in front of him. Eliza sat on the bed next to Alec and placed his left hand within both of her own.

"Mother, are you certain that there is nothing that can be done?" Kristiana hesitated for a moment and then smiled.

"Your father agreed to move both Alec and Oz into quarters more suited for a Lion Hawk and his empathy partner. Oz is already there waiting for you." Both Alec and Eliza's jaws dropped as Kristiana roared with laughter again. After Kristiana's bout of laughter subsided, she calmed her breathing and spoke softly once more.

"You will be asked to gather up your things just as soon as my husband has seen you granted knight's status. The house that you will be moving to is a bit larger than this one and has a balcony on which Oz will be able to take off from and land on once he is bigger." Kristiana paused for a moment as if contemplating something. Alec and Eliza both waited for her to vocalize her thoughts, but after a brief pause took up to question. Kristiana let out a deep sigh and stroked the corners of her eyes.

"I'm afraid that the council is being a rabble of fools. As of now, they are currently unwilling to grant your knights status due to how the trials played out." Kristiana looked to Eliza and Alec and smiled.

"However, I would not worry, your father is seeing to the matter personally," she paused for a moment as if troubled by the thought.

"Although, if things are not settled soon I suppose that I will be confronting them on the matter as well. They would not be so foolish as to deny my council and force my hand." A shiver shot through Alec's spine at the thought of Kristiana unveiling her wrath.

"What is to become of us until then? Is there any need for us at the moment or can we be of assistance in some way?" Alec spoke as he attempted again, to rouse himself from the bed but Kristiana placed her hand over Alec's chest to stop him from rising. Alec winced as if pained as her fingertips traced over the three-raked scar. Kristiana gave him an almost sorrowful glance before turning to Eliza.

"Would you leave us for a moment dear? I will only be but a short while for we must see to your friends and then to your father." Eliza rose from the chair across the room and Alec noticed for the first time as she entered the light that she wore a large bandage upon her brow and she grimaced slightly when bending at the waist. Alec felt sorry for failing to reach Eliza in time but, if she were angry at him for it, he knew that she would have shown it to him. She slowly walked across the room and opening the door let herself out. As the door clicked shut Kristiana turned her gaze toward Alec, leaned forward and hugged him gently. As she pulled away from the embrace, Alec noticed her wiping a few subtle tears.

"Thank you for getting to her, Alec. I know what it meant for you and what it has cost you." She placed her hand about a foot over his heavily battered torso. Alec thought for a moment before answering.

"I froze. I saw that Eliza was in danger and I hesitated. I let my fears get the better of me, and I froze. If I had acted sooner, I could have prevented Eliza and the others from being hurt. I should have instructed Nilus to fire upon the sabre wolves and tended to Zelus, but I just couldn't..." Kristiana stopped him in mid speech.

"You did what you could, Alec. It is easy for any leader to pick apart his decisions and burden himself with impossible "what ifs." Others will question you in hindsight, but the will to act is only granted to a select few. You were presented with a terrible situation and instead of doing nothing, you chose to act. You sacrificed your own flesh for another's. I would say that's commendable by anyone's standards." Alec still seemed unconvinced. Kristiana sighed before continuing.

"Alec, your victory may have been flawed, but you performed to the ablest of your abilities and I think you will find that more support your decision then damn it." Alec did not answer. He knew that what she said may hold true, but he still could not shake the thought that if he had acted sooner things would have turned out for the better. As she rose to take her leave, Kristiana turned her head to Alec once more and smiled.

"I would recommend you stay in bed and rest. It appears that though you killed the beast, it was still able to manage a final bite on your side. I could not detect anything that was broken, but I can only imagine that you cracked at least one rib. The Valdurn definitely banged you up during the fight. You will need to take it slow for a while." Alec looked down to the several purple bruises that decorated his left side, back and arms.

"But since we both know that you will not, you may wish to join us at our home later to speak with my husband personally. Before that however, I implore you to take a stroll and visit the northern watchtower. Your feathered friend has missed you terribly." As she finished, she turned toward the door and exited the room. As soon as Alec was sure that she was gone, he slowly rose from his bed and attempted to slither into a shirt without flaring the intense agony in his side.

As he opened the door, he was forced to wonder exactly how long he had been in the dark. Slowly he lowered the hand shielding his eyes and little by little they adjusted. He tread carefully, but also as quickly as he felt he was able, following the path that would take him to the northern watchtower and to his companion. Sweat decorated his brow as the tower came in sight. A broad smile spread across his face and he reached out and opened the door.

"Great," he murmured to himself as he looked before him at the long winding stretch of stairs. He let out a deep sigh as he placed a hand against the wall and forced his body forward one step at a time. As Alec ascended his first few steps an awful shrill squawking began to echo off the walls followed by the startled yells of several guards.

"I'm coming Oz, do not worry," Alec yelled out fearing that the hatchling might be in pain. He began to scale the steps two at a time pressing most of his weight against the wall as he slowly hunched lower to the ground doubling in pain. Alec's heart continued to race as his pain increased and Oz's wailing shrieks grew ever more hysterical. Alec could hear the alarm in the guard's voices.

"Come on little fella. Just calm down. Go back in the pen, come on." But Oz was not going to have it. Alec could hear a series of loud thuds followed by one of the guards.

"He wants outside, should we just open the door for him?"

"Of course not. We would be flogged if something happened to this creature. We are under orders from the Lion himself to watch over it. I will not have it escaping on my watch."

As Alec scaled the last few steps, Oz's squeals took a slightly different tone and as he opened the door, the griffet readied itself posing its haunches and then pounced at him. Alec pressed his back against the wall as the baby placed a paw on either side of him and began to stroke its head across his chest.

"*Brree!*" Oz purred as Alec lowered himself to a seated position and began to pet him. As the guards attempt to approach, Oz tilts his head to the side and lets out a low growl, halting their advance.

"Oz, be nice. They are on our side." Alec continued to pet him as the guards stood, still on full alert. After several more minutes of Alec and Oz's reunion, a nervous guard spoke up.

"Alec, if I may, is there some way perhaps that you might be able to have your pet accompany you? Not that we are not honored by guarding the Lion Hawk, but I am afraid he has been most ill content under our watch." Alec thought for a moment, but already he knew the answer.

"I am sorry, but I am not allowed to have him about in the city just yet. I must first wait for permission from the council." Oz let out a slight whine and pressed his beak against Alec's chest. Alec stroked his mane for a moment before holding his head between Alec's hands and looked him in the eye.

"Now Oz, I need you to stay here with these two for a while longer, alright?" Sadness filled the lion hawk's eyes. As if it were his own, Alec could feel the overwhelming sensation within his chest.

"Oz, please. You have to stay here, alright? Just for a little while, but I'll see about letting you walk around the city while I'm away." As if accepting a compromise, Oz let out a low chime but then dropped back to all fours and walked back toward the guards who both stumbled backwards. Alec rose to his feet and saying goodbye turned from the watchtower and began to make his way back down the stairs. Finally reaching the bottom, Alec stopped for a moment to check his bandages and thankfully found the stitches along his ribs were still holding. Taking in as deep a breath as possible, Alec pushed himself off from the wall and began to walk toward the town square. As he neared the square, several of the villagers that recognized him from the eye, smiled and waved.

"We support you Alec. We trust in you." Alec smiled graciously and waved back to the crowd as he continued pace. As he walked he came across Zelus, his arm resting within a sling. Alec and Zelus met eye to eye for a moment and a slight smile crept across Zelus' face.

"Good to see you up and about Alec," Zelus tenderly patted Alec on the shoulder as he strode past and vanished into the crowd. Alec stood stunned for several minutes before he remembered to close his jaw, and continued to walk toward Eliza's house. Once there, he rapped on the door and waited for someone to answer.

"Who is it?" Eliza asked as she opened the door and peered outside. Her long flowing hair was damp from washing and Alec could tell that her clothes were thrown on in haste.

"Oh, it is just you, do you need something, Alec?" Alec smiled taken back.

"Just you? Wow, Eliza good to see you as well." Eliza squinted her eyes at him and spoke with the fire that she had become famous for.

"You know that's not what I meant, do you need something?" Alec chuckled to himself for a minute at the oddity that is his best friend.

"You know Eliza, you may bear unmistakable resemblance to your mother but I swear you act just like your father." Alec held back further comments at the bone-rattling growl that he was certain he heard.

"Did you just come by to poke fun, or do you need something?" Eliza was beginning to lose patience with him. Alec turned his hand his palm facing the ground and waved it back and forth.

"More or less." He responded. Eliza rolled her eyes at him before looking back towards him.

"Alec, would you like to come inside? I need to brush out my hair." She opened the door and walked toward a bench sitting before a small vanity. As she began to brush her hair, Alec raised suspicion as to who Eliza was waiting for.

"So, who you were expecting to be at the door, a boyfriend perhaps?" The shade of red coming over Eliza's face was more than an answer to his question.

"That is none of your business, alright Alec. Now, what do you want?" Alec smiled as her feisty side roused again.

"Your mother asked me to stop by later so we could speak to your father more about what is to become of us." Eliza's gaze turned to one of concern, and her tone changed to a much softer friendlier one.

"Well, they are not here right now. You may want to try back later." Alec nodded and turned his back to leave.

"Alec," Alec turned his attention. Eliza looked at him, concern apparent in her eyes.

"Are you sure that you're alright?" She spoke softly as she gestured her head toward Alec's wounds. With a confident smile, Alec looked back at her.

"Yeah, I am fine, do not worry about me." He flexed lazily and struck a bold pose before smiling, then closed the door behind him, and took a deep breath, his hand on his side. He turned his head toward the northern side of the city and debated going back to see Oz, but his side panged at the thought of the stairwell. So, he took the other option left to him, and walked toward the park just outside the castle courtyard. As he entered the park, he noticed the normal crowd surrounding the Sidonis statue. He walked past the crowd over to a vacant bench under a tree, and sat with his back against it, staring at the statue.

Alec closed his eyes and could not help but think to himself that there had been something more he could have done. He played back the events in his mind over and over arriving at different conclusions, but he could not come up with the one answer that he was looking for. The more agitated he grew, the more distracted he became, and his thoughts began to turn back toward his sister.

"There has to have been a way that I could have prevented them from being hurt." The situation continued to unravel between the two until he was frustrated enough that he opened his eyes and looked at the statue of Sidonis.

"What would you have done?" He continued to stare at the silent statue awaiting an answer that he knew would never come. The group of spectators began to clear out of the area, and Alec took the opportunity upon himself to move further into the park to the statue of the goddess Aneira. Alec knelt down in front of the statue and pressed his two fingers to his lips and then to the statue of the beautiful matron. He placed both hands down upon the enormous plaque before him and read to himself the words engraved on its face.

"In the beginning there was only chaos, darkness and brutality the only law of the world. Through the ashes of the destruction came forth Aneira, the matron goddess, mother of all and through her love she cleansed the world and creed that her love unconditional, would be granted upon all those who returned her love. But Aneira's love was not returned by all, and with this she left the outer corners of the world barren and broken. Within these lands she cursed the Forsaken to forever dwell within the depths of despair without knowing the love that they had scorned." Alec stopped himself there and looked up to the goddess and smiled and repeating the tradition touched his fingers to his lips, and then to the statue, rose and walked toward Eliza's home certain that Kristiana and the Lion were home by now.

He knocked three times and waited for a couple of minutes listening to the commotion taking place within. After a short while longer, the door opened ominously and Alec poked his head in and came face-to-face with Eliza.

"What are you standing out there for, come on, my parents are about to get started." She closed the door behind him and they walked across the main hall into the larger sitting room where, Zelus, Dominic and Nilus sat waiting for them. Alec felt an amount of guilt at the different wounds that his comrades bore. Zelus in his sling, Nilus seemed to escape with just a bump to the head, but the way he moved his arm suggested that he had at the very least dislocated something. Although Dominic seemed unharmed with nothing but a few scrapes, he let one leg lay out before him and frequently rubbed his temples suggesting that he had also taken a blow to the head. If they bore any contempt for Alec, they did not show it, because as he entered, each of his companions nodded or smiled to him.

Alec took up a spot behind the pack and leaned his back against the wall and watched as the Lion and Kristiana spoke in quiet for a moment.

"Neither of them seems happy, do they?" Eliza placed her back against the wall near Alec and stretched her legs out.

"They are not happy, but I do not think that means we are lost. There must have been some sort of setback." Just then, Alec sensed something within the back of his mind, excitement. Eliza gave him a puzzling look and Alec shrugged, not knowing what the cause of the sensation was. Alec stole himself away from distraction and instead looked up to see what it was that the Lion was about to say.

He stood with his back straight and his hands behind his back and cleared his throat.

"I have been in talks with the council for most of the day. I warn you, even though I believe that I have made headway, things are still not progressing as I hoped they would." Everyone remained silent waiting for their mentor to continue, but disappointment was evident upon their faces.

"It seems as though the council is of the mind that as warriors you have all proven yourselves well, but they are unconvinced that you have what it takes to become knights of the people of Valoria. It is their opinion, the challenges they set before you should be the challenges, which all of our future cadets will be judged upon. However, with the help of many of the senior knights, it has been brought to their attention, had we known ahead of time what they had planned, you all would have been prepared differently. We will all be meeting with them tomorrow mid-afternoon to discuss this situation. They have agreed to compromise in light of the circumstances and will instead, discuss a different trial. They have agreed to grant you your knight's statuses unless you prove unworthy." Alec could not help but clap half-heartedly joining in with the group who responded with mixed feelings.

Again, the Lion cleared his throat and waited for the chatter and the applause to die down before continuing.

"Since we are all here there is one other matter of note that I must discuss with you. Once you are all knights, you will be moved to more promising living quarters and will each be given a horse that will be kept within the barracks stables. You will also each be allowed to have pets within your homes, but I encourage you to keep this to a minimum as you will be leaving the city from time to time on business as knights." Alec could not help but notice the Lion's gaze, locked on him.

"That was everything I had for you cadets today, I shall see you all in the morning where, after our meeting, I feel at long last I will be able to call upon you as proud knights of Valoria, you are all dismissed." Everyone rose from their seats and began to depart.

"My mom has asked if you could stay behind so that they can talk to you about you know who." Alec knew that Eliza could only be talking about Oz so he merely nodded as Dominic came up to him, limping as he walked.

"Alec, good to see you are out of bed. Are you feeling any better?"

"Yes, thank you for asking Dom. Are you alright?" He looked down at Dom's leg, but the large man only smiled.

"Alec, I know what you are thinking. What happened during the trials is not your fault. As a matter of fact, I was going to tell you that you did a remarkable job in leading us."

"But Dominic, all of you were injured because of what I did." Dominic smiled and shook his head at Alec.

"Better that we suffer a few scrapes and bruises than to lose our beloved Eliza." He reached out and scooped Eliza up in a warm embrace. Eliza struggled for air against the giant of a man who eventually released her when she gasped to catch her breath.

"Well, I am glad that you think I am worth the trouble" she finally managed to gasp out. Dominic smiled again before answering.

"I spoke with Nilus and he and I both agree that Eliza is like another little sister to us." Eliza blushed and Alec smiled.

"Are you sure that you two need another sibling? Aren't there are already four more in your family?" Dominic laughed at the comment.

"Aye, but in the Calnus clan we believe there is always room for at least one more. Our next youngest brother, shall be old enough next year and intends to join the knights. He looks to you all as his inspiration." He placed his hand on Eliza's shoulder, smiled and started to do likewise for Alec, but rethinking the embrace, restrained himself. Eliza smiled and nodded her head to Dominic.

"It was my mother who set the example, though I am proud to hear you say so," said Eliza. Dominic smiled.

"I shall see you two in the morning." He turned and joined his brother who was waiting for him by the door, nodding to them as they left. Alec turned his gaze over to the Lion, who was walking toward him, a rather stern expression on his face.

"So, I hear that you took it upon yourself to go out and find a Lion Hawk before you were granted knight's status." The look that he gave Alec was enough to make his spine quake.

"Aye, sir." He strained to keep eye contact with the powerful man.

"You realize that there are rules forbidding such things, do you not?"

"Aye."

"And you do realize that the penalties for breaking such rules are extreme, do you not?"

"Aye," Alec answered a third time swallowing, a hard lump in his throat.

"Well, I suppose it's a good thing that I don't believe in that particular rule." The Lion let out a laughing roar and patted Alec on the back forcing him to bend in half and gasp in pain.

"Ah, sorry about that, forgot that you banged yourself up for a moment."

Alec attempted to smile as he rose to a standing position.

"Alec, I have talked it over with the Lady Kaldur quite a bit. I was wondering if you would not mind having your Lion Hawk, what was his name?"

"Oz, sir."

"Ah yes, Oz, an odd name, but one that will do. Well, anyway we were wondering if you might not mind letting him stay here for the time being while we wait for the council to grant you your new home. It seems as though the guards in the northern tower aren't aware of the honor it is to guard such a noble beast." Alec was elated to hear the good news.

"Of course sir, that would be most appreciated, thank you. What made you consider such a thing, if I may ask?" The Lion's expression turned darker as if a most heart wrenching thought occurred to him.

"You see Alec, I feel as though I owe you a great debt and, as a rule, I repay my debts. Although this does little to return the boon you have granted me, I feel as though it is a step in the proper direction." Alec thought for a moment, looked to the other room, and seeing Eliza realized what the Lion must be referring to.

"Aye, Alec, she is my only child and my most precious treasure in all the world. The thought that I almost lost her to the ignorance and arrogance of higher powers is most troubling to me. Please, just see this as a means of thanking you for your sacrifice." Alec didn't know how to respond to this. He had never known the lion to speak so heartedly before.

"Thank you sir, I am most grateful." The Lion almost looked as though he would choke up for a moment but then quickly recovered and again became as stone.

"I will. See you in the morning Alec. I will have Oz moved here tomorrow morning. Please try and let him know."

"I will, again thank you." As Alec went to leave, he said a brief good bye to Kristiana and Eliza, made a quick visit to Oz and hobbled home and went to bed.

Chapter 11 – Unexpected Visitor

"Welcome young knight cadets. It is a privilege to have you all here today before us." The five cadets and the senior knights were assembled, standing before the high council awaiting their decision regarding the impending knighthood of the cadets. Alec stood looking around the room to the others, to find that everyone was as equally on edge as he was. The council speaker smiled and after clearing his throat, continued the verdict.

"Upon close evaluation of the circumstances and with careful consideration to all of those involved, we have decided, in general, your knight's status shall not be denied." The group broke out into chorus at the sounds of their achievement. Alec looked around again and saw that the only one not smiling was the Lion. As if understanding what it was that was troubling him, a sudden chill ran down his spine. The speaker raised his hand in the air to call for silence and again spoke.

"But, regrettably, I must inform you that, although it is not our wish to deny anyone knight's status, there are those amongst you that will only be granted status on a probationary basis. Only once certain factors are met shall the title be granted in full." Now Alec understood why Eliza's father chose not to add into the celebration. He must have expected something such as this to happen.

Zelus stepped forward and after receiving permission to speak spoke as respectfully as his anger would allow.

"High speaker, I must ask of you why is it that you decided to postpone our knighthood? Did we not complete the trials?" The councilman stood with an unwavering expression.

"Cadet Zelus, we have gone over the events of your trials as they were viewed through the Eye of Aneira and not once during the footage did it appear as though any of your party managed to make it within the center of the maze and kneel before the altar of Aneira to offer prayer as is the required tradition. However, we are lenient in our decision. As you all managed to make it within the center of the maze and only in your rash behavior, did you fail to enter the center and pray at the shrine. It is on these grounds, we have concluded that although you did not succeed in completing the trial we set before you, you did not entirely fail. We propose you undertake a simpler task, to prove your worth."

"With all respect, High Councilman, Imperius, the only reason we did not make it to the altar was because we tended to our wounded and we were pulled from the labyrinth by a medical team."

"Yes, and this is a further reason as to why we have decided not to fail everyone." Zelus' anger was beginning to grow more apparent.

"But you intend to fail some of us?"

"Cadet Zelus, if you wish for everyone in your squad to fail, by all means press on with your argument but, if you would allow me to continue, we have been more generous than you give us credit for." Zelus stepped back in line afraid of jeopardizing the chances of his comrades.

"Thank you, cadet Zelus. As I was saying, there are those among you that proved worthy of your knight's status and will be granted your titles today. The others may take a secondary trial in order to prove themselves to the people of Valoria and as such, earn back their trust." Alec could feel his anger and that of those around him begin to swell at the insults the speaker had begun to let out. Subtly, he placed his hands behind his back and clenched his fists tightly to vent his anger.

"Cadet Dominic, please step forward." Dominic did as he was told. He stepped forward, placed his hands behind his back, and stood tall.

"During your trials you displayed great courage in facing the challenges set before you, specifically the Valdurn. It is the council's unanimous decision to grant you your knight's status from this day forward until such a time as you prove that you are no longer worthy to bear the seals of Sidonis and Aneira and to tend to her flock and spread the teachings of her love."

"Thank you, High Council. May Aneira live within your hearts." Dominic took as deep a bow as he was able and walked back in line.

"Cadet Nilus, please step forward." Nilus did as he was instructed and shook uneasily waiting for their verdict.

"Over careful observation of your performance during the trials, we have decided you will also be granted knight's status from this day forward until such a time as you prove that you are no longer worthy to bear the seals of Sidonis and Aneira and to tend to her flock and spread the teachings of her love." Nilus bowed his head, walked back to his brother and stood in line.

"Cadet Eliza, please step forward." Eliza did as she was instructed. Alec looked over to the Lion who looked his daughter in the eye and with a gentle shake of his head and gesture of his hand warned her to keep calm.

"It is the council's decision, due to an inability to work within a team environment, you endangered your fellow cadets, which may have been the cause of the resulting failure. It is, therefore, our decision to postpone your knight's status until a secondary trial can be completed. We hope that you will consider taking a more serious approach with your upcoming tasks as had it not been for your father and mother's pristine records and years of faithful service, we would not grant you this most generous opportunity." Eliza's rage was barely contained, but she did her best to smile graciously and walked back in line. Alec let out a deep sigh of relief as Eliza stood and began to take deep breaths.

"Cadet Zelus, please step forward." Zelus followed suit and stood before the council. "Cadet Zelus, you showed excellent promise during your trials and we believe that it was through your leadership and courage that your team was able to survive the hardships that you encountered within the trials. We have granted you the position of squad leader in the hopes that you will continue to lead by example and bring glory to your order. You are now a knight from this day forward until such a time as you prove that you are no longer worthy to bear the seals of Sidonis and Aneira and to tend to her flock and spread the teachings of her love." Zelus bowed his head and stepped back to his place in line.

"Cadet Alec, step forward." As Alec stepped forward, he noticed an uncomfortable stir amongst the council.

"Cadet Alec, we were most displeased by your lack of leadership ability and your rash behavior which led to the injuries and near death of your team. We feel that your lack of honor or noble house has stained the pride of the knights. We believe, as our social experiment, you have indeed proven the worth of "your people." It was the council's decision to deny your knight's status indefinitely until a time that we can determine you are worth a second chance." There was an uproar from the crowd enraged by the council's decision. The head speaker slammed his gavel against the table calling order to the group.

"That is enough! It is within the council's power to determine who is and is not worthy of entering the knight's college. It is our generosity and our pity that allowed Cadet Alec to enter the academy to begin with. He is, and always has been, our little social experiment and should we decide to banish him to join the rest of his lot then so shall it be." The head speaker attempted to calm the crowd, but it was not until a hooded figure walked into the room and pounded her staff on the floor causing a large booming echo to bounce off from the walls.

"What is the meaning of this disruption?" Imperius demanded of the hooded figure. One by one, the crowd began to settle also, curious to discover the hooded figure's intentions.

"I am the head priestess in charge of the worshipping altar within the labyrinth. It was brought to my attention by one of the disciples that there was a disturbance within the waters of the shrine. Therefore, I went to see to the matter personally. I have brought with me a small amount of the water from the shrine, and you will be as surprised as I that there is a message from one of Aneira's nymphs." The head speaker took a step forward and then stopped.

"You mean to tell us that as one of Aneira's messengers who have been silent for centuries has delivered us a message? Pray tell Priestess Mayella, what is your message?" The woman smiled.

"That the cadet, Alec Dante of Highmoore be allowed to enter the knight's college." Alec's heart froze with either excitement or dread, of which one he was unsure. Everyone slowly turned their heads towards Alec and eyed him with a collective combination of anger, excitement, befuddlement and terror.

"Preposterous, sister! Surely, you cannot hope we would believe the nymphs have decided to meddle in such things? This is the trick of yet another Highmoorian sympathizer." As if expecting such an outburst, the priestess had walked across the hall toward the throne room. A young servant boy pushed open the doors for her as she neared them and all who were congregated followed her into the empty room. Alec had never seen the inside of the throne room before and he was not disappointed. The ceilings reached to a ridiculous height supported by enormous marble columns. They walked along the far stretching red carpet that led to the empty throne with a statue on either side, one of Aneira and one of Sidonis. Before the throne sat a fountain that was similar to the one that was supposed to reside within the maze. As Alec stared at the empty throne, he remembered a story his good friend Rowan had once told him.

"Once Valascaa was a proud and peaceful nation, ruled by their most beloved and benevolent King, Caliban. This king had been appointed by Sidonis, to guide the people of Valascaana before the fabled paladin began his journeys. The castle, newly rebuilt with the aid of the golem masters, was rich with ancient secrets brimming with both knowledge and power. The king obtained access to many of these secrets and used them to guide his people into a glorious golden age. It was sometime later, however, that a warring nation attacked the peaceful Valascaana and the king sought out the secrets of the ancient keep for use in his war.

With the ancient power of the golems at his command, the king easily laid waste to his enemies and grew ripe with greed. The king obtained an insatiable hunger for power, such that he was willing to pay any price. That price one day was paid, at the sacrifice of his beautiful queen, Aenora. He was told by consuming the soul of a Divine he could become a god, which no foreign nation would ever dare to challenge again. Caliban paid his price and obtained a great power , though he lost his soul to the lord of malice, Daemon.

With his freedom, Caliban also lost his mind and began to wreak havoc against the people of Valascaana until his eldest son, Baelian, rose up against his father, driving him from his homeland. Baelian vowed neither he nor any other of his house would sit the throne until king Caliban's wickedness had been laid to rest."

Now, Alec stood staring at the empty throne, over two hundred years later, no heir having returned to claim credit for ending the mad king's reign. Alec snapped back to the present as the priestess approached the fountain.

"Please great Aurora, appear before us and deliver your message." The priestess knelt down before the altar and carefully poured the water into the basin of the fountain. The light in the room began to flicker and then a flash of blue light rose from the water.

"I am Aurora, one of the goddess Aneira's nymphs and messenger of her holy rite. It is to be understood that the powers that govern you deem Alec Dante of

Highmoore to be accepted into the knight's college." All eyes in the room shifted to Alec who stood in shock at the impossible odds that had aided him.

Chapter 12 – Repercussions

The eyes of the entire congregation bore into Alec as the nymph vanished with the same flash of blue light. An awkward silence filled the room as if waiting for Alec to produce the answer to the question they were all asking. Why after so many years have the nymphs deemed to interfere with the affairs of mortals, why now, for this one boy? The Lion was the first to react placing himself in between the council and Alec and turned to face Alec.

"Alec, go home, I will be there soon, alright?" Alec was still too stunned to understand what he had been told.

"Alec, I said now!" This time, Alec snapped back to reality and dipped his head respectfully to the council and took a glance about the room at the group before turning his back and leaving. He had only just made it to the door as the arguments renewed. The council began talking aloud simultaneously, changing the usual prepared responses into a clutter of bewilderment. Eliza caught up to Alec as he descended the last of the stairs and entered the courtyard.

"Alec, are you alright?" She reached out and grabbed his arm turning him to face her. He looked into her eyes and saw the severe look of concern that he had witnessed with unsettling frequency as of late.

"Yeah, sure, never better." He mumbled to himself, Eliza punched him in his good arm in response.

"Be serious for once. What we just witnessed isn't natural."

"Eliza, I honestly do not know how to react to this. Truthfully, I think that things would just be easier if I shrugged it off and acted as if nothing ever happened."

"Alec, you cannot just shrug this one off. Of all the nymphs written in Aneira's scripture, Aurora is known as the redeemer, the avenger, the.."

"The angel of death, trust me, Eliza, I am aware of who Aurora is. Of all the nymphs, she tends to be the worst when it comes to dealing with us. Normally it ends in the death of the one that has been named." Alec spoke in as nonchalant a tone as he could muster, which only caused Eliza to overcompensate for his lack of reaction.

"Alec, how can you be so detached about this? How can you not be worried about how immense an omen this is?" Alec could not answer her. The simple fact was that for the second time in his life, he was truly frozen with fear and he knew from experience that such crippling fear would shatter him if he could not come to terms with it.

They continued to walk in silence. All the while, Alec tried to think of something to say, but was constantly drawn away by thoughts of his impending doom. He could hear a voice in the back of his mind calling to him. He stopped and searched in the expanse around them but saw no one even looking his way. Eliza tugged on him gently trying to get his attention. Alec looked past Eliza as her lips mouthed words that bore him no meaning. Beyond her, he could see the ominous girl from his various dreams walking alone, that same sad, foreboding gloom in her eyes.

"ALEC!" Finally, he could hear Eliza's voice and his eyes were redirected toward hers.

"Alec, let's just get you home, you're obviously having a rough time dealing with this. Taking some time to clear your head would do you some good." Alec listened obediently. He arrived at his house only a few moments later and was alarmed upon being tackled by a bundle of feather and fur.

"*Mwerp mwerp!*" Oz curled up on Alec's torso and began to rub its head against his face. Alec's worries washed away for the time being as the adoration for his new friend took precedence.

Eliza laughed and sat on the floor with her legs crossed and reached out and began to pet Oz, who began to purr.

"My father must have had him brought back here for the time being." She guessed as she continued to pet him until she touched something warm and wet.

"Alec, Oz is hurt!" She turned her palm toward him so that he could see the splotch of blood decorating her palm. Alec pushed off from the floor and examined Oz's pelt until he found a small jagged cut on his flank.

"Oz, what did you do?" Alec glanced up from Oz to the shattered glass on the floor and then up to his shattered window. Eliza noticed the same and let out an audible, "aww."

"He missed you Alec he must have known that you were distressed." Alec looked down to the lion hawk and smiled.

"Thank you, my friend, but let's get that bandaged." Alec walked across the room, grabbed some cloth and tearing it into strips, bandaged the wound. Oz fussed as Alec and Eliza attempted to hold him in place and began to pick at the wrap.

"Oz, leave it alone. You have to let it heal." Oz let out a low grumble, but left the cloth on his leg alone. A brief moment later there was a loud knock at the door and the gruff voice of the Lion could be heard.

"It is alright commander, come in." The door opened and the Lion hastily walked and shut the door behind him.

"Alec, we need to talk." He noticed Oz in the room and then, sooner than Eliza and Alec had, saw the broken glass on the floor and the broken window.

"Smart bird," he muttered to himself before continuing to the business at hand.

"Alec, we need to talk." Alec and Eliza committed their undivided attention to him as Kristiana entered. She repeated the Lion's exact response, her eyes moving from the Lion Hawk, to the floor and then the window. As her eyes again fell upon Oz, she smiled to herself but chose not to interrupt.

"As you can imagine, the council is in a state of chaos and panic right now. They aren't sure what to make of the situation and instead of answering with reason, the majority have responded with anger and fear."

"What is to become of us then?" Alec spoke up.

"Well, not even the council's arrogance and ignorance would cause them to ban you from the knights at this point. You will both still be allowed into knighthood, but I believe the council will be eager to keep you far away from the capitol in the hopes of pushing whatever they fear condemns you away from their door. I can only imagine that they will use your exploits to further their own agendas from there."

"Then what is to become of me, father?" Eliza said. The Lion looked to her and let out a long sigh.

"Since the nymph only named Alec, I am afraid they are not going to be lenient with you, Eliza. However, with some help, we were able to convince them to allow you to undergo your secondary trial still. They have decreed that you are to take on a series of jobs that the citizens have asked for assistance with. There are a broad number of things to be done here and in the nearby village of Tarnas. But with the two of you working together, you should be able to have everything taken care of within the next few days and then head out to Tarnas." Eliza let out an angry scoff and even Kristiana let out a snort of discontent. Alec took his chance amongst the silence to speak up.

"Is there any chance that you know more about what the nymph had in store for me?" The tone of the room grew rather grim and it was Kristiana who answered.

"I have asked head priestess Mayella to meet with me later, in order to try and discover the meaning of the message. It will take some time, but I am quite certain that you are still in Aneira's favor."

"How can you be so sure?" Kristiana smiled.

"Alec despite what you may think, you have a pure and noble heart. In Aneira's infinite wisdom, she would never strike down such a person." Alec was shocked at such a bold statement in Aneira's name but chose not to argue.

"Thank you. Please let me know what you discover."

"Of course dear." The Lion looked down at Oz and Alec could almost make out a faint smile.

"I suppose that your friend should stay here with you for the night but please make sure that he doesn't get out again. You would do well to keep the council ignorant of him for the time being."

"I will make sure, sir."

"Eliza it is time to head home. You and Alec will have a long day ahead of you tomorrow."

"I will see you tomorrow, Alec. Please try not to worry so much, alright? Things will be just fine." Alec smirked and nodded his head as Eliza and the Lion turned and left. Kristiana sat down in a chair near Alec and began to speak.

"I do believe that I still owe you an explanation about your empathy partner?" Alec nodded.

"It is a very rare bit of magic so to speak. One of Aneira's more treasured and well protected secrets. I am sure that you have noticed a brand new, yet familiar, presence within your own consciousness?" Alec thought for a moment before remembering the odd sensation that he had felt just a few days ago.

"Well, not so much a presence. It was more like a gut feeling as if it were an emotion or an instinct."

"That is what I am referring to." When one binds their soul with another, the bond, conveys their emotions to the other without words or language of any kind. I know that you are probably too young to understand this now but the closest example I can give you is the bond between two lovers or a dear and relished friend. You need only to know them in order to understand their deepest desires and fears. Normally to know the very soul of another better than you know your own self is an impossible feat but, with such a deeply intimate bond, an empathy partner can do just that. Know your very soul and whether or not you are in danger at any given moment. How do you think Oz knew that you would be here?" Alec was overwhelmed by the information that had just been given to him.

"Can one shield themselves from their partner?"

"I suppose so. Yes, I would imagine that it would be possible, but it would take an immense amount of control. You would have to be in control of your emotions to such an extreme that not even your thoughts would betray you. For now Alec, I would instead focus on deepening your connection with Oz. In fact, with you about to travel, this would be the perfect time for you to learn to locate Oz no matter where you are." Kristiana rose from her seat, but Alec eager to learn more, attempted to stop her.

"Alec, there is no more that I can teach you. I must admit that I am rather jealous of your bond. In all of the years that I have loved my husband, I fear that we will never be able to have the same connection that you and Oz share. Treasure it and use it well to protect the two of you and keep you inseparable." Without another word, Kristiana left the room leaving Alec and Oz alone to expand upon their friendship.

Chapter 13- First Assignment

"Alright, Alec. The best way for us to get all of these things finished is to split up. I will take this half of the list. You take the other half and we will make back here when we are finished. Sound good to you?" This was the question Eliza had asked him early that morning and it had been foolish of Alec to answer with a yes. He was sitting at the same table that they had sat discussing the best way for them to complete their objectives. Eliza was kind enough to leave Alec all of the fairly simple tasks, allowing him to talk to villagers for various reasons, whether to hear their complaints about different policies or to deliver messages.

His favorite task of the day had been to travel into town and collect a list of groceries from the town market. None of the tasks Alec had performed that day was what he would deem a worthy enough cause for a knight to be required, but they were all tasks that had been set forth to them by the council. Now, he sat where he had been sitting for several hours, impatiently awaiting Eliza and he assumed Zelus to return from their half of the tasks. The waitress had already made several rounds toward Alec and he had already eaten one meal there and was becoming increasingly tempted to order again when finally he could hear the sound of a young man and woman arguing. Alec raised three fingers into the air and counted down the seconds before Eliza came barging in and sat next to him.

"What are you counting?" She snapped at him. He rolled his head to the side and saw Zelus sit opposite Eliza, a broad smirk on his face despite the enormous handprint that also bore on his face. From the look of the smirk on his face, Alec knew that Zelus had been laying on a thick layer of sarcasm, and had probably been hounding Eliza for hours, judging upon the look on her face.

"Me, oh nothing. I was just getting ready to flag down the waitress." As if on cue, the young girl who had been flirting with Alec for most of the day arrived.

"Anything I can get for you, darling?" Alec smiled at the greeting as the young woman placed her hand on Alec's. Eliza rolled her eyes already annoyed by the girl. Zeus smirked, hinting to Alec the source material of their bickering.

"Yes, as a matter of fact, my friends and I would like whatever it was that you brought me earlier." The woman smiled.

"Alright then, three bowls of the red fire stew. I'll be right back, darling." The waitress turned and both Alec and Zelus perked up and watched as she swayed her hips as she walked, aware that they were watching. She turned back to match their gaze and smiled as she continued to walk seductively. Eliza cleared her throat loudly to alert them that she was still there.

"So Eliza, how went your half of the list?" Alec asked as he stretched back in his chair and took a deep breath. Eliza glared at him for a few minutes and then looked to Zelus.

"Well, not that he was of any help, but we managed to finish everything on the list." Zelus attempted to hold back a laugh and instead let out a choked gurgle.

"What happened? There's obviously a story here." Again, Eliza glared at Zelus as the waitress came back and sat down three steaming bowls of heavenly smelling stew, three cups and a pitcher of water.

"Is there anything else that I can get for you three?" Sensing the tension, the waitress smiled, winked at Alec and Zelus, while she walked away, giggling to herself as Eliza fumed.

"As I was saying," Eliza started after swallowing a mouthful of stew. "That we had started to finish our half when." A shocked expression crawled across her face as if she had just seen the reaper and then, with panicked intensity, sprang into frenzied action, trying to pour water into her glass. After fumbling around quite some bit, she managed to gulp down three glasses as Alec and Zelus roared with laughter. Eliza gasped trying to catch her breath before starting at the two of them.

"You could have warned me that it was so hot!" Alec and Zelus looked at one another and then very plainly spoke in unison.

"Eliza, it is called red fire stew."

"I did not know what it was called. I was too distracted by that girl ravaging you two with her eyes to pay attention to what she was saying." Alec and Zelus continued to laugh at Eliza's discontent as she gulped down another mouthful of water. As she attempted to recover, by taking in deep breaths of air and trying to exhale the heat out, Alec and Zelus dug into their stew by the spoonful and, through their own deep mouth breathing, emptied their bowls and sat back content.

"Aren't you going to drink any water?" Eliza looked at the two of them with awe.

"Nah, I am good, but are you going to finish that?" Alec looked at Eliza with great curiosity.

"Of course I am, I'm just not used to spicy foods like this. That is all." Alec and Zelus laughed for a moment.

"What's so funny now?"

"Oh, it is just you have lived among the high society for so long you have never had a taste of the local delicacies. Zelus and myself live off things such as this." Zelus nodded in agreement as Eliza battled with another spoonful, each time taking smaller and smaller bites.

"I have not been pampered, thank you. I merely eat what is available to me. Besides Zelus lives in the noble district as well." Zelus spoke up in defense of the argument.

"Yeah, but I practically live on my own since my father is never around. So, I eat here opposed to sitting home alone." Eliza continued to bicker.

"I have not been pampered." Alec and Zelus turned to one another and acted pompous and high strung for a moment until Eliza landed a slug in the shoulder to each of them. Eliza, unwilling to sway from her foul mood allowed, Zelus to continue the story.

"Well, we were working with the locals to try and find a thief and after a small degree of trouble we were able to catch him and return some stolen goods and…" Eliza slammed her small hands onto the table interrupting.

"No, what happened is I chased the thief through the streets, alleys and across rooftops in order to catch him while you were hitting on some random girl you met in the square." Alec looked to Zelus who shrugged his shoulders and nodded before continuing.

"Anyway, it so happens that the thief came back my way and, through my own elaborate methods, I tripped him up and captured him."

"If you call accidently running into someone and falling on them elaborate methods, then yeah you were superb." Zelus smiled again and went on.

"Afterwards, we finished the job that we were initially on and started another, which involved finding a cat. It was hiding in the owner's house and…" Alec leaned forward to interrupt.

"I am more or less just curious as to why Eliza is so upset." Zelus smirked again and as soon as Eliza looked up, Zelus averted his gaze. It was Eliza that finished.

"After spending the entire day hitting on anything wearing a skirt, he had the nerve to kiss me." Alec turned to Zelus, a shocked expression on his face, and Zelus smiled.

"She said that I didn't have the guts to kiss a real woman on a whim, so why even bother." Zelus paused a moment. "She was wrong." Alec laughed and the three carried on their various tales for an hour before finishing up and Alec paying for their meals.

"So, there is nothing left to do on your list?" Eliza pulled the crumpled parchment out of her pocket and began to read through the list.

"No, the one thing that we have left to do is to gather supplies and go to Tarnas and meet with the local barkeep. It seems he has a matter that he must discuss with us.

"Alright. Well. I have already been to the market once today. How about I head there and gather supplies. Then, first thing tomorrow morning, you two and I head out." Zelus leaned forward and spoke up.

"I am sorry, Alec, but I have to meet with the council tomorrow. They have some things they would like to discuss with me. Apparently, I was just helping today to make sure that you two could get through everything."

"Well, we appreciate it Zelus, Eliza and I both." He looked at Eliza who mumbled a thank you under her breath. Alec looked at Eliza and goaded her.

"Come on, Eliza…say it as if you mean it." He spoke to her as if teaching manners to a toddler.

"Thank you!" She looked at Alec angrily.

"That is alright Eliza. That kiss earlier was well worth it." The two men laughed as Eliza balled up her tiny fist and threatened to punch Zelus again. Eliza reared her head towards Alec, who stopped laughing immediately.

"Alright then. Let us go gather some supplies." Alec and Eliza both left the tavern and went their separate ways, each gathering a different set of supplies.

Chapter 14 – The Knight's First Steps

Early that next morning, Alec opened his eyes to see Oz lying beside him, sleeping peacefully, his chest steadily puffing out and deflating with each breath. Alec listened contentedly as the baby lion hawk purred quietly. After a few more minutes of lying in bed, Alec slowly rose and started his morning workout, to the best of his ability. Once finished, he began gathering up his things into a pile and then proceeded to wash himself. As he exited the washroom, he came out to a rather hyperactive griffet bounding from one end of the room to the other carrying Alec's traveling bag with its beak. He smiled and shook his head before reaching out and attempting to wrestle the bag free.

"Come on Oz. Let go of the bag." Alec grabbed one strap and pulled gently. Oz tugged playfully against the bag.

"Oz, give me the bag!

"*Brr brr!*" Oz teased.

"Oz come on. Give me the bag now!" Alec's irritation was apparent.

"*BREE!*" Oz screeched and, pulling himself away, jumped, kicked and flapped his youngling wings and scrambled his way up the wall and rested on the support beam.

"*Brrr!*" He cooed in spite as he stared down at Alec. Alec paced around the room for several minutes debating on what his first course of action should be. He closed his eyes briefly and concentrated on the mental connection that bound them. He could sense an overwhelming amount of excitement flooding into him and knew that Oz thought he was going with him. Alec looked up at Oz with sadness on his face.

"I am sorry little one, I cannot take you with me just yet. I can next time, though." Oz let out a sad cue and turned his back to Alec blocking Alec's view of his face.

"Come on Oz, it's not because I don't want to, I'm not allowed to take you out and about until I have permission from the council." Again, Oz let out another sad cue before there came a knock at the door.

"Alec, I am coming in." Eliza spoke as she slowly entered the room.

"*Brree!*" Oz squealed as he jumped from his perch, nearly landing in Eliza's arms.

"Well, someone is awfully happy to see me. Who is a cute baby?" She cooed at him as he continued to squeak excitedly jumping up and down pawing at her.

"What is got him so excited?" She laughed as she petted his mane. Alec looked at Eliza and closed his eyes focusing on their connection.

"I think he believes that he can get you to bring him with us." Alec focused some more trying to comprehend the jumbled emotions. Eliza turned her head to the side and then realized what Alec must be doing.

"Have you been working on your mental connection with Oz?" Alec nodded his head and then proceeded back to recovering his bag. After a couple of jumps, he resorted to throwing things at it.

"*BRR*!!" Oz pushed away from Eliza and shimmied back up the wall, placing his body over top of the bag. Eliza burst out into a fit of laughter, which after a minute, forced her to bend in half and eventually take a seated position. Alec waited with an annoyed look on his face for Eliza to stop laughing. When she had finished, she took a moment to recover and wipe the tears from her eyes.

"Having some trouble, are we?" Alec made an irritated clucking sound with his mouth and continued to stare at Eliza. She rose from the chair and called to Oz.

"Come here baby. Bring the bag to Aunt Eliza. Come here sweetheart. Give Auntie the bag." She continued to baby talk Oz until he poked his head out and after some more goading hopped down with the pack in his beak and released the strap into Eliza's custody. As she patted Oz on the head and lifted up the bag, she gave Alec a look as if to show him how easy that was.

Alec walked over to her and took the bag from out of her hand and mumbled a thank you before he finished packing his bag. Slinging his pack onto his shoulder, he squatted down and patted Oz on the head and rose again.

"Kristiana said that she is coming over later to play with you, would you like that?"

"*Bree bree!*" The griffet cheered causing Alec to smile bitter sweetly, not wanting to leave his baby behind. Their goodbyes complete, Alec and Eliza walked through the door and, closing it behind them, tried to tear their ears away from the sound of the baby's cries. As they walked, Eliza turned to Alec and spoke to him, walking backwards.

"Hey Alec. I forgot to tell you I invited Zelus to join us. Is that alright with you?" Alec was surprised to find that this news was not a shock to him.

"I thought that he had an important meeting with the council?"

"I am not sure. He told me this morning that he was free now, and so I invited him to come along. Is that alright with you?"

"Yeah, it is fine. It will be nice to have someone else to help handle you." He smiled and waited for the inevitable but friendly shove. They both smiled at one another after she pushed him as she nearly ran into Zelus.

"Oh, guess I should have figured that you would have invited nymph boy as well." Zelus looked at Alec as he caught Eliza by her shoulders and tenderly released her. Eliza smiled and pulled the straps of her pack back up onto her shoulders. Zelus eyed Eliza's outfit which consisted of many garments not suited for travel wear.

"Eliza, you don't plan on traveling dressed like that do you? It's a two day hike from here to the shrine at Tarnas." Eliza smiled as they walked and stopped, tossing her bag to Zelus.

"Of course not, this is our last stop before we leave. I just wore this in town to make my father happy." She strolled into her house and closed the door. Alec leaned his back against the wall and tipped his head down and crossed his arms. Zelus struck a similar pose on the opposite side of the door and spoke to Alec without looking at him.

"Are you sure your afflictions are well enough for travel? Would not want you to wear yourself down." Alec smiled and chose not to ignore the taunt.

"I see you lost your sling, you must have laid off from your, you know, late night activities." Zelus snapped his head toward Alec and glared at him for a moment before looking back to the bustling street.

"You know it was not your fault, right? The trials? Ask the others, Dom and Nilus agreed with your decision and as much as I hate to admit it, I do too." Alec glanced over to Zelus surprised by something so out of character for him.

"I could have done more."

"No Alec, you could not have. None of us could have! You were forced to make a decision and you made the appropriate one! Eliza was all alone and outnumbered. You had no way of knowing that there was a Valdurn waiting around the corner." Alec looked at Zelus who seemed angry now, but it was not usual for him to lose his temper over something like this. Alec questioned the odd behavior but Zelus was not willing to discuss the matter further. At that same time, Eliza opened the door.

"Are you two at it already? I swear you are worse than children." She continued to yell at them but they were both momentarily distracted by Eliza's change in fashion. She stood before them wearing full strider's gear, tanned breeches, tall black leather boots and long leather trench coat, two curved swords on her hips and a bow and full quiver on her back. She held out her arms and spun slightly.

"Much better, do you not think? It was my mother's." Alec nodded his head in agreement and then assisted Zelus in picking up his jaw. Eliza smiled, satisfied with their reactions, and taking her bag from Zelus, slung it over her shoulders and began to walk toward the town gates.

"Do either of you have anything that you need to take care of before we leave? It is still early and we have a few moments to spare." Eliza mentioned and only one thought came to Alec.

"Is there enough time to stop by the Highmoorian sector and say goodbye to the kids? I have not been by the past several days and I would tell them goodbye, if I am able." Both Eliza and Zelus nodded their heads.

"That is fine, we can meet you at the gates in a couple of hours. That will give us a chance to make sure that we have enough provisions." Alec nodded his head as he walked north towards the Highmoorian sector. As he reached the gates to the sector, the knight posted by the gate, tipped his head to Alec as Alec walked inside.

The buildings on either side of Alec were worn, some of which beyond repair. As he walked down the main street, he saw many of his own, who smiled and acknowledged him as he passed.

"Good morning to you, Sir Alec. May the goddess bless you with a swift recovery." One of the many spoke to which Alec thanked.

"Admirable performance," another spoke. Alec smiled and bowed his head to the praises, as he admitted to himself that his performance had not yet been enough to grant his people the break they deserved. As Alec continued to walk down the street, he saw three children, two boys and one girl at play, who immediately recognized him.

"ALEC!" They yelled as they ran up to him. Alec knelt down slowly, placing his pack on the ground and gave them a hug as they ran into his arms.

"Are you going to play with us today?" The little, red haired, green eyed, freckle faced girl asked.

"I am sorry Seera, I cannot today. I just wanted to say goodbye before I leave the city, on my first mission as a knight." The larger of the two boys, Timothy, a brown haired, brown-eyed boy spoke.

"I am going to become a paladin." Alec smiled as the boy puffed out his chest and Logan, the smaller of the two boys looked at him. Logan was blonde haired, greenish blue eyed and was by far the quietest of the three.

"I thought the paladins were gone?" Timothy turned his head.

"The paladins will return. I know they will." He spoke as Alec stood up.

"Are you leaving?" Seera asked.

"I have to but I should be back before too long. You three be good while I am away, alright?" The children nodded their heads as they each gave Alec another hug, before trotting off. As Alec watched them run about, he took a long look at the Highmoorian sector and reaffirmed the reasons for his hard work. Alec turned and walked back towards the gates to Valascaa.

Alec quickly found Zelus and Eliza, looking at the food stalls on the way to the gates. Confirming they were indeed ready to leave, they turned and walked to the southern gate. As they neared the gates, several guards approached and barred their path, weapons outdrawn.

"State your business." The guard grumbled at them, his shield clanking with that of the soldier next to him.

"We have been ordered by the council to travel to Tarnas in order to aid the people there and spread the word of the council." The guard seemed to accept her answer because after examining the group and seeming particularly interested in discussing Alec, they unbarred the path and wished them good fortune.

As the three of them began to march down the road, they all looked out onto the marvelous expanse that lay before them. Grassy plains and roaring rivers stretched out all along it, but then Alec turned his head west and knew it to be west that lay the home of the Forsaken.

"Tarnas is this way." He pointed east by northeast and they began to walk following the long road.

"Eliza, do you have any more information about what kind of job this is?" Alec asked as they walked. There was a pause for a moment and then Alec could hear the crumpling of parchment before Eliza read.

"Speak with Talon, local barkeeper at Tawna's Tavern in Tarnas. Talon has information regarding a suspicious character that we are to investigate. That's all it says." She folded the list and placed it back into her pocket. As they continued to walk for several hours. Often at times, they would take a few minutes rest and they would take turns sparring or just sitting and stretching out their legs for a moment. They had been given additional time to meet the contact and had left sooner than the council had anticipated. That night, they set up camp and built a small fire that they circled their tents around. Alec sat leaning against a log looking up at the sky as Zelus drew circles in the ground with a stick. Alec turned his attention to see Eliza reading a book. He glanced at the title on the tightly bound leather cover.

"The Epitaph of Twilight, Seal of the Nameless God." Alec smirked and shook his head, realizing that it must be some crummy novice author's novel about some alternate world he created.

"You draw often, Zelus?" Alec nodded his head toward the shapes that Zelus was engraving in the dirt. Zelus shrugged in response.

"It helps me to clear my head, drawing, practicing my letters, things such as that." He said.

"Hmm, guess I never considered that. Does drawing them out help you?" Alec thought of the many thoughts that plagued his mind on a regular basis.

"Yeah, I would say so, it just relaxes my mind, gives me some clarity you know?" he looked around him for a brief moment and plucked a twig from the pile of brushwood.

"Here, you try it." Alec took the twig from Zelus' hand and began to draw his own shapes. He started with just simple things at first but after a couple of hours he had made a simple mockery of their camp. He was pleased at his work, never realizing that he could take pleasure in something so simple. Zelus looked over after a while and smirked.

"Not bad, not good either though." Alec threw the twig at him, and they both laughed. Eliza lowered her novel from in front of her nose briefly to see.

"Actually Alec, I think that with some more practice that you might make a decent artist." Alec smiled and looked back at his creation before laying and looking up at the sky. He knew that if they woke early that they would be arriving in Tarnas by the time the sun reached its zenith. He looked to his fellow companions, wished them goodnight and then closed the flap on his tent and went to sleep.

Chapter 15 – The Seer

The woman with the sad green eyes sat on a swing, humming a tune to herself. She continued to swing under the tree playing with something in her hands. Alec tried to watch her hands, but could not quite glimpse what it was that she was doing. Eventually, she turned her gaze toward him and smiled, warming him from within. He walked up towards her and reached out to pull back her hood, revealing her long flowing amber hair.

"I have been looking for you," he whispered to her. She smiled, her sad eyes brightening slightly.

"And I you," she said. Alec smiled, but was suddenly pulled from his peace, his arms reaching out for anything to anchor himself to but he was still drawn away. Alec let out a sigh of discontent as he opened his eyes and sat upright.

"Again, why do I keep having this dream? Who is this girl?" He ran his hands through his hair when an idea struck him. He began rummaging through his pack for anything that would suit his purpose and came upon a piece of parchment. Rushing from his tent without putting a shirt on, he grabbed some char from the fire and began to draw the long narrow lines of the beautiful woman's face. Despite his lack of practice, Alec's hand moved with unparalleled speed and precision having seen her so many times before. Within only a short few minutes, he had created an accurate resemblance to her, and sat now staring at it with awe.

Moments passed before he remembered that there had been a reason for him being pulled from his dream, and began to search the nearby area. There was nothing in sight, to provide reason for concern. Instead, he checked his bandages, strapped on his sword belt and walked out towards the area of camp, where he had practiced earlier.

He made a note not to stand too far from the fire, as the frigid night air was still all around him. Alec tapped back into his memories as a child and began to perform the different stances his grandmother had taught him as a child.

He took a wide stance and carefully drew the sword from its sheath. He looked down to the bandages on his right side, and slowly raised the sword, holding it out. As he did so, he remembered how strict his grandmother had been when training him. He made sure to hold his posture and control every contracting muscle fiber, aware of his body's position and his surroundings.

He had not quite reached shoulder level when he could feel the burning in his ribs, but as it was not unbearable, he continued. He surpassed shoulder height and held the sword over his head for a few seconds. He tipped the blade downward, as he imagined himself defending against an overhead attack and continued to roll the sword over, assuming the next form.

He tipped his body and leaned to the side as he gently stabbed and immediately flowed into a smooth sideways stroke, stepping into the next form. He brought the sword upward slowly and swiped downward across his body, flicking his wrist and bringing the sword vertical in front of his face, clasped firmly with both hands.

"Alright Alec. You can do this." He encouraged himself, and clasping his other hand over the hilt of his sword, eased himself through a series of uncomplicated strokes. He squinted slightly as he felt a rise in his level of discomfort with certain forms, but pushed himself further. As his confidence began to grow, so did the consistency of his strokes against his phantom opponent, until the pain had caused sweat to appear on his brow. He slid the sword back into its sheath, sat cross-legged on the ground, and closed his eyes to think.

"Come on orphan! Get up!" A much larger Highmoorian boy from Alec's past kicked his seven-year-old self, while he was lying on the ground. Alec forcibly spat as his body twitched reflexively. The boy and his friends laughed as Alec slowly rose to his knees. The large boy moved in and kicked Alec again, knocking Alec over as his grandmother, accompanied by a red and gold clad paladin, approached. The paladin had long white hair, pulled back in a ponytail, also possessing no right arm.

"Leave that boy alone!" The paladin called as Alec's grandmother held out her hand to the man.

"ALEC! Do not be afraid to defend yourself. Have I not taught you to be strong? Have I not taught you to overcome all doubt, fear and opposition? Stand up! Defend yourself!" The boy and his friends stared at the old woman and the paladin. Alec rose to his feet and wiped his mouth, as he glared at the boy in front of him. The bully and his friends eyed the two adults, a moment longer, before looking back to Alec.

"What? Do you want some more, orphan?" The larger boy taunted, stepping forward. Alec's eyes narrowed, the feeling of his grandmother's eyes on his back, unnerving him, placing his defenses on high alert. As the boy, swung at him, Alec shifted his back leg, turning his body from the blow, as he swung low.

The larger boy stumbled, as he took Alec's much smaller fist, in the small of his rib cage. Angry, the bully moved on him again. Alec raised both of his forearms, blocking the boy's punch, then wrapping around his arm, Alec twisted, kicking the boy hard in the ribs. After stumbling back once more, the boy backed down and moved on with his friends.

"You see, Alec. It is important to defend oneself. You cannot always allow others to press you." His grandmother chided.

"I did not want to hurt him." Alec whined, wiping the small trickle of blood from his mouth. "I do not want to fight."

"If you wish to shield others, you must first learn to shield yourself. There will come a time, when you will find something worth saving. You must be ready, at any moment, to do all that is necessary, in order to safeguard that, which is most important to you, in this life. I will not be around, forever, to watch after you."

"Alright, grandmother." Alec mumbled, as the old woman turned her head up to the paladin.

"See, Zerendil. You worry too much. The boy is flourishing in my care. Should you not be somewhere, tending to something?" She asked, smiling.

"Of course." The man replied, as he turned and walked away.

"Go ahead, and play, Alec." The old woman smiled at him, as well, before Alec, trotted off.

As Alec continued to meditate, he thought of his first days in Valascaana and of his friend Rowan, who had once been his Valascaan rival. Rowan was built identically to Alec, but had dark brown hair and brown eyes. The same as Alec, Rowan bore no noble name and shared the same headstrong attitude, leading to constant clashes between them. He smiled as he thought of the battles they once waged, until they were both too bloody and sore to continue their fight. Often times, they would continue their brawling until they were forcibly separated by an adult.

After about a year, he and Rowan had become sound friends, being the only outcasts in the knights' academy. It had also been Rowan, who had first convinced Alec, to break the rules, regarding the Aneiran maze. Rowan had eventually returned overseas, to be with his family after the deaths of his older brothers, whom Alec had never met. Alec remembered something Rowan had told him before his departure.

"I must see this world with my own eyes. I must face my doubts, fears and turn my every weakness into strength. One day, I will become a guiding light for my people and for that to happen, I shall see this world and come back, stronger, wiser. I will return my friend, and when I do, I hope you have also found the strength that you seek."

Alec thought to himself of his own need to grow stronger and wiser, in order to protect the ones he cared for. He remembered his various reasons, but mostly his ultimate reason for this, his sister. He continued to ponder about the things that bothered him most, namely, his being chosen by the long silent nymphs. Of the people that had experienced what happened in the throne room, he had been the only one to assume the worst, or so he was told. Not reassured by their comforting words, Alec still attempted to think of reasons that boded well for him.

"Maybe Aurora is not after me, but giving me a chance to redeem myself." Was the best he could come up with, but still found redemption a better alternative than punishment.

"I am not convinced on redemption, but perhaps something closer to forgiveness." Alec had not heard Eliza approach, but he dipped his head toward the ground and smiled, appreciative of her company.

"Ah, I would love to think that Aneira could forgive me." Alec mentioned. "I am afraid some crimes, are simply beyond recompense." Eliza shook her head and sat next to him.

"I meant forgiveness for yourself." She sighed heavily before continuing. "Alec, you cannot blame yourself for being a victim in the war with the Forsaken. You are the one of the few, who survived the attack on Highmoore. The knights and paladins stationed at the town were not even enough. No child had a chance against them. You should be thankful to Aneira for shielding you from harm." Alec did not respond. Eliza waited for him to say anything to back her feelings but knew that he could not, because he did not share them. She patted his scar causing him to tense before whispering in his ear.

"Allow your wounds to heal, brother." She kissed him on the cheek before walking back to her tent to wait morning. After several more minutes of quiet contemplation, Alec rose to his feet and walked back to ready his things for travel. He saw that Eliza and Zelus were already gathering their belongings eager to get an early start on the day. As Alec was packing, he came across the picture of the mysterious girl and stared at it for a moment.

"Who's the pretty girl?" Zelus stood staring over his shoulder.

"Looks as though she could go for a little Zelus action." Alec turned his head toward Zelus and let out a near audible growl. Eliza walked up and flicked Zelus in the forehead and then shooed him away. Eliza could not help but glimpse at the picture herself, however.

"Is that her? The woman from your dreams?" Alec nodded slightly.

"She's beautiful!" Eliza admired Alec's artwork for a moment, before Alec lovingly packed it away in his bag and shouldered the load.

"Too bad I have no idea who she is." He turned and began to walk toward the road. Eliza walked beside him and placed her hand on his shoulder.

"Do you think that she has anything to do with the nymph?" Alec shook his head.

"I have no idea. If she is, then I wonder what it means. I have been seeing her for a while now, Eliza." They continued to talk as they walked down the road, drifting off toward friendlier topics. Just short of late morning, Zelus walked up beside Alec and Eliza.

"How far away is Tarnas from here?" Zelus asked. Alec turned toward Eliza then nodded.

"We should be there within the next few hours." Zelus acknowledged with a shake of his head and began to walk a few paces ahead of them when they came upon an upturned wagon, its horse and owner, an elderly man, lie dying next to it.

"Hurry!" Zelus called back to the others as he threw down his pack and ran toward the man and began to tend to his wounds. Alec and Eliza weren't far behind and took up guard watching the roads carefully. As Zelus worked on stopping the man's bleeding, the man opened his eyes and began to speak to Zelus.

"I was just traveling down the road." Zelus tried to quiet the man.

"Please sir, you need to save your strength. I have to get the bleeding to stop." Zelus continued to work when the man placed his hand over Zelus' and held it in place.

"Too late, save the girl." The man strained to get out the words. Alec spun on his heel and knelt next to the man.

"What girl? If you can please tell us what happened?" Zelus eyed him angrily.

"Found a young girl on the road, said she needed a ride to town. Forsaken came, attacked, and took her." The man was far too weak to speak further so he pointed in the direction. Without regard for his own body Alec dropped his pack and began to sprint in the direction the man pointed.

"Zelus stay with him. Alec, I am coming with you." Eliza began to run as Zelus stayed with the old man. Alec ran, the pain in his side unbearable, as he unsheathed his sword and swung his shield out in front of him. Eliza, likewise, drew her bow and nocked an arrow in flight. Soon they came across the tracks of four pairs of armored boots. They slowed their run to a hastened walk and crouched down low enough so that their heads would be concealed behind the nearby shrubbery.

Alec crouched as close to the ground as he possibly could and peered through the nearby bushes toward the three armored men standing around their camp.

"Why are they setting up camp so close to the road?" Alec asked Eliza. She searched around the site but found nothing of note.

"I do not know, Alec. I do not like this though, something is wrong. The Forsaken should not be sitting about so leisurely within our lands. This isn't good." Alec continued to look around when he saw the fourth armor clad creature walk forward, dragging a child behind him.

"Sit!" It hissed through his metal mask, as he flung the child who stumbled toward the others and sat by the fire.

"We have to save her Alec. What should we do?" Alec thought for a moment and looked back toward Eliza.

"Let me reach the other side of the camp. Is there any way that you can distract them long enough for me to grab the girl?" Eliza thought for a moment and then grabbed something from her pouch.

"Go ahead. Signal when you are ready." Alec nodded and began to make his way toward the other side of camp. As he neared the other side, he could faintly overhear the hissing masks speak of their oncoming party. Alec's heart sank as he listened to the little girl's sobbing. He clutched at the left side of his chest as pain seared in his chest and rage coursed through his entire body. He gripped his fist so tightly that it began to go numb. He made it to the other side of the camp and held his sword out sideways, catching the sun's light, sending a quick flash to Eliza.

"What was that?" One of the creatures seethed through its mask and turned in the direction of Eliza. Alec prepared himself as three of the men rose and began to walk toward Eliza's hiding place. Without hesitation, an arrow shot through the bushes and bounced off the fourth's metal helmet.

"Attack!" This time the four of them charged toward her and Alec slowly walked toward the girl. Just as Alec reached for her there was a loud bang and the first of the four was propelled backward. The others hissed angrily as they were showered with debris.

"Hurry, come with me!" Alec called to the girl holding out his hand toward her. The girl looked at Alec with sheer terror decorating her face, a face that made Alec's worst fears come alive. In his mind, he knew that it could never be true but he could not help but notice how much this girl resembled Rayne.

"Grab the seer!" Alec heard a hiss and a growl as another small explosion sent another armored body through the air. The girl looked to Alec again and grabbed his hand as they ran as fast as they could back toward the road.

"Hurry!" Alec yelled, dragging the young girl behind him, her small legs and feet barely able to carry her. Alec quickly swung his shield over his shoulder and placed the girl over his opposite one. He could hear the men getting closer to him. His side burned and he knew that he would not be able to outrun them for long. As he reached the top of the hill he was scaling, his feet hit the dirt road and he nearly tripped as the ground leveled out.

"Zelus, take her!" He yelled as Zelus rose from the wounded man, drew his own sword and shield, while running towards them.

"Alec, what happened? Where is Eliza?" As he said it, she came running from the other side.

"We have to move now I have wounded two of them but they are ticked, and on their way here now." She whipped around blindingly quick and shot an arrow at one of the armored beasts as it reached the top of the hill. The creature hissed as the arrow lodged itself in its chest plate and black mist oozed from the hole.

Eliza shot several more arrows into it until finally she shot one through the faceplate and the creature buckled and remained still, falling into the tall grass where it vanished from sight. She reached back to grab another arrow as the remaining three arrived on the scene and she found she had none.

"Alec, Zelus we have a problem!" She unstrung her bow and slid it into her quiver and drew out her long curved knives.

"Stay behind us." Alec placed himself between the young girl and the Forsaken, pulling his shield in front of him. As if to laugh at them, the three men hissed in bursts, each standing in front of one of the knights. The one who had once been the fourth, whom Alec had heard speak, stood before him, larger than his brethren. His helmet was horned, where the others masks, were partially covered by hoods.

Alec raised his shield to block the first blow of his attacker and caught a long glance at the black twisted metal that grated against his shield. The blade was sharp and serrated, long jagged spines ran down the back, allowing a kill stroke regardless of which side one was struck with. Alec pressed back with his shoulder and swung his sword in a broad stroke scratching the armor that decorated his enemy's chest.

The creature swung back, knocking powerfully into Alec's shield, causing his right side to buckle. He crumpled slightly as the pain seared through him, but still managed to swing a counter blow. With a flick of his wrist, the armored giant slapped Alec's blade aside and kicked into Alec's chest sending him backward and onto his back.

"Kill them all, and grab the seer to return to the Fallen." The towering monster hissed as it stabbed down toward Alec's chest. Alec rolled to the side and sliced toward the Forsaken's ankles. He kicked at Alec's weapon but Alec still managed to cut into the back of its leg. A horrible squealing emitted from the wound in the leg and Alec had to cover his ears to blot out the horrible sensation. The Forsaken stumbled backward and began to work on his leg until the squealing stopped and Alec uncovered his ears and rose to his feet. He looked from side to side and saw Zelus and Eliza fighting savagely against their opponents but losing ground. He looked behind him and saw the Rayne look alike and then heard a voice within his mind.

"Awaken Alec."

Alec let his shield fall to the ground and, gripping his sword in both hands, felt an empowering rush flow through him. The Forsaken stepped backward for several paces.

"I said kill them!" The more heavily armored one yelled. Each renewed their assault on the knights but this time, Alec's arm felt stronger, his blade felt lighter. As the Forsaken leader swung toward him, he sidestepped and brought his own sword down across its back. He could hear the squealing start again but this time felt no need to cover his ears. Eliza and Zelus however, both covered theirs as the other two Forsaken looked to Alec curiously.

"Why do you not cover your ears? The banshee shriek has the power to kill. Why do you not crumble?" The leader raised his hand to the others to silence them.

"Back away you foolssss. He is one of the blessed ones. Quickly, we must return." Without further hesitation, the troop doubled back and vanished. Alec, Eliza and Zelus all ran toward the hill but knew that with the elderly man in his present condition and now this mysterious girl that they would never catch them. Alec turned to Eliza and Zelus who both stared at him awkwardly.

"What is the matter?" Alec stared back at them as they continued to gawk.

"Alec, do you feel alright?" Eliza asked as she walked toward him cautiously.

"Yeah, I feel fine, confused, but fine, why?"

"Alec, your eyes and your hair started glowing."

"What?" This time Zelus spoke up.

"Yeah man, the big one knocked you down and you lashed out at him. Then, when you stood up, you were glowing." Alec grabbed onto the longer locks of his hair and pulled them out, trying to examine them for himself. Zelus laughed as he watched Alec pull on his bangs.

"You are not glowing anymore but you were. What I want to know is what did the Forsaken mean by a blessed one?" Eliza spoke up after Zelus finished.

"Alec, I think that this has something to do with the nymph but that doesn't matter right now. We have to get them," she motioned toward the man and the girl, "to Tarnas before he bleeds out. We also have to warn the capital of what happened here." Alec and Zelus both nodded as they ran to gather the man and girl and, after some careful consideration, made a stretcher and began to make their way toward the nearby city that rested only a few hours away.

As they carried the old man, Alec and Zelus silently prayed for his safety as the young girl cried. Eliza ran up ahead to inform the guards of their arrival.

"Just hold on sir, we're almost there." Alec spoke to the old man as several guards came running from the open gates ahead of them, Eliza in tow.

"Hurry, young knights, inside, give us the man and report to the commander." Two of them took the makeshift stretcher from Alec and Zelus and sped off with him while the other guards took the three of them in a different direction toward a large stone building. The guards stopped them there before the massive wooden doors.

"Only one of you needs report to the commander, which of you would like to." Zelus stepped forward, his chest pressed forward.

"I am the leader of our squad. I will report. I will need the young girl to accompany me as well. She possesses information the rest of us do not." The guard nodded and led Zelus and the young girl into the building. As he entered, Zelus turned his head to the side and yelled.

"Turn in your report now, then get busy with the rest of your mission." Alec and Eliza asked where they might find the tavern and followed the road toward its location. The odor of sweat, perfume, meat and ale filled their noses as they walked into Tawna's tavern. Men and women of many walks of life surrounded them as they marched their way toward the front of the room and stopped at the counter. A barmaid came over to them and waited for them to speak.

"Is Talon here?" Eliza asked, pulling the paper from her pack showing off both the knights and council seal upon it. The woman smiled and pulled back her long flowing hair, revealing the tattoo of the eagle's talons on her cheek.

"Pleasure to meet you, lass. Are you the knights the capitol sent?" Eliza nodded her head.

"Ah, well there seems to have been a number of abductions lately, young girls. The guards here chalk it up to local brigands, but I am unconvinced. Then, you have the Forsaken sightings, not many at once, but in packs of three or four roaming about. I tried to take this to the commander, but he tells me that I am giving into local superstition and I should leave the investigation to real investigators. That's why you're here." The woman smiled, but turned her attention toward a rabble on the opposite side of the bar.

"It appears that some of my tenants have grown rowdy. This tends to happen often. No need to concern yourselves." Alec turned his head to the large man causing the ruckus who then turned toward two cloaked figures, one was another large bearded man, the other a much smaller feminine figure in a gray cloak, but Alec could not see either of their faces.

"Oy, ow bout you an me go upstairs an make some noise." The man moved into position between the two cloaked figures and the door.

"Out of our way, if you please sir." The bearded man spoke the young woman reaching up, pulling her cloak tighter around herself. The drunkard was not to be deterred however and shoved the bearded man.

"I ain't talking to you, old man, I'm talking to the young lass o'er there." The drunk shoved the man again. Eliza and Alec rose from the bar and walked in between the groups.

"Sir, I must ask you to stand down by order of a Valorian knight." Eliza spoke with the authority her mother and father were both famous for. The drunk was not convinced. However, Eliza turned toward the other two in order to ask them to turn around.

"It is you!" She exclaimed and leaned toward the woman. The bearded man shifted quickly startling the drunk who struck out. Eliza jumped onto the drunkard as Alec stepped in the way to stop the bearded man. As he did so, the feminine figure said something Alec did not catch and stepped forward. The bearded man placed his arm on her shoulder, pressed her back, and shoved Alec away with his free hand. Alec shoved backed against the superiorly powerful man. He caught a glimpse of a symbol, a shining sword and shield with a lion hawk on it, a paladin's seal. The man, also bore a massive broadsword on his hip.

"Sir, please stand down." Alec started to say as the man shoved back again, knocking Alec's right side into the corner of a heavy table. He clutched his side as he felt his stitches open as the man came back upon him and threw him down on the floor.

"Quickly mistress." The bearded man grabbed the young woman's hand and began to drag her away. As if on cue, the town guards showed up and drew their weapons, ending the fighting.

"What is the meaning of all this? Cadet Knights, speak, what happened here?" Eliza rose. Her lip was split badly, but otherwise she was unharmed. She looked to Alec who pulled his hand away from his side showing the blood on it.

"My friend needs someone to reseal his wounds. Those two men were fighting and we tried to break it off." She pointed out the drunk lying passed out on the floor and then to the bearded man. The guards quickly dragged them off. Eliza turned to Alec who was sitting as Talon came over with some rags to help stop the bleeding. Eliza looked around the room frantically for a moment. Alec noticed her distress and then questioned it.

"Eliza, what is the matter?"

"Alec, that was her!"

"Who?" Alec was confused.

"That woman was the one from your picture!"

Chapter 16 – The Paladin

"Are you certain?" Alec nearly jumped out of his chair causing his wound to burn.

"Hun, you are going to need to sit still if you want me to close this." Talon still fussed with his side, working her needle with great speed and skill.

"We'll have to try and find her." Alec looked down at his feet trying to think of a plan.

"You realize that man with the beard was a paladin?" Eliza raised her eyebrow to him.

"What?"

"When I tried to press that man backward, I caught a glimpse at the armor he was wearing, lion hawk symbol and everything. He's a paladin Eliza." Eliza thought for a moment as Talon finished closing Alec's side and cut the thread and cleaned the area around it. Alec thanked her for her help as Zelus entered the tavern accompanied by the guardsmen who had taken him away before.

"I leave for a couple of hours and you two are already starting fights with the locals. What is wrong with you two?" Alec and Eliza were hardly in the mood. Eliza slammed her fists on the table and let out a low audible growl.

"We did not start the fight! We were trying to break it up when we were attacked!" Zelus cowered as Eliza went on with her less than ladylike performance. Eventually she stopped and Zelus took a deep gulp and attempted to clear his throat.

"I see, well then, my apologies. I was not made aware of all the details. I will leave immediately to go and speak with the individuals." Zelus began to walk away when Alec spoke.

"Wait! I am going with you." He began to rise but did so too hastily and the pain in his side seared.

"Alec, just wait here or have someone help you to our quarters. I will go with Zelus." Eliza placed her hand on Alec's shoulder knowing why he was so eager to go.

"Eliza I have to go. I am not going to sit in a room when I know that she is here." Alec finished rising to his feet and slowly straightened out his torso. Eliza smiled and slung her arm around to help steady him.

"Come on Alec." Zelus gently patted Alec on the shoulder and the three of them walked toward the building where the large man was being held. Alec surveyed his surroundings closely as they walked looking for any sign that the young woman might appear. They reached the main building that Zelus had entered previously that day and a guard stepped forward.

"We have just received the prisoners. They are in lock up now." The guard accompanying them stepped forward and spoke with the guard for a moment.

"Come on, knights let's go see your prisoners." The four of them walked into the justice building where they walked down a couple long hallways and down a flight of stairs. They walked past several cells when the guard motioned for them to walk toward their right.

"Hey baby, wanna come in here with me." The large man from earlier blew Eliza a kiss. Eliza stopped and drew her twelve inch hunting knife from its sheath.

"Maybe for a minute, big boy." She mocked as she ran up on him and pressed the knife towards his belt line. The big man gulped and backed away as Zelus grabbed her, pulling her away, as they continued their walk toward the end of the hallway. Alec smiled and shook his head as Eliza sheathed her knife and brushed her hair back with her hand. Alec's smile quickly faded however as they stood in front of the cell they were looking for and inside sat the enormous man, whom Alec now knew to be a paladin.

"Prisoner, you have guests." He opened the door and Alec walked into the cell.

"Eliza, Zelus please just stand guard. I will not be long." Eliza and Zelus gave him a dirty look.

"There is no way that we're leaving you alone with him. No way!" Eliza folded her arms pressed her body against the entranceway. Alec nodded to Zelus and he pried her off and tried pulling her away.

"Eliza please, I only need a few minutes." He leaned in close to her and whispered.

"Do not tell anyone about him being a paladin, alright? I will be right back out." Eliza frowned at Alec but let go of the bars and allowed the guard to close the door behind Alec.

"Call for us when you are done, we will be just around the corner." Eliza, Zelus and the guard walked away. Alec turned his attention towards the man who was still sitting in the corner of his cell biding his time.

"Why are you in town," he paused for a moment and whispered the word, "paladin." The man moved slightly at the word and Alec caught a glimpse of a smile from under the hood.

"I could ask you the same thing fledgling knight. How long do you plan on keeping me in here?"

"If you would please just answer a few questions, I will ask for them to release you tonight. I have not disclosed what you are to them." The man nodded but remained in his seat.

"I appreciate that, however, you do know that these walls cannot hold one such as myself?" The man in the cell looked up through his eyebrows at Alec with a threatening glare in his eyes.

"Yes I do, sir. You would only need prove who and what you are and they would release you. However, I can draw the conclusion that you do not wish for them to know."

"You would be correct. I am on a mission that requires a certain amount of anonymity." Alec smiled for a moment.

"Then why bare the symbols of your order?" The man raised his eyebrows for a moment and then stood, eying Alec carefully for a few minutes.

"Interesting, curious but all the same interesting." He continued to study Alec for several moments before Eliza came back to the cell door.

"Alec are you done yet?" She saw that the man was towering over Alec and the muscles in her jaw clenched her fists balled.

"Eliza, I am alright. There is no trouble here." She eyed the man suspiciously and then looked over to Alec with concern. Alec smiled and grabbed her hand.

"Eliza, please, I am alright. Do not worry about me, please?" She looked annoyed but pulled away from the door and walked away. The man continued to stare at Eliza.

"Eliza Kaldur?" Eliza Alec both looked at the bearded man suspiciously.

"What of it?" The man smiled but refused to allow his glare to cease.

"I know of your father. I am surprised that he lets his only child traipse about so." Eliza turned back to Alec to take her leave before things went south.

"Just do not be too long, Alec. I will be back at the barracks." He could hear the clicking of her boots as she stormed down the hallway and up the stairs.

"Your friend has proper reason to be concerned, Alec." He spoke Alec's name almost mockingly.

"It would not take much effort for me to break these chains and ring your neck." Alec looked at the man with a dismissive stare.

"I am not concerned about that. What is it that you are doing out here so far away from the cathedral?"

"I told you that is a matter of secrecy, I can discuss to none outside of my order." The man looked away from Alec, folding his arms.

"It would be easier for me to get you out of here." Alec thought for a moment.

"What if I told them that you are a paladin on your pilgrimage?" The man shook his head and turned his back to Alec.

"That would make no difference. I will be out of here soon enough. Guard!" The guard appeared from around the corner and unlocked the cell.

"Come knight, let us return to the barracks."

"Alright, I am coming." As Alec left, he turned back towards the paladin who still had his back turned and left the dungeon.

"I need to speak to your commanding officer now." The guard looked at Alec confused.

"Why?"

"That man is another knight of our order. He is in disguise and is in route, to look into the disturbances that have been reported in this area. I would see to it that he be released so that he can be on his way." The guard looked at Alec confused and instead of leading him to the barracks took him around another corner and into the commander's study.

"Commander." The guard saluted and introduced Alec to him. The commander was of an average build, not much taller than Alec. He had a muscular frame, brown, shoulder length hair, matching beard and bright green eyes that rivaled Alec's. Alec bowed his head slightly and addressed the commander.

"Commander, you have a prisoner within your dungeon who is a member of my order in disguise. He is one of our contacts on the investigation that we are looking into." The commander rose from his chair and looked at Alec.

"Knight Zelus made no mention of another knight."

"That is because while he was in here meeting with you, cadet knight Eliza and myself were sent to search for our contact going under the alias Talon. We were instructed to meet our guide at the tavern and when we arrived the gentleman in the cells attempted to connect with us when the fight started." The commander and the guard raised their eyebrows, but did not argue with Alec.

"Is this the truth, young knight?" The commander leaned forward and eyed Alec suspiciously. Alec raised his hand and twisted the truth only enough to convince the guards.

"I swear in the name of Aneira that the man I have spoken of is indeed an ally and is on urgent business requiring him to be back on his mission by night's end." Alec spoke his words carefully but truly. The commander and the guard seemed to be convinced. However, they spoke with one another for a moment and then turned to Alec.

"Do you wish to meet with your contact again?" Alec shook his head.

"That will not be necessary I have already received the information required to carry on my journey. It would be best if he were not associated with the knights."

"Very well." The commander instructed his guard to release the prisoner after escorting Alec to his quarters.

"Commander?" Alec spoke up before he was escorted away.

"Yes?" The tall man answered.

"Regarding the problem with the Forsaken we encountered on the road."

"The matter is being looked into." Was all the commander would tell Alec, and with a wave of his hand, the guard placed a hand on Alec's back. The guard saluted and then escorted Alec back to the room where he and the others were staying for the evening. As he entered the room, Eliza jumped from the bed she was sitting on and Zelus stepped forward as well.

"Well, what happened?" Alec sat down on the bed between the two of them and, after the guard left the room, began to tell his story. As Alec spoke he couldn't help but notice a troubled expression on Eliza's face. He told them of the man in the cell, that he was a paladin and that the guards were not to be informed. He talked about how the man had said that something of interest had happened that Alec had not understood and then spoke of how he arranged for the prisoner to be released.

"You told them that he was our contact?" Zelus looked at Alec in disbelief. "Alec, what's going to happen if they discover otherwise?" Alec put his hands out as he spoke trying to keep the situation calm.

"Zelus, I did not have any other choice. The man was a paladin, on a secret mission from the grand cathedral. What would have happened if he had been forced to stay?"

"If he had been forced to stay, then his friends would have come and collected him sooner or later. It could have saved us a great deal of trouble if you had just let it go at that." The entire time that Alec and Zelus spent arguing Eliza just sat by herself and didn't speak a word. Finally after Zelus had exhausted the subject, he turned away from Alec angrily.

"Fine, I suppose that it cannot be helped at this venture. I suppose all that's left is to wait until morning and head on our way to the shrine in Roak." Alec looked at Zelus and asked why the northern village. It was Eliza that answered, the first that she had contributed to the conversation since it had begun.

"According to Talon, many people have witnessed Forsaken troops walking about, following just off from the roads. They have been spotted frequently around the village of Roak and it was suggested that be our next destination. I have already sent a letter back to father explaining the change in destination." Alec nodded his head and Zelus grunted acknowledging that Eliza had done well. As everyone turned in for the night, Alec waited up, having chosen the bed by the window and leaned his back against the bedpost glancing out on to the street.

He sat watching carefully for the slightest signs of movement. He saw the doors to the guardhouse open and out walked the tall man, whom he had spoken with earlier. Alec leaned forward anticipating what he only knew was soon to come. The man cautiously walked from the guardhouse, stopping every few paces and looking around. Alec opened the window slightly without making a sound and listened. It was in the dead of night, but over the faint sound of crickets and the crackling of the midnight bonfires, Alec heard the man's voice periodically.

A broad smile crept across Alec's face knowing full well that the young woman that the paladin had been guarding could not be far. Finally, another figure came from out of the shadows. Quietly, the young woman crept up to the man with the reins to two horses in her hand. The man helped the young woman onto her horse and then hoisted himself onto his own and they silently rode toward the front gate where Alec's vision was obscured.

Alec felt a sense of relief that the paladin had managed to get back on his way with his young ward but, in the same instance, Alec could not help but wish that for a moment, he had been able to see the young woman under the hood. Alec left the window slightly ajar, the refreshing breeze calmed him as he laid his head down to go to sleep.

"Alec?" Alec opened his eyes to see Eliza sitting near his bedside.

"Eliza?" She had a horribly disturbed look on her face. "Eliza what's the matter?"

"Alec, you know how you told me that man had the mark of a paladin on him?"

"Of course I do Eliza, why, what is the trouble?" She looked around the room carefully before continuing.

"Zelus and I both got a good look at him back at the tavern and at the prison. Alec, I am not sure if you will believe me, but when we looked at him. He was not wearing any armor. He was just in basic traveler's clothes." Alec shook his head and smiled.

"Come on, Eliza, that's not even funny. You mean to tell me that I imagined it?"

"Alec, what I mean to say is, those guards would have recognized the seal of a paladin and of the ten people who saw him, Zelus and myself included, you are the only one who did not see dirty traveler's clothes. I even asked Talon and she said the same." Alec did not know what to say. He knew what he had seen but them why had it not occurred to him, he would not be the only one who could recognize that symbol.

"I am just worried Alec. Are you sure that you are alright?" Alec looked at her and smiled.

"Fine Eliza, just fine."

"You are a terrible liar."

Chapter 17 – The Captain's Warning

Alec woke early that morning from another dream involving the girl with the sad eyes. He sat angry that he had gotten so close to finally meeting the woman in person but had not been able to. He sighed to himself and looked over to the side, seeing that Zelus and Eliza were still sound asleep. Alec looked out the window and judged that he had two, maybe three hours until sunrise.

He swung his legs over the side of the bed and laced his boots. Grabbing his things, he rose from the bed and left the barracks. He filled his lungs with the fresh morning air as he stretched. His side still pained him but only slightly. He strode over towards the training ground and bore down at the row of dummies. Slowly, he drew his sword and swung it in a wide arch above his head, slashing it from side to side for a moment.

He stepped forward and brought his sword down upon the shoulder of a dummy, stepped sideways spun and slashed through the air.

"Thump!" The dummy's head hit the ground several feet from the body. Alec lunged and this time cleaved the sword through its torso. He ducked his head, rolling away from the dummy. During the process of his roll, he pulled his knife from its sheath and flung it into the chest of the dummy opposite of him.

"Clap! Clap! Clap!" Alec turned and saw one the guard's captains approaching, clapping his hands.

"Excellent work, young knight. I would expect no less from one of the academy's elite upstarts."

"I would not exactly consider myself an elite upstart. I am just a fledgling, the same as any other." The guardsman smiled and drew his own sword.

"That is not the story, which has reached my ears." The man smiled.

"Well, despite what you have heard, I am not exactly on the council's list of favorite people," said Alec. The man waved him off, before speaking once more.

"The council rarely enjoys anyone, to whom the people admonish, without their permission. You stick out too much, Sir Alec. The people are excited to see, what you become. The council will wish to control you. Possess you, beneath their cause, or they will cast you aside. I know your heart lies elsewhere, however. You wish to return home, one day."

"I believe we both realize how impossible that will be." Alec replied. The captain shrugged as he whirled his blade about.

"Care to practice against a moving target?" Alec smiled back and nodded his head. He readied himself and stared at his challenger. They circled in closer to one another step by step until their blades connected.

"So, Alec what is it that drives you? Is it fame? Glory? Some sort of misplaced childhood fantasy?" He pressed Alec back and slashed. Alec deflecting and redirecting the blow sent out one of his own. As they dueled, the guard captain continued his assessment of Alec.

"Ah yes, childhood delusions, that is a common one. We see that a lot around here. Boys hoping to become men by taking the fight to the Forsaken in order to win their honor. Pitiful honestly. Do you honestly believe that this war with the Forsaken is one that we can win? Do you have any idea exactly what the situation out there is? It is people such as yourself that cause needless violence and bloodshed." His blows became slightly more aggressive. There was nothing but calm in his voice and demeanor but Alec could sense the searing anger behind the blows.

"Alec, why is it that you and your friend are searching for the Forsaken?" Alec dodged a close blow to the side and thought about the wounded farmer, the destroyed caravans, of the missing women and children.

"Your fight is a hopeless one, why not just give up? This war has too many blunt instruments as it is. Why add to the wealth of those fat pompous crooks in the capitol? Their only motivation is their greed." Alec parried a blow, pressing the tip of the captain's blade down, struck the hilt and spun the sword out of his opponent's hand. Alec struck him backward and pointed his sword down at him. Alec advanced on the guard captain, as he answered his question with a most threatening tone.

"I fight for those who lack the strength to fight for themselves. To protect the weak, from the tyranny of the strong and to avoid unnecessary bloodshed. Innocents are dying every day, captain. How can you sleep at night knowing you sat idly by within the luxurious comforts of your barracks, while villages were plundered and burned and countless innocents were butchered?"

"Alec, that is enough!" Alec pulled away noticing now, he had the captain at sword point, lying on his back, beads of sweat dabbing his brow. The captain panted slightly, but smiled as Alec pulled away and began walking toward Eliza and Zelus.

"Remember your drive, Alec. Soon your faith will be tested as was mine. We shall soon see how truly noble you are with your talk of saving the world. Be warned, however, that your fanciful dreams are merely the unrealistic delusions of a child. When you return here defeated with nowhere left to go and no one to turn to I'll be here waiting." Alec continued to walk towards his befuddled companions pulling his knife from the dummy as he walked past.

"Alec, what was that all about?" Eliza was the first to question the display they had just witnessed.

"Just a duel, he saw me practicing and wanted to give me a try." Alec smiled and attempted to walk by when Eliza grabbed his arm.

"You are a terrible liar." Alec smiled again placed his hand on her shoulder for a moment and then pressed on.

"Here, I grabbed your things, Alec." Zelus lifted Alec's bag, which Alec shouldered and thanked Zelus. The three of them walked toward the front gate without once turning back to look at the humbled captain who had tried to plant doubt in Alec's mind.

They walked the road that would lead them north toward Roak, one of the cities housing a grand chapel to Aneira. Alec knew that their walk would be a long one and he hoped that perhaps he might have another chance at meeting the auburn-haired woman. They walked for several hours entering a path cutting through the woodlands when Zelus shifted and spoke up.

So Alec, what was that display with the guard captain, just now, all about?"

"So Eliza, how long of a walk do we have ahead of us?" Alec attempted to deflect the conversation, but Eliza was with Zelus.

"Alec, please answer the question. That was not a friendly duel. You were about ready to snap. What happened?" Alec looked from side to side and once Eliza and Zelus dropped their bags and folded their arms Alec knew he had lost.

"He was mad, alright? He's lost his vision and forgotten his responsibilities and his duty to his position and more importantly his people. It just makes me so angry." Alec slammed his fist against the trunk of a nearby tree.

"Alec what do you mean?" Alec tipped his head back attempting to regain control of his flooding emotions.

"He told me that what we do is a lost cause. He tried to convince me that we are at war with the Forsaken and that it's our fault that so many die in vain. He told me that we were all tools to keep the capital in power." Alec turned and started walking down the road. Zelus and Eliza shouldered their packs and began to follow Alec silently.

"We will have to make camp tonight but we will be there before tomorrow afternoon." Eliza murmured as they walked. Alec nodded his head but still kept the lead as he marched north toward Roak. They walked for the entire day and even after the sun had sank into the hills, they walked further.

"Alec, we need to rest. Let us make camp here for the night and finish the trip tomorrow." Alec, having had sufficient enough time to cool down, dropped his pack in the grass and walked toward the tree line to gather firewood.

"You two rest. Here, is enough to get you started." He lay down the small amount that he had found along the start of the trees and walked into the woods as

Eliza and Zelus sat and began to build a fire. As Alec walked through the woodlands he thought to himself about what the captain had said and what he could have possibly meant.

"My mission is not futile. Saving lives and defending people from the Forsaken is not a wasted effort." He continued to think to himself about the other items the captain had mentioned. He thought to himself what the guard could have meant about the war with the Forsaken. How they could never win. How was it the fault of the knights and the council, so many had to die?

Alec thought intensely to himself for several moments. The last time that the capitol and the Forsaken had gone to war, was over two centuries ago. He could not remember many of the details but he had remembered learning, that the knights with aid from the paladins, had repelled the Forsaken back over the mountains and into the Scar, the Forsaken homeland. He knew there had been many incursions since, roving bands that had dared enter Valascaana and Highmooria, but he knew none of these stories ever mentioned a full-blown war.

He had been taught this all through the academy, but he could not but wonder if everything he had been taught was entirely true. He gathered more firewood and turned back towards camp, trying to shake the fleeting thoughts that had engulfed his mind.

"What took you so long? Is everything alright?" Eliza looked at Alec with a worried expression as he sat the rest of the firewood down and sat on the ground by his things.

"I will be alright, Eliza. I am just still a little steamed is all." He broke a handful of twigs and tossed them onto the fire, which crackled lively as the flames engulfed the new additions. Eliza sat opposite the flame from Alec poking at a pot resting over the flame that he could only assume was dinner. Eliza continued to stir waiting for Alec to provide a better answer, which he did not. Zelus finally approached the camp from the road and sat down near the fire with his back to the path.

"I think that it would be wise for us to turn in shortly. If we rise early in the morning then we should be to Roak before midday." Alec nodded as Eliza put her feet up on a stump and pulled out her book.

"Still reading that same book?" Eliza nodded and continued to read her book flipping through it page after page.

"Is it any good?" Alec was curious at this point as Eliza was absolutely glued to it.

"Mmm hmm." She answered without actually ever paying attention to Alec. Alec smiled and looked to Zelus.

"Hey, Eliza, do you mind if we put snakes in your sleeping bag?"

"Mmmm." Was Eliza's only response. Zelus smiled and added in on the fun.

"Alright then Eliza, I am going to go find some frogs and snakes to put in your sleeping bag." He rose to his feet and began to walk towards the woods. When he was out of sight, Eliza raised her eyebrows and lazily looked toward Alec.

"I hope he realizes that if he does, I will take my skinning knife and remove his manhood." Alec laughed as Eliza returned to her book. A few moments later, Zelus came back with a small snake in his hands and tried to sneak behind Eliza. He was nearly around to her tent when she pulled a knife from her boot, rolled and threw it.

"Ahh!" Zelus yelped as the knife sunk into the tip of his boot as he was walking.

"Eliza, you could have stuck me through the foot." Eliza turned back to her book and responded with a simple, "Mmm hmm." Zelus continued to go on about the hole in his boot. He pulled the knife out of his boot and whined to Eliza about water leaking into it.

"Zelus I am not in the mood for your crap right now. I am three chapters from the end and I want to have this finished, so I can pick up the second one when we get back to the capital." Alec and Zelus both turned to look at her in unison.

"There are others?" Zelus asked in shock. Eliza let out a disgruntled sigh and rolled away from him.

"It is a four book saga. Book one has been out. Book two comes out soon and the others will come out eventually. Now leave me alone." She reached back, pulled her knife from Zelus' boot and returned it to its hidden sheath. Alec smiled at Zelus who eyed his boot and decided not to bother Eliza further.

Alec lay on his back and stared at the fire intently, while he ate his meal. He watched as the flames engulfed the wood, crackling and snapping. He sat up momentarily, to shift around some of the wood and added another handful of firewood. He shifted back and warmed himself. He closed his eyes and waited for sleep to overcome him. As it approached, he found himself in a place not much unlike where he currently rested.

He came upon a large village with high stone walls and guard towers surrounding it. He turned his head to the side and could see the mountains where beyond he knew lay the Forsaken lands. Just outside of the walls were sharpened fortifications that were mounted into the ground, to prevent riders from approaching too near. He caught a glimpse within the walls, at the people who all looked frightened and ran towards the Aneiran cathedral, as if some enemy were approaching. As Alec approached, the gate slammed to the ground in front of him, leaving him outside alone.

The wind picked up just then, he felt a chill down his spine and then heard the sounds of war from behind. He tried to run but he was much smaller, his legs belonged to those of a child. He caught a glimpse of his reflection and saw himself looking at the young girl Tear. He turned Tear's head toward the noise and could see the Forsaken horde barreling towards them.

Alec bolted up startled and searched around him for any signs of an enemy.

"It was just a dream," he assured himself feeling relieved and then dabbed at the sweat on his brow. He sat hunched over staring down at his lap and took in several deep breaths and released them as steadily as he could. After the feeling had fully passed him, he rose to his feet and began to pack up his things. He was sure daybreak was only just an hour or so off. He confirmed his belief as Eliza and Zelus began to shift, rose to their feet, and began packing their things as well. Together, they all took one final look over their campsite and confidently shouldered their packs and continued along the road leading north to Roak.

"How much farther?" Zelus asked after the sun had already risen and was slowly climbing above the treetops. They climbed over the top of a hill and Alec stopped the wind rapidly escaping his lungs. Alec stared at the village that lay before him, high stone walls, moderately fortified, guard towers resting upon each corner. He turned his head to the side to see the view of the mountains that separated them from the Forsaken lands. The only missing element was the sounds of panic and war.

"We need to hurry!" Alec began to hasten bolting toward the city gates. Eliza and Zelus increased their own speed to keep pace with him.

"Alec, what is the matter?" Eliza tried to catch some meaning behind the mad flight.

"I think that the Forsaken are coming and this town might not stand a chance against them."

Chapter 18 - Roak

"That is absolutely preposterous! There is no way that the Forsaken will attack us here. We are heavily fortified; we also have a full garrison stationed here. There is absolutely no way that the Forsaken would be bold enough to mount such an attack! They haven't marched in such force since...."

"Since the day they destroyed Highmoore. I remember full well I was there!" The guard captain froze for a moment.

"You are the boy from that day?" Alec nodded his head. The guard captain, sat down at Alec's answer, a haunted look, appearing across his face.

"I was born Alec Dante of Highmoore, my sister was Rayne Marina of Highmoore. We lived with our grandmother within the inner wall and I was there the day that the town was destroyed by the Forsaken." The guard captain, Eliza and Zelus, all stood in silence for several moments as Alec stared into the captain's eyes.

"I am sorry Knight Alec. I did not know."

"Alec, please, I prefer Alec."

"Right then, Alec, I am sorry, but I cannot place the entire village into a frenzied panic without even a shred of proof. If you are so confident then perhaps we can compromise. I will send out a band of scouts into the countryside. They will patrol and search the area for any signs of the Forsaken." The guard captain paused for a moment before continuing.

"If they find something, then we will immediately place the entire village on lockdown and prepare ourselves to rid Aneira's lands of the menace. But we must wait for our scouts to confirm the threats existence first." Before Alec could speak up again, Eliza stepped in.

"I wish to head out with your scouts. She began to remove the things from her bag that might slow her down.

"I assure you that my scouts are more than sufficient." Eliza looked over to Alec then Zelus and then back to the guard captain.

"I am most certain that your scouts are more than sufficient, however, it is for more than my sake that I offer my service."

"Very well." The guard captain responded as Zelus began to ready himself in a similar fashion as Eliza.

"I as well. Alec, stay here and see to the fortifications. No offense guard captain, only a fresh pair of eyes may prove useful to you." The guard captain stroked his chin for a moment.

"That is fine. Alec, please feel free to walk around the village and see what sorts of advancements can be made to our fortifications." Alec nodded and placed his hand on Eliza's forearm.

"Be careful." She nodded smiled then she and Zelus took off and ran for the walls. Alec turned his back toward the guard captain.

"Were you also there that night? You seem as though you bear similar scars from that night." Alec could not see the man, but he knew from the sigh that he had been. "Where were you during the attack?" The guard shifted uncomfortably before answering.

"I was sent with my garrison to evacuate the citadel. Even we were unsuccessful in saving everyone. We barely managed to escape with our lives and were lucky enough to even reach the young priestess and her guardian."

"Who were they?" The guard thought for a moment and tried to recall their names.

"I am not sure exactly. He was a rather massive man. He held the Forsaken at bay alone until we arrived. The girl, however, I remember a little bit better. She just seemed to stand out in a strange way. Almost as if she glowed, shined even. She had auburn hair, bright green eyes, poor thing. If you had seen how sad her eyes were, she lost everyone that night." Alec's heart stopped. The overwhelming coincidence of the matter was too much for him to comprehend. Alec turned back to the captain who had grown pale in complexion.

"Please, Knight Alec. If you would excuse me for a time. I am afraid that the memory of that night haunts me still, and I must retreat for the time being." Alec nodded his head and watched as the guard captain walked away. Alec turned toward the eastern facing window and looked toward the tree line where he knew his hometown of Highmoore had once stood.

"Fortifications, alright time to get to work." Alec turned toward the hall that led towards the outer wall and began taking a mental note of everything that he saw. Alec surveyed the solid stone walls and decided that there was not much to be done with them. He walked down the path upon the upper wall and began to look around the outside.

"We need more pikes if we are attacked by horsemen." He attempted to think back to his dream. "The civilians were in a panic and didn't know where to evacuate to." Alec surveyed the area. He could see the temple up upon the hill where the wall was the highest. The temple was made of solid stone and to Alec appeared to be the sturdiest place to hold a line. Any enemy that attempted to get through to the people within would be forced to bottleneck their way in.

"The townspeople will have to be evacuated into the temple if all else fails." He turned toward a nearby guard who introduced himself as having come from the guard captain. Alec began to relay his concerns to him and after a moment the man saluted and ran off to ensure that all of the preparations were made in a timely fashion.

Alec, after spending several hours sweeping the town, made one final round before returning to the town square. He sat for some time eating a simple lunch and resting in the shade when he could make out the sounds of men arguing. Alec stood up and walked towards the source of the distress.

Alec ran around the corner, taking care not to run into any of the townspeople on the crowded streets, where he came to an opening with two men standing in the center. The first man stood behind a grocer's cart and was busy yelling at a small hooded figure.

"I am going to warn you one last time lass, you have to pay for that!" The hooded figure held an apple in front of her staring at it as if confused.

"But sir, I already told you that I have not any of this money you speak of. Could you describe it so that I could go find it for you?" The man scratched his head and went on to attempt to explain the situation further. Alec approached the cart and stood next to the hooded woman who eyed him from under her hood, being sure to not make eye contact.

"Excuse me ma'am, I could not help but overhear your conversation." Alec looked at the apple in the woman's hand. She cradled it carefully as if she were suddenly convinced that it was something much more fragile and valuable than just an apple.

"How much for the apple, sir?" The grocer eyed Alec and caught a glimpse of the handful of coins in his hand.

"Aw, finally a paying customer. Well, they are twenty five copper coins for a bushel, so for that one in the young lady's hand and the others, it will be fifteen coppers." The man held out his hand waiting for Alec to deposit the money.

"What others?"

"Why, for the others the young lady fed to the little wretches." He pointed to a number of children that sat nearby holding apples as if they were edible gold and turned to the girl who was tracing her foot across the ground. Alec smiled again and handed the man some money.

"Here, this should cover that. I will take one for myself and the rest of this should cover any other apples that these children might want." He laced the man's palm with a few more coins. The man stared at his hands for a moment trying desperately not to drop any of the coins as he placed them into his pockets. Alec turned his eyes toward a group of men who had watched the transaction but backed away as they noticed Alec watching them.

"I thank you for your aid, I fear as though I do not understand the customs of this village." Alec raised his eyebrows and looked at the girl for a moment.

"Paying for things applies in all towns that I've ever heard of. Are you a noble, they often at times don't pay for things?" The woman shook her head and Alec smiled.

"That's alright miss, you can tell me the truth. I'm a knight and I promise not to harm you." Alec had placed his hand over his heart when he spoke, a custom that the young woman obviously understood because she nodded and though Alec did not see it he imagined that she smiled.

"I am a priestess of Aneira. I am unaccustomed to this money system. I apologize for any trouble that I have caused." She bowed as she spoke.

"No, no that is fine. No harm done. I was happy to help. There is no need to be so formal either." Alec stopped himself as he noticed three large men approaching him from behind. Alec turned his gaze toward the young woman.

"Go, hide!"

"Tis something the matter?"

"Please go, they are going to try to rob me."

"Rob?" Alec looked at the girl in disbelief and placed his body between her and the three men.

"Is there something I can do for you gentlemen?" The three split apart and formed a line in front of Alec.

"So you say that you are a knight, eh? And you have got a noble with you then?"

"She is a priestess of Aneira and, yes, I am a knight. May I ask your leave?" The leader smiled and spat on the ground at Alec's feet.

"We do not much care for you knights snooping around these parts. Perhaps we ought to teach you a lesson to take back to your friends." The man slammed his fist into his hand. Alec rolled his eyes and looked back to the young woman.

"Please stay behind me." She nodded as Alec pulled his sword from its sheath. "Again I ask, will you leave us in peace?"

"Not likely." Alec's eyes flicked back and forth between his three adversaries, each of which held a bludgeon in his hand and were at least a full foot taller than Alec. The first man charged at Alec, who Alec shoved in the stomach with the hilt of his sword and then struck him in the side of the head, knocking him unconscious.

The second thug approached and struck at Alec, who parried with his sword but was unable to follow up when the man's fist propelled him off from his feet, knocking the air out of him. Alec stumbled and moved to the side, as the man brought the bludgeon down. As the man struck the ground, Alec jumped onto the man's back and pressed all of his weight against the man's head, bringing it down heavily onto a large rock. Two men refusing to move, Alec rose and reached for his sword as he noticed the paladin fighting off the final man.

"Alright, alright. We are going, we are going." The leader approached and kicked his goons until they finally rose to their feet and fled. Alec smiled and sheathed his sword as he turned and looked at the girl whom he had been protecting.

"Are you alright?" This time he caught a brief glimpse of her face as she smiled at him.

"Thank you, for protecting me, Mr. Hero." She curtsied and Alec smiled back, as a large hand grabbed his shoulder and threw him backward.

"Woah!" Alec yelled as he twisted at the last second and managed to get his feet beneath him before hitting the ground several feet from where he had been standing.

"Naïve, how dare you approach the priestess!" The man was so enraged, he drew his sword and came after Alec.

"Calm down man, same side, same side!" Alec pleaded as he lunged to the right narrowly escaping the blow from the man's massive sword.

"You must pay for such an outrage!" The man still yelling swung at Alec again who had just managed enough time to draw his shield and blocked the blow, his knees nearly buckling from the weight behind the man's blow.

"Sir Marec, please be still, he meant no harm!" The young woman was frantically jumping at her guardian who continued to wail against Alec's shield.

"Mistress Talia, please step back this instant." Marec kicked against Alec's shield, propelling him backward. Alec drew his sword, battering it against the side of his opponent's and continued to fight for his life. This continued for several minutes, Marec swinging angrily at Alec, who did the best he could just to defend himself. The much more powerful man continued to hammer away at Alec blow after blow and Alec could feel the life leaving his arms. Finally, with one loud ringing "clang," Alec knew the fight was over as both his sword and shield were stripped from his lifeless limbs and his body was sent through the air.

Alec landed with a hard thud and began to rise when a large armored foot was pressed against his chest holding him in place. If only to emphasize his victory, Marec pressed his sword to Alec's throat before pulling back and sheathing his weapon.

"You are lucky that milady wants you spared, else I would flay you where you lie." He backed away as the young woman bowed her head and apologized to Alec.

"Please forgive him. He is a little protective of me. It was a pleasure meeting you. I am sorry I must go, but I wish to see you again...." Alec began to rise as she was trotting away after her guardian.

"My name is Alec." He called to her. She looked back and called out to him.

"My name is Talia...Talia Degracia." She waved and smiled to him as she continued to run after the man whose name had been beaten into him. Alec watched them leave and rose, clenching his stomach all the while trying to catch his breath.

"Talia Degracia," Alec repeated to himself, and a broad smile spread across his face, even though he still could not breathe. He turned toward the front gates and began to slowly walk back toward the barracks. As he walked, he could hear the sound of panic. He took off at a run as best he could. As he neared the front gates, he heard sounds that were only too familiar to him.

"Hurry, run. Get the civilians to the temple. Man the walls. Archers to your posts." Alec rushed forward as Eliza and Zelus ran in, each supporting a wounded scout and bearing several cuts of their own.

"What happened?" Alec ran up to them as medics rushed forward to grab the wounded. Zelus didn't speak instead he began to tend with Eliza's wounds.

"We were out scouting the trail. We found tracks, three Forsaken. Thought they were the ones from before. We followed the trail and were ambushed. Alec, you were right. I do not know how you knew but you were right, there are hundreds maybe thousands of them on their way here." Alec turned his attention toward the gates and a searing pain rose to his temple. Frantic voices began to cloud his mind as if he were hearing the cries of multiple people all at once. Then, he realized they were the Forsaken, marching in unison and one voice caught his attention.

"Hold the gates," he called out to the men who were turning the wheel. They paid him no mind and just continued to turn the wheel. Alec searched around frantically and, grabbing Eliza's bow and quiver from her, ran over and mounted a horse.

"Hyaah!" He yelled and patted the horse on the flank and began to ride past the gates.

"Hold the gate!" He screamed as he barreled through the gates, knocking an arrow as he rode. The voices continued to press within his mind but he focused on the one that he was now searching for.

"TEAR!" He cried out as he rode around the bend and could see the army in the distance down below in the valley. He rode down the hillside for another moment and he could see five horsemen, riding toward his direction.

"Help!" He heard the little girl scream and rode to intercept the Forsaken riders who were after her. Quickly, Alec pulled back the bowstring and focused hard, breathing in deeply and slowly exhaling as he released the string. The arrow struck the first horsemen in the chest causing him to lean backward in his saddle. Alec could hear the wail of the banshee shriek and his horse nickered with discontent as Alec pushed it to press forward. Three more times Alec shot at the riders and still all five of them pressed forward.

"Tear, take my hand!" Alec reached out and grabbed Tear's hand and lifted her in front of him onto the horse's shoulder. He turned his head around and attempted to shoot backwards at the horsemen but missed as a black veil pressed around the lead rider. Alec looked again at the veil, as another whizzed harmlessly to the side and instead or firing back, he pressed the horse harder, until the gates were within sight.

"Close the gates! They are coming! Start closing the gates!" Alec continued to ride as he saw Eliza running from post to post with a watchmen's bow shooting something into the trees.

"Alec, duck!" Alec slowed and lowered his and the steed's head just in time as he could see the barbed snares as they passed underneath them. He watched as Eliza launched several more arrows and began throwing her small contraptions from the last attack beyond him. As Alec approached the gate, he was riding at a slow trot but made it through just before the gate came to a close.

"There are five of them out there!"

"BOOOOOoooooommmmm!" Alec hopped off the horse's back and lowered Tear as Eliza stood above the wall smiling.

"They are ensnared. Hurry, kill them." Thirty archers began to launch out a volley of arrows and all Alec could hear were the wails of the dying Forsaken. He quickly guided Tear toward the temple where he looked her over quickly.

"Are you alright?" She nodded her head but Alec could see that she was crying.

"It is alright Tear. I will protect you." He wrapped his arms around her and gave her a warm hug. He held her until her sobs stopped and then he let her go.

"I need you to stay here, alright Tear? I will come back for you once this is all over, alright?" Again, Tear nodded as Alec ran back towards the walls. Eliza and Zelus were standing atop the wall looking grimly toward Alec.

"Alec, we can see the Forsaken beyond the valley and there are too many of them.

The village will be lost and we cannot escape."

Chapter 19 – Battle Preparations

"How many of them?" Alec continued to pass glances between Zelus and Eliza waiting for one of them to respond. Zelus and Eliza both turned and looked down to their feet, and Alec knew that they both feared the worst.

"I estimate one thousand soldiers." They all turned their attention to Marec who was approaching them from behind.

"Everyone, this is Marec." Zelus looked him up and down for a moment.

"He does not look like a paladin. Alec, are you sure?" Marec turned his attention toward Alec and raised his right eyebrow slightly. Alec shook his head, ignoring Zelus, and turned to Marec.

"You have more experience than any of us. What do you recommend?" Eliza and Zelus both turned and looked toward Alec with disbelief.

"Alec, you cannot be considering taking orders from his man. He looks like some wandering drunkard." Zelus gestured toward what he believed to be a battered old cloak and tarnished clothing but which still gleamed brightly to Alec. Marec looked upon the trio and smiled.

"Please, give but just one moment. It appears as though my anonymity is of little concern at this point in time." Marec began speaking in a low whisper to himself and began to trace a symbol that Alec could see on his belt.

"Oh, wow! Alec I had not realized it, but you are right. That is the mark of the paladin. I can see it now!" Zelus continued to exclaim but Eliza looked confused. Alec turned and looked at Marec whom to his eyes had not changed.

"Are you two joking? He looks the same as always." Marec smiled at the conundrum and stroked his chin.

"Alec, I believe what your friends say is the truth. Up until this point, my appearance was of a drunkard. I am unsure of how or why but what you have seen this entire time was my true appearance. This rune you see here on my belt is a rune used for creating illusions. Paladins use sigils and runes in order to manipulate magic." The trio looked to the paladin stunned. Alec's confusion was due to his ability to see through the illusion the entire time, Zelus and Eliza, the concept of magic.

As the three of them stared at Marec awaiting further instruction, Marec drew out his sword and shield.

"Alec, please draw your weapon. I noticed several holes in your defense when we brawled earlier that I would help you to correct."

"That kind of sums up Alec," Zelus agreed and Alec gave him an insinuating look. Alec was confused on whether he should be grateful or insulted by the man's remark, but, in light of arguing, he drew his own sword and shield, before looking to Marec.

"First off Alec, when you block an attack with your shield, it is important that you support the weight of the blow with more than just your arm. If you wish to endure several attacks, your arm must only be the fulcrum, which directs the force, but your body must bear it. Attack!" Alec stepped forward and swung his sword bringing it down upon Marec's shield. The sword bounced off harmlessly propelling it back towards Alec. Alec could feel the energy within the sword as if his own attack had just been reflected back. Marec smiled and raised his hand for Alec to stop.

"My apologies, my shield is still enchanted. Allow me but a moment." Marec began tracing a symbol in the air, and for a moment, Alec thought he could see a gleaming veil dissipate from around the shield.

"What was that?" Alec asked assured that Marec had finished what he was doing. Again, Marec raised an eyebrow to Alec and then turned toward Eliza and Zelus who had obviously not noticed.

"Would you mind leaving young Alec and I for a while? I will have him ready to fight in just a short while." Eliza and Zelus both nodded their heads and trotted off at high speeds in order to begin the preparations for the battle to come. Marec turned his attention back toward Alec and began to whisper to himself as he drew. This time it was Marec's armor that lost its sparkle.

"How did you do that?" Alec asked as he pointed to Marec's armor.

"How is it that you can see?" Marec paced around Alec asking him several times to please face forward and assuring him that he was not going to attack him. Marec walked a full circle around Alec and then stood in front of him facing him.

"You are most intriguing young knight. I am unsure of what you are." Alec looked at Marec disapprovingly. Marec shook his head after a moment of contemplation and then looked to the sky.

"I am afraid that we have wasted too much time. I must be off, so that I may help prepare for the attack. As Marec walked away Alec couldn't help but notice the sparkling glow return to Marec's shield and armor and Alec was unsure of what that had meant. As Marec disappeared from sight Alec turned his attention toward the walls and scaled up so that he could see how things progressed.

He could see nearly half of the entire village's occupants out working on fortifying the walls. They were placing various traps to use against the Forsaken as they neared, varying from pits, horse and rider snares and other concealed contraptions that would release rocks and boulders. These particular traps would tumble their payload down the hillside or release a mass of flammable materials. He continued to walk about the village and noticed Eliza aiding in the effort, to create more arrow shafts and heads. He smiled as he noticed she already had several quivers by her station, filled with arrows as her dexterous hands quickly created more. He could see Zelus on the other side of the street helping to work the forges.

Alec walked over toward the forges and looked to see if there was anything, he could do to help the effort. Zelus was standing there, pounding away at the piece of hot steel that he was shaping. He looked up and nodded at Alec, acknowledging him.

"Is there anything I can do here to help?" Alec asked as he walked up to the owner of the forge.

"Afraid not, your friend here is a natural at the forges. If we all live through this, I think I will ask him to be my apprentice." Alec smiled in response and walked back to see if there were something else that he might be able to do. He ran to several different stations trying to help, but was continuously directed toward the next station. After seeing that everything was in place and that everyone was well staffed, Alec decided that there was only one other thing to be done. He turned his head toward the temple and walked towards it. As he entered the temple, he could not help but feel the enormous statue of Sidonis was staring at him, judging him as if to deem his worth.

It was at the temple that he saw the rest of the town, all of the elderly, the children, and the expecting, or nursing mothers. He walked the stone steps, searching about for Tear and the mysterious Talia Degracia. Alec walked within the temple, and gazed upon the cathedral ceiling, admiring the beauty of the stained glass. There were depictions of Aneira, represented as either a light or a maiden of indescribable beauty breathing life into Valoria and banishing the Forsaken who had removed her from their hearts. Alec could see depictions of Sidonis in full battle armor wielding his famed sword against those who threatened Aneira's flock.

Alec took his eyes from the ceiling and caught the eye of a priestess whom he had met earlier during his previous visit. He walked up to her and she smiled at him sweetly.

"Oh, why hello, Knight Alec, what may I assist you with today?" A temple priestess asked, wearing the silver and blue gowns of her order.

"Priestess, I was wondering if you could tell me where my young friend is that I brought in earlier, and if you have seen a young woman with auburn hair and bright green eyes?" The priestess thought for a moment before answering.

"I am sorry, Alec. I am not certain of the young woman, but little Tear is in the altar room praying to Aneira. I hope you realize that she is a most exceptional young lady. Poor dear, to have been captured by the Forsaken and only now that she has reached safety, do they come to our very doors."

"Yes, it is most unfortunate, but if you would please excuse me I would like to go speak with her and see how she is doing." The priestess nodded and Alec passed by and strode into the altar room where he could see Tear praying before the altar of Aneira. Alec walked into the room and he heard the faintest of songs. This one, however, reminded him of beauty and peace. He strained to hear the words, but could only catch the melody; he was taken away to thoughts of his home in Highmoore. The scar on his chest stung him for a moment snapping his attention back to reality, and he approached Tear, kneeling beside her. He too bowed his head in reverence. They sat there in silence for quite some time until Tear finally lifted her head and spoke.

"I prayed to Aneira for help." She looked at Alec with small tears in her eyes.

"I did as well." He thought for a moment as he stared into the child's face and tried to think of something encouraging to say in order to shield her from the reality of the situation.

"She will answer, do not worry Tear. Aneira will protect us as she always has." Tear nodded her head as if she believed Alec, but then she confirmed it.

"She says that the Divine will rise and that her shield shall appear, gleaming green and gold, to guide and safeguard them to strike at the heart of malice." Alec stared at Tear for a moment in disbelief.

"Was that a passage from one of Aneira's scriptures?" Tear shook her head.

"There was a lady that lived with me and my family for some time. She is the one that taught me about Aneira, before…" Tear couldn't finish her sentence.

"Before the Forsaken came?" She nodded her head, another trickle of tears flowing down her innocent face. Alec reached his arm around her and gave her a gentle hug.

"She says that everything is going to be alright and that if we stay together everything will become clear." Alec stared at her even more confused than before.

"Stay with who?" Tear looked at Alec and smiled.

"Stay with you, silly."

"Tear, is that why you came all the way here from Ternia?" She nodded.

"Who told you that you needed to stay with me?" Tear laughed as if Alec were playing some sort of game.

"You know, the lady in the water, she said that her name was Aurora." Alec's head began to swim at the words that just left Tear's mouth. At this point, two things had been confirmed to him. The first was that something terrible was about to happen. The second was that at least in some part that she was involved.

"Tear, are you certain that her name was Aurora?" Alec asked hoping that it were all a joke that Eliza and Zelus had put her up to but to his horror, Tear nodded. Alec took in a deep breath and tried to focus his thoughts. His attempt proved to be in vain as at that moment he heard someone shouting from in front of the cathedral.

"Quickly, everyone inside, the attack has begun!" As Alec rose and moved toward the door Tear who still knelt at the altar spoke aloud.

"*When the heart of malice beats again and the one who has fallen enacts her unholy vengeance, the Forsaken shall march with fire and death upon the lands of Valoria. In their time of need, Aneira's shield shall appear among the people gleaming green and gold and safeguard the divine as they rise to again seal away the heart of darkness.*" Hearing the recital in its full form was even more disturbing to Alec than Tear's shortened version. As chills seared through his spine, he heard the first of many cries to arms.

Alec rushed to leave the cathedral but felt his hand being clung to by Tear.

"Tear, I have to go and make sure that the Forsaken don't make it passed the walls." She continued to hang on him with a look of confidence on her face.

"I know. I am going with you."

"Tear, you need to stay here where it's safe. You can't go out there."

"Alec, I have to go out there, I have to stay with you, remember?"

"Yes, I heard you the first time but it's too dangerous out there."

"I will be alright Alec. Lady Aurora told me that I have a much larger role to play." Alec stared at Tear for a moment and then turned to the priestess.

"Please make sure that she stays here." Tear flailed and yelled to Alec as another priestess ran to help.

"No, Alec I have to go with you, please let me go with you. I'm scared Alec please!" Alec did his best to ignore the child's cries but all the while, her sobs made him anguish. Alec walked outside and took a deep breath.

"I am sorry Tear, but I cannot go through that again." He closed his eyes as he felt the scars on his chest throb.

Chapter 20 – The Siege

"On my mark, FIRE!" A wave of arrows launched into the air toward the black hearted beasts that marched below. The Forsaken raised their shields above their heads to protect them from the volley and continued forward.

"Blast, they just keep coming!" The head guardsmen searched over the top of the walls for a sign that the army ended someplace within sight. Eliza's snares and traps had so far proven to slow their climb but they all knew that it would only be a matter of time before the Forsaken reached the walls and only a matter of time later that they discovered a way to breach them.

"Fire!" The guardsmen swung his sword through the air again signaling for the attack. The archers released their bow strings and the arrows as before pelted against the hardened shields of the Forsaken, dropping several of them but never enough to cause much damage to their ranks. Alec looked down upon them from behind his shield and was surprised by what he saw.

"They do not wear any armor?" He turned and looked to the guard captain who shook his head.

"Only the officers wear armor, all of the others are expendable. They fight in just those leather garments and cloaks that you see, but do not be fooled. They still fight just like any other demons. They are all strong, lethal and very vicious." Alec continued to gaze upon the battlefield and noticed several clumps of clothing where one of the Forsaken had fallen. The guardsmen by Alec's side must have noticed and cleared up his confusion.

"The Forsaken are physical beings, but they leave behind no flesh. When a Forsaken dies, they just disappear. Only the little they march into battle with remains." A shudder ran down Alec's spine and he cringed to think of what lie beneath the cloaks. Another volley of arrows rushed over the walls and, as they had the previous times. The Forsaken raised their shields and marched upon the corpses of their fallen.

"We need to find a way to slow them down." Alec began to look around, trying to think of a method of attack that might work when another of Eliza's traps released, this time causing a large number of logs to go tumbling down the hillside.

"Fire!" He could hear Eliza yell from the sidewall and Alec watched as a stream of flaming arrows rained down upon the logs and the Forsaken. Alec smiled as he realized that the rolling tree trunks and branches had been treated with some sort of chemical ahead of time and they burst into flames once the arrows struck them. As Alec stared at the flames, he noticed several of the armored Forsaken for the first time whipping their arms and weapons around frantically issuing commands to their troops.

Alec saw another wave of the flaming arrows launch into the air, but this time, was surprised to see the Forsaken throwing themselves before the volley to prevent the trees from igniting.

"Hopefully, Eliza can keep them busy for the time being. How are things looking from our end, guard captain?" The man stroked his chin for a moment before answering.

"I think that if we can combine your clever friend's tactic with something of our own, we can split their forces, cause them to strike in two separate places. Our attacks will not be as concentrated, but neither shall theirs. It could buy us valuable time and allow us to find a weak point to press upon." Alec watched as another volley of flaming arrows fell from the sky. Alec thought for a long moment and turned toward the captain.

"Captain, am I correct to assume that this is a trade city?"

"Sure, you could say that. We have no port, so little trade comes from overseas, but we see our fair share of merchants. Why do you ask?"

"So, would I be correct to assume that your tavern is well stocked?" The captain's eyes lit up with both hope and despair simultaneously.

"Oh, I am afraid that Travis is not going to like this plan."

"But do you think that it would work?" The guard captain turned and looked toward the Forsaken who were nearly upon the walls.

"Captain, we cannot keep them from scaling the walls for long. What should we do?" The captain waved his hand toward the man for a moment.

"Soldier!" He turned toward the nearest swordsman who stopped in place and saluted.

"Tell innkeeper Travis that I will be needing several barrels of his strongest to defend the walls. But do tell him gently and we will do our best to see that he is compensated." The soldier gulped and ran off as instructed.

"And you!" Another soldier stopped and saluted.

"Gather as many torches and grease as you can possibly find. We are going to make ourselves a rather large fire." The soldier ran off and soon thereafter had returned with a pile of torches, and barrels of grease. A moment later, the first soldier returned with a rather large, cross-looking man, and with them, they pulled a cart with several large casks.

"The items you requested guard captain!" They both saluted and awaited further instruction.

"Alec, southern wall, quickly!" Alec turned his head and could see Zelus' men fighting savagely trying to keep the Forsaken from advancing.

"Aneira's Nymphs! Guard Captain, please carry on with the plan." Alec ran along the upper walkway toward Zelus' men as more of the Forsaken ladders raised to the wall.

"Push back!" Zelus cried as his men attempted to halt the Forsaken, but several still managed their way over the walls. Alec drew his sword and shield, placing himself beside Zelus, began adding his own slashes to the fray.

"How is Eliza's team faring?" Alec smiled as he blocked a sword blow and severed what should have been a head, the body wisping away, leaving nothing but clothing.

"In comparison, she is beating both of us.

"Drat!" Zelus yelled as he landed killing blows on two more Forsaken. Alec slashed at several more of the hooded beasts and moving close enough to the wall, slashed at the hooks, holding the ladder in place as he pushed it to the ground. Zelus followed Alec's lead, and soon after the row of ladders had been cleared, the Forsaken began to scurry back to the main force.

"Booooom!" Alec and Zelus both turned their heads to see that the south wall, where Alec had just been, began dumping flaming casks of ale over the side of the wall, causing intense fires to begin to lick their way across the bushes and fallen trees. Alec smiled as he heard another yell from the grounds.

"The Forsaken are within the city!" Alec turned his head and saw several of the hooded devils slashing their way through some of the guards who did their best to hold them at bay.

"Zelus, come with me!" Alec yelled and they both started at a run as Eliza ran to move herself into better position, grabbing a fresh quiver of arrows from a soldier.

As Alec reached the end of the walkway, he, Zelus, and several of their men bounded down behind an advancing troop of the enemy and began to slash at their flanks as the soldiers pressed back from the front.

Alec swung feverishly, dodging and blocking one attack after another, until several of their adversaries lay dead before them, in powdery clumps of ash and cloth. Alec turned his attention toward their method of entry and held his shield before him. The gates lay in ruins, but still held enough that only a few of the Forsaken could enter at once. Alec and Zelus both pressed forward until they were holding the gates but he could see them giving way.

"Fall back! Create a wall. They move no further!" As instructed, his fighters stood side by side and raised their shields. The gates burst and several enemies poured through the opening when they heard the order, calling from behind he and his team.

"Fire!" Alec had not even had a chance to turn his head before the wall of arrows came down upon the invading troop and toppled the first wave. As the second wave cleared the gates, several of them were shot down as well. The few that managed to escape the repeated waves of arrows, only managed a few more steps. The Forsaken were quickly cut down, at the wall Alec and Zelus' teams had created. Before too much longer, the wall was no longer being breached. Alec and Zelus both fought to catch their breath and turned to smile at Eliza when they heard the call.

The voice that Alec heard could not be described accurately. It was by far the most horrible and terrifying growl of a voice that he had ever encountered but the message was clear.

"Shields up!" Alec cried at the top of his lungs as a cloud of black fell from the sky. Everyone threw their shield skyward and leapt against the nearest wall as thousands of arrows rained upon the town. The sound of the metal on metal rang so loud and clear that it took a long while for Alec to make out the other sounds, screams.

As the blackness lifted, Alec lowered his shield and ran out into the open, slashing his way through the forest of arrows. Zelus and the survivors of their squadron followed suit and began to call for their comrades.

Again, Alec heard the booming terror of a voice and another volley of arrows blotted out the sun.

"Shields!" As before, the sky rained with arrows and Alec caught mere glimpses of the chaos that was being rained upon their forces.

"Alec!" Alec turned to see Marec approaching him.

"The southern wall is overrun! The Forsaken will have it within the hour, sooner, if these waves continue on. Sound the order to fall back. We can hold them at the temple. They will not be able to breach the walls. We can hold them there." Alec knew that they would not be able to survive much more of this. There was only one thing that they could hope to do.

"Fall back! Make post at the temple. Quickly begin fortifying its defenses. Move all available weapons to the temple. Move the civilians and the wounded to the catacombs." Alec turned his head and could see Eliza, who was cut badly, but still scurrying about collecting arrows and helping the wounded retreat to the temple.

Alec looked toward the front wall, fearing for the worst, but caught a brief glimpse of several men running from the wall with supplies moving toward the temple. As they retreated toward the temple, another group of Forsaken barred the path.

Alec, Zelus, Eliza and Marec all drew their weapons and safeguarded the way for the retreat.

"You three! Cover for me!" Marec began to trace invisible runes through the air and chanted to himself.

"What are you doing?" Eliza demanded of him. Marec continued his chant for a moment longer as the three of them fended off a group of swordsmen. As the three of them fought, Alec could see a translucent shield appear around them.

"Marec, what did you just do?"

"It shall protect us from enemy arrows." It is imperfect, but shall at least defend us from another attack like before.

"Why did you not do that sooner?" Zelus screamed at the man as he sliced clean through a Forsaken's cloak.

"I only have so much energy and the ward consumes a lot of it, alright. Now, quit complaining and fight." Alec and the others continued their attack as another wave of fighters broke in on the action.

"There are too many of them!" Zelus yelled but Alec was not to be moved.

"Not until our troops are safe."

"Sidonis shield us and Aneira guide us." Marec growled as the troop advanced towards them.

"*Ssccrrrreeeeee!*" A large shadow swooped down from above, tackling into the onslaught of Forsaken and began to tear into their ethereal bodies with its razor sharp claws and beak.

"Oz!" Alec and Eliza called excitedly together. As if in answer to his triumphant entrance, the Lion Hawk reared its head again and let out another powerfully deafening battle cry.

"*SCCRRREEEE!*"

Chapter 21 – The Daemon Knight, Belias

"Oz?" Marec stared at the Lion Hawk in bewilderment, at such a beautiful force of nature.

"*Screee!*" Oz wailed as he finished the last of the Forsaken and casually tossed their ruined clothing to the side.

"How have you come to know this Lion Hawk?" Marec asked.

"He belongs to Alec." Eliza yelled.

"My sister found him in the woods when…"

"*Screee!*" Another wave of Forsaken began to flood into the street. Oz, Eliza, Alec and Marec all charged forward while continuing their conversation.

"My sister found his egg when we were younger," Alec paused for a moment as he sliced through a Forsaken's cowl. "His egg was her most treasured possession."

"Might you repeat that for me?" Marec brought his enormous sword down, crumbling the frame of his adversary.

"His egg was my sister's most treasured possession!" Alec yelled as he too took on another opponent. The creature swung his weapon wide, a novice mistake. Alec forced his shield forward knocking the creature's head backward before severing it.

"These ones are not all too fearsome, are they?" Alec turned his head toward Eliza who raked both of her knives across the chest of another.

"They are not even putting up a fight."

"I fear something is afoot! We should hold back at the temple."

"*Screee!*"

"Woah, what is that?" Zelus ran up from the rear. Alec turned around having thought Zelus to have been there the whole time.

"Where did you go?" Zelus leaned toward Alec and gestured toward the bushes a little ways off.

"Had to, you know." Zelus mumbled.

"In the middle of battle?" Alec asked in complete disbelief.

"Hey it happens, alright. What is that thing?"

"What did you get scared?" Zelus glared at Alec as if he were ready to attack him.

"NO! I was simply preparing myself in case I needed to storm in heroically and save the day." Zelus attempted to recover.

"Hey Zelus, your flies' down." Alec gestured below.

"AH!" Zelus shrieked as he looked down and quickly corrected his situation. After a moment, he looked back to Oz and pointed.

"Now, what is that thing?"

"Tis a Lion Hawk, Knight Zelus. The symbol of Sidonis, one of Aneira's most beautiful creatures."

"Zelus where have you been? We could have used your help?" Eliza was standing behind him staring at his back awaiting an answer.

"I had to take care of something, alright?" He looked back at Alec for help as Alec was fighting off another wave of Forsaken.

"Alec? Little help here?"

"Where?"

"No, not like that, Tell Eliza I had to take care of something." Alec could not understand Zelus through the clanging of sword on shield.

"Eliza took care of something, shut up and fight someone!" Zelus looked back to Eliza who had drawn her bow and began firing into the crowd of Forsaken swarming the courtyard. Zelus looked around for a moment, drew his sword, and then began to help press the wave backward. Oz pounced, stabbing with his beak and raking through enemies magnificently with his claws.

"Marec, I fear that something has gone terribly wrong?" Marec turned toward Talia who had walked out into the courtyard and stood behind them.

"Milady, please return to the safety of the temple. You must not be out here." Talia looked up at Alec fighting alongside Oz. Tears began to well up in her eyes and she clutched her chest as if she were in excruciating pain.

"It hath begun." Talia gasped.

"Milady?"

"Marec, I detect a shaman, one most powerful. I have come to lend aid." Talia stood behind Marec and the others and waited. As Alec and his team continued to push through wave upon wave of Forsaken, a terrible thought crept upon Alec.

"Eliza?"

"What is it Alec?"

"You do not suppose that these are decoys do you?" Marec looked to Alec, the thought just now striking him.

"Everyone to cover!" Alec cried out as he pulled his shield up and swiped his sword through a nearby beam dropping a wooden roof that had withstood previous arrow attacks.

"Shields up, everyone together!"

"What is the matter?" Eliza asked as she and Zelus both drew their shields and placed their backs together. Marec and Talia joined their group along with Oz. There was silence for a moment and then the hair on Alec's neck pricked before he had even heard the word.

"FIRE!" Alec watched as the cloud of black arrows rose into the sky, blotting out the sun.

"Hold your shield arm firm and we shall prevail." Alec called out to everyone, noticing the fear in his or her eyes. Marec had his shoulder pressed against Alec's back, holding his shield above his and Talia's head.

"Will your ward protect us all?"

"Nay, I am afraid I lack the strength for such a feat, but hers shall." Alec turned his head toward Talia whose eyes were closed and her lips moving slowly in silent prayer. Alec raised his shield higher, and waited for the cloud to descend.

"Benevolent mother, shield us!" Talia finished her chant and her green emerald eyes shone brightly, her auburn hair glowed bright as if on fire.

The arrows began to fall. Alec could feel them striking against his shield but his arm felt stronger and he pressed forward against the strain with ease. He looked over and watched the arrows bounce harmlessly against Eliza and Zelus' shields and then he turned towards Oz who sat on at ease beneath the partially collapsed stand watching as the arrows bounced lazily off from it.

Lastly, Alec turned his eyes towards Talia who was concentrating intensely on the task she was performing. Her eyes were still bright, her hair still aglow. Rays of sun began to shine through the darkness as the last of the arrows struck the ground. Alec rose to his feet and brushed the arrows from his shield. Quickly, he threw his shield down on the ground as he noticed Talia's knees growing weak as the light left her. Alec lunged forward and instinctively wrapped his arm around her waist, catching her as she collapsed.

"Milady, are you alright?" Talia however, did not answer. She gazed up into the face of Alec, his strong arms wrapped around her, her hand on his chest. Marec spoke to her again and she awoke from her dream like state and placed her feet beneath her.

"Yes, Marec, I am alright. I have only tired myself and grew light headed." Alec released his grip from around her and could not help but notice Marec glaring at him. Marec began to lead Talia away but stopped and continued to look toward Alec. Before either Alec or Marec could speak, Eliza intervened with a warning.

"Look out behind you!" Marec reacted too slowly however, as a large group of adversaries reared from around the back of the temple. They were led by a cloaked figure baring a huge staff and a headdress that proved his status as a shaman.

Talia spun around and threw her arms out, as the shaman whirled his staff around, projecting a ball of fire toward her. A faint bubble formed in front of Talia's hands, shielding her from the initial blast, but did very little to defend her from the concussive force. She was thrown backward against the stone wall. She crumbled to the ground as Eliza, Marec, and Alec all ran to her defense, Oz and Zelus remaining behind, fending off an assault from the opposite flank. As Alec placed himself between Talia and the Forsaken, the booming voice returned with thunderous terror.

"Bring me the Divine! Kill any others!" The shaman whirled his staff and another jet of flame bounded from it. Alec stood with Eliza as Marec tended to Talia. With no other options before him, Alec raised his shield and again felt the surge of energy rise up within him. He pressed his shoulder into the shield and let out a fearsome cry. The burst made impact with his shield and Alec pressed back as his feet began to slide backwards. Alec took one step and then another as the flames continued to curve around his shield.

"Another blessed one. He dies first, and then bring me the Divine!" Alec could hear the shaman croak to his allies and they rushed forward, each carrying two curved, serrated blades. Marec slowly helped Talia to her feet but failed to see the archers atop the steeples.

"Look out!" Eliza cried without thinking and rushed forward shield raised. Alec turned his attention toward her for a brief second, as the creatures with the serrated blades rushed forward.

"Blast!" He yelled as he blocked the blades with his shield and pressed them backward. Three arrows struck Eliza's shield. Alec slashed at the blade wielders and tried to move toward Eliza. The shaman waved his staff, releasing another blast of fire toward her. Alec ran to intercept the flames, as the archers prepared to fire again.

The blast hit Alec's shield at an angle unbalancing him. Eliza turned at the sound of the blast as Alec's shield was forced from his hand.

"Eliza, look out!" Alec yelled as the archers fired upon her. The first arrow pierced through her shoulder, the second through her hip and the third through her leg. Eliza fell to the ground as Marec managed to get his shield over her and block the remaining arrows. Alec began to rise to his feet, as Oz descended upon the Forsaken and Zelus ran to Eliza.

"Kill the Lion Hawk!" The shaman screeched as Oz began to tear into his troop. Marec rose to his feet and looked to Zelus. Zelus pulled his knife from its sheath and threw it into the air, the blade wedging itself into the ribs of one Forsaken archer, who fell from the roof a pile of clothes. Eliza managed to roll onto her back, and pulled the arrow from her leg, with a pained cry. She quickly knocked the arrow and shot over Marec's shoulder, killing another archer. Alec strapped his arm through his shield swiping an arrow from the sky as he did so.

"Take them inside now, young knight. Alec, the Lion Hawk and myself, shall hold the entrance." Marec commanded Zelus. Zelus ran over to Eliza, who had managed to reach her quiver and shielded her as she fired a continuous stream of arrows, finishing the archers. Zelus helped Eliza to her feet as Forsaken swarmed them. Alec raised his shield in defense as the beasts with the serrated blades returned to attack. They held their ground as Zelus helped Eliza over toward Talia.

More Forsaken attempted to come from the rear, upon the rooftops. Oz soared high into the air and began to knock them from the buildings and shredding anything else, that neared to close to him. As Oz swooped back down beside them, Alec could see Zelus helping Talia rise to her feet. Talia took Zelus' place in supporting Eliza and shouldered her weight as everyone else returned to the fight.

Alec, Marec, Oz and Zelus stood side by side trying to encircle Talia and Eliza as more Forsaken began to swarm them, blocking their path back into the temple. Alec turned his head towards Talia and Eliza and felt the burning in his chest. Alec could feel strength coursing through his veins, his vision, hearing, and reflexes all felt enhanced. As his opponents rose to fight, he read their movements and parried their attacks as if they had been choreographed.

Oz screeched out fiercely as he raked his claws across the chests of any who neared too close. Zelus slashed as if a cornered beast, tearing through anything that dared take a step in his direction. They all knew however, that they were outnumbered and had only a matter of moments before they would be overwhelmed by their attackers.

"And the Divine shall rise to strike down the heart of darkness!" Alec heard just before he saw something he could not comprehend. It was as if the very earth had risen up in defense of them. Tree branches swung on invisible joints and vines rose from the ground entangling and strangling the Forsaken warriors. Alec and his team used the distraction to their advantage striking back at the enemy.

As they fought, they slowly pushed back toward the temple. Eliza and Talia leaning upon one another for support. Alec caught a glimpse of the source of the rampant trees and vines.

"Tear!" He yelled out to the young girl but noticed that she was glowing. Her hair whipped about behind her as if being blown by a heavy wind and her eyes glowed bright. She held out her hands as she walked and the supernatural destruction she wrought continued to follow in her wake. Talia reached forward and placed her hand on Alec's shoulder.

"We must help her. She cannot hold the trance for long."

"Trance?" Talia nodded her head.

"Yes, please allow me to explain later but we must help her." Alec nodded his head and turned toward Zelus and Oz.

"Take Eliza and Talia inside, defend them and the others. Don't open those doors until I tell you!"

"Alec I must go with you!" Talia stepped forward beside him. "Please take Miss Eliza inside to treat her wounds. We shall not be but a moment."

"Mistress, would you please reconsider?" Marec rose to stop her but Talia was already approaching Tear and the massive hoard of creatures that were swarming the square.

"The Divine must defend one another." Talia stepped forward and began to rush toward Tear.

"To battle then!" Marec called out as Alec ran to Tear and stood by her side, along with Talia.

"Alec, I sense another spell-caster." Talia spoke. Alec turned his head from side to side searching about as he defended them from oncoming attack. As he struck out at the invading parties, the booming voice from before returned.

"STEP ASIDE, THE DIVINE SHALL BE MINE!" As Alec struck down another opponent, two lines began to form and the Forsaken parted ways. The air around Alec began to grow cold and he felt a shiver travel through the length of his spine. Alec searched through the crowd and saw a lone figure approach. The goliath's frame was covered by large amounts of thorny armor, which covered every conceivable part of its body. It bore a massive shield on one arm and on the other an equally massive sword that made Marec's seem meek in comparison. Even from a distance, he could hear the metal grieves pounding into the ground, the concrete groaned in protest with every step of the massively armored man.

His armor was black. His helmet resembled something from a nightmare, horned with a metal face. The armor he wore covered his entire body with shoulder pauldrons, defending his neck. Not a single semblance of flesh was left exposed, beneath the protection of this armored form. Alec looked down to his greaves, which were as was the rest of his body, over abundantly armored with plates of a metallic origin Alec had never seen.

His gauntlets bore three spines on each forearm but it was the sword and shield that still commanded Alec's attention. The shield was massive, reminding him of Dominic's tower shield only one that had been crafted by some sadistic giant, spikes pointing out from its extremities. The sword must have been a full foot in width and another five or six in length. It could easily be large enough to be doubled as a shield and must have weighed more than Alec, perhaps even twice as much.

The armored beast raised its hand into the air, forgoing its sword, and a great pulse ripped through the air. Alec raised his shield to divert the blast and felt it slam against him as if he had been rushed by a wall. As the blast subsided, Alec dropped to a knee and felt his arm groan in protest. Alec felt in the back of his mind that Oz was in pain. He turned his head to the side to see that his beloved Lion Hawk had also been forced to the ground by the blast.

"Come to me youngling, my master has plans for you." The creature motioned towards Tear, who seemed to be unaware of Alec's presence. Alec pressed his legs beneath him and raised his shield and moved between Tear and the armored hulk.

"Step aside!" The beast commanded again and raised his hand. Alec raised his shield and felt the hammering blow against it but this time he was ready and resisted the blast, allowing it to pass around him. Alec lowered his shield still on his feet and caught a glimpse at the dent that had formed within its center. The thorn armored beast stopped for a moment in hesitation and it was then that Alec realized that he stood alone, his friends and even the Forsaken had been knocked to the ground.

"Sir Alec, I am at your side. We can defeat him!" Although ever confident, Alec could not help but notice that Marec spoke as if even he himself were unconvinced. Alec turned to Talia who approached behind Marec. Zelus had been knocked to the ground and was rising to his feet, helping Eliza to hers and continued his retreat to the temple.

"Intriguing" The creature began to speak in its deep evil voice. "You are not a Divine that is certain. Yet, I sense that you are not as powerless as these other mortals are. My master shall have your heart as well." The demon raised its hand again. Alec raised his shield in preparation but did not anticipate the man's target.

"I shall consume your heart myself." He spoke as he turned his hand toward Marec and Talia and shot a force pulse toward them. Alec did not have enough time to get in the way and was propelled sideways by the blast as Marec and Talia were forced backward. Marec shielded Talia with his body, breaking her fall but he did not rise.

"Capture both of the Divine, while I tend to this one." The Forsaken began to swarm around Tear and Talia and both began to retaliate with magic but Alec knew that it would not be enough.

"Oz, protect them!"

"*Scree!*" The Lion Hawk lunged into the fray and began to strike at the Forsaken alongside Tear and Talia. Alec squared off against the armored man, his shield arm aching but his sword arm firm. Alec slashed at his opponent and the man allowed his sword to bounce off from his armor and laughed at Alec's dismay.

"It will take more than mortal steel to harm me boy. I am Belias. I am undying!" He swung at Alec who foolishly blocked the blow with his shield and cried out in pain as he felt his bones give way. Alec landed upon the ground several feet away and his ruined shield several more feet from him. He could hear Oz screech horribly as Alec caught the blow. He could hear Talia cry out to him, but the ringing in his ears was too intense and he failed to make out the words. Alec raised himself from the ground with his remaining arm and lifted his sword confidently in the air, his crippled arm, hanging limp at his side. He focused his vision and watched as the titan slowly walked toward him.

"Give me your heart, boy!" The monster swung, but this time Alec avoided the blow and brought his sword against the back of the man's armor. Belias howled with annoyance even though Alec could not see a scratch upon the armor. Belias swung back. Alec moved out of the way in time to avoid being severed in half. Alec turned his eyes back toward Oz and the others and saw Tear had returned to normal. Apparently, her trance had ended and she looked terrified.

Alec winced as he saw and felt a Forsaken sword rake Oz's wing. At that moment, he could not help but feel a surge of desperation. In Alec's moment of distraction, he was flung through the air again as he narrowly dodged a blow. He felt the tip of a blade run across the length of his back. As he spun from the force behind the blow, his legs failed him and he fell to his knees. He looked up toward Talia straining to keep his eyes open as she cried out to him, her eyes filled with tears.

"You have power, boy, but I have neither the time nor the patience to test it. I shall end this all now." He took a step back and let out his booming voice.

"Fire!" The words seemed to barely touch Alec's consciousness. He was in a daze. He continued to look at Talia and a shadow grew over her face. She looked skyward and raised her hands into the air as the arrows descended. Alec watched the arrows falling around him and his friends as Talia concentrated hard to keep her ward on all of them, but he could see the strain on her face. He also saw the Forsaken shaman crumble to his knees in an attempt to keep his men alive. He succeeded in saving many, but evaporated as an arrow struck him through the chest.

One of the surviving Forsaken lunged forward and stabbed toward Talia who was partially shielded by Oz. Oz cried out in pain as the sword grazed his shoulder and stabbed Talia. Talia clutched the wound in her stomach and Tear ran to her side. Oz pierced the Forsaken's body with his beak as Talia fell. Belias raised his hand and immediately Oz crumbled to the ground as it appeared that gravity had begun to fight them as well. Tear fell forward and strained to hold her body up. Oz, who was already wounded, fell to his side and Talia, who was already lying in anguish, let out a pained cry as her body crumbled further.

Alec grasped at his chest as he felt his scars throb and burn. He could feel desperation begin to well up within him. He could feel his blood boil and his desperation began to change within him. As he could feel the tug in his chest, he watched as Talia fell to the ground and another surge of energy flowed within him. His desperation turned to will and he felt power radiant through his body.

Alec rose to his feet as he felt his shield arm grow strong. He looked to his side and watched as the bones mended. He clenched his teeth in pain, but knew now that his arm would move should he command it to. He reached forward and grabbed his sword and ran toward Belias who had his back turned.

"Awwww!" Belias howled as Alec raked the sword against the joint in his armor and saw upon it the slightest of scratches.

"Aw, so the boy has great potential after all." Belias turned toward him and swung his sword. Alec moved swiftly and using both hands guided his sword toward a strike at the hip joint. The blade struck leaving behind another small scratch and Belias laughed.

"It has been over a century since an opponent has landed a blow that could scratch my armor. You should be proud boy but you are still not nearly powerful enough to damage me." He swung again and Alec allowed the blade to pass overhead where he jabbed toward Belias' shoulder.

Belias reached out with blinding speed and grasped Alec's sword, catching the blade in one hand and snapped it in half.

"Too bad!" he laughed as he kicked Alec in the stomach sending him flying backward tumbling across the ground. Alec looked over again at his friends and saw Zelus running from the cathedral side of the temple to lend a hand. As Zelus neared them, his movements slowed as he entered the gravity aura. Immediately, it appeared as if nearly an additional half of Zelus' body weight burdened him, but he pressed on towards the others. Alec knew this new power of his would never be enough to defeat Belias. Zelus would not be able to save the others, should Alec fail.

Belias kicked Alec, sending his body against the cathedral wall. Alec fell to a slump as his body collapsed. Belias held out his hand causing several more of the kinetic blasts to strike Alec.

Alec's body flailed violently from the stream of blows. The force of his body striking the outer temple wall caused it to crack. Belias' attack ceased and Alec's body fell to the ground again, his head resting against the wall. He looked around him to his friends lying on the ground. Zelus was still attempting to stand against the strange gravity increasing aura that was assaulting them. Marec was still collapsed, Oz and Tear, still pinned. Alec placed his hands beneath his body and pressed himself from where he had landed, coming face to face with Sidonis. Alec closed his eyes and prayed for salvation.

"Aneira please give me the strength to defend my friends. Even if I must fall to protect them, lend me your strength. Aneira, I swear to you and Sidonis upon my life that should you aid me I shall save them!" Alec opened his eyes and saw the bloodstained patch on his armor glow. He dabbed at it and pulled his hand away as a rune began engraving itself within his palm using his blood as the ink. Three curling, symmetrical stems sprouting from one another, curled to the left as a small shield formed within the center. Alec watched as the rune finished tracing and glowed brightly as it activated.

"I swear upon my life that I will save them!" He yelled out raising his hand in the air. A large burst of thunder cracked the sky and the force from it shook the ground, crumbling the statue of Sidonis. Alec turned his eyes toward the ruins and within them, he saw his prayers, answered. All eyes fell upon Alec and time seemingly froze as Alec placed his hand upon the hilt of a brilliantly gleaming sword, resting within its sheath. He pulled the blade from the sheath, lifting it into the air. The blade sang as one of five runes on its face glowed, while lightning glistened across it.

Chapter 22 – The Fabled Blade

Alec gripped the hilt of the sword and felt the massive power within. He searched the length of the two and a half foot blade, running his fingers across the several runes etched into it. The blade ended in a unique twisting hilt that reminded him of thick entangling vines. Within the vines, rested a brilliantly gleaming emerald and ended in a smooth handle with a hollow pommel.

He swiped the sword through the air again, feeling, and hearing the air hum, as he cut through it. Belias stared at Alec for a moment before drawing his own sword. Alec walked towards him, unburdened by Daemon Knight's strange aura. Belias let out a deep throaty laugh and shot a kinetic burst at Alec.

Alec watched intently, able to see the energy rushing towards him. He swung his sword horizontally from left to right, striking the head of the burst and with great strain propelled the blast sideways crumbling the far wall, well away from everyone. He felt a large amount of energy suddenly leave his body and he collapsed to a knee for a moment as his head spun.

After a moment, Alec rose to his feet realizing a second attempt would probably cause him to pass out. As such, he decided such action, would be ill advised. Alec looked up and though he could not see Belias' reaction, which was veiled by the sheet of metal covering his face, he caught the sense that Belias was beginning to grow concerned.

"Why are you still standing?" Belias approached him realizing his kinesis would no longer aid him and swung his sword. Alec moved to the side as he had before and brought the blade across Belias' armor. He felt the blade connect to his armor and felt as a portion of it gave way.

Belias howled with pain and stepped backward, holding his side. Alec could see the wound and saw the shifting of spirits within the armor. The faces of countless enslaved souls moaned and cried from beneath the ebony armor as if calling to Alec, asking him to free them or join them.

Alec turned his head to the side and saw that his comrades were all collapsed on the ground, covering their ears, crying out in pain. Alec looked back towards the assembly of souls and remembered the Forsaken captain from outside of Roak.

He remembered, while the others had been paralyzed by the banshee wail that he had mysteriously grown immune to its effects. After a moment, Belias pulled his hand away and Alec could not help but notice the wound continued to move about, as if it possessed a life of its own. Alec could also see the twisting souls slowly reaching out to one another, as the hole in Belias' armor shrank.

"Excellent strike! It has been quite some time since someone has been able to wound me." Belias raised his hand and released the force pulse. Alec could not react in time, to avoid the blow. Possessing no shield to block with, he threw himself to the side, but felt the blast striking him in the stomach. The blast continued onward and struck the barricaded temple door, which burst from the force.

Alec's lungs were on fire. He tried desperately to fill his lungs with air and, once it reached him, he let out a hard cough. He noticed that his limbs were trembling violently and that blood was flowing from out of his mouth. He picked up the sword again and the blade continued to hum. As Alec grasped it, however, he began to feel the strain from holding it. His arms felt as though he were attempting to hold up the sky.

"Ah, so you have noticed the downside to wielding that weapon. That sword's power is legendary but it comes at a price. It channels the energy of the user. Use it too much, and you will die." Belias approached Alec and this time Alec was too weak to dodge the blow. Instead, the swords clashed and sparked as they were struck together repeatedly. Alec could hear Oz screech triumphantly, confirming they had overcome the increase in gravity and would be safe from further attack. Alec was also aware that Talia desperately needed medical attention.

Belias swung at Alec relentlessly. One strike followed immediately by another, each time, Alec knocked the blade backwards and did his best to land a blow. As Alec and Belias squared off against one another, their blades connected and Alec took stance to try to repel his attacker.

"You are strong warrior. That is certain but you lack the strength necessary to wield that blade for long. Even now, I bet you grow fearful and weary. You are most wise to be afraid. That sword, it is not fatigue that it has made you feel, you are dying." Alec did not want to admit it but he knew that Belias was right. Even now, Alec could feel the warmth leaving his hands, the strength in his arms was failing him and worse yet, he could feel his heart beat beginning to slow. He was fighting for his life so that he could save Talia and yet the only instrument he had at his disposal, was killing him.

Alec pressed forward with his legs, doing his best to push Belias backward, but the goliath did little more than shift the positioning of his feet. Alec attempted the one last thing he knew he would have strength for. Alec's knees buckled and he fell to the ground, prompting Belias to laugh at his weakness.

"Too bad, young knight. I was hoping for more zeal from you, but I suppose that the master has no place for you after all." Belias raised his sword in the air and Alec coughed blood again but smiled as he gripped the sword tighter. Belias swung his sword toward the ground and Alec leaned forward, rolling just before the blade cut into him. The force from Belias' stroke unbalanced him, exposing him from the rear. Alec kicked off from the ground and twisted his body using both of his arms to channel his remaining strength through a final stroke.

"AWWWWWW!" The booming voice screamed, tearing the sky apart and causing Alec to go deaf for a moment, as Belias' sword arm fell to the ground with a powerful clang.

"YOU SHALL PAY FOR THAT!" Belias turned and with an open palm sent his force pulse directly into Alec's stomach. Alec's body soared through the air and landed painfully on the ground, but he continued to glow brilliantly. More hot sanguine spewed from Alec's mouth as he brought himself to a seated position, just in time for Belias to send another shockwave at Alec, forcing him back to the ground.

"I WILL KILL YOU SLOWLY!" He continued to rage as a mounted Forsaken rode into the street, a second steed by his side.

"Sire, the knights are here we must make haste."

"I AM NOT FINISHED YET!" Belias turned back toward Alec and began to approach him when the blinding flash of gold, brown and white rammed into him causing him to topple.

"*SCREEE!*" Oz cried out as he slashed and pecked at Belias, who attempted to shield himself with his remaining hand. Coming to the lion hawk's aid, Talia and Tear joined the fight, whirling spectacular flashes of light and whipping vines toward him. Belias continued to roar out in rage, but was in no shape to continue the confrontation.

"REMEMBER ME, KNIGHT! I WILL SEE YOU AGAIN ONCE MY ARM RECOVERS! I SHALL BE BACK AND MERCILESS, I WILL I BE!"

"Good! I will be taking your other arm next time!" Alec croaked as the armored man fled. Talia, Tear and Oz descended upon Alec. Oz was the first to be by Alec's side, poking and prodding at him.

"Please great Lion Hawk, I must tend to knight Alec's wounds. If I may, please allow me to treat him?" Talia waited for Oz to allow her to pass and she knelt by Alec's side.

"Is everyone alright?" Talia looked down at Alec and smiled.

"Marec is only unconscious, Zelus is helping him to his feet now, and everyone, including Eliza, is safe within the temple. I will be tending to knight Eliza's wounds the moment I have healed yours." Alec looked up without lifting his head and saw Talia's wound. He placed his hand by it and Talia winced.

"Heal yourself first." He choked out the words, gasping for air as he felt his lungs failing him.

"No need. My wound is not as severe as yours. I shall heal you first." She leaned forward and attempted to roll Alec onto his side but he refused. Talia sighed. Placing her hand onto her stomach, she began to concentrate. Alec watched as the flesh began to heal and Talia's wound sealed itself. She opened her eyes and looked to Alec, still baring a smile, kindness in her eyes.

"May I?" She placed her hands out toward Alec who strained to roll to his side, coughing uncontrollably all the while.

"Tear, please have the other priestesses join me. I fear that my power alone, will not be enough." Tear ran for the temple and Talia turned back toward Alec. Alec coughed again and could feel his eyes steadily rolling into the back of his head.

"Sir Alec, please stay with me you must hold on!" Alec strained to keep his eyes open but could feel his life rapidly leaving him, as if still being siphoned from his body. Alec's limbs grew weaker and he no longer possessed the strength to hold Talia's hand. He could hear Zelus and Eliza calling out to him in the distance as the light radiating from his body began to fade.

"Alec! Alec, are you alright?" Alec could not answer, his throat was dry and he had not the strength for speech. Zelus ran up to him and kneeled by his side, placing his hand on Alec's shoulder, while Eliza held his limp hand. Talia lifted up Alec's head and placing it on her knees, stroked his hair trying to keep him awake. Marec joined the group as the priestesses ran out into the ruined courtyard.

Alec turned his eyes towards the sword in his hand, trying to alert anyone of its effect but could not speak. His world began to slow, growing hazier with each passing second. Alec's consciousness began to slip back and forth as if in and out of a dream.

"How is he? Will he be alright?" Marec spoke as he looked down at the weapon Alec was wielding and quickly placed it within its sheath. Talia shook her head, tears in her eyes.

"I am unsure. Please stay with me brave knight, please."

"Alec, just hang on." Zelus chimed in.

"Alec, if you die, hide, because, because I will be coming after you, come my time." Alec tried to smile at what was a moment of great affection for Eliza. As everyone crowded around him, Alec's eyes closed but a bright light still burned at his eyes.

"Alec, you have been granted a great responsibility. From this day forth, it will be your charge to protect Talia and Tear, from the Forsaken and the forces of Daemon. You have in your possession, the sword of the fabled Sidonis. You must travel with Talia and Tear and find the pieces of his armor. There are other Divine in need of your help and you must be ready to aid them. Accept Marec's offer, to teach you the ways of the paladin and grow stronger so that when the time comes you will be ready to undergo the ultimate test. Talia knows your next destination. Remain vigilant young knight. You shall be tested."

Alec opened his eyes, blinking them several times in an attempt to clear the haze that blurred his vision. Although his sight was obscured, he could tell that he was inside. He attempted to gather as much visual information as possible, noticing the floor was brown, wooden he imagined, as it matched the ceiling in color. Weakly, he moved his fingers and clenched his hands, working on his other limbs, until he came across his torso, which was weighted down.

Alec looked down and the fog began to clear as he saw Talia, fast asleep, her head resting on his chest. Her hair had been let down and was sprawled out across his torso. He reached up with his hand and gently stroked her cheek, brushing her hair back behind her ear. He stared at her beautiful face for a moment and took his first chance to marvel her. After envisioning her for almost a year, he felt comforted that he had never imagined her and was now in the same room, holding her.

"She never left your side." Alec could not turn his head but he knew that Eliza was sitting near to him. Eliza sensed Alec's first question and answered, before he had the opportunity to ask.

"We are still in Roak. Father and the rest of the knights have been out on patrol for the last two days searching for signs of any surviving Forsaken. Father felt that it might be dangerous if we tried to move you far, so you were brought to the tavern to rest." She giggled lightly at the sight of Oz, who was curled into a ball at the edge of the bed, fast asleep.

"He gave the medics a wretched time. It took four of us to pull him away from you so that they could tend to you." She laughed again and Alec could tell by the crack in her voice that she was crying. Alec strained to move his arms, but was able to stretch out his hand, which Eliza grasped and held within her own.

"I thought that you were gone." She had lost composure and her voice trembled as she spoke. Alec knew beyond a doubt that she was crying terribly. "Your heart even stopped for a brief moment."

"I am fine, Eliza. This is nothing but a couple of bumps and a bruise here or there." Eliza stopped crying and Alec flinched knowing that he was about to be punched. Eliza stopped her hand only a few inches from him, one finger pointing upward as she listed her conditions for restraint.

"I am going to let you off with a warning this time, Alec. If you pull another stunt like that, I swear once you wake up I am going to put you back under." She stood up and began to walk from the room but turned her head toward him and smiled.

"I am glad you are not dead." She turned and walked through the doorway.

"That makes two of us." He called back quietly and turned toward the young woman lying on his chest. Alec brushed her cheek some more as the young woman smiled and slowly opened her eyes.

"Good morning, Sir Knight." Talia spoke, sitting upright, still holding his hand in her own.

"Are you alright?" He asked her, to which she laughed nervously. Alec felt his breath leave him as her face illuminated, when she smiled.

"I am quite, thank Sir Knight. How are you?" She spoke as she held out a glass of water to him. Alec drank what he could, before he could feel his throat clench.

"Glad to see that you are alright?" He replied. Talia's smile only broadened.

"You gave us all quite a fright. You have many kind friends who were loath to leave your side." Talia told him. Alec relaxed as Talia began to hum a melody aloud. He closed his eyes and felt as though he had been returned to Highmooria. Though he could not recall where or from whom, he knew that he had heard the melody before, in his childhood.

"My apologies, priestess but what is that melody? I have heard it before, though I cannot place it." Talia's eyes sparkled as she smiled again.

"Tis a melody I learned from Sir Marec. Twas quite colloquial, I understand." Talia answered though it did not give Alec any clues. "Please Sir Knight, rest thy head."

"Alec...please, call me Alec." Talia closed her eyes as she bowed her head.

"Of course. Sir Alec, please try and rest." She requested of him as she began humming her beautiful melody once more. Alec laid his head back and closed his eyes, allowing for the sound of Talia's lullaby to guide him back to sleep.

"Sir Alec, please wake up, we need to speak with you." Alec opened his eyes and quickly his field of vision was filled with near everyone that he knew. Eliza, Tear, Zelus, Talia and the Lion, all circled around his bed. Oz sat perched on the balcony above his bed surveying the room, ready to strike if anyone moved too quickly. Dominic, Nilus, Marec and several of the other knights from the academy, filled in the back of the room.

"Ah, Sir Alec, there you are. Welcome back." Talia smiled at him and turned her head toward the Lion who spoke up.

"Alec, who was this enigmatic armored man you fought with? We have heard the details of your fight, of your discovery of the Sidonis sword but we know nothing of the general who led the attack." Alec's eyes grew wide at the mention of the sword and he began to choke.

After catching his breath from the shock, Alec cleared his throat, which had grown severely dry. Eliza handed him a goblet filled with water that he hastily drained. Opening and closing his mouth several times spreading the moisture, Alec answered.

"I did not realize that it was Sidonis' sword. Are you certain?" Talia smiled and nodded her head. Alec silently counted his blessings and doing his best not to continue choking, resumed. "As far as the armored man, he said that his name is Belias. He told me that he had been sent by his master to collect the Divine, who he identified as Tear and Talia. He also told me that he was an immortal, or rather he said that he was undying."

"And, I hear that you managed to wound this Belias?"

"Yes? I cannot quite describe it, however, but when I cut him, it was as if his body was not made of flesh, but instead something of the spirit. He moved unlike anything that I have ever encountered. It was definitely not a creation of Aneira." Marec stood in the back of the room gripping the backrest of the chair firmly enough that it snapped within his fingers.

"Excuse me, I shall be in the courtyard." Marec turned and left the room, a host of confused faces staring into his back as he left.

"How badly did you manage to wound it?" The Lion asked.

"I left a gash on one side and severed its right arm, but he said that it would heal." The Lion scrunched his face, a sign that he was thinking deeply.

"And one more thing, we have heard that you were glowing throughout the battle, enduring wounds that would have killed any other man. I can only imagine that has something to do with your current state?" Alec sighed and looked to Talia for help.

"Well, as far as my wounds, many were given to me by Belias while others were from the sword."

"Did you impale yourself?" The Lion asked, but this time Talia chimed in to help Alec.

"Sir, if I may. Sir Alec is what is often referred to as a blessed one. A mortal who is blessed by Aneira and in extreme circumstances can manipulate her light. The Sidonis sword however, feeds upon the strength of those blessed by Aneira. Only a blessed one can wield it, else the user would die. With the case of a blessed one however, the sword feeds upon the strength of the spirit, but if used for too long a time will kill the wielder." The room stirred uncomfortably as they stared at Alec.

"Alec, I would recommend not using that sword again anytime soon, understood?" Alec nodded his head but Talia shook hers.

"I am sorry senior knight but this Belias that Sir Alec faced is no mere enemy. It will take a weapon such as the Sidonis sword to defeat him and we already know that he intends to return."

"How do we prepare him for such a thing? Wielding it alone is enough to kill him." The Lion asked. Alec thought about the dream he had and considered what it told him to do.

"I would like to speak with Sir Marec, if I may? I would like to learn the ways of the paladin."

"What!?" Was the collectively astounded response of the room.

"I cannot explain it, but I feel that if I learn the ways of the paladin that I will be able to better endure the toll the sword takes." The audience thought as a mob for a moment.

"I agree with Sir Alec's suggestion." Talia faced the group trying to keep her face as straight as possible, so not to alert them to her excitement. "I only mean that Sir Sidonis was a paladin. If Sir Alec were to also learn the art from Sir Marec, he may be able to better endure the weapon." The Lion stood for a moment, stroking his beard.

"Alec, is this truly what you wish?" Alec nodded his head.

"It is sir. With your permission, I would seek Sir Marec's aid so that I might be able to better defend the people of Valoria."

"Very well. Should Marec decide to take you on as a student, I shall grant you my blessing. First however, allow me a moment to speak with him." The Lion rose and left the room. Eliza sat on the bed next to Alec, with her back to him.

"So you think that you are just going to leave the knights, just like that?"

"Eliza, I have to do this. I cannot explain but yes, just like that." Eliza tipped her head backward and let out a deep sigh.

"Well then I guess that means I will be going with you." Shock spread across the faces of the group.

"Eliza, you cannot be serious. You must return to the capitol to be granted your knighthood." Zelus attempted to deter Eliza.

"Zelus, you know that I will always go wherever Alec goes. He would not last a couple of minutes without me watching his back. He is hopeless."

"Come on, Eliza. Cut me some slack, would you?" Eliza turned her head towards him and gave him her devilish smile.

"Not a chance!"

"Thank you." He smiled back at her as Zelus pressed forward and looked her in the eye.

"Eliza, seriously, you need to return to the capitol. Otherwise, you may never get another chance." Dominic stepped forward and placed his hand on Zelus' shoulder.

"Peace Zelus. Eliza…Nilus and I will return to the capitol with the commander and inform the council of what has happened here. Surely, they would not interfere with a direct order from the commander to escort a priestess of Aneira on her sacred pilgrimage?" Eliza smiled.

"Thank you." The room grew quiet for some time before Nilus turned toward Zelus.

"We all know that you are going with them anyway. Why are you still just sitting there pouting?" Zelus folded his arms and turned his back toward Nilus.

"I have not decided whether or not I intend to travel with them."

"That is alright Zelus. You run along home, I am sure Alec and I can handle whatever trouble we encounter along the way." Zelus grumbled to himself for a moment before grabbing his things and then headed outside. Dominic turned and smiled at Nilus.

"I suppose brother that it shall be you and I returning with the commander then." Nilus nodded as they left the room leaving Alec, Eliza and Talia alone.

"Miss Eliza, Sir Alec, I welcome thee to join myself and Sir Marec on a sacred pilgrimage to the shrines of Aneira." Talia curtsied as she turned and left the room herself. Alec took a deep breath, swung his legs over the side of the bed and reached for his boots.

"Are you sure that you are ready Alec?" He nodded and stood his knees slightly wobbly.

"Oh yeah, not a problem." Eliza gave him a playful slug in the shoulder as he steadied himself and walked outside. Just as she passed through the doorframe, she rested her arm upon it and looked back at him with a smile.

"You are a lousy liar." Alec smiled at her as he slowly followed her lead. As they walked outside, they were unprepared for what their eyes beheld. The Lion and Marec were squaring off just outside and were lashing out at one another violently, with sword and shield.

"Your strikes still lack courage, knight commander." Marec taunted as he brought his sword down across the Lion's shield.

"You still fight as if you were a child!" The Lion struck back at Marec, sparks dancing across the blades of their swords. Marec swung upward. The Lion's blade flew free of his hand. Marec struck again as the Lion feigned and tipping the sword behind his back, twisted, Marec's arm and wrenched his sword sideways. Everyone from the room stood watching the two massive men fight with their bare fists pummeling one another until they both began to laugh maniacally. As they both buckled at the knees and panted to catch their breath, the two men began to pat one another on the back.

"How have you been all of these years Marec? How long has it been?" Marec halted his laughter and stood straight.

"Nearly a decade I would wager. Tell me brother, how has life been for you of late?" All of the assembled knights gasped in unison and Eliza approached.

"Father?" The Lion wrapped one of his massive arms around Eliza and pulled her in closely.

"Marec, this is Eliza, my pride and joy and heir to all of our house." Marec bowed his head and looked Eliza in the eye.

"Your father has told me much of you, I apologize that I have not had the pleasure of meeting you beforehand but I fear that the path I walk leaves little time for family."

"Are you my uncle?" Marec smiled.

"I am." Marec answered. Eliza looked back to her father and then to Marec.

"You never told me that my uncle was a paladin. Why?" Marec answered on his brother's behalf.

"I am afraid that was upon my behest. You see under normal circumstances it is imperative that I remain anonymous due to the nature of what I do."

"And what is that exactly?"

"Perhaps another time. Brother, what was it that you needed from me?" The Lion looked towards Alec and motioned for him to come forth.

"This, as you already know, is Alec. He has been as a son to me for the past eleven years and it is my hope that you would take him on as your student." Alec bowed his head and watched as Marec's surreal smile transformed back into the seemingly loathing glare, which Alec had accepted as Marec's usual face.

"We shall yet see if he is worthy but I shall not deny him the opportunity. I do expect however, that I shall be referred to as master or another equally respectable title." Marec hardened his gaze upon Alec, bearing down into him. "And should he prove unworthy and I suspect he will, then he will be cast out, never to return to the paladins or the knights. Does this satisfy you brother?"

"No, but I am unable to argue with your ways."

"Uncle, why would Alec be unable to return to the knights should he fail the paladin trials?" Eliza asked.

"If Alec should learn the age old secrets of the paladins and fail, then, in order to protect their sacred order, he must remain among them as an unproven or he must be cast into the Forsaken lands with his weapons and supplies never to return." Alec remained unfazed as Talia leaned in.

"It is of course your decision to make Sir Alec. The path you choose must be the path that lies truest to your heart." Alec held his head high and looked over his friends and then faced Marec.

"I still wish to be your apprentice."

"Very well then Alec. From here, we travel east toward the shrine in Remora. There we will pray to Aneira and along the way I shall begin your instruction." Alec took a moment to swallow his pride.

"I am eager to begin, master."

"Very well then, fetch your belongings." Marec turned his head to face Eliza and Zelus. "You two, are of course, more than welcome to join us, however, we must continue to keep a low profile and you are not to speak to Alec of the content matter of his studies. Am I clear?" Both Eliza and Zelus nodded their heads, their things already slung over their shoulders.

"Eliza, I shall speak to the council on your behalf and explain the situation. I am sure that you are already made aware of our story?" The Lion turned his head toward Dominic and Nilus who nodded their heads. "Good," He continued, "Alec do not disappoint us. I would hate to have one of my finest cadets go to waste chasing some boyhood dream of becoming a lowly paladin." Marec snorted but Alec smiled at the only man whom he may have related to as a father.

"I will become more than you ever hoped for sir."

"I look forward to that day, but, we both know, that the day you become more than I have ever hoped will be a long ways off. Too much potential, my boy." He patted Alec on the back and turned towards Zelus.

"Zelus, you know what your mission is, correct?" Zelus stood tall and saluted.

"To defend the innocent, spread the blessing of Aneira's love and to protect Cadet Eliza at any conceivable cost."

"Well enough, see to it that you do not fail me knight. Her mother shall be most worried once I bring her this news." Eliza rolled her eyes at her father.

"We both know that if mom were here she would tell you to leave me be and would have already begun the march home."

"Very well then, Eliza." He turned towards his men. "Knights move out!" Alec watched as his friends marched away in file. Alec turned his attention back towards Marec and Talia.

"We are ready, master."

"Very well, to Remora then." Alec shouldered his pack and was pulled backwards.

"Bree!" Oz continued to tug on Alec's shoulder strap.

"Alec, the Lion Hawk is not a beast of burden, I will ask that you carry your own belongings." Alec attempted to pull his pack from Oz's beak but he would not relent.

"Oz, let go!" He pulled again and the Lion Hawk purred as if playing with Alec. Zelus, Eliza and Tear shook their heads, broad smiles upon their faces. Alec's face flashed deep red however, as he saw Talia staring at him, giggling merrily at the expense of his forever shame.

"Oz, come on, you are embarrassing me in front of everyone!" He whispered to Oz and as Alec pulled his bag, again, Oz released his grip and Alec stumbled backward falling on the ground, his bag landing on his face.

The entourage of spectators could no longer contain their laughter as they all howled with merriment. Marec turned at the sound of the laughter and everyone did his or her absolute best to recompose. Oz sat upright, straightening his back and holding his head high. Eliza, Zelus, Tear and Talia, all coughed down their last chuckle and hastily wiped the tears and smirks from their faces, leaving Alec still lying miserably beneath his bag wishing for death.

"Alec, what are you doing lying about? We have a great distance we must travel today. I expect much better of you young apprentice!" Alec was no longer embarrassed but irritated. He quickly sprang to his feet, lifting his pack onto his back but knew there would only be one answer Marec would accept.

"Yes master, I will try harder."

"Unacceptable! Trying is for those who intend to fail. Do better, I trust that you will not continue to disappoint forever." Marec turned his back and Alec took the opportunity to glare at Oz angrily and then turn to his friends again who smiled and quietly laughed some more.

"Stupid bird." Alec thought to himself and Oz sensed his frustration and began to pick at Alec from behind as they walked. Oz would tip his head down at just the right angle and snort causing Alec to shiver as the hair on the back of his neck was pricked.

"Oz, leave me alone." Alec thought again and Oz backed away for a moment before he began to paw at Alec. Alec reached out and patted him on the head and seemingly contented Oz backed off and walked near Tear and Talia.

"Bree!" Oz leaned in to Talia and brushed her arm with the top of his head. Talia smiled and patted him as Tear scratched the underside of his chin.

"Tis a pleasure to meet you Oz. You are quite friendly indeed." Oz stayed by her side for some time giving Alec a chance to cool off. After walking for several hours, Marec halted the pack.

"We shall make camp here tonight. Unfortunately, now that we have your training to consider we shall need to stop earlier than usual. Alec, come with me. Eliza, Zelus, could you please do me the favor of setting camp?" Eliza and Zelus nodded their heads and began to set their things down.

"Of course uncle, would you like for us to prepare supper as well?" Zelus stood behind Eliza shaking his head vigorously, gripping at his throat with his hands and distorting his face pretending that he was dying painfully. Picking up the hint, Marec turned to Talia who was looking confused at Zelus.

"Mistress Talia, if it wasn't too much to ask. Would you please do us the honor of aiding Miss Eliza?" Talia still rather naive to the world answered.

"It would be my pleasure Sir Marec. Was that what you were trying to recommend Sir Zelus? I am afraid that I am unfamiliar with the communication technique you use." She placed her hands around her throat and tilted her head still baring an extremely confused expression. Zelus' face turned ghost white with fear as Eliza turned her head towards him and glared with promise of pain and prejudice.

"What's...wrong...with...my...cooking Zelus?" She spoke each of her words slowly so that he could fully appreciate the anger behind them and the grave nature he was in, should his response prove unfavorable.

"Uh...um, nothing Eliza, your cooking is sublime the best," he gulped, "Right, Alec?" Zelus turned to where Alec had been standing, but he and Marec had already begun to walk away. Alec smiled as he heard Zelus yelp with pain, a sure sign that he had just been decked by Eliza. He turned and saw Zelus sitting on the ground holding the top of his head as Eliza yelled at him and Talia still observed, confused.

Oz trotted beside Alec searching about the woodlands as they walked. Turning to face his friend, Alec patted him on the flank.

"Oz, if you would like, you may go hunt. Sir Marec and I will be fine, I promise." Oz turned his head from side to side as if contemplating, and then trotted off excitedly. Marec turned towards Alec.

"Spirited young griffet isn't he?"

"Very, he is a handful."

"Being considered a pact partner with a lion hawk should never been thought of as a burden. You have been granted a great honor that few before you have ever shared."

"I know master, I did not mean to imply."

"Alec, I understand that you are young and far too much responsibility has been forced upon you, but you must learn to accept it."

"Yes, master," Alec replied, hoping not to say anything that would irritate his instructor further. Marec stood, his hands folded behind his back.

"Alec, what do you know of the war between Aneira and Daemon?" Alec thought for a moment before answering.

"Just that it has continued on into the present day. It is the knights' sacred duty to defend the people of Valoria against the Forsaken." Alec smiled; pleased with himself for knowing the answer to the question, but Marec shook his head as if disappointed.

"You have much to learn Alec, much indeed."

"What have I to learn? Was that not the answer?"

"I am afraid not Alec, your answer was incorrect." Alec was astounded that he had answered the question, after having been so certain of himself.

"That is what we have been taught at the capitol. Are not the Forsaken the evil legions of Daemon's former armies?" Marec massaged the corners of his eyes as if pained by Alec's confusion.

"I do not blame you for your ignorance, Alec. Tis the way of the ignorant to believe all that they are told. Never thinking for themselves or daring to learn and form their own beliefs. Ignorant and lazy, young knight, I will expect better of you in the future. Now, I want you to look to that rock over yonder." Marec pointed, not to a rock, but a boulder that was half again as large as Alec.

"Move it." Were his only words.

"Master?"

"Move the rock, Alec. Do not return to camp until you have." Alec stared again at Marec. Alec stared at the rock for a moment and, determined to find a solution, rolled up his sleeves. Placing his hands beneath the rock, he positioned his feet under him to support the weight and began his attempt, at lifting the boulder.

Chapter 23- The Warrior Who Stands Tall

"You see Zelus, I told you that there was nothing wrong with my cooking." Eliza looked over at him, and held out an empty bowl. Zelus looked over at Talia, who smiled and nodded her head.

"Miss Eliza has done quite well. She has the workings of a great culinary master." Zelus turned his head from her and looked over to Oz, who was busy tearing at the collection of rabbits he had caught. Zelus tried slowly to reach his hand out towards one of the lion hawk's rabbits. Eliza, Talia and Tear stared at Zelus, as he looked at them, unaware of the lion hawk who was currently watching him.

"*Scree!*" Oz flapped and kicked at Zelus as he touched the ear of one of the bundle.

"Ah alright, alright. I just thought that yours might be the safer option, is all." Talia giggled, but once she saw Eliza glaring at Zelus, she took to straightening out her dress and then folded her hands in her lap. Eliza looked over to Zelus and shrugged.

"Fine, then. Go hungry, see if I care." She filled the bowl, sat back, and began to eat. Tear sat next to Talia and was eating quite happily. Zelus' eyes moved between Eliza and Oz several times before he finally gathered the nerve and scooted forward, grabbed a bowl, and slowly began to spoon her creation into his dish. As if a scared and wild creature, he surveyed his surroundings carefully and hastily hobbled back to his seat and sat staring at his bowl. Zelus sniffed at it casually and then sat it down next to himself, as he leaned towards his bag.

"*Brr.*" Oz leaned forward and stuck his beak into Zelus' bowl eating half of the meal as he turned away to grab a spoon. The three girls all strained to keep from laughing as Zelus turned and examined his bowl. He turned his head toward Oz, who had resumed picking at his rabbits, and then looked to Eliza who was now attempting to hold back the tears.

"What?" Zelus asked as he poked at the bowl disturbed at what might be in store for him. Finally, before he took the chance and risked a bite, Eliza spoke up.

"Zelus, why do you not grab another bowl and set that one back down."

"Why?"

"*Bree!*" Oz face planted back into Zelus' bowl, devouring the rest of his food.

"That is why." Talia, Tear, and Eliza laughed, as Zelus dropped the bowl and crawled backwards, eventually grabbing another bowl and setting opposite from Oz.

"Well, how is it?" Eliza eyed Zelus.

"Yeah, this is good. Are you sure, you made this Eliza? Owwh!" Zelus yelped as Eliza threw a pebble across the campfire, which pelted him in the forehead.

"Of course I made this, you were sitting right here the whole time. You saw Talia helping..." Eliza trailed off for a moment as she turned her eyes toward Talia and noticed the very large spider that had crawled near her hand.

"Talia, spider, look out!" Eliza despite her usual character, had grown quite desperate in the presence of the hairy eight-legged crawler. Talia looked down at the spider on her hand and stretched it, allowing it to crawl into her palm and turned back towards Eliza, whom Tear had joined in fearful repose.

"Oh, this, I would imagine that he was just trying to get warm, is all." She held him out towards Eliza and Tear who scurried backward, hiding behind Zelus.

"Talia, are you not afraid of spiders?" Zelus asked, flexing his body, taking advantage of his role as the savior.

"Well, no I suppose. Why might one be afraid of such a thing?" Eliza pressed passed Zelus and walked away as he stepped towards Talia.

"Well Talia, it is just that most girls are afraid of spiders, snakes, slimy and many legged things in general. It is just odd to see someone who does not fear them."

"Should I be afraid of such a creature?"

"No, I only meant that if your aim was to blend in, you would be better served to pretend to fear them."

"Alright, I thank thee for the advice. I shall make an effort to do better in the future." Zelus and Eliza looked to one another and then back to Talia.

"You might also want to be careful about the way you speak as well."

"Thou believe tis something improper in mine speech?" Again, the others smiled.

"Only that you do not hear others speak in such an old tongue." Talia nodded her head again placing the spider on the ground where it scurried away.

"I shall improve." She turned and took her place within the campsite and began to study a scroll as Marec returned from the woods.

"Ah, that smells like just what we need right about now." Marec stopped before the fire.

"May I?"

"Of course, uncle, but where might I ask is Alec?"

"I assure you that he will be quite alright, however, I do not expect him back before night fall."

"Might I ask why?"

"Do you remember our agreement?"

"Of course uncle. I merely wished to know Alec's circumstance not the particular exercise."

"I am attempting to strengthen him. That is all you need know for now." The five of them sat back and enjoyed their fire as Marec turned his attention over to Tear.

"Your name is Tear then, is it? Please tell me, young highness. How is it that you came across my niece and her friends." Tear wiped her mouth and began to recall her story to Marec as they warmed and stretched their limbs.

Alec

"Grrraaaaahhhh!" Alec strained against the boulder every muscle in his body tensing as he fought against its weight. He could hear the ground beginning to crack, when his legs gave out, he fell forward and was forced painfully onto the stone.

"Aneira's Nymphs!" He yelled and in his anger stood, breaking a branch off from a nearby tree. Alec looked down at his scraped and bleeding hands and then dabbed his forehead to find that he had cut his brow as well. He looked up at the sky and already he could see the stars, he had been trying to move the rock for several hours now.

"This is hopeless. This boulder weighs much more than I do. How does Marec expect me to move this?" He turned and kicked another rock with the heel of his boot and watched it roll away. Alec looked down at the branch within his hand, placed it behind the boulder and attempted to pry it forward.

"Grrr!" He strained against it but his arms were too tired. Alec lifted first one foot onto a neighbor rock face and then the other and used the strength of his legs to press as well. To his delight, he could feel the boulder budging. Alec rocked the boulder back and forth in an attempt to gain momentum, when his branch snapped in half and he landed on his back, on the cold hard stone.

Alec closed his eyes for a moment, holding back a long series of curses that came to mind. Waiting a minute for the throbbing to end, he placed his hand on the back of his skull and found that he was bleeding slightly. He rolled his head to the side and stared at the bloodstain that rested upon his shoulder. His body still able to move, he took several deep breaths and prepared himself. After a brief moment, he strained to rise and began to search about for a larger branch. After stumbling in the dark and tripping on various things decorating the woodland floor, Alec found a large thick branch which may have once served as the trunk to a young tree.

"One more time then." Alec reassumed his attempt at prying the boulder and this time, as he rocked back and forth, he could feel the boulder gaining momentum. Finally, it began to roll backward and he fell, twisted his body and caught himself on his knees. He panted aggressively for several minutes. Wiping the sweat and blood from his brow, he placed his wobbly legs beneath himself, and began to walk back to camp in the dark.

He stumbled nearly blind for several minutes before the smell of smoke and a dim light in the distance caught his attention.

"Food!" He tried to increase his speed but his legs failed him and he fell on his face in front of everyone.

"Oh well, we assumed you would want to eat before bed but if you insist." Eliza teased as she rose to help him.

"Food!" Alec moaned still face down in the dirt. Eliza patted him on the back and he began to push himself to his feet. Marec's boots were at Alec's eye level as he lifted his head from the ground.

"Is it done?" Alec nodded his head in response.

"Yes, master!" Marec looked at his pupil for a moment.

"We shall see. You may eat after you have cleaned yourself. There is a bucket near to where Oz sits and the stream is only fifty paces in that direction." Marec pointed just off from the opposite side of the road. "I shall return after I have inspected your work." Marec trudged off into the woods, an odd light glowing from an unknown source guiding his way. Alec rose to his feet and walked over to Oz and, seeing the bucket, lifted it.

"Alec, are you alright?" Eliza walked with him for a moment.

"Yeah, wash, food." He continued his dazed zombie walk away from her towards the stream and took off his shirt before filling the bucket and beginning to wash himself. The water was icy cold but still it felt rejuvenating to his aching body. He started with his clothes scrubbing clean his shirt and then beginning to work on his breeches. After he had finished his clothing, he splashed the water on his face and over his torso and began to wipe away the dirt. Several minutes later, when he was shivering from the cold, he began to ring out his clothes.

"Here you are." Marec handed Alec a blanket, which he gladly accepted.

"Clever work using the branch to pry the boulder from its resting place. Clever is a great place to start Alec, but I do intend for you to be strong enough to lift the boulder in the future."

"Master, I do not believe that I will have the strength to attempt to lift another boulder tomorrow."

"You will not be lifting a boulder tomorrow. However, do keep in mind Alec, if you fail to lift the boulder, you will never be able to break it. Dry your things by the fire and get something to eat." Marec walked away as Alec gathered his clothing and trudged back to camp. As he arrived, the others sat, staring at him, as if waiting for him to share the evening's events.

"You know that I cannot tell you what I did today right?" They all looked to him stunned at what he implied.

"Of course we do Alec. We would not dream of pestering you about your training, the thought had not even crossed our minds." Eliza started in as Talia searched about confused.

"But Miss Eliza, you and Sir Zelus were just mentioning the...mmm mmhh." Was all Talia managed to get out as Eliza clapped her hands over the puzzled priestess' mouth.

"Yeah would not dream of it." Alec laid out his wet clothes on a stump and sat near Oz.

"Did you have a good hunt?" The stream of emotions Alec received from the excited lion hawk was more than enough of an answer. Alec reached out and scratched the space right above Oz's beak and he cooed approvingly. Talia wriggled free of Eliza, moving to the place next to Alec and began to pet Oz. Oz folded his wings and rolled onto his back allowing for Alec and Talia to scratch at his chest and underbelly while he kicked his feet and wormed about.

"He is most friendly, is he not?" Talia continued to scratch Oz's underside as Zelus slowly stood.

"*Brr!*" Oz rolled over quickly and glared at Zelus.

"Hey come on Oz, I just want to pet you, that is all." Zelus slowly began to reach his hand outward. Alec could sense Oz growing on edge.

"Zelus, you may not want to do that." Zelus raised his hand palm facing towards Alec as he slowly leaned in for the petting.

"No, Alec it is alright. If we are going to be traveling together, we need to be familiar with one another." Zelus continued to crawl towards the lion hawk.

"I do not think you want to be as acquainted with him as you are about to be." Eliza chimed in.

"Do not worry Eliza. I know what I am doing. I had this cat once I found him when he was just a stray in one of our gardens and this trick worked famously."

"That is not a cat that you are reaching towards, Zelus." Oz began to puff out his chest towards Zelus.

"No everyone, I think I have got this. Look, he likes me already." As Zelus touched the tip his beak, Oz snapped into action.

"*Brree*!' Oz flung out his paw too quickly for Zelus to react and he was struck in the chest, sending him tumbling across the campsite. Everyone within the group began to laugh as Zelus frantically, pat out the flames that had caught on his sleeve.

"I can tell. The love truly is instantaneous." Eliza joked, as she pulled Zelus back to his feet.

"Is Master Zelus alright?" Talia approached Eliza and Zelus.

"I am alright priestess, just took me by surprise is all." Zelus rose and began to brush himself off. "Stupid bird." Zelus muttered to himself as he walked back towards the campfire and turned his back to the others.

"He just tricked you, did he not?" Zelus turned his head back around and began muttering to himself.

"Clothes are ready." He eventually grumbled and Alec rose to collect his things. As Alec plucked his things from the line, Tear came around towards the front of the camp with a long willow branch in hand. Alec began to turn his head away but stopped as he noticed the greenery on the branch.

"Oh Tear, what have you found there?" Eliza leaned forward towards the branch in Tears hand.

"A fallen branch from a Jasmine Pixie. I was walking along the woods and I heard hums from the earth that led me to this." She held up the branch again, and Alec caught a better glimpse at it. The leaves resting upon it danced and swayed in the wind when there was none.

"The wood is enchanted Sir Alec, that is why it reacts in such a fashion when held by a blessed one. It responds to Tear's touch, because she is blessed." Talia informed him.

"What would you do with such a thing?" Alec asked.

"Simple, Tear could use it as a staff in order to help her channel her abilities." Alec walked behind the row of tents and began to put his clothes on in private.

"*Scree!*" Oz rang out as he ran from the row of tents with Alec's shirt in his mouth.

"Hey, give that back!" Alec yelled as he ran, pulling on his left boot, while giving chase to the mischievous griffet. He chased Oz around and around the campfire, until Oz quickly ascended to the top of a tree and cooed down at Alec.

"Come on Oz, not right now. Give me my shirt back."

"*Brr.*" Oz turned in his perch so that his back faced Alec. Alec let out a long sigh before walking back and setting near to the campfire. The wind picked up and blew across his bare back. Alec shivered and, looking between the campfire and Oz, decided to at least wait where he would be warm. Alec turned his head toward Tear who was still smiling, trying to hold back her laughter.

"He would not give it back?" Alec shook his head at Eliza's question. "Do not be so sour Alec. He is just playing is all."

"Then take your shirt off and give it to him to play with." Eliza crossed her arms over her chest and looked at Alec.

"I think not. You two" she pointed at Alec and Zelus, "would enjoy that far too much!" Alec looked up at her and smiled.

"Meh, seen it. It was good enough I suppose, but not enough to catch my attention." Eliza turned a deep shade of red and was too paralyzed from embarrassment to even retaliate. She stood in front of them pointing a shaky finger at Alec, all the while, Zelus sat staring at Alec, his jaw dropped to his lap.

"You...saw her," he swallowed hard and then whispered the final word of his sentence, "naked?"

"*CRACK!*" Was the sound that Eliza's hand made as it was brought down upon the side of Zelus' face. Eliza turned back towards Alec who was smiling quite smugly. She opened and closed her mouth, while pointing at him several times but as if the words had left her, did not speak. Finally, Eliza had managed to find the words she was looking for.

"You just forget what you saw that night, alright? I do not need to know anything about your enjoyment." Alec smiled as he looked at the lion hawk, who still shook the shirt merrily within its beak.

"The only thing I would enjoy is hearing you admit how much fun you would be having was that your shirt." Eliza rolled her eyes at Alec and turned her attention to the campfire. Alec sat down beside her and began to warm himself. Accidentally grazing the gouge on his shoulder, he instinctively twitched.

"Alec, are you alright?" Eliza leaned toward him.

"Yes, I am fine." He answered as he tipped his back away from her making sure to avoid her seeing his gash.

"Oh dear, Sir Alec, you are wounded. Please let me tend to that." Alec turned his head not realizing he had shown his shoulder to Talia.

"Honest priestess, it is nothing. I will be quite alright." This time as he turned to face Talia he turned his back towards Eliza.

"You see Alec, I told you that you needed to have that looked at. It looks terrible." She remarked as she poked her finger at the gash.

"Yaaah!" Alec jumped as Eliza poked her finger in his wound. As he twisted around, he nearly barreled Talia over. As she attempted to back away, she fell over, as Alec tripped and landed on top of her.

"Sir Alec, I, I uh.." Talia stuttered and stumbled as she rested her hands on Alec's torso and felt the strength of the muscles that lay above her. Alec looked down at her face, which was beginning to turn shades of red as she looked up at him and, as if waking from a trance, backed away.

"I beg of your pardon Sir Alec. Please allow me to heal your wounds." Alec's tongue was glued to the roof of his mouth for a moment until he too awoke from his dreamlike state.

"Oh no, priestess, the fault is mine. Please accept my deepest apologies." Eliza rolled her eyes at the awkward nonsense. Zelus sat shaking his head, rubbing his temples, a large mark running across the side of his face. Tear paid no heed instead spending the time to annihilate her food. Her new staff was still humming, its leaves mysteriously blowing in the still air. Alec turned his back to Talia, and this time, she placed her hands upon Alec's shoulders and inspected the gouge.

"Tis not as bad as it looks, you shan't require stitches. Will take me... but just...a moment," She spoke between slight pauses as her attention was again drawn away for a moment. Oz sat in his perch, cooing as the party ignored him. Eliza looked

"Well, if you are certain that he will live. I suppose that I will turn in. Tear, are you ready for bed, sweetheart?" Tear nodded her head and walked to her tent. Eliza made sure to pat Talia on the back as she passed, again snapping her to attention.

"Right, of course, if you would please allow me?" Talia recited a quick singing chant and Alec felt the severe tingling of his flesh knitting itself together. Alec's spine quit tingling the moment that the spell ended and Talia noticed the knick on the back of his head.

"May I?" Talia pointed to the side of Alec's head. Alec tilted his head downward. Talia gently placed her hands upon either side of his head and found herself staring into his eyes. Alec slowly reached up to place his hand over hers, when his shirt was dropped promptly over his face.

"OZ!" Alec growled from beneath the shirt his voice slightly muffled.

"*Bree*." Oz cheered triumphantly as he bounded about the campsite barreling Zelus over in the process.

"Watch out stupid bird!" Zelus growled at Oz who turned and knocked Zelus down once more before rushing into Eliza's tent where he remained. They could hear Eliza and Tear yelp with surprise as he most undoubtedly knocked both of them to the ground. Again, Alec could hear the sound of Talia's singing chant and he felt the massive fuzzy tingling this time by his left ear. Once the feeling dissipated, Alec looked up to her and asked.

"Priestess, if I may, where did you learn to cast healing magic?"

"I was instructed in the healing arts by the maidens within the chantry. Where else might one learn of healing magicks?"

"I am unsure, perhaps my question was foolish, my apologies. I just find them to be unfamiliar and I am curious."

"Tis quite simple once one has obtained the proper discipline. Would Sir Alec wish of me to show you?" Talia asked as she subtly scooted toward him.

"I would be most honored if you would." Their moment was soon interrupted, as Marec returned from his venture. Loudly, Marec cleared his throat announcing his presence while also startling the two.

"I would recommend that you get some rest, young Alec. Your current amount of energy and vigor suggests to me that today's lessons were not challenging enough for you. To bed, for tomorrow we awake much earlier than the others to continue your training."

"Yes, master, of course." Alec rose to his feet and bowed his head to Talia.

"May Aneira watch over your dreams, priestess." Talia blushed and returned the parting gesture as Alec walked toward his tent. As Alec rose to march off to his tent, Zelus sidled over to him being sure that no one was watching him.

"Alec," Zelus whispered barely capturing Alec's attention. Alec turned his head slowly towards him and looked at him befuddled.

"What?" He whispered back. Zelus again looked from side to side ensuring that he had not been found out.

"Did you actually?"

"Did I actually what?" Zelus' face became much more mysterious before he answered.

"You know…see Eliza naked?"

"Oh, yeah, sure all the time." He brushed Zelus off as though it was nothing, and closed the flap to his tent as Zelus collapsed with envy. Alec sat on his bedroll for a moment and thought to himself of the last time that he had heard such a song. As he sat, eyes closed, he remembered his days in Highmoore.

"You will have to do much better than that, Alec." His grandmother chided, as she tapped her cane aggressively on the ground. Alec stood, doubled over, breathing heavily as sweat poured off from his face, which also bore a few bruises and a couple of bumps.

"Grandmother? I do not want to practice anymore." He whined as looked up at her.

"I did not ask you if you wanted to continue or not. You need to practice if you are to protect your sister and I." Alec, only six years old, looked back at his baby sister who was crawling around on the floor. He gripped his wooden sword tightly as he turned his back toward his grandmother. He could remember clearly, that the old woman smiled, the wrinkles on her face running smooth as she grinned widely.

"Much better my boy. Now, again!" She continued to smile as Alec began to practice each of the forms that his grandmother had taught him. First, he began to bring his sword up into the air and walk through defensive stances as she called them out to him. "Excellent. You are showing much improvement." As Alec continued walking through his forms, his grandmother began striking at him, forcing Alec to defend himself once more.

As Alec began to grow even more exhausted, his grandmother drilled him harder until Alec dropped his sword. As his grandmother's cane descended towards Alec's head, he flinched, closing his eyes, ready for the blow. After a brief pause, Alec opened his eyes and saw the cane floating just above his forehead. His grandmother gently tapped him on the head and smiled once more.

"That is enough for today, Alec. You have done well but you must never accept defeat. Never falter, never surrender, you are the warrior who shall stand tall, when even the sun and moon cower before the darkness." Alec nodded his head as his grandmother hugged him gently and sang to him, stroking his head. Alec could feel the tingling sensation upon his brow, as his wounds were healed.

"Now, my boy. Come help an old woman prepare a meal for you and your sister." She spoke as she walked back inside their house and Alec scooped up his baby sister as he walked inside.

Back from his memory, Alec opened his eyes and stared at the canvas in front of him. He took a deep breath and laid down on the bedroll as he closed his eyes and awaited sleep to claim him.

Chapter 24 – The Cost of Power

"Arise, young cadet. It is time to begin the day's training." Marec prodded Alec in his side for a moment until Alec arose and began to scurry about gathering his things.

"Leave them. Bring only your weapons and shield."

"Yes master." Alec dropped everything else, grabbing his sword and shield he trotted after Marec who wandered to the river. Marec stood, turned away from Alec.

"In order to wield the Sidonis sword we will need to prepare both your mind and your body. The blade will feed primarily off from your inner spirit, the power of Aneira's blessing. Once the power of your spirit is drained, it will begin to siphon off the energy of your body." Alec thought to himself about the feeling that overcame him when he wielded the sword before.

"So, am I to strengthen my spirit or my body?"

"Unfortunately, you possess desperate need of both. If the spirit is weak, then you will lack control of the Sidonis sword and will be unable to use any runes. If your body is weak, it will be unable to resist the weapon and your heart will stop. We will begin this morning by training your body." Marec turned and held out his claymore and tower shield.

"You will be using my weapons today." Alec approached and reached out for the shield. Straining against its weight, he placed his left shoulder beneath it and held on the best he could as he reached out for the sword in the other hand. The sword was nearly as heavy as the shield, but with his strong arm, he managed to lift it into the air and perform a couple of slow sluggish slashes.

"Are you ready?" Marec reached to his side belt and pulled from it his longsword.

"I am, master." Alec raised his sword arm and attempted to make the first swing, which Marec lazily parried. Alec swung again and, this time, Marec retaliated with a downward stroke. Alec swung his entire body into the shield and was spun around by the force of his move and the weight of the shield.

"You must learn to master your physical and spiritual self!" Marec yelled as he kicked Alec hard in the ribs, rolling him back onto his side, shield and all. Alec coughed aggressively and stood, lifting the shield as quickly as he could, Marec's blade barely tipped away but grazed Alec's face leaving a gash from his cheek to his ear.

"Try harder!" Marec yelled to Alec. Alec yelled in anger as he swung the sword again. Marec knocked it away with his gauntlet and, this time, smashed against the tower shield with the hilt of his sword. Alec's left arm went numb as the shield thudded to the ground.

"You are unworthy!" was the last thing Alec heard before Marec's fist deflated his torso and sent his body hurdling through the sky.

"Scree!" Oz cried out as he rushed to Alec's side and began to slice at Marec with his talons.

"Your weakness will be the end of both of you!" Marec yelled at Alec as he defended himself from Oz's attacks and, with a hastily spoken chant, pinned the griffin to the ground with invisible chains. Oz fought desperately against the force as Marec approached Alec.

"Oz is dead now, because you were unable to defend him! Who else has suffered as a result of your weakness? Your allies? Your friends? Your sister?" The nightmares clouded Alec's vision and the decision to forego logic was made.

"How dare you speak of Rayne!?" Alec's hair turned bright yellow, his eyes shimmered green." He lifted the shield from the ground and the claymore into the air. Marec came after him with all of his might as the spectators began to emerge. Alec and Marec sliced and slashed at one another for several moments before Marec with his superior swordsmanship forced the claymore to the ground and kicked Alec's wrist. The claymore flying from his hand, Alec reached for the only weapon he had remaining.

"Alec, what do you think you are doing?" He heard Eliza's voice but not her words nor their meaning. He noticed Marec's eyes widen, but almost as if, he expected the attack. Marec jumped to the side and lifted his shield as Alec struck out at him.

"You will soon feel the burden of your weakness." Marec spoke as he took up the defense, occasionally striking back at Alec. Their battle continued for several moments until Alec brought the Sidonis sword down upon the top of the tower shield and looked at the blade within his hand. The blade, which had once been sparkling and brilliant was now black.

Alec dropped the blade to the ground and stepped away, his eyes met with Talia's for a brief moment as he walked away from the group.

"We are not done Alec. You have yet to learn the significance of what has just transgressed." Alec stopped and turned back towards Marec.

"You have squandered the holy mother's gift. Not because you meant to, but because you lost control. You are still unworthy and you wielded the Sidonis sword out of nothing but anger and hatred. It is such weakness that allows one to become claimed by Daemon." Alec looked up from the ground and saw the looks in the faces of his companions. Eliza just shook her head in disappointment while Zelus smirked smugly, as if he had confirmed that Alec was inferior to him.

"Again!" Marec called from behind Alec, who turned and stared at his master.

"Forgive me, master."

"Raise your weapon." Alec turned and, picking up the Sidonis sword, slid it back into its sheath and began to remove his belt.

"You will be needing that weapon. I will, however, be taking back my own." Alec hastily retrieved Marec's sword and shield and strained to bring them to him.

"Master...are you certain?"

"Yes, I need to measure the extent of your spiritual energy." Alec closed his eyes for a moment, took a deep breath, raised his extremely sore shield arm and drew the Sidonis sword from its sheath. As it had every time before, the blade hummed and resonated with Alec as he could feel it drawing on his strength.

"Now, young disciple, come at me!" Alec did so, running toward Marec and making the first strike. His stroke bounced off from Marec's shield, but he could see the paladin buckle slightly from the force of the blow. Alec struck out several more times, with each blow being blocked by the shield.

Marec followed with a swipe from his claymore. The sheer power behind the blow knocked Alec's arm sideways causing him to stumble backwards. Before Alec had time to recover, Marec came at him again with even more attacks. Alec feigned with his shield, tipped the claymore off its edge, and ran in close for a strike.

As he ran forward, Alec could feel the strain from the Sidonis sword weighing upon him. He attempted to swing the sword, but he could feel his body moving increasingly sluggish, his breathing becoming shallow and his heartbeat slowing. Marec must have noticed Alec's weariness for he stood in place and waited for Alec to approach him. Alec tried his best to swing but instead Marec knocked him backward with his shield. Alec stumbled and fell to a knee.

"Rise!" Alec pushed with all of the might in his body and attempted again to run at Marec. Oz shrieked angrily in the background. Alec could feel his worry in the back of his mind and did his best to ease the terrified griffin, but Alec himself was beginning to realize his own limitations. He was weakening ever more quickly. Already, he felt as though he were at his end.

Alec coughed and could taste the bitter swell of blood in his throat. His vision began to blur and he fell face first onto the ground.

"Sheath your sword Alec, so that it desists its drain on your energy." The words sounded alien to Alec. He rolled his eyes around for a moment and looked at his hand bewildered.

"Here Alec, let me help you." Eliza ran up to help Alec.

"Eliza, do not touch that hilt." Marec's warning came too late. Eliza touched the handle of the sword to pick it up and then, as if struck by lightning, tossed the sword backward and fell to the ground.

"By Aneira, what was that?" She yelled out as she clutched her hand in agony. This time, Talia approached and, grabbing the hilt of the sword, lifted it from the ground and gently slid it back into its sheath.

"Are you alright Mistress?" Marec looked to his ward.

"Quite. I am surprised that he was able to resist the sword as long as he had. Just that simple touch, and I could feel it pulling my strength."

"As for you Eliza, please do not attempt to carry the Sidonis sword again. Even just a simple touch can have extremely damaging effects for one who has not awakened Aneira's inner gift."

"I understand uncle, it will not happen again." Marec turned his attention from her to the sun rising over the horizon then toward Alec.

"Please rise, we are done for now. We must be moving, I still expect us to reach Remora by tomorrow evening." Alec slowly placed his palms down in front of him and pressed against the earth. With a great deal of strain, he managed to rise to a knee and from there to his feet. He stumbled backward and Oz was there to catch him.

"I will inform Tear that we are leaving." Eliza spoke as she walked from the party. As Zelus and Marec walked away to begin packing, Talia approached Alec and Oz.

"Sir Alec, may I?" Talia held out her hands gesturing towards his scrapes and bruises.

"Oh, thank you." Alec waited as Talia began to recite her chant and then he felt strength returning to his body. A moment later, he could feel the gash on his cheek healing.

"So, does everyone use magic that way?"

"Forgive me Sir Alec, in what way do you mean?"

"By chanting like you do." Talia shook her head as she checked to ensure that Alec was healed.

"No, only the Divine cast spells in such a way. There are a few spells may be activated with a phrase, though they are uncommon and require a paladin or blessed one of a most advanced level. Most others would require a rune or a seal of some sort."

"Just like when Marec touches the runes on his belt or draws a symbol in the air?"

"Quite."

"So what is the difference between your singing and someone using a rune?"

"For a Divine of Aneira, we harness the true potential of Aneira's gifts through chanting. It is said when someone sings a song to Aneira that is well received, the tribute is rewarded with good luck and prosperity. It is also said that when a divine sings to Aneira, they call upon and wield the power of Aneira."

"So using a rune is simply channeling magic. Where for you, singing to Aneira allows you to borrow her power?" Talia nodded her head. "That explains a lot then. Aneira must love your voice. It is most beautiful." Talia blushed and turned her attention towards the camp.

"We must prepare. To reach Remora by sunset will require time and a hastened pace."

"Right, of course." Alec and Talia walked towards the campsite. Eliza and Zelus had already collapsed their respective tents. Marec stood with both his and Talia's things. Alec looked back at Talia and then to his own things that still needed to be collapsed and packed.

"Where is Tear?" Zelus peeped up after a moment.

"She is just beyond the treeline at the mouth of the river." Talia spoke much to the surprise of everyone save Marec. Alec, Zelus and Eliza all turned and looked toward the place Talia specified.

"Talia, how can you be so certain? Can you see something that I cannot?" Eliza asked. Talia smiled as if the answer were obvious but humored the pondering trio.

"No Miss Eliza, it is just that we divine have a way of sensing one another's gifts. Tear is chanting a hymn just beyond the treeline. I can sense the power of her hymn." The three smiled in unison, accepting yet still confused with their answer. After a few moments Tear appeared from within the trees which they had just been staring.

"I am sorry, are you waiting for me?" Tear chirped with her delicate voice.

"Actually, we are awaiting young Alec to close his jaw and begin packing."

Marec's voice in contrast to Tear, sounded similar to stones grinding against boulders, which in Alec's opinion suited the paladin.

"Right away master," was Alec's response as he hastily began tearing apart his contributions to the campsite. As Alec finished packing his bedroll into his bag, he looked up to see Oz and Tear playing together while Marec spoke with Eliza. Zelus was standing with his back to everyone looking toward the road they had walked thus far. Alec shouldered his belongings and walked to Zelus' side.

"Homesick?" Alec asked as he stood by him. Zelus scoffed as he watched the rolling hillside.

"Hardly, I merely wonder what is to become of me once we head home."

"You will return to the command of the knights, I suspect." Alec suggested.

"Perhaps."

"Have you different plans now?"

"This quest of yours has me wondering if the path laid before me is actually the path that I was meant to follow." Alec thought to himself for a moment before answering.

"Perhaps you are on your given path to find the true course you must steer." Zelus nodded his head.

"It is worth considering at the least." Zelus and Alec both turned as Marec approached from behind them.

"Are we ready?" Both Zelus and Alec nodded in response, taking stride towards the road.

"Good, Alec I want for you to take up the lead for the day. Milady, Sir Alec will be escorting us until we reach Remora. I must request you do not heal him in the future." Talia shied away, approaching and looking Alec in the eye.

"Please lead the way Sir Alec." Alec turned his head toward the road that would lead them to Remora and began walking. He checked back and saw Tear, Oz and the others following a few paces with the others close behind them. As they walked, Alec paid heed to the environment around them being ever watchful for the dangers that could await them.

"Is something troubling you, Sir Alec?" Alec turned his head to Talia who was walking just behind his right side.

"No milady, of course not. I am just keeping an eye out for any who may wish to harm us." He renewed his search of the landscape while Talia spoke to him again.

"Is there some way with, which I may assist you in your search?" Alec turned his head to the side and smiled. Talia had cupped one hand over her eyes blocking out the sun, careening from side to side as if looking through a far seeing eyeglass.

"Well, if you do not mind, I would love to know more about you." Talia returned Alec's smile.

"What would you like to learn, Sir Alec?" Alec only needed one second for his head to be filled with the infinite number of questions he had in regards to Talia.

"Anything you have to offer. For instance, what are your hobbies? What drives you? What is your family like? What was life in the Grand Cathedral like? When is your birthday?" He began to blurt out a number of them excitedly as Talia attempted to keep up with him. She frantically attempted to slow Alec's excitement long enough for her to answer.

"First off, I enjoy reading, singing and tending to flowers in the cathedral. These were among my privileges within the shrine. Sadly I do not know much of my family though I have this to remember my mother by." Talia pulled a necklace from beneath her clothes. Alec stared intently at the necklace, examining every detail from its long, blue, rose red and pink beaded band to its Aneiran talisman at the end. Alec smiled at Talia.

"It is a beautiful necklace. Your mother must have loved you greatly." Talia gripped the necklace lovingly before responding.

"I miss her so much." She paused for a moment. "What of your family?" Alec shook his head.

"Lost along with Highmoore, eleven years ago. Talia frowned, remorseful for asking.

"I am terribly sorry Sir Alec, I did not think."

"It is alright priestess," he assured her as he smiled at her. "What would you like to know?" Talia thought to herself as a moment.

"What were they like?" Talia asked,

"My sister was adventurous, curious. I remember that she was always running off and getting me into trouble." Alec began remembering his sister and his childhood. "My sister, though younger and much smaller, often picked fights for my benefit." He laughed slightly as the thought came to his mind and Talia saw a slight tear appear in the corner of his eye. Eliza looked up towards Alec with concern, as Zelus tried to avert his eyes. Even Marec wore a solemn expression, as the tone in Alec's voice suggested the weight behind his words.

"I was rather small, compared to many of the other children my age and even though I lived within the inner wall, I bore no formal title, no blood family to claim me. Many of the noble born children would push me around or spit at me when my sister and I walked by."

"I am sorry, Sir Alec, that sounds awful." Alec shrugged.

"It prepared me for life in Valascaana." He continued. "Besides, I never allowed it to bring me down. I did have a few friends, Mariah Aetrian, for instance. Her and I lived near one another and my sister and I would often visit her. The only time the other children ever bothered me was when they would harass my sister." He shook his head as both eyes bore signs that they were soon to shed tears.

"Whenever the other kids would make fun of us or speak ill of our grandmother, my sister would take one look at them and know instantly of their insecurities, doubts, fears and would relay them aloud. I still to this day, do not know how she managed to do it but the fights that were started as a result made full use of my abilities. I was only fortunate that grandmother had trained me well." Talia eyed Alec curiously.

"Your grandmother taught thee, the rules of combat?" Alec nodded his head.

"Yes, ever since I can remember, I have been trained in swordplay. My grandmother was tough but I never forgot the lessons that she taught me."

"Such training must have been most beneficial at such a young age." Talia commented as Eliza spoke.

"Alec was one of the top cadets, his first year in the college. He was already more proficient in most forms of combat than many who were older than he." Alec smiled at Eliza before turning back to face Talia. After some consideration, Talia thought of another question.

"What is thy earliest memory?" Alec thought for quite some time before answering. He tried to think back as early as he could and after pondering for several minutes, a blurred vision of the past came to him.

"I am in a large room, bathed in red and gold…." He started. "It is as if the sun has risen within...everything is so bright." He thought some more as everyone listened intently. "And there is a woman...I cannot see her...but she is singing to me. I cannot place the song but it is there, just out of reach." Alec continued to strain with the memory as he lost it.

"The gold and red, bathed in light might have well been a troop of paladins." Marec began. "You said that you lived within the inner wall. We performed regular demonstrations. Surely, that explains a part of your account." Alec nodded his head and smiled at Talia. Talia returned the smile before continuing through the list of questions.

"Thank you for sharing. What was your next question?" Alec thought for a moment lifting his gaze skyward in an attempt to recall.

"Well, I think I understand life in the grand cathedral, so the next one was when is your birthday?" Talia smiled at Alec.

"Well, my birthday is in the middle of next month. It is on the seventeenth of the sixth month." Alec thought for a moment.

"That is only a few weeks away."

"That it is."

"Well then priestess, I will be sure to get you something." Talia shook her head as they rode.

"That will not be necessary, Sir Knight." Alec was not about to accept such a thing.

"Nonsense, I am going to get you a present for your birthday, I only need to think of the perfect gift." Alec insisted. Talia shook her head and smiled at Alec's determination.

"Enough about my birthday, when is yours?" Talia asked her cheeks slightly blushed. Alec frowned and looked down at the ground.

"I do not have one." He spoke. Talia looked to him with a shocked expression on her face.

"What do you mean? Does not everyone have a birthday?" Talia asked him. Alec shrugged his shoulders and responded.

"Well, I never knew mine. It was not something my grandmother, sister and I celebrated." Talia was shocked into silence and they walked on for several awkward moments. Desperate for the conversion Talia thought of an appropriate conversation.

"Would you wish for me to train you in the ways of healing magic, whilst we walk?" Alec's head snapped over to her.

"Very much so, milady. Do you feel as though I have the proper gifts for such a thing?" Talia smiled at his underestimation.

"I would imagine that should one wish to become a paladin, they ought to possess the proper talents."

"Then, if you would tutor me, I would consider it a grand honor." Alec bowed his head to her out of sincere respect. He could hear Marec clearing his throat and looked over his shoulder to see that he had only done so in an attempt to continue his conversation with Eliza. He turned back to see that Talia had also looked toward her guardian and, concluding the same, continued to speak with Alec.

"First, you must come to understand the runes used by the blessed ones and how to activate them. The first thing you must do is to draw the rune you desire. I will start with a simple rune, the rune for mending." Talia pointed with one of her elegant fingers and began to draw into the air. At first, Alec followed her finger through the air until he noticed a blue spectral image appearing before him.

"How did you do that?" The sight amazed Alec. Talia simply kept walking as she explained and Alec sped up to keep in stride.

"The second thing one must do is dig into themselves and reach for Aneira's gift within. Summon the power from within and, with it, craft your symbol creating the magical effect you just saw."

"What happens once the symbol is cast?"

"Then you need only apply the effect to the individual who is to receive it."

"And how do I do that?"

"Some runes will apply to you and others you must direct the enchantment by touching the target."

"How does one come across new runes?" Alec asked.

"There are many old libraries scattered across Valoria that still hold scrolls and tablets from before the dark times. There were once academies where those who possessed Aneira's gift could learn the ancient runes." Alec thought for a moment, reaching to his side and began to unsheathe the Sidonis sword. The blade began to hum at his touch and he turned to Talia with it.

"There are some runes on this sword. Do you think that you could tell me what they are?" Talia leaned toward Alec and looked at the blade, confused.

"Sir Alec, I see no runes upon this blade." Alec pulled the blade back towards him and looked upon its surface, seeing that the runes were clearly there. Unsure how to continue the conversation, he diverted slightly.

"Do you know where I might find one of these libraries?" Talia thought for a moment when the obvious occurred to her.

"Why yes, in fact at the grand shrine, where I am from, there exists such a library. Once our quest is complete, you may accompany us back there to learn more. I know many of the basic runes, as does Marec, however, many of the old runes have been lost over the millennia."

"I would love to see the grand shrine with you." Alec turned toward Talia who was looking ahead.

"Perhaps one day you may see it." Talia paused for a moment as if something were troubling her. Alec saw that look in her eyes that he had seen so many times before in his visions. Her beauty was marred by a deep longing sadness that permeated the soul. As they walked in silence for a moment, Alec began to practice drawing the rune in the air.

First, he pointed straight in front of himself, then traced his finger skyward the length of his forearm. Then he sliced down diagonally toward his left side, stopping half way down his first line. He swiped his finger the length of his forearm, straight across again, up in sync with the top, diagonally across to the bottom left extreme and then connected it to the first point he had drawn.

He stared at his mark for a moment and grew disappointed that the blue hue never appeared. He drew up a deep breath and attempted to write the symbol again. He attempted several more times with no result and decided that for the time being that he would desist.

"Keep practicing Sir Alec. In time you will discover the way to unlocking your potential. It will not be from thought that you achieve this. It will come to you through desire, decision and instinct."

"Thank you, I will be sure to continue practicing. Is there anything else that I should know?"

"Not until you are able to call upon the rune. Master its power and I will show you more." Alec again traced the three bladed windmill that stood for mending and, yet again, he saw nothing.

They continued to walk down the winding path for hours on end until Marec called out.

"Zelus, once we reach Remora I need for you to arrange lodging for all of us. Eliza, I would like for you to practice that which we discussed earlier today. Alec, Tear, Talia and myself all must go to the temple. We will meet with you at the inn once our business is settled."

"How much further to Remora, uncle?"

"Another few hours at the most, we shall be there by midday. I do suspect however that the hour of our return shall be most late. I would advise the two of you to brush up on what we have discussed so far today." Marec spoke as he looked at Eliza and Zelus.

"What will you have me do, master?"

"You will follow Talia, Tear and myself to the temple. Whilst the three of us meet with the head priest here, you will head down to the altar of Aneira. Just as

Sidonis before you, you shall drink from the fountain of Aneira and pray to the holy mother."

"What then?"

"That is not for me to determine young Alec. Do as I have instructed, and you will be given further guidance." Alec nodded his head and turned his attention back towards the road ahead. After he had finished speaking to everyone, Marec turned his attention back to Eliza asking for a moment in private. Zelus walked toward the front of the pack and walked alongside Alec.

"Are you still homesick?" Zelus took up his usual aggressively defensive stance.

"Hardly, in fact, I have come to find this trip rather rewarding."

"Is that so?"

"Yes, it appears that Marec has more to teach than just paladin tricks and old legends. I suspect that once I have mastered what he has shown me, I will be the greatest knight in all of Valoria."

"Only because I will be a paladin and unable to claim the title, myself." Alec joked causing Zelus' ears to grow bright red.

"You just wait, once I am ready to show off my new abilities you and I will spar again and we shall see once and for all who is better than whom."

"We will see." Alec and Zelus turned to face one another and deadlocked as if a malevolent force bound them in that position.

"Crack!" Alec's entire world spun around him. He was unsure which discomfort was making him more delirious, the massive booming sound of their heads colliding into one another or the fact that he and Zelus' heads had just been forced together.

"Ha! It appears that once again I am victorious. All hail Eliza, Queen of the universe!" She laughed as she walked past the two men who groaned in pain, her arms raised high into the air taking her victory stance. Alec rolled to the side and saw Zelus lying on the ground face down his body arched as if trying to balance on his head.

"Oh my, Miss Eliza, you are most fierce." Talia said softly recovering from the startling attack.

"A warrior, be they knight, paladin or disgruntled farmer should always keep their wits about them and be ever mindful of imposing danger. Had she been an enemy, you would both now lie dead, unsung and forgotten." Marec spoke as he stepped over top of them and continued walking. Pulling up the rear Talia and Oz passed them, Tear jabbing Alec with her stick as if prodding to check a cadaver. Alec could feel Oz's merriment as he let out a broken scree that could only be laughter.

"Stupid bird." He could hear Zelus mumble followed by another violent grunt as Oz stepped on him as he walked past. Slowly, Alec rose to his feet and steadied himself, the world still spinning violently around him. In his drunken vision, he could make out Zelus and his twin stumbling beside him after the others.

"One day, soon, I will make you pay for that." Zelus shook his fist angrily toward Eliza, Alec full well knowing that Zelus would never harm Eliza, even if he were able to. Their vision refocused, they easily managed to catch up to the rest of the group who had taken a slightly slower stride allowing them to do so.

"Alec, I feel that, from henceforth we will begin conditioning your body during the day outside of training. That way, when there is time for training, I can more effectively focus on your spirit." Marec said, causing Alec, to grow excited by the thought.

"What will you have me do?"

"Carry these." Marec stated as he threw his pack to Alec, causing him to stumble backward and land on his rear.

"For now, I shall be carrying my own weapons and, for now, you shall be carrying my and Miss Talia's belongings. The additional weight will do your body good." Alec squinted at Marec's back angrily as he threw the extra-large pack over his shoulders and felt the increased burden bearing down on him. With the increased workload on his shoulders, he could not help but feel the intense throbbing sensation between his eyes. He reached up with his hand and already could feel the massive welt forming from Eliza's sneak attack.

He placed his finger out in front of him and began to again practice the three bladed windmill insignia Talia had just shown him. Again, nothing happened. Alec could feel his temple's pulse, as he grew increasingly frustrated with this "rune thing." He continued to trace the rune again and again and became so involved in the process, he stopped paying attention to the task at hand, running into the back of Eliza.

"Hey watch it, or do you want a pair of horns on your forehead?"

"Sorry Eliza, why are we stopped?"

"We are here genius." Alec looked up from Eliza's annoyed stare and saw before him the town of Remora.

Chapter 25 – The First Shrine, the Town of Remora

"Mistress, might you be willing to take young Tear ahead with you while I guide Alec to the shrine?" Talia nodded her head to Marec.

"Of course, Sir Marec, we will wait for you in the cathedral." Alec watched as Talia and Tear walked pass the building, which now stared at Alec and Marec. Alec was not impressed.

"Is this the shrine?" Alec turned to his instructor and asked as they walked up to the small building that lay before them. It was no bigger than was the guardhouse in Roak.

"Yes, it is not as illustrious as many of the other shrines but things have become much more difficult in these outlying towns since the fall of Highmoore." Alec flinched at the name of his old home. Marec continued as though he had not noticed Alec's reaction.

"A great deal was lost that day. T'was my first station as a paladin. I served there for many years before I was appointed to be mistress Talia's defender. It was a truly beautiful place."

"It was my home." Alec solemnly moaned.

"I had heard such. It was also mine for many a year. One day, Alec, we may yet be able to reclaim our home. If only you had been able to see the noble's district and the grand temple. The paladin order was much greater back then. Not so great as it was before the dark times, but we had reclaimed much of what we had lost." Marec sighed. "To have spent countless lifetimes in hopes to restore our former glory, just to have it blinked out within a single eve." Alec kept his eyes on the ground, holding his composure, the pain excruciating, but necessary, he needed to know more.

"He was there that night. The black knight." Alec's eyes met Marec's, and Marec noticed that glimmer in Alec's eyes.

"Belias?!" Alec asked in shock. Marec nodded his head.

"He was not alone however, he had another with him."

"Another?"

"Yes, in the Forsaken lands, there exists an order of what you could call "anti-paladins." They refer to themselves as the Daemon Knights and are each masters of dark and terrible magic."

"How many are there?" Alec asked. Marec shook his head in response.

"I have no idea, but I once read that no more than twelve have ever existed at one time."

"Why twelve?"

"I would imagine two for each of the great nations of the world. Beyond that, your guess is as good as mine. I also read that Daemon will only create as many as he can control. Too many knights armed with his power could turn against him."

"So even Daemon's power has its limits?"

"I can understand why you would think that, however as far as a mortal such as us could fathom, his power is still beyond comprehension."

"And the knights are immortal?" Marec did not answer but simply nodded his head. Alec thought back to his fight with Belias and a dark shiver overcame him.

"How many of these knights are you familiar with?" Marec placed his fist in front of his face and rested his chin upon it in thought.

"Belias, we have met. There was Abaddon from the days of Sidonis, the mad king Caliban and the witch of the Tartarian wilds, Cecille." Alec was not overly familiar with Tartaria, a country to the south, across the ocean. All he knew was that the entire continent was covered in woodlands and mountain ranges.

"There are Daemon knights in lands other than those on the Exodon?" Marec nodded his head.

"Quite. As I was saying, I believe that there were many others amongst the stories from my days as an initiate. There was Calyptus, the vagabond, who was felled long ago and Calleus, his brother. I seem to be forgetting about someone. Once you have an opportunity, we shall consult the old records, to fill in the gaps."

"Was Belias the first Daemon knight that you encountered?"

"He was but enough talk of the past young cadet. Let us attend to the business at hand." Marec pulled his and Alec's packs from Alec's back and set them on the floor just inside the temple doors. They walked inside a few steps and were greeted by a man in long flowing brown robes.

"Ah, Sir Marec, welcome back. It has been quite some time since you last visited us. Is this a new recruit, I presume?"

"Not exactly Triam, this cadet was chosen by another. I have, however, taken it upon myself to fulfill the sacred duty of training this cadet." Triam looked most confused by the news.

"With so few paladins left in the region, who by Aneira's name could have selected him?" Marec nodded his head towards Alec's hand which now rested upon his sword belt. Alec took the queue and delicately removed the Sidonis sword from its protective sheath. Triam gasped at the sign of the sword and Alec could swear that the old man wept as he stared upon the blade.

"How did you come upon this sword?" Alec looked to Marec who nodded. Alec cleared his throat and then answered.

"I encountered a Daemon knight and in a moment of desperation I pledged an oath in blood to Sidonis and Aneira that if they granted me strength that I would protect the priestess Talia from the forces of Daemon." Triam grew silent for a moment and Alec feared that he had said too much.

"The time it seems is finally at hand. To be honest I had hoped that it waited for the next age or so but it appears that it is time."

"Time for what sir?"

"*When the heart of malice beats again and the one who has fallen enacts her unholy vengeance, the Forsaken shall march with fire and death upon the lands of Valoria. In their time of need, Aneira's shield shall appear among the people gleaming green and gold and safeguard the divine as they rise to again seal away the heart of darkness.*" Alec's eyes opened wide.

"That was what Tear said when she went into trance!" Marec nodded his head at Alec's recollection and then spoke.

"That hardly surprises. Tear is a divine and as such, she has had some access to Aneira's prophecies. Triam, is there not more to this prophecy?" Triam nodded his head.

Yes, there are several pieces to this puzzle. However, much of it has been stricken from record by order of the grand priestess but what I do recall says something like…

"*To flame and ruin, he of one thousand blackened souls shall call upon the sword of his nemesis and by Aneira's spilt blood, shall reclaim what was taken from him. Aneira's shield shall fall by the hand of the sentinels' betrayer.*" Triam stopped and Alec looked to him an expression of horror across his face.

"I am sorry young cadet, I do not remember the rest. It has been sometime since the old scrolls were lost."

"What does it mean?"

"It could mean a great many things. One thing that I can tell you is that Aneira's blood often times refers to the death of a nymph or to the blood of a divine and that Daemon's nemesis is Aneira and you hold her sword." Triam pointed to the blade by Alec's side. Alec looked down to it and nearly dropped it to the ground.

"Then we must be rid of it. We must take the Sidonis sword somewhere that Daemon will never find it." Both Marec and Triam shook their heads at Alec.

"I am afraid that it is not that simple. Even if we hid the sword in the Grand Shrine, Daemon would still find a way to claim the blade for himself. The only way that we can protect the sword and thereby negate the prophecy is to train you in the ways of the paladin so that you may keep the sword safe. There is no other way." A terrifying rush of emotions flooded through Alec as he considered all that he was being confronted with.

"What must I do?"

"Triam will take you further inside to the shrine of Aneira. Once there you must do as I asked, pray to the goddess and drink from the fountain. The rest will be presented to you from there." Alec looked to Triam with renewed purpose guiding him.

"I am ready."

"Very well then young cadet, this way." They walked down a long hall which opened up into a large courtyard. Alec surveyed the courtyard picking out the statues of Aneira and Sidonis along with a rather illustrious fountain.

"I believe that you already possess all the knowledge you need to continue on without me young Alec. May Aneira guide you."

"And Sidonis shield you, Sir Triam." Triam smiled and bowing his head left Alec alone in the empty courtyard. Alec stood before the statue of Sidonis and bowed his head in reverence.

"I shall defend the sword. I shall not fall to the darkness." Alec turned to the fountain, and kneeling drank from the water. The water was cool yet flowed down his throat as if comprised of angelic nectar. Alec bowed his head once more and offered up his prayer to Aneira.

Tear and Talia

"Talia, why do we have to come here?" Talia smiled and looked over to the small child beside her.

"I must speak with the head priest here in order to gain access to the archives. I must also determine if they have any information in regards to my visions."

"Like the ones of Sir Alec?" Tear asked, curiously. Talia turned her head to Tear with curiosity in her eyes.

"Tear, what do you mean?"

"That is how I found you on the road. I saw Sir Alec in my waking dreams and they led me to him." Talia began to rack her brain for an answer to such a strange twist. Talia smiled and looked back at Tear.

"Well then, my dear Miss Tear, we shall see if we can find an answer to both our questions." They walked side by side until they came to a large pair of oak doors, which Talia forced ajar. Talia found herself wondering why Tear was having visions as well, not to mention ones that involved Alec. Talia could not help but wonder just how and why Alec had become so entangled in the web of the divine.

The room opened up into an enormous chamber, complete with cathedral ceiling decorated with murals celebrating Aneira and her nymphs. Talia and Tear walked the red carpet toward the altar that lay at the farthest end of the room where an older man knelt.

"Father Mathias?" The man turned his head and looked at Talia for a moment and as if her name suddenly dawned upon him.

"Ah miss Talia. My, my it has been some time. Look at how much you have grown." He rose and bowed before her. "How, my dear priestess, may I be of service to you?" Talia curtsied in response to Father Mathias.

"I wish to speak with you on a delicate matter?"

"Of course, but what may I ask is so urgent that has brought you here from the Grand Shrine?"

"I have been gifted with Aneira's sight and am in pursuit of answers to certain questions. I seek access to the sealed archives." Father Mathias nodded his head as if he had anticipated her saying so.

"I had presumed that you were in fact a Divine, once High Priestess Angelica ordered for you to be sealed away. Please, Priestess, follow me, you shall be granted full access to the archives." He walked off to the side of the altar and shifting a statue to the side revealed a keyhole.

"Thank you, Father. I shall see to it that your efforts in preserving the legacy of our people are well rewarded." Father Mathias shook his head and smiled.

"If it is all the same to you Priestess, I would much prefer that my services to the preservation of Aneira's teachings go unheard of." Father Mathias spoke as he removed a small key from within his robes.

"I understand Father. It is shame that things have come to their current state."

"I would agree, Priestess. Now, if you please." He inserted the key into the slot and turned it. The wall pressed forward slightly allowing Father Mathias to grab onto the edge of the wall, where it pulled away easily, revealing a hidden corridor. Tear and Talia moved forward passing through the doorway.

"If you would please excuse me, I must be away. Everything that you need should already be waiting for you within." Talia and Tear bowed their heads and Father Mathias took his leave. They journeyed further into the archives following the light of the torches.

"How much further is it Talia?"

"Just ahead Tear." They walked further on until they came to the end of the lit torches.

"Please allow me." Talia let out a light humming sound and then, from the torch to her right, flames began to leap out across the room landing upon the once invisible candles that when lit illuminated the room. The entire room lit into a spectacular display of flickering flame revealing rows upon rows of various scrolls and tomes. First, Talia removed her cloak and placed it onto a hook, which may have once been a part of a mantelpiece. She then began to search through the dusty web covered shelves and delicately began to pull several of them away from their resting places.

Talia walked towards the nearest table and, as if laying a babe to sleep, lowered the various writings and its smooth surface. Hastily wiping a chair, she sat and began to carefully unroll her first scroll.

"What is it that you are looking for?" Tear asked her, still tiptoeing around the spiders' webs.

"Something that will help me on my mission and anything that might help Sir Alec."

"You like him, do you not?" Talia's only responses were silence and blushing.

Eliza and Zelus

Eliza looked at the small trading village before her, noticing the severe lack of abundance she had grown accustomed to within the confines of the capital. She could only hope that this quaint little town possessed the many necessities that they would need in order to continue their journey. She walked a few paces and noticed the first of many food stands. A significant amount of her list depended on a varied selection. She peered at the many stands before her noticing, considerable choices ranging from different fruits, vegetables and, strangely, a large selection of cheeses. Loaves of bread and rolls decorated the sides of buildings resting along window ledges where they must have been left to cool from the oven. It appeared to her that she might yet fulfill the list her uncle had given her. Reaching into her pocket she pulled from it two slips of paper and placing one back into her pocket, unfolded her list.

We shall be needing enough provisions to last six of us for five days:

Fruit, some vegetables, medical supplies, bandages, bread in case of an emergency, any variety of bean not meant for consumption – will need a modest amount, perhaps 2 pounds, 1 large sheet of leather, one dozen leather straps, lots of cheese, any meat can be more effectively gathered and kept on the road, no eggs unless you come across a suitable means of transporting them.

The list continued on, but consisted of items in which Zelus had already left to acquire. Eliza thought to herself for a moment attempting to reason why they would need two pounds of beans that were not meant for consumption. Shaking the thought from her mind, she flipped her list over to the opposite side so that she could read the one she had made for herself. It contained, in her opinion, everything that a young lady should need. Quickly skimming through her list, she ensured that it did indeed contain a complete list of her own "private" essentials.

Barbs, arrowheads, 2 whetstones, straps, bowstring, book

She determined that in fact all essentials were listed. Eliza approached the first food stand, which contained the cheese. Its neighbor, contained fruit, which would account for the majority of her shopping. The shopkeeper, after finishing with another customer, turned to her.

"What can I get fer ya miss?" Eliza sat her list on the countertop between them and began to read off it. The shopkeeper began reaching behind herself, while carrying on a conversation with Eliza and the other patrons as she gathered all of Eliza's items. Finishing at the stand, Eliza paid the shop keep, and packing her things into several large bags, carried on with her business. As she walked away, a haunting thought came to her.

"Have I bought enough? Talia, Tear and I would be fine for weeks but Alec and Zelus never stop eating." She thought to herself for a moment and decided that if they could not control themselves, then they could go hungry or hunt. Convincing herself that she was in fact finished with the food portion of the list, she began to walk down the row of stands in search for her uncle's score of non-edible legumes. Upon the fourth stand, she came to, she found one which carried a suitable amount of coffee beans. This she determined, should suffice and, purchasing the two pounds needed, continued on her way towards the smithy.

As she walked, she noticed large numbers of burly men gathered in droves around the weapon racks and armor displays. She began to feel increasingly outnumbered as the amount of women in sight quickly diminished. She could feel the heat of the forges growing hotter as she neared the smithy. She stared at the wooden bench that served as the counter and noticed the many notches within from long years of use. She peered into the shop beyond, everything dark in color yet brightly illuminated by the flames within the forge and the embers of the coals. A man came around the corner covered in black dust, sweat and grime.

"Something I can get for you miss?" Eliza reverted back to her list and held it out before her.

"Yes I will be needing barbs, arrowheads, one large sheet of leather, two dozen leather straps," she continued on with the list making sure to include both Marec's and her items. The blacksmith before her began hastily rummaging around his shop gathering everything Eliza specified.

"Anything else you need miss?" Eliza pondered for a moment looking around before gently declining. Eliza paid the smith and, gathering up her things, sat them down next to her massive bundle of groceries and supplies.

"Where in the world is Zelus at?" She looked down one side of the street and then turned her head towards the opposite side. No sign of Zelus. "Where in the world is he?" Eliza waited for several minutes, in the hot sun before growing angry, and straining to gather all of her things, attempted to drag them back toward the approximate location of the inn.

She marched through the streets bearing her load, scanning about in an attempt to find the inn. Taking off her overcoat and unfastening her vest, Eliza removed them and draped them over her sweating shoulders. Her arms strained from the weight of everything, and she could not help but imagine the tortures that Zelus had in store for him.

She wound around many busy roads and followed the density of the population toward the obvious solution. More people would gather around the bar and therefore lead her to the inn. At long last, the inn came in sight. Eliza wiped the sweat from her brow and looked to the sign, which read "The Pilgrimage Inn." Eliza dragged her bags the rest of the way.

As Eliza entered the Pilgrimage Inn, she immediately, as if her vision were drawn to him, locked onto Zelus, who sat at one of many round tables stuffing his face.

"Zelus!" Eliza yelled as she slammed her bags down next to him and flopped into a nearby chair. "Where were you? You were supposed to be helping me today, remember? Go to the inn, secure a room, help Eliza get supplies." She continued on with her tirade whilst Zelus collapsed into himself and daringly pointed a lone finger towards the bar.

"Free food for knights of the capital. First night's stay only." Eliza slowly rolled her eyes back toward Zelus unsurprised and even angrier.

"You bailed on me for food?"

"Not just food, Eliza, this stuff is delicious and FREE! We have not had a decent meal like this since we left the capitol." Eliza glared at Zelus and he swallowed hard, suddenly realizing the error in his ways. Eliza turned her head slightly to the side and Zelus could hear the sounds of the bones in her neck popping, releasing the building tension.

"Eliza I did not mean it like that. Your cooking is amazing. It is just, you know, out on the road things tend to lack a certain…homemade zest, that is all. It had nothing to do with your culinary abilities." Eliza stood from her chair and watched as Zelus shrank into his.

"Zelus I ought to…" Zelus continued to cower as he placed his hands above his head in an attempt to shield himself.

"Everyone quickly the cathedral is on fire!" Eliza and Zelus turned from one another and bolted through the door.

Chapter 26 – Wolves in Sheeps' Clothing

"Hurry everyone, grab some water. We must protect the cathedral!" The screams of the panicked populace quickly flooded the streets as Eliza and Zelus exited the inn. Eliza looked into the sky and could see the flames atop the cathedral rapidly soaring higher.

"We have to hurry Zelus! Everyone is still in there?" She turned her head to where Zelus had been and already could see him at work. Zelus quickly unfastened his cape, removed his armor and dove into the nearest horse trough, cape in hand. He threw his cape back over his shoulder, pulled himself out from within the trough, placed his shirt over his nose and top of his head, before yelling, as he ran towards the fire. Eliza shook her head in disbelief and followed his lead, removed her water resistant clothing and, wearing only her undershirt and a pair of trousers, doused herself as well.

Their first inclination had been to use the front door but, as they approached, they found that it had already collapsed into itself. Quickly, Zelus corrected course and dove headfirst through the nearby window. He tucked his body, rolled over the top of the shattered glass and began his search. Eliza came in shortly after him and narrowly avoiding a flaming banister that fell between the two of them.

"You go left Eliza, I will head this way and search." Eliza nodded and sprinted off in the direction Zelus had pointed. Zelus looked around and, pulling his hood tighter, ran down the first corridor.

Zelus

Zelus tore into the flaming ruin, his eyes stinging from the heat and smoke, rendering his vision poor. Pushing fallen beams and sconces out of his way, Zelus foraged through the blaze, in search of his friends or denizens of the town.

"Is anyone in here?" He called out at the top of his voice. The only response was the cackle and roar of the inferno before him. "Hello! I said is anyone there? I am here to get you to safety." No response came to him and so he pressed on. He turned down the hall and threw more wreckage to the side. Several feet away from him he saw a man lying on the ground, partially buried by rubble.

"I am coming do not panic. I am here to help." Zelus ran to the trapped man and began throwing the debris off him. "Hang on, sir, I can almost get you out of there." Zelus worked more frantically yet and, removing the last beam covering the man, gently rolled him over.

"By Aneira!" Zelus exclaimed as he fell over and backed away abruptly, his hands dripping with fresh blood. He sat for a moment in shock staring at the downed man, a large dagger sticking out from his ribs. Clearly, this fire was more than a mere accident. Somewhere close by there must have been a murderer and this fire was meant to conceal it.

Zelus contemplated for a moment, should he move the body outside or spend the precious time looking for others who may still be trapped. He heard a large crash and someone crying out for help. Shaking himself to attention, Zelus tore a cloth from the man's robes and wrapping the murder weapon, placed it on his side and continued inward in search of any survivors.

"I am coming, where are you?" He yelled out against the deafening roar and scanned the area frantically. Suddenly he saw a hand shoot out from behind a collapsed pillar. Zelus ran to it and gently held the young girl's hand.

"Do not worry I am going to get you out of here." He examined the column that barred his path attempting to determine the best way to remove it. "Stand back," he called to the young one.

"I am back as far as I can go." The girl yelled back. Zelus reached out and began to pull himself atop the column being careful not to force any more debris down on the child. As he reached the top, he realized why the child had been difficult to spot. She was nearly buried alive. So much rubble had fallen on the column that perhaps the pillar was the only thing that had kept her alive. Zelus began to peel away stone upon stone in an attempt to unearth the child. He bore through the stone so quickly with such ferocity that he could see his own blood begin to decorate the lumps he tore away.

"Please hurry, the flames are getting closer." The girl struggled between coughs. Zelus could feel the panic welling inside of him and he hastened his pace. He could now see the girl who let out an excited yet still terrified cheer. Zelus could feel the heat of the flames striking his face as he grew closer and closer to pulling her out.

"Give me your hand!" He called and, reaching out, he was able to secure the young girl's hand and pull her from her demise.

"Thank you, thank you," the child cried to him but, as Zelus turned, he realized their plight was far from over. Flames had completely encompassed the area he had entered through and he saw no viable way of escaping. The room they were in was surrounded by fire on all sides. Zelus found himself staring back into the hole he had just dug. The flames were a few feet thick, not nearly as bad as what now lay behind him. He tore his cape from his body and wrapped it around the child who he lifted into his arms and jumped into the hole.

"Close your eyes child. I do not want you to see this." He spoke softly as he covered her head with the still somewhat damp cape and sprinted as fast as his body could manage. Almost immediately, he could feel the flames scouring his flesh as they passed through the wall. The child screamed as the heat increased but he knew her to be alright. The room he entered into was just as flame filled as the previous, with one exception. He turned his head toward the only safe path and noticed an armored man standing there.

"Sir, is the path that way safe?" But, as the words rolled off his tongue, the man turned. Zelus knew otherwise immediately by the torch in one hand and the alcohol in his other, he had trouble. The man smiled and pulled out a rag, placing it into the end of the bottle. Zelus looked around, spotted a window and took flight. The man threw his flame bomb, Zelus jumped through the window just as the alcohol erupted against his back.

Eliza

Eliza raced through the blaze, calling out to any who might still be alive. She turned back to the window she had entered through. Fire now decorated the walls, the doors also, were ablaze. Eliza decided that she would need to search further in to find the exit. She ran down the only path that lay before her.

"Is anyone there? Is anyone alive?" Eliza continued to cry out against the flame.

"Hurry help!" Eliza ran around the next corner to see several armed men cornering a group of worshippers.

"What is going on here?" Eliza called out to the men, who bore no marks or insignias, upon their chests.

"Just taking care of a few blasphemers. Looks like we have one more to add to the collection." Two of the men drew their weapons and began their charge. Eliza had no weapons, only her wits and skill to defend her. She looked to either side and grasped a nearby sconce, hot wax still within its tip. Both men came at her simultaneously as the other four sat back watching. Eliza stepped to the right avoiding the attack from the left and blocked the attack on her right.

"Hrah!" She grunted as she pressed her body against the man in front of her, pushing him back a step allowing her to power kick him in the chest and whip the wax end of her makeshift weapon straight into the face of the unsuspecting assassin.

"Aah, my eyes!" He wailed in pain as he fell to the ground. His friends moved in from the sidelines and her unbalanced attacker recovered. Eliza dove upon her downed assailant and, removing his own weapons, quickly finished him off. His sword was bulky, too slow for her uses and the shield would only slow her down. She took in a deep breath and stood her ground, honing in her senses, dagger drawn. She could see the man she needed to attack, curved sword to his side. She tightly squeezed the hilt of the dagger and prepared herself.

As the first man swung, she dipped, stabbing him in the back of his leg, crippling it and threw the blade into the throat of the curve blade wielder. She lunged upon him taking his weapon as he fell to the ground and rolled. She stopped in front of another man, jumped, forcing the blade skyward through his torso, and spun gliding the blade horizontally across the chest of another as he swung his own weapon.

"Aah!" Eliza cried as the enemy's sword grazed her across the stomach. She clutched her stomach and turned towards the other men.

Eliza stood with the blade pointed out in front of her and focused on the remaining two men. The one she wounded eyed her ready to strike as the other attempted to flank her. Pulling her attention from the wounded one, she poised herself ready to lash out at the more imminent threat.

"Ooof!" The armored man in front of her fell to the ground. Eliza looked where the man was and saw one of the parishioners holding a flaming beam in his hands. The wounded soldier knowing that he was hopelessly outnumbered, dropped his weapons and surrendered.

"Aneira, forgive me," the parishioner spoke as he dropped the beam.

"You did what you had to. I cannot imagine Aneira being angry. Is there anyone else within?" The preacher looked around as if counting those around him.

"Brother Mathias is still missing and the four from out of town."

"Do you mean the ones that I came with?"

"I am unsure; there was a young priestess, a little girl, a young man and an armored individual."

"That is them, where are they?"

"They are further within, but you must hurry. These guards were not the only ones that attacked us." Eliza looked around her with furious intensity.

"Do not worry yourself, the remaining soldiers are within, we shall find the exit." He added. Eliza turned her head towards their new prisoner.

"And him?"

"Do not worry. We shall see to it that this one is escorted to a cell." The wielder of the flaming beam assured her.

Eliza nodded her head and darted off toward the inner sanctum. As Eliza ran, she could not help but notice the increasingly potent pain in her stomach. She pulled her hand from her navel and noticed it was covered in blood. Eliza turned her head around a corner and saw the corridor filled with flame.

"Is anyone there?" She approached the blaze and what she saw horrified her. Amongst the rubble she found a tunic bearing the insignia of the Aneiran knights.

"Alec! Where are you?" Eliza began sifting through the rubble unearthing Alec's shield and longsword. She slung them to the side and continued digging, as she heard a loud groaning from above.

"Alec if you are there help me. Please call out to me, Alec!" She heard the groaning sound again and looked up as the beams above her cracked in half and began to tumble. Eliza dove to the side as the room around her collapsed.

"Alec!" Eliza screamed and attempted to get up but the agony in her stomach and a new pain in her leg caused her to collapse. Eliza looked down to her leg to see a large splinter of wood penetrating her calf, a deep gash forming around it. Eliza turned her head and closed her eyes before grasping the wood. She squinted her eyes even more tightly and took a deep breath before quickly tearing it out.

"Ah!" She yelled followed by a line of curses. She examined the wound and, tearing her sleeve, wrapped her leg. As she breathed she traced her eyes back toward the pile of rubble, heaped ever higher and she knew no one could have survived the weight. She rocked back and forth for a moment attempting to deal with the loss when she heard the sound of men's voices. Eliza slowly braced herself and rose to her feet.

"Just a little further Eliza, keep moving." She coached herself as she placed one foot in front of the other until she could hear the sound of swords clashing.

"Alec!" Eliza hobbled towards the sound but, instead of Alec, she came upon the vision of Marec being assailed by another group of assassins.

"Uncle Marec!" Eliza yelled as she limped over to the aid of her uncle. He was already managing against seven combatants and Eliza could see several more on their way. She could see that Marec bore several wounds of his own and was having an increasing amount of difficulty fending off his attackers.

"Eliza are you alright?" Marec spoke with his back turned toward her as he struck down his enemy.

"I will live." She answered as she drew herself upon one of the armored men as Talia and Tear turned around the corner.

"The archives are on fire!" Talia called as two of the remaining men turned toward them.

"Talia can you help us?"

"I cannot cast any magic in here. It could cause a collapse." Eliza looked around and knocking her opponent down took his sword.

"Talia heads up!" Eliza threw a sword towards Talia, which skidded across the floor to her feet. Talia reached down and awkwardly lifted the blade and held it in front of her at an unusual angle.

"What do I do?"

"Hit him with the pointy end!" Eliza yelled as her and Marec both pressed through another attacker. Talia wobbled uneasily as the swordsman approached her.

"Mistress! Get out of there!" Marec yelled at Talia who stood her ground placing her body between the armored man and Tear. The man approached and Talia swung her weapon. The guard laughed as he lazily parried the blow to the side, knocking Talia backward. Marec and Eliza both struggled to quickly fend off their own adversaries as the man whom Eliza assumed was the leader toyed with Talia.

Talia gripped the hilt of the sword tightly and regained her posture.

"Harm her you shall not!" Talia raised her voice as she prepared herself. The armored man laughed at the shaking priestess.

"Harm her? I believe you have misunderstood. I am not here to kill you, I was only sent to kill the knights and the paladin. My orders included recovering the weapon, but, alas, the one I killed did not have it."

"You are the one that killed Alec?" The man turned his head toward Eliza and smiled.

"I was hoping for a bit more sport but hopefully the paladin will prove to be more of a challenge." The armored man ran up on Talia and again knocking her blade sideways kicked her hard in the stomach, knocking her backward against a wall. Eliza continued to lash out at her attacker when she was interrupted.

"Lay down your weapons now. I was told to take Talia captive, not Tear." Eliza turned her head to see Tear pinned to the wall, the man's blade against her throat. Blood was already leaking from it. Without hesitation, Marec and Eliza dropped their weapons to the ground and kicked them away.

"Good, now into the tunnel." He motioned towards the flaming corridor to his right. Eliza and Marec hesitated yet still could see no other choice.

"Good," the man called back as he turned his head towards Tear and lifted his sword pressing her chin and her body up. "In you go little one. Time to join your friends." He turned her to face away from him and then kicked her in the lower back, forcing her into the backs of Eliza and Marec.

"Farewell." The man pulled a pouch from his pack and lit the end before throwing it against the wall causing an explosion, which filled the hallway with rubble. Eliza ran back towards the collapsing rubble and screamed out a slur of threats and curses. Marec was right behind her, pounding against the debris, doing his best to clear out the mess. Tear chimed in and together the three of them threw as much from the pile as possible before they came upon solid slabs of stone.

"There must be another way out!" Marec began to search around to see that there was, in fact, no viable option within sight. All around them flames danced upon the walls and floor. They were trapped. Eliza hobbled across the room in a desperate search for hope. She looked all around and found a door.

"Allow me!" Marec approached the door and drew a rune in the sky. Eliza watched as against the flame, she could see a narrowly visible bubble form around her uncle. Marec stood in front of the door and carefully reached out and turned the handle.

"Brrrrrooooooaaaarrrr!" Marec's body was covered in flame and propelled backwards across the room, where he hit the wall hard.

"Uncle?" Eliza began to limp towards him.

"I am alright Eliza, I feared that may happen so I used flame shield."

"Flame shield?"

"It is a paladin technique used to protect the user and his allies from fire. I am afraid, however, that I regrettably lack the strength to use that ability again." Eliza carefully walked to the door and peered within. The doorway would prove impassible. The flames were too thick and she could already feel the air around them beginning to grow thin.

"What do we do?" Eliza turned toward Marec as Tear began chanting.

"We wait and hope that the Divine may shield us." Eliza listened as Tear chanted, Tear opened her eyes and forced her hands forward. Eliza watched as the flames began to rise up and move under her control. She stepped forward and the flames leaped backward.

"Back!" Tear called out to it and the flame responded.

"Should we follow her?" Eliza turned to her uncle who was still struggling to rise to his feet.

"I suppose..." He started to speak as he noticed the strain that the feat was causing Tear. She did not whine. She did not stumble but the bleeding from her neck intensified and her knees began to shake.

"Eliza get back!" Marec yelled as he ran ahead to catch Tear. Eliza noticed Tear beginning to stumble and ducked down behind a pile of rubble. Marec reached out and scooped her into his arms, turning his back as the light of trance left Tear's body. The flames roared again and Marec was once more thrown through the air. This time, he failed to rise. Tear lay next to him, gently wriggling in an attempt to rise to her feet. Eliza knelt down next to her friend and her uncle, prepared for the worst.

"Crash," Eliza shielded herself and the others as glass shards showered down from the ceiling. Eliza looked up and saw another of the armored thugs standing above her twenty feet in the air. A rope dropped down from the ledge and landed next to Marec.

"Tie the rope around him and we shall raise you up." The metallic voice called down to her. Eliza searched around again and, seeing no other option, tied off Marec and wrapping one arm around Tear grabbed ahold of her uncle.

"We are ready." She called and, immediately, they began to rise from the ground. It was not until they nearly reached the top when Eliza first heard the sounds of a familiar friend.

"Bree!" Oz grunted as he and the armored man finished pulling them to the rooftop. The armored man ran to Eliza's side and without warning began drawing a rune into the sky. Eliza felt her entire body begin to itch as her wounds began to knit themselves together.

"Do not worry, Talia is safe. We got her out right before we tracked you all down." The man spoke as he healed Marec who groaned a barely audible thank you. Once everyone was healed, the man began aiding everyone in climbing down the side of the tower where Eliza could see Zelus and Talia resting against a tree awaiting them. Eliza aiding Tear the last several feet allowed herself to take up the rear and drop the last few feet.

Eliza rested her head up against the wall for a moment. She noticed the rescue crews breaking through the blaze and scouring the area then looked to their rescuer.

"Thank you, sir." The metallic man laughed beneath his helmet before removing it.

"Eliza, you know that I will always be there for you." He spoke as he dropped the black helmet to the ground, revealing his light brown wavy hair.

"Alec? Alec!" Eliza called out as she rushed to her not so dead best friend and tackled him to the ground.

Chapter 27 – The Lady Seraphina

"Oh, by Aneira, I am so glad to see you safe. I thought for sure you were dead." She sobbed as she hugged the life out of Alec and kissed him feverishly on his cheeks and forehead. He did his best to escape, suddenly fearing for his very life. As he pulled himself free from Eliza's grasp, he caught a glimpse of the disapproving looks on Talia and Zelus' faces.

"Yes Eliza, I am alive, but we are still in danger. You can calm down now, alright?" Eliza stared at Alec tears still in her eyes.

"I thought you were dead. I found your things in the temple and that man said he had killed you. I did not know what to do." Alec put his hands on Eliza's shoulders steadying her. Then he lifted her chin and wiped away her tears.

"It is alright, Eliza. I am not leaving you." He hugged her again gently as Marec tended to Talia. Zelus cleared his throat loudly, announcing his presence.

"Well, now that we have determined we are all still alive, do you think we could start trying to get to the bottom of this event?" Zelus grumbled, after clearing his throat loudly. Marec turned towards the party.

"Zelus is right. What happened here tonight must be unearthed. I fear what happened here, was in direct correlation to our mission."

"You are right uncle. I had begun to fear the same. One of the men I encountered told me he was there to throw down some blasphemers. Do you think there is someone within the church of Aneira that does not approve of our mission?" Eliza asked, Marec considering her question before answering.

"It is a possibility, though it is one I had not considered possible. Our mission, while unsanctioned by the high priestess, would never warrant an attack."

"But they did say their orders were to take Talia alive and to recover the Sidonis sword, an important religious relic, no?" The party all turned their attention over to Marec, who paused for a moment before deciding to avoid the question.

"It is of little importance at this juncture. We must prepare for our journey. We leave in the morning. Everyone please return to the tavern and rest, Alec stay here with me." Everyone rose, while Alec could not help but feel the looks of discontentment Zelus and Talia shot at him with. Alec waited for everyone to leave, before he approached Marec.

"Yes master?"

"Sit. Tell me what happened at the courtyard." Alec sat down next to Marec and began to relay his experiences.

The first thing Alec noticed was his ears being assailed by a hauntingly beautiful melody. There was a miraculous symphony of mixed voices, which rang out in a chorus, which made Alec both blissful, yet at the same time, filled with heartbreak. He searched about the marble room for any sign he was still in the temple.

"Where am I?" Alec searched around him noticing all of the ghostly faded images. It was as if he were sifting through a screen of fog. He looked down at his own body noticing the lack of his weapons and equipment. He pulled at the strange clothes that he was wearing and recognized the insignia they were adorned with. On his right breast, brilliantly gleaming in gold was an image of a lion hawk set in front of a glamorous shield.

"This is the symbol of the paladins of Highmoore but there is no way I am there." He slowly spun around in circles in search of any clue to his whereabouts.

"Is anyone here?" He called out again as he attempted to find anything that looked familiar to him. He slowly revolved examining his surroundings. As far as he could tell, he was standing within the center of a large open balcony. He could see the shrine of Aneira before him, yet it looked different. Instead of standing tall and proud, a vision of strength and glory, she stood with her arms held out as in a welcoming gesture. Alec looked into the face of this unique goddess statue and could not help but realize why she was the goddess of beauty.

He continued to look around. There were two doors leading out of his present location. He walked towards the edge of the balcony and looked below. A city lay below that bustled with activity, surrounded by a tall wall, wrapping around it, entirely. The tower he was in, seemed to touch the sky. He looked upward and saw how the building rose into the clouds, leaving the moon, still visible in the distance. He took in the view and decided he must be within his trial and should begin. He walked across the room and grabbed the door handle. He tugged on the handle but it refused to open. Alec walked further across the room and tugged on the next door.

"Both locked." He thought to himself for a moment before attempting to place his shoulder into the door. The door refused to budge but he continued to slam into the door until it began to come ajar.

"That is more like it." He opened the door the rest of the way and walked through.

"AAAH!" He yelled as he fell into nothingness and dangled by the door handle. He looked down and all around, seeing nothing but air. Carefully he pulled himself back skyward and, taking one-step in, closed the door behind him, the sounds of the haunting melody again filling his ears.

"You are not yet ready to go in there." Alec looked across the room and saw a young woman standing in a beautiful long flowing dress. Alec looked into her gorgeous face with her crystal grey eyes and her long blonde hair.

"Hello, my name is Alec. I am here to undergo the paladin trials." The woman walked to Alec with such elegance and grace, her whole body seemed to flow as if with the tide. The woman eyed him up and down as she floated around him. Alec hunched his shoulders defensively, feeling an immense chill as he was thoroughly examined.

"Welcome, Alec of Highmoore, I am the Lady Seraphina. I have been expecting you for some time." Alec looked up into her face, which dazzled magnificently against the moonlit background.

"Are you a Nymph?" Lady Seraphina smiled at Alec before answering.

"Ah, Lady Seraphina, yes." Marec interjected at this time causing Alec to cease his story telling.
"She was once the leader of the paladins, founder of Highmoore. It was she who gave up her mantle of nobility in order to allow for a council to rule the people on her behalf." Alec looked to Marec with a perplexed look on his face.

"Master do you wish for me to continue my story?" Marec waved him on so Alec continued where he left off, with Lady Seraphina's story.

"I was once a paladin, in truth, the leader of the paladins, before I gave my life in battle and was resurrected as a nymph in the service of the Holy Mother." Alec looked again into the maiden's face, yet could not bring himself to imagining this woman as a fierce warrior in command of the greatest legion in Valoria. Seraphina sensing what Alec was thinking, smiled brilliantly before speaking.

"I was once the ruler of Highmoore, your home. I am surprised you are unfamiliar with my name and renown." Alec looked down from the face of the angelic figure and stared at his own feet.

"Highmoore was destroyed when I was but a child. Much of the culture and history of my birth home was destroyed. Little written script is made available to commoners within the capital."

Again, Marec interrupted.

"That was one reason I never returned to the capital. The reason Eliza rarely saw me. So many horrors committed in a single eve just for the council to wash everything under the rug, burying the truth of what happened that night." Alec had never seen Marec look so solemn as he did when speaking of Highmoore. Alec gave his instructor a moment and then continued his story.

"I see not much has changed since my death," said Lady Seraphina. "The council sounds just as corrupt as I remember. In time Alec, I will teach you about your home. Behind you, I am certain you noticed two doors. Beyond each door lies a room that can only be revealed to you once you are ready to complete the appropriate trial. If you complete this trial, I will ask for you to complete another. Once you reach the next shrine, drink from the fountain of Aneira and offer your prayer. You will reappear here where you shall open the next door. Is this simple enough for you?" Alec nodded his head to Lady Seraphina after moving back from the doors, which, he feared had just nearly killed him.

"I sense something is bothering you?" Alec was shocked that she had noticed the thought scratching away at the back of his mind as if a swarm of insects were eating away at it.

"Yes, actually I was wondering, where are we?" Again, Lady Seraphina smiled hauntingly. She spread out her arms and slowly spun.

"Do you not recognize it? This is your home. You are in Highmoore." Alec stared at her alarmingly and began to look around in search of the Forsaken.

"What about the Forsaken? How did we manage to slip past them?" This time, when he looked to her for answers, Lady Seraphina only held sorrow on her face.

"I am afraid that this is not the Highmoore of your world. This is, in fact, only a memory of the once great bastion." Alec could not help but notice the extremely sad tone in her voice.

"I wish to one day reclaim the old fortress," said Alec. "Hang the banner of Highmoore amongst the clouds as it once was." Seraphina snapped out of her lament and looked to Alec.

"Good, you will need much preparation before you will be able to do so. Are you ready to begin the first trial?" Again, Alec nodded his head.

"You will have no need for your weapons. This test shall be a trial of the spirit. I will be testing the extent of your gift with Aneira's blessing. Before we begin, what training have you undergone thus far?"

"I am currently learning to perform the mending technique, though I have yet to create it." Seraphina thought for a second, her smile never once leaving her face. She looked up to Alec and spoke.

"We will not be worrying about that at this venture, however, if you would follow me." Seraphina glided in the direction of the fountain and Alec followed. She stopped floating above the surface of the water before turning toward Alec.

"If you would, step into the waters." Alec did as he was instructed. Immediately the water began to glow brightly and he was encompassed in waves of green and gold.

"Lady Seraphina, what is happening?" The nymph smiled and watched as Alec's hair began to wave as if within a gust and turned gold. His green eyes intensified. Alec could see Seraphina staring at him and attempted to look upon his reflection. The water now glowed so brightly it felt as if he had stared into the sun. He rubbed his eyes and instead focused on the nymph floating just beside him.

"You have wonderful potential young cadet, though I must wonder if you have yet harnessed your gifts." Seraphina raised one finger into the air and began to draw a rune. Immediately, Alec recognized it and began to trace the rune for mending. He finished drawing his rune, yet was unable to produce anything, as was normal from his experience. Alec grew frustrated and looked up to explain to the great lady, but instead she smiled.

"Rise from the pool, Alec. I understand what it is you need." Alec dipped his head to the side in confusion but all the same rose from the pool of churning water. As he did so, the water stayed, the surface of the water again clear and crystalline.

"This place is becoming increasingly strange." He muttered to himself and Seraphina began to laugh. For a moment, he was lost in the sound of her merriment. He knew Aneira was predominately known as the goddess of beauty and song, but he had never imagined exactly how that related to the nymphs. The sound of her glee, made his heart lift up and he had to catch himself to wipe the ragingly blissful grin from his face. Calming herself, Lady Seraphina turned toward Alec. This time her smile bore all of her perfect teeth.

"You do understand this place, though a memory not your own, represents you, do you not? As you grow more aware, more doors will open. As you become increasingly prepared for knowledge, information that has been lost for over a decade may reveal itself to you. Perhaps once you are ready, knowledge, which has been lost for centuries, shall reveal itself. You stand within the living ancestral memory of what may have once been the greatest city in all of Valoria." Alec paused for a moment in an attempt to understand.

"This place represents me?" He asked. Again, another melodious giggle escaped the nymph.

"That would be all you would grasp. Not much has changed. Are you ready for the lesson I have to teach you?" Alec nodded his head.

"Raise up your hands in defense." Alec did as he was told.

"I am going to teach you an offensive rune, simple, practical and powerful. As you become stronger, so will it." Seraphina raised her hand and drew a diamond in front of her. Alec watched while she flattened her fingers against her palm as if preparing for a palm strike. Alec watched her handprint appear within the center of the diamond, and suddenly he felt as though he was struck in the stomach. The air escaped his lungs and he was knocked off from his feet.

"What was that?" He moaned as he attempted to rise to his feet and regain his breath.

"That was force. A simple, basic, yet necessary rune for a paladin. This will be my first lesson to you. Now return the attack." Alec placed his hand to his breast, assuring to himself that air was again flowing into his lungs, then straightened himself.

Alec placed his hand out in front of himself and repeated the process he had been shown. A blue light radiated from the lines he had traced. He held his hand as Lady Seraphina had done and pressed it into the center of the diamond. A faint gust shot out from the rune, enough to cause the nymphs hair to blow backward in the wind.

"Well done, Alec. You have successfully cast your first rune. I expect you already possess the potential to cast a great many runes, just not the necessary control. Cast your rune again, this time with more power." Alec began to trace his rune and threw his palm into the center. This time he almost thought he could see the energy he had created. It shot out and flew toward Seraphina who, with a graceful wave of her hand, brushed it to the side.

"We will continue this until you have gained proficiency." Alec nodded his head and again drew the symbol. Hours passed and Alec continued to force out the blasts one after another until he began to grow exhausted. Sweat poured off from his brow and he buckled at the waist placing his hands upon his knees.

"We are not yet finished cadet. Cast the rune again, you must be ready when you return." Alec looked up and wiped the sweat from his eyes.

"Ready for what?"

"Your friends are in danger and have need of you." Alec rose to the occasion and took up a fighting stance.

"Then send me back!" He yelled. Lady Seraphina, unfazed by Alec's tone continued to speak calmly.

"I cannot, not until you have learned to use your gift. If you leave before a trial is completed, then I am afraid you have failed. They are fine for now. Time here is different from time in your world. In the hours you have spent here, only a few minutes have passed in your world."

"Can I not return once I have helped my friends?" He asked. Seraphina looked to Alec solemnly.

"I am afraid you cannot. If you fail my test, then you may never return and all will be lost." Angrily, Alec clenched his fist and realized all he was doing now was wasting time. He drew the rune as he had already done nearly one hundred times but, this time, exhaustion kicked in and he buckled.

"This is pointless. My body is too tired to continue."

"Then revive it." The nymph commanded. "Surely you do not think all of this time spent casting force would only prepare you for casting that one specific rune." The thought had not occurred to Alec. Quickly, he rose to his feet and drew the seal for mending. For the first time, the blue lines appeared and glowed brilliantly before him. He remembered what Talia had told him about selecting a target for the rune. He pulled his hand back towards himself and the rune followed his hand and struck him.

"I feel no different."

"You have just cast the rune for mending. Allow me to teach you a rune of my own creation, the rune of regeneration." Lady Seraphina began to trace her rune. She drew a large circle before her and sliced two lines through it, one vertical, the other horizontal, slicing her circle into four identical pieces.

Alec repeated the process and, as he had just done with mending, he pulled the rune of regeneration back toward himself. Light soaked into his skin and instantly he could feel his body energizing. He took a deep breath and stumbled, feeling slightly light headed. He stabilized himself and turned to his teacher.

"Why did I…"

"The body has two forms of energy, life energy and spirit energy. Life energy of the body affects your physical self, while spirit energy is drawn upon using you gift. You will have to train your spirit as if it too were a muscle. Now cast your rune." Alec placed his hand before him and drew out the rune for force. This time the concussive force emitted was nearly enough to push him backwards. Lady Seraphina stepped to the side avoiding the blast but, as she did so, Alec could see she was again smiling.

"Very well, you are ready to return."

"So I have completed my trial?" Seraphina smiled her glorious smile.

"The moment you stepped into the pool, your spirit was placed on display before me. The test was for me to determine the caliber of your spirit. The runes were so you do not wind up killing yourself before our next meeting."

"Wait, you lied to me?" Alec turned around to see Seraphina had already cast the rune for force. Alec was blown backward, landing into the fountain he had stepped in earlier. As he sank into the water, the world around him began to spin.

"Goodbye, Alec. I hope you survive long enough to come visit me again. I shall wait for you to arrive in Trias, where your next altar awaits." Alec felt himself spinning out of control. He closed his eyes to keep himself from growing even more nauseous, when his world suddenly grew still and he fell backwards and landed on the cold hard stone floor of the shrine.

"Am I back?" He opened his eyes and tried to make sense of the still spinning, blurry images. After another moment, his eyes refocused and he saw he was in fact back. He heard screaming out in the distance and, gathering his things, quickly ran towards its source. Alec ran around the corner to see the hallways already filled with flame. He could hear voices around another corner. Alec approached said corner and peeked around to the sight of an armored man threatening two cowering people in robes.

Gripping his sword and shield, he attempted a stealthy attack. As he crept behind the armored man, he could not help but catch the attention of the people the man was assaulting. Alec attempted to place his finger in front of his face to signal the two to be quiet.

"Drat!" He thought to himself as he made eye contact with a frightened young man. The guard, seeing the boy look, turned toward Alec.

"Hey who are…" was all the man could muster out before Alec dove into his side, losing his sword and shield in the process. With no other option, Alec began to pummel the man viciously as the armored man struck back at him.

"Run!" Alec turned and yelled to the two cowering parishioners who had remained on the floor leaning against the wall. They seemed to understand as they rose and began to flee. Alec found he had been turned away too long as an armored fist drove into the side of his skull, sending him towards another twist in the hallway. Alec lay on his back facing upward towards the now sword wielding man. As Alec began to back away, he noticed the beam that rested above the man's head. Quickly, Alec traced the rune for force and thrusting his palm into its center, shot out a massive gust that shattered the beam.

The man cried out as the beam fell on top of him. Alec was unsure if the man was alive or dead, but, he could hear the sounds of another man approaching. He turned toward his fallen victim and began to tear off his armor. He threw the helmet and gauntlets to the side, just managing to pull on the chest plate when the man came around the corner.

"Hey what are you doi.." Alec had already fired off force interrupting the man and sending him against the wall with a loud bang. Quickly, Alec grabbed the man and dragged him across the room, throwing him on the other side of his initial pile of rubble. Alec removed his boots and greaves and slipped them on.

"Now, I need to hide the evidence." He began to look around for a place to hide the men as he placed the Sidonis sword on his hip.

"I heard it from down here hurry!"

"Blast!" Was the first of many choice words to course through Alec's mind. Frantically, he began to trace runes against the walls, each one booming with an exciting chorus of demolition.

"Stay back! One of the firebombs landed in the kitchen. There are bags of flour in there exploding!" Alec yelled to them as the walls came crumbling down. He forced on the gauntlets and crammed his head painfully into the helmet, diving out of the way of the crumbling walls. He thought to himself for a moment and realized his actual sword and shield were beneath the rubble still. The armored thugs ran up on him and saw the collapse he had just caused.

"Are you alright?" Alec looked around and realizing they were speaking to him turned and nodded his head. The men looked over at him with gestures of confusion.

"Must be in shock." Alec gave a forced nervous jitter that the men seemed to buy.

"Alright then, follow us we have work to do." Alec fell in line directly behind the armored men and followed them around a corner, where more members of the church were corralled within the inner sanctuary.

"Alec!" Marec again cut Alec off during his regurgitation of recent events.

"Yes master." Alec tried to answer without an annoyed tone in his voice.

"Did you save them?"

"Yes."

"Good, if this were a book most readers would be ready to set you down right now. You need not explain every last detail of every moment. After a point, it becomes most excessive and you lose the interest of your audience. I think we are done for tonight. Your use of the third person whilst speaking of yourself has grown quite disturbing."

"I am sorry master."

"Just do not allow it to happen again." Alec rose and began to walk away from Marec.

"Alec?"

"Yes master?"

"Seeing as how you have passed the trial of spirit, tomorrow will be the start of a new type of training. Be sure to acquire sufficient rest. Things will be much more difficult henceforth."

"I will master, thank you for the warning." Alec headed back toward the direction of the inn. He looked back toward the church. The flames had not been completely dissolved as of yet but there was little left for him to do with all of the various different teams working on it already.

He confirmed things would be alright without him. Stopping in front of the door to the inn, he tapped into his link with Oz to check on the lion hawk. His connection revealed that Oz was in the stables sleeping. Alec decided not to bother him and walked inside. He eyed the counter as he walked in and debated to himself if he was in need of some of the free food Zelus had been raving about. Alec opted out and walked up the stairs to find their room.

He reached the top of the stairs which opened up into a second large lounge area where sat his friends. He looked around and saw Tear sitting in a chair, in the corner, drawing quietly. He saw Talia sitting in a chair next to Tear reading various scrolls. Finally he looked toward the fireplace, where sprawled out on opposite couches lay Eliza and Zelus both reading intently. Alec cocked his head to the side in order to catch a better view.

"*The Epitaph Saga: The First Elder Born*" Rested in Eliza's hands while "*The Epitaph of Twilight: Seal of the Nameless God*" was held firmly by Zelus.

"What are you two reading?" He asked. Neither Eliza nor Zelus looked away from their respective novels. Alec cleared his throat and repeated the question, this time loudly enough to receive the attentions of both readers. Eliza and Zelus looked up at Alec with awkwardly giddy, childish grins on their faces. Alec looked specifically to Zelus who was cradling his book, as if kin.

"Zelus? Seriously?" Zelus stared back at Alec with a defensive look on his face.

"What? It is an enticing book." Eliza nodded her head in agreement with Zelus and turned back to her own book, ignoring everything else around her. Alec stared back at Zelus and shook his head.

"For shame Zelus, for shame. You have been turned astray and lost to romantic feminine bewitchery." He smiled at his rival who attempted to defend himself as Alec walked away in search of his room. He expected to be thoroughly ignored by Zelus and Eliza, so instead he approached Talia and Tear, sitting across from them.

"Are the two of you alright?" Alec asked. Tear looked up at him and smiled before returning to her drawing and Talia glanced at him ever so slightly.

"Quite, thank you for your consideration." She spoke as mannerly as usual, yet somehow Alec could not help but catch the feeling the emotion behind it was bitter and cold. He paused for a moment, scratching the back of his mind contemplating his next move.

"Um, do you know which room is mine?" He asked nervously afraid of the response he might receive.

"Sir Marec said he would be rooming with you and Zelus for tonight. You are the first room nearest the stairwell." She immediately began to study her scrolls. Alec turned away from her, seeing she was preoccupied and preceded toward his room for some much needed rest. Alec reached for the door handle, and pressing open the door, walked inside toward the bed where his things sat.

He rested his body upon the bed and stared out the window to his left. It was dark, yet the village was still quite alive with activity. He stared outside and his mind was filled with questions from the day. Not just questions of his trial, but questions regarding the attack on the shrine, as well. He wondered to himself why anyone would attack a holy site, when even most bandits refrained from such actions.

Alec turned from the window, removed his traveling clothes until he sat with just his tunic and breeches. He reached his hand out in front of himself and began to slowly trace out the rune of force. As the glowing blue lines appeared, he ever so gently, placed his hand up against it and caused for a kinetic burst to leave his hand. Alec smiled to himself as he began tracing out the rune of mending again and watched, as it too, activated.

"I am going to become a paladin. I am going to bring about a change about this world, the no one has ever dared hoped for." He smiled to himself as he took off his boots, swung his legs over the side of the bed, and closed his eyes.

Alec's dreams that night, were filled with unexpected curiosities. He once again, could hear the sound of Talia's lullaby but it was not being sung to him by Talia. He could not place the voice but something about it, felt familiar, soothing even. He could see through blurry vision, he was surrounded by vast amounts of red and gold, which made him assume his dreams had taken him back to Highmoore.

"You shall be my gift upon this world, my little Alec. It shall be upon your shoulders that the fate of all things will balance. Guard yourself well, my son. For the dangers you shall face, will be unspeakable. But know this, even within the depths of darkness, a light shall shine and it is you, my son, who guides the flame."

Chapter 28 – The Priestess' Secret

Alec awoke the following morning to the sight of Zelus bent in half. His back was arching upward toward the ceiling, placing the majority of his weight onto his face, which still rested next to his book. Alec shook his head in disbelief and rose from his own bed.

He looked out the window and saw it was still dark out. He looked around and noticed that the third bed, likely reserved for Marec, was empty. Alec forced his feet into his boots and walked from the room. He had not managed to walk far when he heard the voice of his teacher from behind.

"You should rest while you still have the opportunity. As soon as the others rise we will be leaving for Trias."

"How far is Trias?"

"We will be there by nightfall. I asked Zelus to secure some horses for us."

"I wonder how Oz will feel about that."

"Considerate, however, I would be more concerned as to whether or not Oz will attempt to eat them."

"Another thing to consider." Alec nodded his head, the thought of Oz pouncing on a full grown steed would not surprise him. "Oz mostly goes for rabbits though. A horse would be much too large."

"Aye, but the lion within him may search for sport even if he is well sated." Again Alec had a moment to himself whilst he imagined Oz prowling through a savannah in search of game.

"I am just going to head down to the river, clean up."

"You may also want to check on Oz. He remained in the stables all night. He is probably cooped up." Alec nodded his head as he marched down the stairs and entered into the dining room.

"Good morning sir knight," Alec looked to see the innkeeper standing behind the counter as usual. "Are you headed out so soon?"

"Just to go wash up is all."

"Aye, well, how's abouts some breakfast for the road?" The man quickly scurried about in the kitchen behind and came out with a small parcel of food.

"Thank you sir, how much do I owe you?" The innkeeper waved his hand at Alec.

"After what you and your friends did for us yesterday, think nothing of it." Alec smiled, accepting the gift.

"Again, thank you sir. Was Oz alright last night?" The man turned his head up and to his left as he scratched the stubble on his chin.

"Oh, I suppose you mean the strange cat bird that you brought in with you. Why, yes, he was most agreeable. A little full of energy but I took him some meat scraps and that seemed to calm him down in a hurry."

"That usually does the trick." Alec said as he walked outside into the early morning dimness. He took an immediate turn to his left and followed the building around towards its exterior to find the stables. Alec pushed open the gate, allowing himself access to the pens.

"Oz" Alec spoke softly as to not stir the horses too much. Alec could hear a light coo coming from the back of the stables. He walked towards the source to find nothing but an empty pen.

"Oz!" Alec called more sternly and, this time, he noticed that the sound of the coo came from up above. Alec looked up to see his griffet staring down at him with curious eyes.

"Come on down Oz, we are going outside." Immediately a rocketing ball of feather and fur came bounding down next to him and began to trot off in the direction of the town gates.

"Wait for me, Oz." Alec called as he ran to catch up with him. As they approached the gates, the guards arose from out of the shadows to greet them.

"I was just leaving to go freshen up below. My friend needs to hunt and will be accompanying me." The guards nodded without protest and pulled the massive doors to the gate apart. Alec eyed the view as the lush scenery came into sight. The landscape around him was heavily wooded, with abundant wildlife and greenery.

"Go ahead Oz, I know that you are wanting to stretch your wings." Oz bounded off merrily toward the tree line and vanished within. Alec turned toward his left and followed the path off road towards the river. As he strolled down hill towards the river, he took a few moments to stop and take in several deep breaths.

The air here was entirely different from the air in the capital. There was no apparent abundance of filth about, no over powering pollution of noise. Alec felt peaceful in a way that he had never come to experience within the walls of the capital. It lacked the clarity that he often felt when in the heat of battle yet he possessed a sense of focus that was new and welcome.

He came down another slope and he heard the sound of water. A few more paces confirmed visually what his ears had already told him. The river was wide but did not look to be dangerously swift. The water was clear as crystal he touched the surface and found it to be refreshingly cool. Alec stepped into the churning river and began to feel the water splashing against his legs. He waded deeper within until he was submerged up to his waist.

Alec waded in the water, looking around and stared up at the bright blue sky. He tilted backward and allowed his feet to float up to the surface. Tipping his head backward ever so slightly, he noticed a nearby waterfall, which fed the stream. Alec rolling onto his stomach, breast stroked his way over to it. As he neared the waterfall, he could feel the current to pick up. He looked up and squinted his eyes as the falls crashed over the rocks spraying water into his face.

Alec reached up and pulled himself onto the rocks. Immediately, he could feel the strain hit his body, making it difficult for him to even lift his body off from the rocks. Alec smiled at the challenge and pushed as hard as he could slowly raising himself onto his knees. He growled aloud against the roar of the water and, placing his legs beneath him, slowly stood up against the falls.

Alec could feel his body giving way and quickly began to draw the symbol for regeneration. He could feel his spirit revitalizing his body. He straightened his back against the fall of the water and, for a moment, felt the benefits of his training.

"I see that you are coming close to mastering that technique." Marec's announcement caused Alec to lose his concentration and his balance simultaneously, falling backwards onto the rocks and then sliding into the water. Alec floated for a moment, waiting for the pain to leave his body.

"Concentration is still a little lacking though I see." Marec muttered, as his student remained inanimate. Finally, Alec recovered and looked up to face Marec.

"It was easy once Lady Seraphina showed me how to use it." He groaned. Marec sat looking at Alec.

"Can you explain to me how it works?" Marec asked. Alec nodded his head as he attempted to remember what Seraphina had told him.

"It uses the energy of the spirit to replenish the energy of the body."

"What else has Seraphina shown you?" Marec asked, strumming his beard, contemplating.

"Well, I can cast mending now."

"Is that all?" Alec shook his head and facing the waterfall began to draw the symbol for force. He shoved his hand through the center of his rune causing the water to divert. A shower poured down atop Alec's head as he turned back to face Marec.

"Most impressive. Alec, today I am going to begin training you on the use of more advanced runes. We are going to start with elemental shielding."

"Sounds self-explanatory, how does it work?"

"Well, in the case of conjurers, they simply casts the rune they wish and shield themselves from the element. With the case of paladins however one must cast the rune and instead focus intensely on redirecting the energy behind the elemental force."

"Why such a difference between the two?" Alec's intrigue had only grown since Marec's explanation.

"Conjurer's have a severely unique ability. While some have the power to utilize Aneira's blessing, others have the ability to tap into elemental forces similar to the Divine."

"Similar to the ones we faced at Roak?" Marec's expression grew grim.

"Exactly like those from Roak. Even the Forsaken have conjurers amongst them. Now, that is enough of the lesson on conjurers. Today we shall begin with a simple water shielding spell." Marec began drawing out his rune. Alec strained his eyes in order to focus on the blue lines, which appeared against the blue sky that lie beyond his teacher.

Marec drew out a blue line in the shape of a shield, and within its center, he drew what to Alec looked to be the shape of a typical drop of water. Next, Alec watched as the rune spread out and formed a protective bubble around his mentor. Alec cocked his head from side to side examining the bubble, which seemed to form around him. He measured the circle's diameter to be approximately five feet. Marec took up his stance and called out to Alec.

"You cannot see the shield, but I shall approach the waterfall and you will be able to better see what has happened."

"But master, I can see the shield. You are surrounded by a large bubble about five feet in diameter."

"What do you mean, you can see my barrier?" Marec said, snapping his head back toward Alec.

"Am I not supposed to be able?" Marec scratched his chin for a moment contemplating his most peculiar student.

"Once again, you surprise me. Typically, the effects of magic are invisible. Yet, before your eyes, their most intimate secrets reveal themselves. I suppose that showing you the effects at this point are moot, however, to humor an old man." Marec reached out with his hand and Alec watched as the shape of the barrier morphed to accommodate the change. He reached out and grazed the water's surface. Alec watched in awe at the water bounced off from the shield, as if bending to Marec's will and ran over its edges, as if hitting a rock or an awning.

"With this type of rune, it is best to cause for the element to warp around you. You will expend much less energy manipulating an element than you will to deflect it. In the case of fire shield, try to focus on using the water in the air as a combating force and, similar to using the force rune, cause the flames to bend around your body. To completely dispel an element could drain you of all of your body's energy."

"I will try master, how long would you like for me to practice today?" Marec smiled at Alec's enthusiasm.

"Actually, we will be practicing whilst we travel. Until we have adequate time to stop and rest, you will be practicing with wards. Once conditions are suitable, we shall carry over to elemental shielding. The ward you will be fighting with for the time being will be the projectile ward." Marec began to draw out the symbol. Alec watched as he again drew out the shield shape and this time drew another symbol. He drew out an "x" on the left extreme of his shield and drew an arch stemming from that to the far most right.

Alec watched as the water shield dissipated and was replaced by that of the projectile ward. It was only slightly different from the water shield. The projectile ward, as Marec called it, was slightly harder to see but looked to be comprised of a similar energy type as created the force rune. "Now Alec, take a pebble from the river bed and throw it at me." Alec did as instructed, removed a small pebble from the riverbed and threw it at Marec. Alec could hear the light tapping noise of the pebble hitting the supposedly invisible shield and bouncing off from it.

"You see now Alec what it is that you must learn to do? To learn a skill such as this is the very reason why paladins are renowned as superior protectors."

"I understand master, please allow me to try now." Alec began to draw out the symbol as shown to him. He mapped out the rune and the barrier began to form around him. He closed his eyes and waited for its effects to surround him but instead when he opened his eyes he saw that to his disappointment the effect was limited to a small wall that formed around his hand. Marec laughed heartily at Alec's frustration as his face grew comically annoyed.

"You shall require much practice, but, in time, you shall see that the ward shall become yours to command." Alec removed his hand from its outstretched position and lowered it back to his side. As he did so, he marveled that the ward he had cast still remained in front of him, remaining within the place where he had cast it. Alec reached out with his hand and pointed to the ward, which moved as he did so. Marec laughed as Alec continued to play with the ward in front of him.

"You will have mastered the technique before long. For now, we must carry on. Please Alec, rise from the pool, pass through my ward, and your clothes will be dried for you." Alec's head shot up with curiosity and he rose from the water. As Marec recast his rune of water shielding, Alec passed through it and noticed his clothes drying themselves. He watched in awe as the water flowed from his skin and off of his body as if he were a raincloud wringing itself dry.

"That is incredible!" Alec exclaimed as he watched the last of the water droplets flow out of his hair and onto the ground.

"Quite, one day, you will be able to do this as well." Marec dispelled his ward. "For now we must be away. Our companions are waiting for us to leave." Alec searched the tree line meticulously as they walked.

"I have to find Oz before we set out."

"There will be no need. Oz shall come to you when he is ready. Surely you are aware of the connection you two share?"

"The empathetic link, you mean."

"Quite. Your link shall allow for the two of you to find one another regardless of where you might travel." Alec, trusting in his master's words, followed the paladin back towards the gates of town, where mounted on horseback, sat his traveling companions. Two horses remained without riders, one with Alec's traveling clothes resting upon its back. Alec pulled his clothes from his horse's back and began to put them on. Amongst his things, he saw a new sword and shield.

"I suppose I forgot to mention that we took the liberty of replacing your sword and shield. I had Eliza and Zelus pick it out for you so I am sure it will be what you are used to. I also picked these up for you. I want you to begin training with them immediately." Marec walked to his own horse and pulled from his bags a large shield and a halberd. He handed them to Alec who received them gratefully but immediately felt his arms drop at the severe weight of the items.

"Thank you master, I shall begin mastering them along with my other weapons."

Fastening his sword belt securely around his waist and slinging the shield and halberd over his shoulder, he lifted himself onto the back of the horse and turned towards Marec.

"We ride to Trias. I expect us to be there by nightfall, if not, we ride until we arrive. Once there, we shall attempt to learn what news there is to be had about these armored men. I have already ordered a messenger send word to both the grand shrine and to Valascaa. They will deliberate on the matter and send what aid is needed. It would be best for us to finish our business within Trias quickly as we will have one more stop to make before we can return." They rode southwest toward Trias. Marec, who was in the lead, slowed his place so that the others rode in sync with him.

"Alec I would like for you to lead us. The road to Trias is a simple one. Just keep following it southwest and we shall arrive. The only thing between us and our destination is a road leading toward the border, so navigation shall be quite simple.

Eliza, I believe I shall ride next to you to discuss a few matters with you in regards to your training and your father."

"Of course, uncle," Eliza spoke as she shifted aside allowing for Marec to ride in between her and Zelus. Alec rode beside Talia and Tear who shared a horse being the smallest two who were unburdened by their belongings.

"How are you this morning priestess?" Tear was still fast asleep so Alec attempted to make conversation with Talia.

"I am well, Sir Alec, merely eager to conclude my journey and be back amongst my fellow priestesses." Her demeanor was still as pleasant as normal, yet to Alec she felt cold.

"Marec has begun instructing me in the ways of warding runes. I have already learned to cast the projectile ward."

"That is impressive progress. You are nearly a paladin. You should be proud." Still Alec could not help but shake the feeling of something being amiss.

"Priestess, is everything alright? I do not mean to be intrusive but you haven't seemed yourself since last night after the fire." Without looking at Alec, Talia spoke.

"I have much on my mind is all. A great many things have occupied my mind which must be considered." After a particularly long pause, Alec turned his head towards Talia.

"What of your family?" Talia turned her head towards Alec oddly.

"What of them?" Alec quickly clarified what he meant, knowing full well that Talia had lost her family as well.

"I was only wondering what sort of people they were, while they were still alive? I am not sure, I just feel that I wish to know more about you." Talia's confused expression changed to one of acceptance and understanding.

"My father's name was Dormund and my mother's, Relina. My father was a senator while my mother was a priestess for the Aneiran order. She reported directly to Lady Angelica and they were both beyond kind. I did not lose them in the Fall, however. They both died long before, attacked by a band of Forsaken." Alec's eyes grew wide as he absorbed the information.

"I see, I am sorry to hear that. I had only assumed…"

"We do not all walk the same path, Sir Alec. Each of us has seen our own struggles and faces our own trials." Alec clamped up and ceased his conversation. He stared at Talia for a moment and wished that he had not asked his question.

"I apologize, priestess." He spoke softly. Talia nodded her head but was otherwise, quiet.

Their conversations continued this way for several long awkward hours before Alec decided to call it a quits and resign himself to practicing his wards. He carefully drew out his ward and watched as the bubble grew before him. After several more hours of practice, he began to tire and gave practicing a rest. Alec looked up to the sky to see that the sun was dipping low and soon it would be sunset.

"Hold Alec, we are here." Alec eased his horse to a halt, as did the others. They turned toward Marec waiting further orders. "Eliza, Zelus, and Alec, I will have the three of you train together as I go and secure our lodgings for the eve. Mi'lady, young Tear, if you would be so kind, might you be willing to stay behind and watch everyone."

"That will be fine, Sir Marec. On what terms shall they be fighting?"

"I wish for Alec to fight against Zelus and Eliza. If Alec manages to best you both, Eliza I wish for you to use your bow while Zelus combats Alec with his blade." Zelus looked at Alec and began punching his fist into his opposite hand. Even Eliza smiled.

"Sorry, Alec, I guess that we are just going to have to pummel you." Eliza taunted as she swung her legs onto the same side of her horse and dismounted.

"Alright then, if you head a little bit further down, there is a small barracks that you can practice at." Marec pointed down the path and everyone else continued onward while Marec separated from the group. Securely tying off his horse, Alec approached the nearest knight being sure to show the symbol of the Valorian knights which he wore on his chest.

"Might we use the training ring? My fellow knights and I were hoping to get in some practice." The knight looked at Eliza and Zelus who had also produced their separate seals. The knight nodded his head and pointed them in the proper direction. Alec, Eliza and Zelus all marched into the center of the ring, where they stood ready to square off against one another.

Alec decided that now would be a perfect opportunity for him to practice fighting with his new weapons and so he carefully removed his sword belt and lovingly placed his new longsword and the Sidonis sword up against the wall next to where Tear and Talia now sat. Pulling his new shield and halberd from off his back, he did his best to adjust to the extreme increase in weight. Carefully, he placed a leather cover over the blade to keep from killing anyone and looked to his friends.

"Alright, who is first?" Alec turned his attention back and forth between his two potential opponents. Both had already grabbed practice weapons but Eliza was the first to step up.

"I suppose that will be…"

"Oh no, Eliza, if anyone is going to get to pummel Alec first, it is definitely going to be me." Zelus stepped up as Eliza shoved him.

"Hey, I called it."

"He is my rival." Alec shook his head and laughed as the two squabbled back and forth. Finally, after several minutes of senseless arguing Alec chimed in.

"How about the two of you fight each other to determine who I will fight? I'll stand over here and practice with my new equipment so I will be that much more ready to face whomever." Eliza and Zelus looked at one another and got into their respective ready positions.

"Sounds like a great idea to me." Eliza spoke as she pulled out her curved sword and gave them each a few practice swings. Zelus pulled his weapons to the ready and pounded on his shield tauntingly.

"Normally, I would not fight a girl but, seeing as how you are only technically one, I should be fine." Eliza glared at Zelus, and Alec knew this battle would probably end in a fistfight with Eliza being crowned the champion.

"Alright, well whatever you are doing, FIGHT!" Alec called and turned his back to them as they ran at one another and began to brawl. Alec walked over to the other side of the ring and began to test out his new equipment. Talia walked over to Alec all the while keeping an eye on the duelers. Eliza dodged a swing from Zelus' sparring sword and jumping into the air spun, kicking him hard in the face.

Talia frantically tried to gain Alec's attention flailing her arms back and forth in front of her as the background brawlers continued to duke it out.

"Sir Alec," Talia stared at him, wincing in pain as Eliza climbed on Zelus and began punching him. "Sir Alec, should you not be watching them?"

"Watching who?" Alec asked over the slew of curses from Zelus' mouth as he flung Eliza off from him and renewed his assault. Alec turned his head, watching Zelus and Eliza begin flailing at one another as if actually trying to kill each other.

"Nah, they will be fine. We practice this way back in the capitol all of the time." He waved them off missing the part where Eliza pulled her bow and began firing dummy arrows at Zelus' head. Zelus began running for his life as he attempted to dodge the barrage that flew past him. Talia, however, turned and saw the confrontation and began to jump up and down with anxiety. In her frenzied tension, she noticed Tear standing up close picking up the stray arrows. Zelus screamed in as high-pitched a tone as Talia had ever heard a man emit. He fell to the ground and barely escaped with his life as arrow after arrow pelted at his feet and passed his head.

"Oh Tear, please you must not get too close." Talia said, as she ran to the child in a panic. Alec gave a few practice swings of his weapons, completely unaware of the chaos behind him. Eliza had nearly depleted her supply of arrows, fetching a handful of them from Tear and launching them back at Zelus. Still in his high-pitched squeal, Zelus yelled out at Tear.

"What are you doing? Whose side are you on anyway?" Tear continued to pick up the arrows as they began flying in every which direction conceivable. One rogue arrow flew past Alec nearly blasting him in the forehead, though he turned having parried an invisible blow and was otherwise unaware.

"I thought it was obvious…the bow lady's side." Tear spoke to Zelus unsure why it was not obvious. Talia nearly tackled Tear as she ran to defend her from the crazed onslaught of onslaught. Running for their lives, Talia and Tear ran back to Alec's side and pulled at his cape as Zelus and Eliza, having broken their practice weapons, resorted to using grappling techniques. Alec turned his attention towards the two divine as if confused.

"Yes? Is something the matter?" They both bore stern expressions as they pointed over toward the two brawlers.

"They are wrestling, so?" He turned back towards his practicing for a few more minutes. Tear and Talia walked further past Alec and sat behind the trunk of a nearby tree as more hammer arrows whizzed through the air, the grappling having lost its appeal for Eliza.

Alec performed a few more practice thrusts and swings against his invisible opponent before turning around to watch the two fight. Zelus was now fighting with a broken hilt and shield while Eliza was chasing after him with her two broken blades. Zelus reached the weapon rack, and pulling another weapon from it, spun around hitting Eliza hard in the side making her drop her blades.

"Ha, now I can finish this." Zelus charged in to make the winning stroke.

"I will never lose to a second rate fighter." Eliza yelled as she jumped up at the last second, landing on Zelus' shield. Using it as a springboard, Eliza launched herself, knocking Zelus onto his backside. As she flew backwards through the air, Eliza pulled her bow and fired a hammer arrow dead center into Zelus' forehead. Zelus' head lurched backward aggressively and he failed to rise, though the occasional twitched confirmed, that he was still alive.

"Alright, Eliza is the winner." Alec called as his best friend brushed off her clothes, and thanking Tear, took her arrows back.

"Thank you! Thank you!" Eliza joked as she bowed to an invisible audience.

"Hey where did you get the arrows?" Alec asked her looking at the strange heads.

"Oh, Uncle Marec helped me to make them on the way here. He had me buy leather pieces and beans to mount onto the ends of my arrow shafts so that I could have some practice arrows to use while we sparred. I suppose they would be great for knocking someone out without killing them." She leaned to the side to see passed Alec at Zelus who still lay sprawled out on the ground, a welt already forming on his forehead.

"I will get you next time." Zelus moaned as he weakly shook his fist in the air. "Does anyone else smell coffee?" Alec laughed at him for a moment before proceeding to healing his and Eliza's wounds. Zelus finally sat upright and rubbed his forehead.

"Was it totally necessary for you to pull out the hammer arrows?"

"Was it totally necessary for you to insult my femininity?" Eliza turned her nose up to him and scoffed.

"What femininity?" Zelus began to laugh after insulting Eliza again. Again, Alec could see the anger in Eliza's eyes. She stared at Zelus as if she were trying to explode his head with the power of her mind.

"Do you want me to shoot you again?" She threatened as she readied another arrow and pointed it between Zelus' eyes.

"No, no, no, I do not think that will be necessary. You won, so just go on ahead and fight Alec. I am good." He spoke as he scooted backwards, being sure to keep one hand in front of his face at all times as a shield. Eliza looked to Alec.

"Alec, do you mind if we do this later? I will not admit it to Zelus, but after riding all day and then sparring with him, I am pretty tired."

"Ha, I heard that." Zelus called from by the weapons rack. "I tired you out, and here you're keeping up your tough "MANLY" visage." Without warning or hesitation, Eliza pulled a hammer arrow from her quiver and shot it at Zelus. Alec laughed as Zelus howled in pain after receiving the blow in his buttocks.

"That is quite alright Eliza, I can always practice alone. It will take me some time to get used to the feel of these weapons anyway." He turned from Eliza and began to occupy himself with the target. Eliza turned towards Talia who had finally calmed herself from the commotion.

"Hey Alec, if you have the time, you should help Talia with her swordsmanship." Alec looked at Talia.

"Talia would you like for me to teach you?" Talia blushed and began to play with her hands as if she had been afraid to ask.

"I am certain that I am not nearly as gifted with a blade as either of you three, but I would be willing to learn..." She paused for a moment before her compulsion for being overly proper kicked in. "If you would be willing to teach me, of course."

"Talia, I would be honored to teach you. In fact, it would be my pleasure." Alec approached Talia and taking a practice sword from Eliza, handed it to Talia.

"Alright now, the first thing we need to do is make sure that you have a proper grip on your weapon." Alec became distracted for a moment as Zelus bounced passed them in the background still holding his rear, limping as he tried to make his getaway. Shaking himself from the moment, he placed his hands over Talia's and began to help her adjust her grip so that it was proper. Alec could not help but notice that the young priestess' hands were trembling from the contact but Alec made no attempts to acknowledge that he noticed.

"First, you must have a strong grip on the weapon, otherwise you will just lose it. Second thing we need to do, is work on your form." Alec began to critique Talia's posture, advising her to take up a better defensive stance. It was apparent now that Talia was having some difficulty as her entire body was trembling.

"Priestess, is something the matter?" Alec and Talia's eyes met for a moment and to Alec it seemed as though she were about to cry.

"Everything tis fine, though I must ask your leave. Thank you for the lesson, Sir Alec. T'was most educational." She handed Alec the sword and spirited away. Eliza looked over to Alec.

"What did you do?" She asked him before running off after Talia. Alec remained where he stood, absolutely befuddled. He looked to Zelus who shrugged his shoulders and shook his head.

"Women, man, I just do not get them." Zelus spoke. "Hey, enough about them already. How about you and I train like Marec told us to?" Alec nodded his head, picked up a practice weapon, and removed his brand new shield.

"Should I use my new equipment?" Alec asked. Zelus waved him off as he stretched his lower body.

"Nah, let us finish the match we started back in Valascaa. I have been waiting for far too long now to continue." Alec nodded his head as he walked over and stood before Zelus, raising his sword and shield. They both smiled at one another, as they both saluted the other, by holding the sword vertically before their faces and slashing out sideways. Next, Alec and Zelus squared off and began to attack one another in friendly competition.

Meanwhile, Eliza had finally managed to catch up to Talia, who was catching her breath, beneath a beautiful tree within the gardens that overlooked the sea. Eliza cautiously approached behind Talia and stopped for a moment as she noticed what the tree was doing. She watched in awe as the tree blossomed rapidly. Small white flowers bloomed, glowing a magnificent white. She watched the flowers, as just as soon as they had fully bloomed they fell from the tree and danced elegantly through the sky, then landed upon the blanket of blossoms, which had already fallen.

"Talia are you alright?" Eliza edged closer to the young woman being sure to announce her presence before joining Talia on the swing where she sat. She looked at the young priestess and saw that she had streams of tears pouring from her eyes. Eliza reached toward Talia and pulled her close and began to stroke her hair.

"Talia honey, what is the matter?" Talia leaned into Eliza and sobbed into her chest. Talia did not speak. She merely continued to weep on Eliza's shoulder. Eliza continued to try calming the priestess. She began to swing them both, as she petted her hair. She whispered hushing noises to Talia as she began to calm her uncontrollable sobs, changing them to a simple whimper.

"Talia, please tell me what is the matter?" Talia looked up to Eliza, her sad eyes magnified by the immense number of tears that had fallen from them. Eliza looked away for a moment, as she felt a wave of her own sympathy tears being summoned.

"Do you swear not to speak a word to Alec or the others?" Eliza looked at Talia with extreme concern in her eyes. Talia stared at her waiting for an answer. "Please Eliza, they must never know." Eliza's conscience began to attack her. She had never lied to Alec before. They had been best friends since they were young but all the while she couldn't help but feel that this once she had to do this.

"I swear." Talia leaned into Eliza and began to tell her the secrets behind her infinite sorrow. Eliza trembled as Talia relayed the events of her life and collapsed inside at their meaning. Eliza attempted to remain strong for Talia yet once the priestess was finished, Eliza found herself kneeling in the pool of blossoms beside her weeping frantically.

"Talia, you have to tell him." Talia shook her head.

"He can never know, he would only try to stop me and I fear I lack the courage to resist should he ask it of me." Eliza held Talia to her chest again, to offer comfort her and also, to hide her own stream of tears.

"I will not tell him not until after we have returned home."

"Thank you Eliza. You are the first friend I have ever known." They sat together for several more minutes watching the Aneiran blossoms fall around them.

Chapter 29 – A Vision, Fulfilled

Alec and Zelus, both continued to exchange blows in a furious flurry of metal. Both had grown, in the time they had spent on the road, the merits of their training, showed in their attacks. Alec with his impervious defenses, continued to parry blow after blow from Zelus, who fought fiercely offensive. Both bore equally broad grins, on their faces, as they sought to settle once and for all, which was the best.

"You know I have always been better than you." Zelus taunted as he slashed at Alec. The young, paladin in training smiled, as he blocked yet another blow, returning one of his own. Zelus deflected Alec's sword with his own blade and stepped into his friend. Alec, moving with Zelus, leaned slightly as he kicked against Zelus' shield, knocking him off step. Charging forward, Alec let out a downward stroke, which narrowly missed his nimble ally. Zelus retaliated with a back handed swipe, which Alec caught on his shield.

"Have you had enough yet?" Zelus panted as sweat dripped from his brow. Alec stood opposite him, equally exhausted from their battle thus far.

"What are you talking about? I am still waiting for Eliza to come back so I can fight you both." Alec smiled, the additional weight of his new weapons upon his back straining him. Alec smacked his sword on his shield challenging Zelus to continue. Zelus returned the smirk and charged Alec, lashing out at him again and again. Alec continued to repel Zelus' assaults until he saw his opportune moment to strike. Alec jabbed and Zelus smiled as he spun around the blade, locking Alec's wrist and forcing him to drop his weapon.

"I told you that I was better than you." Zelus cheered for himself as Alec began to see the results of Marec's training on he and Eliza. Zelus swung at Alec who blocked the blow with his shield and slammed into Zelus knocking him backwards. Alec dove for his blade as Zelus placed his foot over it.

"You cannot beat me now, Alec. I have learned much from Marec." Alec thought of reaching for his halberd, but then realized he did not actually want to kill Zelus. He looked up as Zelus continued his taunting. "You have spent your time learning paladin tricks, while I have mastered my abilities with the sword."

"Would you like to see one of my tricks?" Alec asked as he began to draw the force symbol with his weaponless hand.

"What are you doing?"

"Winning." Alec replied as he forced his palm through the rune sending Zelus flying backwards. Alec picked up his blade and pressed it to Zelus' throat before he had the time to recover.

"I win." Alec told Zelus who looked at him wide eyed with astonishment. Quickly recovering from his surprise, Zelus slapped the blade away and rose to his feet.

"You cheated. You underestimated me. I tired you, I beat you, and then you resorted to your paladin tricks."

"Zelus, you would not have me beaten," Alec drew out the symbol of regeneration and Zelus watched as Alec's body reversed all of the effect that stress, fatigue and battle had wrought upon him. Zelus watched as even the sweat that had begun to drench him evaporated from his skin.

"You see, I am not the only one who has underestimated his opponent. I am proud to call you my rival, Zelus. May we both continue to improve in our own fashion." He reached his hand out to Zelus who, after a moment, smirked back at him and shook it.

"I will beat you next time, and I will not take it easy on you when next we fight."

"I shall be prepared to be overwhelmed. We should train more often." They began to walk back towards town to find their friends, Tear having taken off long before they had finished their duel.

"Hey Alec."

"What Zelus?"

"Do you think that you could use that trick on me?" Alec smiled, already aware of what Zelus meant.

"What trick?"

"You know that thing you just did to reverse your fatigue." Alec smiled at his friend's importuning.

"I am afraid that it only works for me, on me. Marec already attempted to test it himself. He told me that it was a special technique that only I may master."

"Well then, what good is that? You better not use that again next time we fight. I would have beaten you for sure had you not done that." Alec smiled but chose not to tell Zelus that he had not used it during their fight. They marched toward the top of the hill where the town sat. They saw Tear sitting in front of the inn, playing in the dirt with a stick.

"Tear, do you know where everyone is?" The small girl looked at them, nodded her head and smiled. She stood up and as if she had been practicing a speech, began rapidly relaying the details.

"The bow lady has gone to the archery range after speaking with the prayers lady." She was speaking so fast that Alec and Zelus had to lean in to hear her properly. "The prayers lady is waiting down by the sea in the gardens after the beard guy asked her to wait for Alec." Alec smiled that he was the only one whom she addressed by name. "Beard guy also asked for whiny guy to go and practice with the bow lady." At this, Alec started cracking up laughing as Tear finished her story. Zelus elbowed Alec in the ribs and then turned to Tear.

"Hey, what do you mean whiny guy? I am not whiny." Alec continued laughing as Tear returned to her doodling. Zelus looked from Alec to Tear then from Tear to Alec.

"I am not a whiner." He nearly sounded as if he were whining as he said it but, after another moment, the thought seemed to pass him. "Well, you better get going then. You do not want to keep the prayers lady waiting for you." Alec turned to Zelus.

"What?" He asked.

"Did you not hear Tear. She said that Marec wants you to go practice your wards with Talia. I swear sometimes you are dense." Alec turned to Tear.

"I am sorry I did not hear you, Tear. I was too busy laughing at the whiny guy. Thank you for delivering the message. I will head that way now. One more thing before I go though. Tear, do you mind keeping an eye out for Oz? He should be back before long. Beard guy said that he would find us after he finished hunting and I do not sense his usual excitement."

"Alec, you are silly. That is why Tear sits here. She has been waiting for the kitty to come back. He will be here soon." Alec thanked Tear and began to walk away from her. Alec was unsure of where the gardens were, but the fact that the sea lay south, was an easy enough method for him to follow. He headed south and followed the path with the most greenery. Finally, he found the gardens and he entered.

"Talia, I am here. Where are you?" Alec looked around as he walked.

"I am over here, Sir Alec." Talia stood just beyond the next wall of vines and Alec stopped to take in the vision before him. Talia stood with her back to him watching the sea as the blossoms fell around her. Her cloak rested on a swing that was to her right. Her long beautiful auburn hair was let loose and flowed in the wind. As she turned to face Alec, her magnificent green eyes burnt through him; he felt the fatigue from his battle with Zelus hit him again.

"Please come here Alec, Marec has asked for me to practice the projectile ward with you." Alec did as she asked and removed his armor and weapons before approaching her.

"What would you have me do, priestess?" Talia smiled at Alec as she led him beneath the tree.

"Watch." She looked up at the tree and blossoms began to rapidly pour from the trees branches. Talia sang a melodious hymn. Alec watched as a blue bubble similar to Marec's enveloped her. Alec watched as the petals landed on the bubble and floated in midair. He felt his breath being forced from him as he watched the already beautiful maiden being enveloped by the flowers.

"Now you try, Sir Alec." Alec nodded his head and did just as he was asked. He cast his rune of projectile ward and focused intensely on the palm of his hand. He watched as his shield began to bloom. The shield reached out to be about the width of his forearm, but still was not as impressive as the wards cast by Talia and Marec. Alec held it out above him and watched as petals began to accumulate over his hand.

"Remarkable progress, for having only just learned your first runes. Please release thy rune and use it once more." Alec nodded his head as he released his rune and the falling flowers landed on and around him.

Alec traced out the rune again and focused on the palm of his hand. He willed the rune into being and commanded it to grow before his outstretched hand. Talia stared intently at what was invisible to her but to Alec he saw as the rune grew again to the length of his forearm and despite his will, grew no further. Alec held his hand into the air and watched as the petals landed on it and floated around its surface.

"Well done. I believe that you have the necessary strength and talent to create a powerful ward, though it appears as though your trouble lies with focusing the required energy." Talia walked closer to Alec and placed her hand gently upon his breast, just over his heart. "Close your eyes, Sir Alec. Feel the beating of thy heart." Talia closed her eyes as she leaned in and concentrated. Alec did as instructed and closed his eyes.

"In thy mind's eye, picture the image of thy body. Picture thy beating heart, transmitting a current of energy through thy entire being. This is thy life's energy that thou feel, coursing throughout. Focus on that and thou will feel beside it, a second current. This is the current of thy soul." Alec focused for a moment in silence until he could sense a light flooding his body as well as blood.

"I feel it priestess! I can sense a light within me!" Talia smiled, though neither could see as she spoke calmly and continued.

"Focus on that light. Feel its embrace, spreading through thy body and picture its light spreading throughout thy entire being. From thy toes, to thy legs, up into thy core. Allow the light to illuminate from and envelop everything." As Talia spoke, the light he held in his mind began to swell, until he felt as though he were connected to the world around by invisible threads.

"I can feel the light and see it surrounding me. I can sense its presence now!" He spoke again as Talia removed her hand from his chest, releasing her connection to his energy. As she did so, Alec felt as his energy grew closer to his body, yet maintained its brilliance.

"Now, Sir Alec. Cast thy rune once more." Talia walked back from Alec and cast her own rune as Alec did the same. Talia's ward grew all around her as before while Alec began to trace out his rune.

"This time, when thou releases thy rune, focus on channeling thy radiant light into thy rune." Talia added as Alec released his rune and imagined the floodgates of his spiritual reservoir, spilling out into his rune. He could feel the rune growing and as he opened his eyes, he witnessed that his rune had grown nearly the size of his body. As Alec lifted the shield over his head, petals accumulated in abundance, landing several paces on either side of him."

"That is most excellent, Sir Alec. Thou shalt become a fine paladin." Talia dispelled her shield and Alec watched as the blossoms she had accumulated fell around her. Talia looked up to the tree lovingly.

"Tis a most beautiful sight, is it not?" She spoke, but Alec could not take his eyes off from her. Alec stepped in closer to her, released his ward and placed his hand on her cheek.

"The most beautiful sight I have ever bore witness to." He leaned in toward her. Talia looked up at him with wide frightened eyes but did not resist him as he held her close and kissed her. She met his embrace and instinctively wrapped her arms around him and returned with her own affection. They stood there under the shade of the Aneiran blossom conjoined in heart as much as in body.

"I have been looking for you." He whispered into her ear. Talia looked up at him, still very much in the embrace of his arms.

"And I you." She answered as she nuzzled her head into his chest; he held her close for a moment. Alec took in a deep breath and reveled in the moment. Their embrace lasted for several more minutes as Talia could feel her heart pounding in her chest for the love she felt. She took great pleasure in being in Alec's arms, but the closer she neared bliss, the more she was reminded of her sorrow.

Finally, her joy grew to a point where her remorse overwhelmed her and the ecstasy she felt was replaced with an unbearable pain. Talia could feel the tears welling up within her. As much as she was in love with Alec, his touch felt so intensely warm to her that it burned her skin. She pushed away from Alec's embrace and turned away.

"I am sorry Alec. I cannot give thee what thee seek." She spoke as she ran from him. Alec stood confused and heartbroken at the same time. He lacked the strength to chase her and instead his knees buckled and he took up a seat upon the swing. He looked down to his side and gathered up her cloak in his hands. He sat there alone in silence for over an hour. Finally, Oz came to his side, Tear riding on his back.

"Hey Oz." Alec spoke softly as if any higher a decibel would cause his body to shatter. "I see that you found him after all." Tear nodded her head as Oz capered toward Alec's outstretched hand and laid his head on Alec's lap, allowing Alec to pet him.

"Of course he did, I told you that Tear was waiting for the kitty and kitty came to Tear." Alec smiled as he helped Tear down off from the "kitty's" back. Tear petted Oz gently on the snout, and grabbing her staff, spirited away, her tiny legs carrying her at a slowed pace. Once she was out of sight, Oz turned back to Alec as he reassumed his seat upon the swing.

"I am alright Oz, just a little confused." Alec lied not for Oz's sake, he knew that Oz could sense when he was lying even easier than Eliza could. He knew that he lied because without the lie he lacked the strength to renew his emotional armor. Alec stared down at his empathy partner who turned his head at the sound of someone approaching.

"What is it Eliza?" He did not even attempt to block the blow that he was sure she was ready to land on the back of his head. Instead, however, Eliza placed her hand on Alec's head and began to stroke his hair.

"Alec, I am not sure what to tell you at this point, other than this is probably for the best." Alec batted Eliza's hand away as he rose from the swing.

"Honestly Eliza, please do not start with me right now. Is everything ready?" Eliza was stunned for a moment but knew that Alec had reassumed his defense and no matter how hard she tried, nothing she could say would give him relief.

"Yes. Uncle Marec has secured rooms for us for tonight. He suggests that we leave early tomorrow. It will be a long journey back to Valascaa. He has a few small matters to attend to before he and Talia return to the shrine." Alec nodded his head as he passed Eliza.

"I agree with him. It is probably for the best that we go our separate ways as soon as possible. Please tell everyone not to expect me back tonight." Alec said as he walked away. Eliza tried to stop him but settled for an explanation instead.

"Alec where are you going?"

"I have a trial to complete. If I go now then we will be able to leave even earlier." Eliza watched as Alec vanished into town.

"Oh Alec I wish I could tell you why it is better this way. I am so sorry that you suffer but, if you only understood, you might be able to see that Talia is trying to save you. She is so much stronger than any of us." Eliza marveled at the mysterious priestess her brother had fallen in love with.

"I am the paladin initiate, Alec. I wish to be allowed access to the shrine so that I might offer prayer to the goddess." The priest nodded his head and opening the door allowed Alec within. Alec followed the priest deep into the temple where he gestured Alec beyond with an open arm.

"The shrine is just through here. Feel free to take anything you might need, I will likely retire before long." Alec nodded his head graciously to the man as they parted ways. Alec knelt down before the statue of Aneira and offered his prayer. First touching two fingers to his lips and then raising his hand out to touch the goddess statue he spoke softly.

"Aneira, I have returned to you to offer my prayer. I ask that you allow me the opportunity to grow stronger so I may be a defender of the weak. I ask for you to instill me with the privilege and honor of serving as one of your paladins. I swear to you that I shall remain strong and vigilant in the depths of greatest despair and that I shall safeguard your children as best as I am able." Alec lowered his hands to the spring and cupped a handful of water and brought it to his lips. Alec closed his eyes as he grew dizzy and felt himself lifted away.

Chapter 30 – Seraphina's Second Trial

Alec's eyes opened and he knew that he had returned to Highmoore. He rose from his knees, walked towards the balcony and, looked out to the memory of the town that had bore him.

"It was once beautiful, Alec." Alec continued to stare off from the balcony as Lady Serpahina approached from behind him.

"I have returned my lady. I have come to undergo my next trial."

"You have learned much since last me met. I am glad to see you prospering so well, yet I sense that something is troubling you."

"Nothing that shall interfere with my training, I assure you." He replied. Seraphina watched Alec as if studying him.

"We shall see. Follow me, young Alec. Your next trial awaits you." Seraphina floated off and Alec turned from the image of his hometown and followed her. Seraphina lead him across the only room of the tower Alec knew of and stopped in front of one of the two doors.

"I believe Highmoore deems you ready to enter the next door young Alec. Choose your door, explore its contents, and prepare to be tested." Alec thanked Serpahina and approached the door to his left. Steadily he eased towards it and turned the knob, opening it. Instead of falling into nothingness and nearly dying, Alec walked in an opening that left him with three choices, a staircase leading up, one leading down and a room that lay just in front of him. Alec examined all three options and, noticing that both staircases ended in nothing, he opted for the route that lie ahead of him.

As Alec entered the room, he noticed a ghostly man sitting across from him.

"Are you too part of the memory of Highmoore?" Alec asked, prompting the ghostly man laughed at Alec as he rose from the table.

"I am your next trial, the trial of might. Defeat me and your trial shall be complete." The man rose and pulled out a large ethereal blade. "Now young Alec, fight me and prove your worthiness." Alec looked to his arms as both sword and shield materialized for him. He weighed them in his hands and their weight felt perfect to him.

"In this place, your memories are your arms. What you feel to be ideal is what you summon." The ghost approached him and made his first stroke. Alec blocked the blade and was almost shredded as the blow passed through his shield. The ghost laughed at Alec as he tossed aside his ruined shield.

"I see that this lesson shall be short. You obviously lack the talent to defeat me." The ghost pressed forward again, cornering Alec. Alec thought to himself about the first thing the ghost had told him. Your memories are your weapons. Alec looked down at his empty hand and another shield materialized before him. As the ghost approached for another strike, Alec began to trace the symbol for force with his shield hand. Before Alec could press his hand through the symbol, the ghost swung. Alec instinctively raised his shield, accidently forcing it through the rune.

"Ah, so the cadet does have some promise." Alec looked up to see that he in fact had blocked the attack with his shield still intact. Alec looked at the shield in wonderment, narrowly dodging the ghost's next attack.

"You must learn to keep your eye on your opponent. Lose that focus and you will die." The ghost lashed out at him again and again, Alec, becoming more and more confident with the strength of his ward, began to return the assault.

"Very good, young cadet. Such strength in your blows. Too bad your strength is meaningless when attached to a simple mind. Alec swung several times stabbing at the phantom from over the top of his shield. The apparition seemed to take a poor stance and Alec saw his opportunity. The ghost's poor footing allowed for Alec's down stroke to pass through him. The phantom brawler laughed as he split, allowing a second apparition to appear.

"Defend yourself Alec, we will kill you otherwise." The spirits laughed in unison as they both lashed out at Alec.

Alec did his best to protect himself against both assailants simultaneously, using a series of parries and thrusts. One phantom swung his blade upward, knocking Alec off balance. The other phantom took up the opportunity to swing at Alec.

"I am not dying today." Alec yelled as he thrust his shield out in front of himself. Both phantoms were struck backward by the force of Alec's shield arm. He looked at the shield with wonder and saw the force rune engraved upon it. He turned his attention to the phantoms to find that only one remained. Alec began drawing his rune again as the ghost attempted to bring itself to its feet.

"Impressive technique, I suppose that I will have to try." The phantom split forming his second apparition again.

"I have seen this already, show me something new," said Alec. If the phantom had the ability to smile, Alec imagined that he was doing such now.

"If you would like to see something new, all you had to do was ask." The two ghosts each split and then each split again. Alec watched as eight phantoms now glared angrily at him. "Are we still so confident? Do you still insist on seeing more?" Alec watched as the phantoms flickered in the light as if they were made of shadows.

"As a matter of fact I would enjoy that."

"Then so be it. I should warn you, however, that your death here shall also be the death of your body." Each phantom split again. Nearly the entire room was now full of apparitions. Alec smiled again as each division caused for the phantoms to shimmer and sparkle even more intensely. Alec even noticed that the last batch of phantoms was created without swords to bear.

"Now…we…kill…you." The phantoms spoke between long pauses. Alec smiled at them as he raised his shield.

"That is the best you can do?" He taunted. There still are not enough of you to survive one blow from my force rune." The phantoms looked to one another and back to Alec.

"There are more than enough of us to kill you. Your pride has become the end of you." Only the original phantom spoke as the others rushed in for the kill.

"Haaaa!" Alec screamed out as he forced his shield forward into the bulk of the phantom hoard. He made sure to pull every last ounce of himself into the blast sending phantoms in every which direction. Alec's eyes shifted attempting to find the one amongst the many. His eyes locked onto the one he was looking for and he approached and placed his blade against the phantom's throat.

"Yield." He called to the phantom. The phantom looked up to him and again made that look that resembled a smile.

"We have already proven that I cannot die. There is nothing stopping me from summoning my troops and devouring your flesh."

"No, what we have proven is that your strength is limited to the power of my mind and within my mind I say that you hold no power."

"If you are so confident in this, then strike me down."

"I can sense that you are not a malevolent force. If you were a being of evil, then you would not be suffered to exist within the memory of Highmoore. You are merely here to test my mettle and test you have though still I have passed." The phantom vanished and several feet behind Alec appeared the Lady Seraphina.

"You have done well Alec, even if your methods were a bit excessive." She turned her attention towards the crumbling wall, which lay behind her. Alec reached his arm behind his head and performed his best "whoops" face.

"Sorry?" He finally answered. Seraphina shook her head and motioned for Alec to follow her to the wall.

"This wall would have fallen anyway as soon as you had completed the trial. The trial was a test of your might, yet not just the might of your body. This test also tested the strength of your mind. You are now worthy to continue into the archives. You have one more trial to complete, to determine that you are indeed ready to find the Sidonis relics." Alec looked to Seraphina, stunned at her last statement

"Am I not already on the path?" He asked.

"You are." Seraphina smiled. "Yet, the trials you are undertaking, are to prove you are indeed worthy. Once you have proven your worth, you shall begin your journey to reclaim the legendary paladin's legacy. Only then shall you be able to call yourself a true paladin, worthy of your oath." Seraphina gestured for Alec to proceed toward the hole that had appeared in the wall. Alec approached and carefully stepped inside.

"It is dark in here." Alec spoke to Seraphina who entered behind him.

"The world is dark." She replied.

"Is there a light?" Alec asked.

"You are the light, Alec." Alec looked up to her confused by her answer. Seraphina smiled and began to explain.

"Think of every Valascaan as a candle and every soul a light. Once a soul realizes its potential, the flame ignites." As she spoke, Alec could see a candle ignite. "Each time a lit flame comes in contact with another, there is a chance that the spark from one soul shall ignite another." As she spoke, another candle burst into flame. "One by one, soul touching soul, with each flame lighting the next, it is possible to save this world from darkness." As she spoke, Alec looked all around him as the room continued to self-illuminate. Yet as Alec continued to watch, he noticed that only a small portion of the room was lit.

"Why is only part of the room lit?" Seraphina looked back to Alec.

"How is it, young cadet that you expect to ignite the hearts and potential of those around you, if you have yet to ignite your own? If one has yet to fall in love, how would they describe it to another?" Thoughts of Talia rushed to Alec's mind and quickly he forced his armor back on.

"There are some things that can never be." He whispered to himself as Seraphina continued.

"Alec, allow me to grant you a warning. Here, sooner than you may care to think, you will have to make a choice. Your decision will impact the lives of thousands of people maybe more. You will be given a true test to determine how brightly your light will shine. Think to yourself, if you were chosen to sacrifice your life for the greater good, what would you do?"

"Consider the source to determine who's greater good I was serving." Alec spoke, a tone of defiance in his voice. Seraphina smiled again.

"You may not be as naïve as I once thought you were. When you are finished, you need only return to the pool. I shall see you again after your return to Valascaa." Seraphina left Alec alone to himself. He turned and began to sift through the various scrolls and books that had mounted up. He gathered a few, sat down at a nearby bench and stretched one out.

"It is blank?" He sat the scroll aside and stretched out a second, which was also blank. Three more blank scrolls in and he rolled them to have a better look at the seal.

"*Advanced tactics and battle runes,*" "*Advanced medical runes,*" "*Physical manipulation of the body.*" Were among the scrolls he had initially gathered. He turned back and sifted through the piles again and found another cluster of scrolls he thought might be helpful.

The words "*The Golem Masters of Valascaana,*" were etched along the side of the scroll. Alec had heard of the golem masters before in his history lessons as a boy. They had once been a strong founding tribe of Valascaa and were rumored to have once helped build the palace back in the days of Sidonis. Alec found himself increasingly curious, and he pulled the two ends of the scroll apart unraveling the parchment so that he could claim its secrets for his own.

"The golem masters of Valascaana were among the original tribes to settle the Exodon and were renowned throughout the world as seekers of knowledge as well as being pioneers of the modern age's architecture. They were said to have been the first to produce the mighty fortresses that scatter the world of Valoria, and it was with their aid that Sidonis was able to erect the capital city of Valasca. It was even said that the golem masters were the ones that helped build the labyrinth of trial, which are still used to this day to test heroes from around the world as Sidonis was tested in his youth when he sought to prove himself to Aneira.

Although little record of the golem masters exists before the dark times, it was believed that they initially arrived from the country that existed before the Scar came to be. This would explain the god defying, monolithic statues and mountains that litter the coastline of the Scar. Though archeologists and adventure seekers often avoid incursions into the Scar, it is said by one, Charisma Mitra, that the ruins of an ancient statue exist within the ocean. It was never confirmed where Charisma's statue was located but upon further incursions into the uncharted waters, the remains of what might have once been a grand city were found and researchers suggest that perhaps a peninsula had sank into the depths carrying the secrets of the golem masters with it.

As far as further attempts to uncover the lost golem masters, all met with failure. At one point a breakthrough was believed to have been found as diggers happened upon a long stretch of tunnels that seemed to extend far below sea level, suggesting that there may have been a path to the theorized city below.

Unfortunately no attempt to reach the city ever succeeded and the legend of the golem masters was set back upon the shelf. The only other records of their existence remain in the guarded vaults of Valasca." Alec set the scroll back, fascinated by the tales of the golem masters and knew that one day he would have to search for these secret records. He looked over to his next scroll and held it before his eyes.

He unrolled *"Runes of the Sentinel Volume 1,"* and began reading about runes to use in life or death situations. Alec did his best to commit to memory as many of the runes as he could remember. He started with a rune to purify water, and another to start a simple fire. He sifted through others that to him were not exactly sentinel class runes. Eager to learn what he could, he quickly skipped to volume four and unrolled it. He carefully examined the scroll, which was mostly blank except for a couple of runes. One in particular caught his eye.

"Rune of the martyr," he read aloud to himself as he studied its significance.

"This rune will save its target from any wound at the cost of the caster receiving it instead. If martyr is cast on an individual with a broken leg, the caster's leg shall shatter, yet the recipient's shall be restored. This rune is best reserved to save the life of a loved one or one whom the sentinel protects. Simple wounds can easily be recovered with mending or revitalize.

If martyr is cast to save the life of another, the caster shall slowly have their life force drained as it replaces the life force of the recipient. Using martyr in this fashion will kill the caster if enough energy is taken. A note about the rune of martyr, should an individual cast the rune then be warned that its effects will become irreversible until such a time as the recipient's life force or wound has been restored.

Once the rune has taken effect, the caster may not be healed by an outside source, as all benefit from the healing rune will be transferred to the recipient of martyr. If either the recipient or the caster of martyr should attempt to heal the caster, then the effect will also benefit the one receiving aid from martyr but at the cost of the martyr casters energy." Alec thought to himself the significance of this rune and, as terrifying as it sounded to him, he committed it to memory.

He carefully traced his finger over the octagonal shape of the rune's body, and then he memorized the overlapping hearts, a line slicing through the dominant heart from right to left. A chill struck Alec and he quickly rolled the scroll, setting it aside for later and began to read another.

"Imbuing runes upon objects: beginner," Alec unrolled the scroll and began to read within. He examined the details within learning of various different uses for runes, such as imbuing healing runes on gemstones. He also came across an entry, which detailed how to imbue runes upon your equipment such as Alec had done with his shield. As he read through the scroll, he felt as though his understanding of imbued runes had been greatly improved.

Setting the scroll aside, Alec looked upon the shelves in the library, seeking something that caught his attention. A number of scrolls presented themselves to him. *"Tale of the Windrider Paladins," "The Knights of Falcanos: Kingslayers," "Outposts of the Lost Realm,"* and *"Ancient Paladin Traditions."* Seeing these, Alec set them aside for future reading as he reached for another and turned it to the side and read the engraving. *"Runes of the Sentinel, Volume 2."* Alec unrolled the scroll onto the table and began reading.

"Not every rune has one single means of use. There are runes that exist, which possess multiple properties once their applied method or the base of the rune is altered. For example the rune of force, a staple amongst paladin runes, can be used for more than simply knocking away an opponent. One such alternate use for the rune is with the retaliation rune. Where typically the rune of force is cast with a diamond shaped rune base, the rune of retaliation is inscribed within a circular base, giving it a slightly different effect.

With the force rune, one might cast it on its own or simply inscribe it upon their equipment so that when activated, the rune shall fire off at the caster's discretion or upon being stricken by an opponent. In the case of retaliation, however, the rune may only be activated once the rune has come in contact with an outside force.

Once the rune of retaliation has been activated, a force, similar to its more basic relative will be emitted, although in this instance the energies assault the outside force directly, instead of simply releasing kinetic energy. In this fashion, retaliation may be considered one of the most misunderstood yet most beneficial defensive runes a paladin might learn as it allows one to deflect even magical attacks should enough energy be released.

It is to be noted that the rune of retaliation is a more advanced version of the force rune and requires additional amounts of effort to cast, though its effects are worth merit. Other examples of multi-use runes would be using the runes of the elemental wards as a means to guide the blocked element. For instance, the rune of fire ward can be used to not only defend the wielder from harm. It can be used to guide a flame along a desired course..." The scroll continued on for some time, explaining the many different ways that Alec could use elemental wards to guide elements or manipulate them to his will. After further study, Alec sat the scroll aside and reached for one from his pile.

"Tale of the Windrider Paladins." Curious, Alec laid the scroll out and began to read the information contained within. *"Paladins have long been known to be explorers of the natural and supernatural realms, though none save Sidonis and his conquerors of the lost realm were as highly admonished as the fabled Windrider Paladins. The Windrider's were founded by a young paladin elite, Cairon Ronak, who gained his post amidst the Battle of Windy Peak on the border of Highmoore and the southern coastline to the Scar.*

The Forsaken, led by Calleus the Bloodletter, had led an assault on

Highmoore's southern border in an attempt to flank the city whilst Sir Sidonis led the main force into the Scar from the north. Sir Cairon's commanding officer, Karlon Barge, had held an admirable defense at Windy Peak, though there forces, siege ridden and desperately outnumbered, were forced from the keep.

Barge was killed, while defending the retreat of his men and Cairon, Barge's second in command took up the assault afterwards with one daring attempt. As its name suggests, Windy Peak was a paladin fortress built upon the plateau of a mountain range in southern Highmooria where unusual wind patterns ravage any who take to the air.

Surrounded and heavily outnumbered, Cairon faced the wind atop his Lion Hawk, Silver Wings and flew high over the enemy forces, marching through the canyons. Desperate for victory, the other paladins in the troop who could, mounted their Lion Hawks for one last attack.

Cairon led the assault on the Forsaken front line, using the unusual patterns of the wind to his advantage, Cairon plummeted towards the enemy with blinding speed, only to unleash blasts of force and other offensive runes directly into the enemy and the sides of the canyon walls.

Following his lead, Cairon's men, rode the wind beside him, unleashing their combined might against the walls of Windy Peak. The resulting avalanche sent massive rockslides down upon the forces of Forsaken. As Calleus' forces were crushed beneath the rubble, Cairon and his paladins plummeted once more and struck a mighty blow to Calleus, defeating the Daemon Knight, allowing Sidonis and his men to strike into the heart of the Scar.

After the war, stories of Sir Calleus Ronak and his Windriders, spread across the Exodon. A new type of paladin was trained, ones which excelled above all others in aerial combat. Theirs was a separate order from the main body of paladins, flying high above the enemy and dropping behind enemy lines, using various runes to slow their fall and ambush their adversaries. The practice is still quite common, though since the days of Sir Sidonis' death and the resurrection of the old kingdoms, there has yet to be a war on Highmoorian soil. The Windrider order has since become an order of thrill seekers."

He studied for several more hours, reading each of the scrolls he had laid aside along with several others that he had discovered afterwards.

Laying down, *"The Knights of Falcanos: Kingslayers,"* Alec smiled as he read about the knights destined to defeat the mad King Caliban, knowing that his friend Rowan had traveled to train with their order and to lay to rest, his brothers. Eventually his eyes burned from the strain of reading. He rose and stretched his sore muscles before exiting the room. He reached the balcony and saw that it was past sunset. He knew from before that time ran differently while he was within the memory, but he was certain that if he were not back soon, that Eliza would begin to worry. He turned to face the pool of water and walking up to it and dove in.

"Ooph!" He grunted as he face planted into the ground. "Mental reminder, do not dive into the pool." He groaned some more before rising to his feet and left the church. He finally made it back to the inn and found Marec standing guard outside of Talia, Tear and Eliza's room as usual.

"How went your trial."

"I have succeeded, my next trial awaits me back in Valascaa."

"Very good Alec, you are very nearly a paladin. Soon you will be able to bear our insignia."

"I look forward to that day." Alec started to walk away, eager for rest.

"Alec, might I have a moment?" Alec stopped and turned back towards Marec.

"Alec, I know that you and Talia have become close. Normally I would only be cautious, as paladins are not forbidden from pursuing relationships. In the case of Miss Talia, however, I must lean beyond caution and forbid such a relationship. Milady has spent her entire life preparing for a sacred duty. One that I am afraid prevents the two of you from being together. Please do not make things harder on either."

"You need not worry master, she has already made things abundantly clear to me. Good night." He spoke quickly as he darted inside the room and falling onto his bed, quickly went to sleep. Marec remained outside of the room head down, remorseful of the many things, which he lacked the courage to tell his apprentice.

Chapter 31- The Rise of a Paladin

Zelus awoke in the middle of the night to the sounds of chatter pouring from the other side of the wall. Zelus attempted to hear, but could only make out the sounds of someone crying. Zelus leapt across the room and began to shake Alec in a panic as he attempted to wake him.

"Zelus what is it? Is everything alright?" Zelus placed a finger over his lips and silently signaled for Alec to be quiet.

Alec silently mouthed, "What's the matter?" Zelus took his finger from his lips long enough to point to the wall. Alec leaned his head to the side.

"Eliza and Talia…" Zelus pounced on Alec and covered his mouth.

"Shh, shh, shh, shh," Zelus went off in a rapid-fire burst as he continued to silence Alec. Alec attempted to shove Zelus, causing them to squabble and wrestle one another until Alec finally managed to press his legs into Zelus' chest and shoved him away.

"I am going back to sleep, leave me alone." Alec rolled over. Zelus, too curious to let things go, crept back over to the other side of the room. He leaned his ear to the wall but, unable to understand what was being said, looked for a better way to eavesdrop. The nearby window caught his eye.

Zelus walked over to the window and carefully opened it. He looked out the window and to his relief he found that there was a balcony. "Ah, drat." He spoke to himself as he climbed out to the edge of the balcony and looked straight down, remembering that they were on the third floor. Zelus placed his feet on the rail and preparing himself jumped to the next balcony. He hung there for a moment making sure that no one had heard. Swinging his legs over the railing, he slowly leaned against the edge of the window and being sure not to peek inside intently listened in.

"I have never had feelings such as these before. When I lived among the clergy at the grand shrine, I was frequently in contact with men, yet never before, have I possessed such unbearable feelings."

"Talia, what you are feeling is called love. There is no reason for you to be so upset by that."

"But Eliza, I am forbidden from feeling such things. It is an offense against Aneira for one in my position to feel such things."

"Talia, Aneira is the goddess of love. How could such a thing ever be forbidden?" There was a long pause, Zelus feared that they were being quieter so he leaned in more. Still no voices remained on the other side of the door and he leaned in just a little bit more.

"Ha!" Was the noise Zelus heard as the window was forced open and he fell into the room face first.

"Zelus you filthy letch, what do you think you are doing?" Eliza yelled at Zelus with a whisper as she kicked him a couple of times. Zelus turned his head upward his hands securely over his eyes.

"I know what this looks like, but I swear to you that I was not here to peek."

"Yeah, right you lewd freak. As if I am about to believe that."

"Honestly, I swear on my honor as a knight of Valoria. I only listened in. I overheard someone crying and I was worried. However, now my concern for you two has turned into concern for my friend. Why are you two whispering about Alec?" Zelus still could not see but he imagined Eliza was doing her best to come up with a cover.

"I swear Eliza, if either of you are out to hurt him, I will be coming after you. He may be my rival but his training is too important for you to be attempting to sabotage him." Without proper warning Zelus was slapped hard across the face, causing him to land face down on the ground again.

"Zelus, you insensitive prat. You have no idea what Talia is going through right now. If you so much as breathe a word of this to Alec I will be coming after you!" Zelus rubbed his face as he continued to keep his other hand over his eyes. Zelus felt a pair of gentle hands on his own.

"Sir Zelus, please open thy eyes. There is naught to fear." Zelus opened his eyes to see Talia's were bloodshot and swollen.

"Priestess, are you alright?" Talia shook her head at him. Zelus patted Talia's hand gently as he looked into her grief stricken eyes. "Talia, please do not hurt my friend." Instantly, a renewed stream of tears began to pour from Talia's eyes and she reached out and hugged Zelus. Zelus was unsure how to respond and simply patted the priestess on the back while attempting to comfort her. Eliza placed her hand on Zelus' shoulder and then looked Talia in the eye.

"Zelus, it is not what you think. Talia has no intention of hurting Alec." Zelus pushed Eliza's hand away and rose to his feet.

"Well, that is exactly what's happening right now. Have you seen him? He is shattered. How do you plan on rectifying this?" Eliza nearly struck Zelus again but knew that, in his ignorance, his intentions were still noble. Talia was still sitting on the floor nearly collapsed into herself.

"Zelus, I feel tis time for me to tell thou of a deep secret. The very purpose of mine birth." Zelus froze in place as Talia began to relay her story to him.

Alec slowly opened his eyes and began to survey the world around him. His eyes glanced upon the open window and he saw that it was nearly daybreak. He turned and searched across the room to see Zelus sitting on his bed, his back to the wall, staring off into space. Alec searched his face to find his eyes were red and swollen.

"Are you alright?" Alec asked but received no answer as Zelus continued to stare at the wall opposite the door. "Hey, are you alright?" Zelus twitched as if snapping from a dream before looking at Alec.

"Yeah, I am fine." He answered with a sullen tone in his voice. Alec turned his head from side to side examining Zelus' face.

"Have you been crying?" Zelus jerked again this time much more violently before turning on Alec.

"Of course not! Why in Valoria would I be crying? I am not upset. Nothing has happened. Maybe you are crying and it makes it look like I have been. Jeez, Alec, you without a doubt are sad, not even daybreak and you are balling like a babe." Zelus rose abruptly and left the room.

Alec sat confused and curious as to what exactly had just transpired. He sat for a moment contemplating the possibilities but instead found himself horrified by them. No longer able to remain still, Alec rose from his bed and walked out into the common area. There already waiting were Marec as usual, Tear, Zelus who was attempting to be extremely interested in the wall and Eliza. Alec looked around for signs of Talia but figured she must still be in the room. Alec turned towards Marec.

"Master, do I have time to go practice my wards?" Marec nodded his head.

"We shan't be leaving until about midday. Miss Talia and I still have a matter to attend to within the sanctuary." Alec nodded his head as he began to leave. He neared the bottom of the stairs as Zelus and Eliza both dashed the length of the room to catch him.

"Alec we would like to accompany you." They spoke as a mob. Alec turned to them.

"I am going to practice my wards."

"We know." Again as one voice.

"What does Marec say?" They both looked in the same direction in sync and then began walking down the stairs.

"He says it is fine." Alec shook his head as the three of them walked outside. The sun was not yet over the horizon and the air still smelt damp of morning dew. Alec took in a deep breath and exhaled, filled with vigor.

"You two do realize that I will have to concentrate right?" Zelus and Eliza looked at one another accusingly as if declaring that they themselves would never be the cause of distraction.

"We know, Alec. Marec has been working with the two of us, briefly. He has given both of us a basic understanding of what you have been doing and we have both taken oaths of secrecy." Alec looked at Zelus who confirmed what Eliza had said.

"Alright, well then in that case, I could use some help. During my last trial I learned the rune for water shield. Once I cast the rune, if one or both of you could splash water on me that would be helpful." Zelus and Eliza looked at one another and shrugged. The three of them continued down the road until the stream came into sight. Alec walked up to the stream and stared down into the water and focused.

"What do you need us to do?" Eliza asked.

"I will let you know when I am ready." Eliza nodded and stood patiently waiting for Alec. Alec returned to concentrating. He focused on his own energy, trying to imagine the wave flowing through him. He struggled, still angry at how things had transpired between he and Talia and found it difficult to identify the well within his spirit.

He found the connection and began to trace out his rune. First, he drew out the diamond shape that was the base of defensive runes then he drew the water symbol, a simple tear drop. Alec knew that Eliza and Zelus would not be able to see it but he watched as the water shield began to creep around his body, its borders expanding so that the circle's diameter was about the length of his sword sheath.

"Alright, I have it now. Can you see my shield?" Eliza and Zelus both looked at Alec.

"No," Eliza responded. Zelus continued to stare awkwardly at Alec.

"Do you mean that small circle?" Alec and Eliza both jumped in surprise causing Alec to lose the shield.

"Wait, you can actually see it?" Zelus did not answer as he continued to stare.

"I thought I could but seems the fuzzy light is gone." Alec realized that he had lost the rune.

"Actually, Zelus that is my fault, I am sorry. Here, allow me to cast it again." Alec renewed his process and cast his rune again.

"Yeah there it is. It is right here." Zelus traced his finger around the exact location of the shield.

"Zelus, that is incredible. I thought that I was the only one that was able to see the barriers."

"Well, I am not sure if I am actually seeing it or sensing it."

"What do you mean?" Alec and Eliza both asked him.

"Well it is strange. It is not like seeing something, but I can feel as if the air around it is vibrating." Zelus spoke as he batted at the air, trying to feel out the invisible barrier. Alec and Eliza both stared at Zelus for a moment.

"Alec, what is Zelus talking about? What barrier are you talking about?" Alec, still confused by Zelus' strange ability, turned to address Eliza.

"When I cast a rune, it leaves an energy trail. For some reason I can see the energy. Marec thought I was the only one, but now it seems that Zelus has the ability to sense the energy. I will have to ask Seraphina next time I see her."

"Who is Seraphina?"

"She is the one I have been undergoing my trials with." Eliza and Zelus both nodded their heads knowing full well that even if Alec wanted to say more that he probably could not. Snapping back to the task at hand Eliza asked.

"Alright Alec, so what are we supposed to do now?"

"Just take and splash water at me. I will attempt to block it with my ward."

"You mean the invisible energy bubble that you can see, Zelus can feel and I'm not sure exists?"

"That is the one."

"Ok then." Eliza spoke as she kicked a jet of water up at Alec who placed his ward in front of it. Eliza was so startled as the water stopped in midflight that she stepped backward, tripping on her own feet and then fell with a splash. Alec spun his ward up high and deflected the water that rained over him.

"Alec, that is AWESOME!!!" Eliza cried as she sat in the water still ecstatic.

"Here, Eliza, come here." Eliza stood and walked to Alec.

"Marec showed me this." Alec spoke as he ran the shield across Eliza's clothes, instantly drying them. Again, Eliza exclaimed as she began to turn around examining herself. Zelus looked at Alec.

"What else have you learned to do?" Alec thought for a moment. He knew they had both already seen the mending runes effect and he knew that regeneration would not work just yet.

"Well, I am learning the projectile ward. Would you like to help me practice that one?" Zelus and Eliza nodded their heads. Alec prepared himself and cast the rune.

"I am ready."

"What do we do?"

"Throw rocks at me." The two members of the audience stared for a minute before shrugging to one another and both picked up a small cluster of rocks. Initially, they took turns throwing their pebbles one after another and, as Alec's shield continued to repel them, the spray of pebbles grew more rapid until their supply was depleted. After the flying rocks desisted, Alec released his hold over his ward and looked at his friends.

"Alec, you are going to actually become a paladin." Eliza was so proud of Alec.

"That is the plan. I swore a blood oath to Aneira, should she deem me worthy, to become a paladin." Zelus raised an eyebrow to Alec.

"And, what exactly was this oath?" Alec cleared his throat as if preparing for a long-winded speech.

"I vowed to protect the innocent, to hold up the weak and be an icon to the strong so that they stray from the dark." Eliza and Zelus stared at Alec, looked to one another and then began to crack up.

"You should listen to yourself." Zelus puffed out his chest and began mocking Alec. "Be an icon to the strong." They continued to laugh at Alec who just stared at them. "Who exactly is it that you plan on protecting." Alec turned away from them for a moment and saw Talia at the top of the hill, talking to a priest. Turning back towards his friends, Alec stared beyond them, his own thoughts, clouding his mind. Their tone instantly changed, as they sensed the pained nature behind his gaze.

Eliza and Zelus both averted their gaze away from Alec, wishing that there was some way they could tell him the truth. Zelus and Eliza looked pass Alec to Talia who waved at them and smiled. Alec turned again and she quickly turned away for a moment and then peeked back. She fussed with her hands for a moment and then slowly approached them.

"Marec says that he has one more lesson for each of you before we leave town. He says that Sir Alec is to learn one of the most useful tools a paladin can have." She smiled and nodded then froze as soon as her eyes met Alec's. "I would also like to see how you perform. It would be an honor to see the rise of a new paladin. It has been quite some time. Marec was the last Valascaan to be granted the title." Alec smiled at Talia and reaching out placed his hands on her shoulders. Talia smiled and touched the hand that rested on her left shoulder. She tilted her head to the side and embraced it lovingly.

"Sir Alec, I am sorry but I thought…" She stopped as Alec placed a finger over her lips. She shivered from the touch.

"Talia, I do not understand why you want to keep me out but I just want you to know that I know you and I are connected. I have dreamt about you for over a year now. I know that I am meant to be by your side even if you can never feel for me the way I feel for you. If you need me to remain with you as only your protector then I can live with that. I will not lie to you or myself about my feelings however, Talia Degracia I am hopelessly, irrevocably in love with you and I swear to Aneira that I shall protect you."

He leaned down and gently kissed her on the cheek. Her face was pressed up against his chest. She could smell his scent. How she wished she could bask in it forever. Talia tilted her head to the side longing for the touch of his lips on hers but she resisted. Alec removed his lips from her cheek and pressed past her. He took in a deep breath as he scaled the hill. He felt better somehow, more focused.

Back on the hill, Zelus and Eliza watched as Talia began to quiver, the warmth of Alec's embrace having left her. Talia looked up at them and began to cry. Zelus and Eliza approached Talia and comforted her as Alec turned around.

"Hey, are you coming?" Eliza and Zelus hollered a boisterous "Yes!" back to him as they turned back toward Talia who nodded for them to leave. The duo left the priestess on the hill to battle their friend. As they disappeared from eyesight, Talia turned back to make sure she was alone and then collapsed to the ground, sobbing, her heart thoroughly broken.

Alec reached the top of the hill to see his instructor sitting on a chair waiting for them. Marec rose from his chair to greet them as they arrived.
"Ah, you are here, excellent. Our time together is running short, but it seems as though I have one last lesson for each of you." The trio approached and Marec handed to each of them a rolled scroll. As they began to unroll, Marec shot up his hand stopping them. "My gift to each of you is for the recipient alone. Eliza, Zelus would you please excuse Alec and I for a moment, my gift to him must be delivered personally." Zelus and Eliza nodded as they smiled and ran off in separate directions, eager to unroll their scrolls.

Marec waited for them to be out of sight before addressing Alec again.

"Alec, please unroll your scroll." Alec did as he was told, finding the scroll to be completely blank, with the exception of a small rune, the shape of his thumb.

"Master, what is this?" Alec pressed his thumb into the rune, activating it. Alec watched as ink and letters bled across the parchment forming written instructions. Alec read the newly formed words running across the top of the roll revealing the title.

"Rune Inscription: Inscribing Casting & Sustainable Runes"

Alec began to read the scroll as Marec waited patiently.

"Rune Inscription varies from normal rune casting in the sense that the rune need not be drawn whenever needed. The purpose of rune inscription is to take a piece of equipment or gemstone and in essence "pre-cast" the desired rune before it is needed. The paladin who inscribes runes on their equipment will be able to access a runes power by simply holding the object the rune is engraved upon and think of the spell they wish to cast.

Recommended inscriptions would be placing wards on a shield, healing runes upon a gemstone or even something as advanced as adding an effect to a weapon. Even with the case of this document inscription is used to seal away the secrets within until the rune is activated by a paladin or paladin initiate. With inscription, the possibilities are nearly endless.

Materials required in order to inscribe runes – First one must obtain a focus crystal, a gemstone or a suitable piece of equipment and knowledge of the desired rune.

How to inscribe runes – Hold the focus crystal firmly in hand and begin to trace out the desired rune. As you are writing the rune begin to focus a steady stream of your energy into the crystal, causing for the rune to be engraved upon your desired object.

How to use inscribed runes – Simply hold or touch the inscribed object and focus upon the desired rune as if you intended to cast the rune normally. The inscribed rune shall answer the paladins call and be cast as if the paladin had indeed drawn the rune. Sustainable runes shall remain in effect until dispelled as normal. Casting runes shall perform their function and await the paladins next cast.

Warning on inscribed runes – As is the case in normal rune casting, a certain amount of the paladin's energy shall be expended every time a rune is cast. This law applies even when casting inscribed runes. In the case of sustainable runes, the rune shall continue to absorb the caster's energy until either the rune is dispelled or until the paladin's energy is entirely expended. Use your runes wisely and they will carry you through the darkest of times."

Alec reached the bottom of the scroll and saw another circular rune at the bottom of the text. He pressed his thumb against the rune and just as it had appeared, the text began to bleed back towards the top of the page slowly erasing the words as it went on. Alec rolled the scroll and looked up to Marec with a smile on his face.

"When do I begin?" Alec asked. Marec reached backward and from his satchel pulled a large, clear, glassy stone. "What would you like to inscribe first?" Alec reached out gently for the crystal, which Marec relinquished. Alec reached to his back, removing his shield and held it out in front of him.

"Have a seat, Alec. Lay your shield on the table so that you have a steady surface to work from." Alec did as he was told and began to think to himself.

"What was the single most important rune for him to place on his shield?" He continued to think to himself for a moment and then decided on his first rune.

"Before you begin, I would caution you that the more runes you place on a shield the less effective the shield will be at amplifying your individual runes."

"Can I place more than one rune on an object?"

"Yes, though the object's ability to amplify a rune is limited to the percentage of mass the rune is allowed to occupy. For instance, if you were to place a single rune on your shield then that shield shall amplify that single rune with one hundred percent effectiveness. When more than one primary rune is chosen the amplification potential is divided between the number of primary runes.

In the case of secondary runes, however normally the capacity of a shield is limited to three. I can tell you that, normally, the recommended placement of runes on a shield consists of three defensive runes or two defensive and a healing rune, while most prefer an advanced ward as their primary. This will allow the shield to amplify the effect of the rune to protect more than one person without additional strain upon the paladin. Do you understand everything as I have explained it?" Alec nodded his head and looked back to his shield in order to determine his first rune.

Alec thought again to himself, considering the new information, and making his decision, began to inscribe his first primary rune. First, he drew the diamond shape that would serve as the runes body. Then, placing his left hand on the shield, began to trace it. Once his rune of force was completed, he picked up his shield and looked it over carefully. Holding it up for Marec to see, his teacher approved.

"Next, you must select up to three secondary runes. Choose wisely." Alec returned to his pondering as he determined his three runes. Carefully tracing each one out, Alec decided upon the projectile ward, the healing rune, and regeneration. His shield completed, Alec turned to Marec and showed him the finished project. Marec looked it over carefully and gave it back to Alec with his approval.

"Not my personal choice, but your shield shall serve you well. Are you ready to go and test your inscriptions?"

Without further warning, Alec jumped from his seat, and slinging his shield on his back, took off towards the training ground. Once Alec reached the training ground, he paced back and forth eagerly awaiting Eliza and Zelus' arrival. Alec noticed Marec rising over the top of the hill, followed closely by Zelus, Eliza, Tear, Talia and Oz.

"Oz! You are back!" Alec exclaimed as he ran to the griffet, which eagerly received his love and affection. "You were gone an awfully long time." Alec spoke as he stroked the lion hawk's mane. Oz purred for him as he brushed his large body across Alec's torso. The griffin now sat at the size of a pony.

"Alec, are you ready for your final test before you undertake the last trial?" Alec nodded his head. He patted Oz again as the lion hawk trotted off to stand by Tear and Talia.

"I am ready, master." Marec turned to Zelus and Eliza.

"The both of you shall fight Alec together. I wish to see how Alec fares against more than one opponent who fights with differing styles." Eliza pulled two dulled curved swords from the weapon rack. Zelus drew his regular long sword. Alec also approached the weapon rack and grabbed a dulled long sword.

Alec walked into the center of the circle, and raising his shield, prepared himself. Eliza and Zelus both faced him, dividing and readying for the attack. Eliza had her bow on her back. Alec could only imagine she had a quiver full of hammer arrows at the ready.

Alec smiled as he focused himself and carefully watched Eliza and Zelus. Eliza had not yet drawn her bow, so Alec instead focused on his force rune. He waited for Eliza to take up the first strike.

"Hyaah!" She cried as she lunged at him. Alec ducked to the side as he stuck out his shield, allowing Eliza to slam into it with both swords. Eliza flew backward as both of her blades rocketed from her hands, nearly impaling Zelus who blocked them with his shield. Eliza turned her head to Alec with a shocked expression on her face.

"What was that?" Alec smiled as his knees buckled slightly. He had underestimated the amount of energy the rune would take. Her swords had struck at different times causing his shield to fire two charges.

"Now it is my turn." Zelus yelled as he ran forward. Alec retracted some of his energy before he allowed Zelus to strike his shield. Zelus stumbled backward after the force rune struck him. Alec pressed forward and lashed out at Zelus but resisted as an arrow shot close to his head, which he narrowly avoided. Alec looked up to see Eliza smiling at him from behind her bow. Alec quickly focused on the projectile ward and watched as the energy expanded in front of him nearly twice its normal size. Eliza shot again and Alec moved his ward in front of it, deflecting the shot.

"Eliza, the ward only covers him from the front. Get behind him and this is over." Zelus yelled. Alec found his ability to sense the displacement around Alec's ward most impressive. Alec blocked another of Zelus' attacks knocking him backwards. Alec felt the drain on his body from using both wards and so he dispelled force as he continued to defend himself from both fighters.

"His shield has become disenchanted, grab your swords." Eliza grabbed both of her swords and rushed at Alec. Marec turned his head to the side, intrigued by the interesting test for his student. Zelus and Eliza lashed out at Alec and so he dispelled his other enchantment, relying on his physical strength and skill to save himself. He began to block blow upon blow, as the duo assaulted him. Alec would capture the weapons of one but be forced to release them to defend himself from the other.

"There is no way you are ever going to beat both of us." Zelus taunted as he continued to wail on Alec. They had been fighting for almost an hour at this point and they all knew that the three of them were tiring. Alec smiled as he captured all three swords and propelled them backward. Quickly, Alec focused on the force rune on his shield and launched a massive blast, then charged at his opponents as they were stumbling backwards.

The first blow landed with a pat on Zelus' ribs, declaring that he was dead. As Alec charged for Eliza, she pulled her bow, while still flying backwards through the air. Eliza fired an arrow. Alec attempted to summon his ward. Eliza's arrow banked to the side striking Alec in his shoulder as he patted her. As the battle ended, Alec could hear the sounds of Marec clapping.

"Great job Zelus. Excellent work, Eliza. I am most pleased with how you two performed." He applauded their efforts as they walked from the battlefield.

"We lost uncle, there is no need for applause."

"Ah, but on the contrary, you have faced a paladin, I was expecting Alec to prevail."

"Then why did you have us fight him?"

"I needed to test Alec's limits. He is soon to be put to an impossible task and he will need all the strength and courage you two have to offer." Eliza and Zelus felt slightly better about their situation yet, as they looked back to Alec, he seemed unhappy about his victory.

"Do you know where you went wrong Alec?" Alec had already returned his sword to the rack and was now standing facing down at the ground.

"I misjudged my power. I used too much of my spirit energy and was unable to defend against Eliza's final blow. On the battlefield such a mistake could be the end of me."

"And the end of any whom you were sworn to protect. Such a mistake is unacceptable for a paladin. You must learn to control the release of your energy without incident. Become the master of your mind, body and spirit!" Alec continued looking down at his feet. Talia rose from her seated position.

"He was still quite remarkable, was he not?" Talia ran up to Alec then stopped suddenly as if backing away from a hungry lion. Alec looked her in the eye and smiled, yet still he felt ashamed of his battle performance. Marec looked at Alec.

"You must press yourself harder. You will begin training your physical body to the point of exhaustion every morning. You will then use your regeneration technique and train throughout the day. You must push yourself beyond mortal limits. Most paladins must train their entire lives and some die in the process, yet you have the power to perform such a feat without risking your life."

"I will try…" Marec began to yell at Alec, whose words seemed to strike a deep-rooted nerve within him.

"You will have to do better than try. Trying is for those who plan to fail. Should you do any less than succeed then you are not worthy of the title of paladin. Raise your sword, Alec. You and I shall fight with our weapons." Alec was stunned, yet knew that his teacher was serious. "Draw your weapon, Alec. This is your final test." Marec pulled his claymore and his tower shield from their resting place behind him.

"Sir Marec, I must protest. This exercise is highly unnecessary. Sir Alec has already exhausted his spirit energy in the last fight." Talia called out to Marec in an attempt to stop him.

"Priestess, please, this is necessary for me to complete my paladin training. This test was inevitable." Alec spoke to her as he untied the Sidonis sword from his belt and handed it to her. "Please hold this for me. I fight to prove to you that I am worthy to remain by your side." He walked away from her as he drew his longsword and brought out his shield. Alec raised his weapons and prepared to battle.

Marec and Alec faced one another preparing for their fight. Alec knew that Marec was not about to take things easy on him. Marec took up the first offense, Alec knew that he lacked the energy to summon another force impact and so he decided that he must resort to relying upon his physical abilities until he could have the chance to recover some of his spent energy.

Marec struck out at Alec, chasing up to him and slamming his claymore down. Alec had enough time to see that Marec's sword bore the force enchantment and so he placed his shield between them as he pressed off the ground with his legs, propelling himself backwards. The sword struck the ground like a hammer, causing a massive shock wave to emanate outward in an explosion of energy. Alec flew across the arena but managed to land on his feet. He continued to slide backward for several feet, until his heel connected with the walkway and he was able to force himself to a stop.

Marec came at him again this time slicing horizontally through the air. Alec rolled under the blade, which barely missed him as he did so. Marec adjusted his grip in mid swing and stabbed the blade into the ground. Alec was propelled in circular motion by the blast. He hit the ground several feet away, which stopped his spin. He began to rise to his feet but already could feel his strength draining. Alec activated his regeneration and felt his physical strength returning.

"You should have spent more time practicing. Your energy is too easily depleted. You must never allow that mistake again. You must push your body to its limits as often as possible. Do this and your body shall become stronger and that will push lengths beyond what once would have killed you. We paladins have done this for centuries. We are the masters of the art of transcending death."

Marec charged again as Alec began to think of his options. He could see that Marec was coming at him again with his force rune intact. Alec began to think very carefully about his next move. An idea struck him as he dodged around Marec's next assault. He could feel his limbs growing steadier as his regeneration rune continued to perform magnificently. His arms felt stronger. He vaulted himself forward and ran ahead a few steps.

Alec knelt to the ground and began to draw out his force rune. Marec turned and renewed his charge. Alec reached into his boot and pulled out his knife, concealing it behind his back.

"Master, is this fight for real?"

"I want you to fight me with EVERYTHING YOU HAVE!" Marec yelled. Alec closed his eyes as he prepared to make his move. He managed to store a small amount of energy since his battle with Eliza and Zelus and now he focused himself to use it.

"I understand master, please forgive me." Marec lifted his sword high into the air in preparation to bring it down like a hammer. Alec flicked his arm and wrist, sending the knife straight through the rune.

The knife shot at Marec with blinding speed. He barely had time to react, quickly summoning his projectile shield. Marec's entire momentum was reversed as he stumbled backwards from the force of the two runes.

"HYAAAAAH!" Alec cried as he lunged forward and bashed Marec with his shield being sure to use the fully amplified power of his force rune. He could feel the first strike, completely destroying Marec's defensive runes. He struck again, knocking Marec's shield from his arm, breaking both his arm and his hand. Marec groaned in agony as he attempted to slash horizontally, his only option at close range with such a weapon.

Alec swung his sword skyward, focusing the power of his force rune through it. Marec's sword shot out of his hand and into the air along with his body as his other arm was dislocated. He landed several feet away and lay on the ground. Alec approached Marec and gently placed his blade to his master's throat. Marec smiled at Alec with great pride in his eyes.

"Well done Alec, you are now worthy of the title of paladin." Alec pulled his sword away, the duel now over. Marec, without using his arms or hands, sat upright, the weight of his armor straining him. Everyone including Oz and Tear rushed into the center to either congratulate Alec or tend to Marec.

"You performed most admirable, Sir Alec. I should expect the day you are granted your seal shall be a day of grand honor for you." Alec smiled at Talia who blushed under the gravity of his gaze. Alec collapsed to his knees as Eliza ran to Marec's side.

"Uncle, are you alright?" Eliza had ran to Marec to check on his wounds.

"I shall be fine Eliza. Miss Talia, would you mind aiding me? I am afraid that I cannot draw a rune in this state." Talia snapped back to the world of reality and bowed her head as she ran to her defender's side.

"Of course Sir Marec, please forgive me." Talia kneeled down next to him as she began to chant and though Marec's facial muscles made no sign of discomfort. Alec could hear the bones realigning and popping back into place as they were rapidly mended. Alec rose and walked to his master's side, too exhausted for much else, and allowed himself to drop to his knees beside him.

I am sorry master, are you alright?" Marec placed his newly healed hand on Alec's shoulder.

"Be not ashamed Alec. I told you to come at me with everything you had and you performed admirably. I am very proud to call you my student." Alec smiled as he fell onto his face completely drained of all of his energy.

"Come on Alec, on your feet...paladin." Talia smiled as she helped Alec rise to his feet. Alec stood and tried to stabilize himself. Talia leaned into him helping to support his weight.

"Bree!" Oz chirped at Alec as he bounced alongside of them and aided Alec on his opposite side. Eliza and Zelus helped Marec to his feet and he tested out his newly healed limbs as he began to follow Alec, Talia and Oz toward the stables. As Alec and Talia walked, Alec glimpsed down at Talia's waist and saw the Sidonis sword strapped around her.

"Looks good on you." Alec motioned towards the sword and Talia looked down at it and smiled.

"Why, thank you Sir Alec, Paladin of Valascaana. I shall take your compliment with highest honors." She returned Alec's smile and he felt as if things between the two of them were better than they had been for some time.

"I would like to think of myself as a paladin of Highmooria, though I am glad to see you acting yourself again priestess. I was afraid that you were going to leave me forever." Alec did not see but Talia quivered slightly as he spoke. Talia nodded her head and made her correction.

"Sir Alec, Paladin of Highmooria, I wish for you to have this." Alec turned to look at her as she pulled her necklace from around her neck. Alec placed his hands over hers and looked into her eyes.

"Talia I cannot accept this. This means so much to you." Talia nodded her head and stated her feelings quite factually.

"It does. It was my mother's. She died when I was young. I loved her very much. Alec, please, I want for you to have this." Alec could not refuse such a meaningful gift. He took the necklace from her and placed it around his own neck.

"I will treasure it always." Talia smiled to him and kissed him on the cheek. They spoke very little the rest of their trip as Talia continued to guide him until they reached the stables. Marec and the others arrived just behind them, Tear pulling up the rear.

"Alright everyone, we must now return to Valascaa. Lady Talia and I have one last task we must complete before we return to the Grand Shrine, and Alec has one last meeting with the Lady Seraphina." Everyone shouted as they mounted their horses and together began the journey home.

Chapter 32 – The Proof of Their Bond

"Sir Alec," Marec began, the first time he had addressed Alec in such a way. Alec turned his head towards his master.

"Yes master," he responded.

"I want for you to dismount your horse and see if Sir Oz will allow you to ride him." Alec stared over at the Lion Hawk, who turned his head sideways. As they stared at one another, everyone else eyed them from behind. Alec did as he was told and dismounting his horse, handed the reins to Eliza.

Alec walked over toward Oz as the Lion Hawk continued to stare at him. As Alec reached out his hand, Oz placed his hand beneath his outstretched hand and began rubbing himself on it. Alec walked to Oz's side and attempted to climb up onto his back.

"*BREE!*" Oz reeled as he tipped up into the air, knocking Alec down before beginning to prance around him. Everyone, Marec and Talia included, began laughing at Alec as began picking himself up off from the ground. Oz's bouncing only intensified as the young griffin began to joyously pounce.

"Oz!" Alec began as he wiped the dirt off from his shirt and spat out the last of the grass that had gotten into his mouth. Oz stopped momentarily and stared at Alec as he eyed him sternly. "Oz, may I please ride on your back?" Alec asked as Oz again turned his head sideways to stare at him.

Alec cautiously walked up to him and pet his head. As Oz calmed down and lowered his head, Alec approached his side. Carefully Alec proceeded to mount the Lion Hawk once more. First he swung over his right leg, without incident and carefully lowered his weight, resting it onto Oz's back.

"BREE!" Oz exclaimed as he began bucking, flailing and lurching about in an attempt to throw Alec off. Alec gripped Oz's mane tightly while trying to maintain his position. The laughter only increased as Oz began spinning in circles, Alec, whipping helplessly about the whole time.

"Communicate to Oz through your link. Ease him. Assure him why is it that you wish to ride on him." Marec began instructing as Alec tried to focus on his words. Alec could feel Oz on the other side of their empathy link and reached out to him.

"Oz, please. I wish to ride on your back is all. I am not going to hurt you." Oz continued to lash about, Alec sensing Oz's stubbornness and agitation as if Alec were trying to tie him down. "Oz I do not wish to subdue you. I only wish for us to be able to be paladin and Lion Hawk. Able to work as one to fend off the Forsaken." Oz calmed slightly though Alec could immediately tell that he was unconvinced.

"Oz if you please let me down, I would gladly speak with you on the matter." Oz slowed his lurching and came to a halt, allowing Alec to swing his leg back over. As he landed on the ground, he turned to face Oz as everyone stared at his back. Oz stared into Alec's eyes, beak to nose as Alec placed his hands on either side of the Lion hawk's face.

"You are my friend, Oz," Alec began, speaking through their empathy link. "I do not wish for you to submit to me, nor do I wish to break your spirit. I desire, that as your friend, that we be able to rely upon one another in all situations." Oz gently pressed his forehead against Alec's as Alec continued to pet him.

"What do you say, my friend? Might you lend me your aid?" Oz gently bonked Alec in the forehead once more before turning his body and bowing. Alec walked over to Oz's side as the Lion Hawk lifted his wing out of the way. Alec gently lifted his leg over to the other side of Oz's back and slowly lowered his weight onto his back. Oz fidgeted slightly under Alec's weight, while Alec could sense his nervousness. Alec pet Oz's mane and Oz turned his head back to face Alec and began to purr.

"Excellent work, Sir Alec. Fine job indeed." Marec spoke as Eliza, Zelus, Tear and Talia all dismounted. As they walked up to Alec, they looked up at the two of them.

"Alright, Alec! You two are official now!" Eliza commented as Zelus approached.

"*SCREE!*" Oz screeched as Zelus grew near, whipping himself about and knocking him over.

"Stupid bird," Zelus muttered as he crawled away and climbed back onto his horse. Talia and Tear began to laugh as Oz glared evilly at Zelus.

"Cannot say as though I see him warming up to you any time soon," Eliza spoke in between snorts. Talia looked up at Alec and smiled.

"I...," she began though she lost the words. "I..." Talia tried several times to tell Alec how she felt but unable to find the words, smiled at the two of them before returning to her own horse.

"Well done," Marec spoke. "You are sure to become a fine paladin, worthy of recognition." Alec smiled at the compliment and followed the rest of the troop east after they mounted their horses.

"Sir Alec, I would have you ride Oz the rest of the way back so that you might be better synchronized once you are ready to continue your studies." Alec stroked the back of Oz's head as he rode beside the others. Alec made sure to remain in tune with Oz's emotions and conversed with him through their empathy link. Oz was still slightly unsure of the situation, however, he no longer attempted to throw

Alec.

Alec and Oz rode together for several paces, feeding off from their empathy link. Alec gently steered Oz by tugging on his mane in the direction that he wanted to go. As he did so, he could sense Oz's reluctance to being led about in such a way but followed Alec, all the same.

"You should use your link. Guide him as Paladin and Lion Hawk, not as master and beast." Marec suggested and Alec, letting loose his hold on Oz's mane, began speaking to the griffin.

"Oz?" Alec began, utilizing their connection to speak to his friend. He felt Oz, honing in on his thoughts as Alec continued. "Oz, can you veer to the right, please?" Oz did as asked but began to move away from the group. Alec quickly thought hard, to ask Oz to readjust their course but over corrected and steered them directly into Eliza's horse. Eliza's horse whinnied as it reared slightly.

"Sorry Eliza." Alec spoke as he attempted to straighten Oz's course, again steering him with his hands. As they steered true, Alec released Oz's mane and again attempted to communicate with him through their link. Marec, his eyes still on them, watched for a brief moment as Alec began to veer to and fro.

"There is no need to overthink every detail, Alec. Communicate with Oz as if you were willing your own legs to move. Oz is attuned to your thoughts, just as you are to his. If the two of you can synchronize your thoughts, you will be able to react more effectively. Oz's naturally heightened senses will be yours to command just as Oz will possess your skills. Paladin and lion hawk, two bodies, two souls, but one shared mind. It is this connection that allowed the paladins of old to conquer Daemon's forces."

Alec sat silently as he and Oz followed alongside the others. He thought to himself of what Marec was saying. Looking down at Oz, the Lion Hawk turned his head towards Alec and he could feel Oz's elation.

"I will not disappoint you, Sir Marec. I will make you proud." Everyone smiled as Marec's gaze locked onto the two empathy partners.

"I believe that you will. One day, when we return to Highmoore, you shall sit proudly, overlooking the world you helped create. It will be on that day, which your real work shall begin."

As the day progressed, Alec continued to silently communicate with Oz as they traveled west. Alec, through thought alone, began to lead Oz, having him run away from the road and back towards it. Upon Marec's commands, they ran in circles and weaving in between the others.

Alec found that the more that he communicated with Oz, in this fashion, the more he enjoyed the experience. Again, he could also feel Oz's level of excitement increase, while they rode. Oz let out several loud, trumpeting cries of excitement. Talia and the others, each began to laugh as Oz's animated screeches pelted the countryside.

Later that night, they made camp just off from the road. They had built a small campfire, which Zelus, Eliza, Tear and Talia, sat near. Oz had gone off on another of his hunting trips, while Marec and Alec stood at the edge of the hill. Alec stood, Marec's weapon drawn, slowly walking through offensive and defensive postures. Alec's muscles, within mere minutes, already screamed with discontent as Marec continued to call out forms.

From their position on the hill, Alec watched as the sun set just ahead of them, its magnificence, so ominent, Alec was nearly tempted to reach out to it. Alec began to recite the paladin's pledge, as Marec had taught it to him, while he maintained his stances. After a moment, Marec gave Alec a brief rest as he turned his gaze towards the setting sun.

"Enjoy this moment, Sir Alec. Each of us may only enjoy a handful before our time has come to return to mother's embrace. Do not waste a single one." Alec sat on the ground, staring at the sunset as his rune of regeneration began recuperating his body. He sat for several minutes and listened as Talia, began to sing her lullaby. Alec closed his eyes briefly, as the priestesses' melodious voice, filled him with peace.

"Alec," Marec began, "Once we have returned to the capital and you have completed your final trial." Marec paused for a moment as if searching for the words. "I was wondering what you intend on doing?" Alec considered the question before answering.

"I had not placed much thought on the matter, other than remaining one of Talia's guardians."

"Once Talia has returned to the Grand Shrine, she will no longer need be accompanied by you or myself. Even I have been pondering on what I might do next." Alec dwelled on the matter further. He knew that he would want to visit Talia as often as possible, though he needed to consider what else remained to be done.

"I suppose that I will travel abroad. Move from town to town, uniting those who might become paladins themselves, one day. Naturally, I would begin in the capitol but slowly work my way out. One thing that I have learned in my travels with you, Talia and the others; is that no matter the strife, it is up to us, to safeguard the fire of hope, for the next generation. I have gained wisdom, from you teachings, and it will be with this wisdom, that I shall uplift all peoples. I cannot leave all of the work to Talia. I will give it my all, to ensure that all of her desires can be birthed into the new world, she is working towards."

"A fine answer, to be true. I look forward to seeing what you make of yourself." Marec spoke.

"What of you, Sir Marec? If Talia no longer needs your protection, what shall you do?" Marec thought for a moment.

"I cannot yet say. I have been milady's guardian so long, I am not sure what I will do, once I am no longer needed."

"You do not have to say it, in such a way." Alec started. "I plan on visiting Talia regularly and writing when I cannot. I promised her that I would take away her sadness. I will start by never again allowing her to feel alone." Marec smiled at Alec's words.

"I am sure that milady will enjoy that. Do not become so entangled, that you fail to live your own life, however." Alec silently nodded his head as he stood, grabbing the claymore as he did so.

"This time, Alec. I wish for you to practice your wards, while moving through your stances. I will call out a ward and you shall use your free hand to cast, while flowing through your forms." Alec nodded his head and began as Marec called out a series of wards to him, one, briefly after the other. After running the circuit, several times, Alec had a thought.

"Sir Marec? How long have you been Talia's guardian?"

"Thirteen years, seven months and twenty three days." Marec responded, without a moment's hesitation. "Nearly her entire life, have I been by her side. Ever since her parents were killed." Marec again paused briefly before speaking again. "Alec, soon, you shall be free to travel the world, as a paladin of Aneira. One day, when our order is reunited, shall we march into the lands of our enemy. Until then, however, you are free to spread goodwill and peace, as you see fit. I only ask, that in doing so, that you, without exception, put your entire being into everything that you do. We never know how long we have, in this world and it is imperative, that you live life to its fullest, so that you might die empty."

"Do you mean without regrets?" Alec asked to which, Marec nodded.

"At the least, yes."

"Do you have any regrets, Sir Marec?"

"Aye. More than one," Marec responded as the sun sank below the horizon.

"Might I ask what they are?" Marec paused, for the longest length yet and Alec believed that he was about to learn much more about the solitary paladin.

"The hour is growing late. We must rest, so that we might travel swiftly tomorrow. I would ask that you ride atop Oz again." Marec spoke gruffly as he walked back towards the fire. Alec stood, confused and after a moment, shrugged his shoulders and walked down the hill. There he set his things beside his traveling pack and placed the claymore near Marec's pack.

Everyone gathered, they sat and enjoyed a silent meal together as they each contemplated how their lives might look, once they returned to the capital.

The following morning, Alec awoke before the others. As he exited his tent, Oz trotted up to him and brushed his head against Alec's chest. Alec latched onto the griffin and hugged him gently.

"Do you want to practice some more?" He asked psychically. Oz without hesitation, slammed into Alec, scooping him up onto his back. Alec carefully grabbed onto his friends and righted himself before they rode a short distance from the camp. After reaching a safe distance, Oz began to run excitedly, flapping his wings joyously as he and Alec both shared in laughter.

As they did so, Oz's flapping caused for the griffin's legs to lift off from the ground slightly. Alec instinctively clung onto Oz's back as he felt the hovering rise. As Oz slowly settled back to the ground, Alec perked up and smiled.

"Do you think that we can? We are not carrying any additional weight?" Alec could feel Oz's competitive side kicking in. The griffin's entire body flexed as he sprang into action, flapping his wings, while dashing across the grassy plains. Slowly, they began to achieve lift. Oz flapped frantically, attempting to gain altitude but gradually sank back to the ground.

That was a great try Oz!" Alec began. "Do you wish to keep trying?" Oz did not waste time answering as he tried again to gain altitude. After a couple of hours had passed, Talia, Marec, Zelus, Tear and Eliza stirred and left their tents as the morning sun began to break free of the horizon.

"Sir Zelus, can you please alert Alec, that we shall soon depart?" Zelus nodded his head and walked toward Alec's tent as the others began gathering up their belongings.

"Hey Alec, it is time to wake up," Zelus spoke as he rattled the flap of the tent. "Alec? Are you awake?" Zelus carefully pulled back the flap and looked inside. "Sir Marec, Alec is gone!" Marec and the others, all turned their heads in wonder as they looked around the campsite.

"Uncle Marec, Oz is missing as well." Talia turned her gaze to Zelus and Eliza.

"Did the two of you…?"

"No priestess, we did not say anything. We promise." Zelus and Eliza confirmed and she turned away and walked towards the hill slope, where Tear was standing.

"What is it, Tear? Do you see them?" Talia asked as the small child pointed up into the sky.

"They are right there." She spoke calmly as she pointed towards the sun. Talia stared in the direction of Tear's outstretched hand and searched the hillside. She squinted her eyes, in an attempt to block out more of the sunlight but could not see.

"I cannot see them, Tear. Which hill are they upon?" Tear looked at Talia and standing in front of her, turned her head upward.

"Not on the hill, there. On the sun." Talia focused more on the rising sun as a black form darted across its surface. Eliza and the others slowly walked towards the two divine just as the spot on the sun began to grow.

"What is that?" Zelus asked, his hands over his eyes. Marec however smiled.

"They have learned to think as one." He commented as Oz and Alec, soared overhead, screaming their fool heads off, merrily. Everyone smiled as they witnessed the first flight of paladin and lion hawk.

After a moment, Oz and Alec landed. Alec carefully dismounted the lion hawk and pet his friend's mane. Everyone approached them, at their own, individual speeds, Talia, taking up the rear. Eliza, Zelus and Tear, at the front and Marec just beyond them. Zelus kept his distance from Oz, as Eliza and Tear both ra up on Oz and began petting him.

"That was amazing, you two!" Eliza began. Tear wrapped her arms around Oz's neck and hugged his head as the griffin lifted her up and placed her on his back.

"I want to ride too!" Tear exclaimed as laid flat against Oz's back and held on firmly.

"Sir Alec…" Marec spoke slowly with an aggressive tone. "Of all of the irresponsible things that you could have pulled. You are not even a fully proficient rider, possess no proper saddle, have received no instruction on flying and you in all of your infinite wisdom, decided that it would be a swell idea to try." Alec eyed his teacher, in shock.

"I am sorry, Sir Marec. I did not think too hard about it before we tried."

"Had you fallen from Oz's back, you would have surely died and all of our work would have been for naught!" Again Marec continued with his aggressive tone and the others, save Talia began to cower.

"I am sorry, Sir. I will think it over more carefully, next time."

"I most certainly hope not," Marec spoke, causing everyone's eyes to quickly look up and see his broad smile. "Relying on instinct, instead of overthinking is the reason that you succeeded. Excellent work, Sir Alec. Excellent work, indeed." He laughed as he patted Alec on the back. Everyone else joined in on the laughter before they prepared their things and set off on the road.

Chapter 33 – On the Road Home

They rode at a steady pace for two days, nearing closer and closer to Valascaa. Alec noticed that, once again, Talia had become prone to long periods of time in silent contemplation. He noticed that Eliza and Zelus also seemed extremely glum. The last two days, neither of them had barely spoken a single word to Alec. Alec could not have been more excited. However, soon he would be granted the title of paladin and his trials with Seraphina would reach completion.

Alec's heart could not have been lighter, save the pain he still felt at Talia's rejection. He continued to think to himself about what awaited him back in Valascaa and the adventures he would have once he was granted his paladin status. He looked back to Talia and felt bad for her. How he wished he could take away her sorrow. He continued to watch her, the way her hair blew in the wind, the way her skin shone in the sunlight, the glint in her eyes as she stared back at him. Alec snapped back to reality once he realized he had been caught.

They continued to ride at a steady pace. Alec began to search the landscape and noticed several things that seemed out of place. The land looked as if it had been scraped. There were large areas where the grass off to the side of the road had been trampled and lay dead. He looked from side to side, trees had been torn down, and fires had been set. He looked to Eliza and Zelus and they began to worry about the same things.

"What happened here?" The three of them turned to Marec.

"It looks like the enemy may be moving in force now." Alec's jaw dropped at the thought.

"You mean?"

"Yes, it appears that the Forsaken have returned to the lands of Valascaana. I had feared that it was only a matter of time before such an event occurred. The warning signs have grown ever present lately."

"What do you mean, master?"

"Ah, yes, about that Alec. You need not refer to me as master any longer. You are now a junior level paladin and shall be treated as my equal. I shall still be your instructor, but please from here on out call me Marec."

"Of course maste…I mean Sir Marec."

"Better, now in regards to your question. When Miss Talia and I first left the grand shrine, we encountered a small roving band of Forsaken the likes of which I had not seen for quite some time. Then, there was the attack on Roak, it seems as if history has begun to repeat."

"Uncle Marec, when exactly was it that you last saw a roving horde of Forsaken? And what do you mean that history is repeating itself?"

"The last time I saw this many Forsaken marching was many years ago. It was right before the attack on Highmoore." The group gasped audibly in unison.

"If the Forsaken are indeed on their way, we must return home quickly." Eliza stated.

"I would agree, though I fear that the council will meet us with some resistance." Alec said. Zelus, Marec and Eliza, all nodded their heads in agreement.

"Ever since I was boy looking out over the walls of Valascaa, the one thing the council has always been good at is ignoring the important issues facing their people." Marec spoke as Eliza rode up next to him.

"That is something uncle Marec. You have not told me much about you and my father growing up as kids." Marec looked around to everyone in the group who had all begun to move in closer.

"I suppose we do have time for a story. We will not arrive in Valascaa until tomorrow morning." Marec took a deep breath as he began to recall his early child with his two brothers.

There were three brothers, Marec the eldest, Talic and Talos the youngest of the three.

At this point in the story, Alec and Zelus were compelled to interrupt.

"Wait! Which one is Eliza's dad?" Marec and Eliza looked at them suspiciously.

'Why, Talic of course." Alec and Zelus looked to each other, the clouds departing light beaming from the sky as the ultimate question had finally been revealed. "Wow, Talic the lion, all this time we never knew." Eliza rolled her eyes at her friends and turned to her uncle.

"Uncle, please continue your story."

"Of course, Eliza."

The three brothers were born into a poor family. Their mother had died shortly after Talos was born. The trio of brothers was infamous even from a young age as notorious street urchins. It was well known that the blood of the beastmen flowed through their veins as their mother had once belonged to one of their tribes. The brother's actions, temperaments, and wild side paid much credit to their ancestry as they consistently found themselves within the middle of mischief. Over the years, their father had managed to gain a knight's commission and received honors after turning the tide in an important battle overseas. Yet, when the three arrived within the noble's quarters, they were not received warmly.

They were looked down upon by everyone as if they were nothing more than dirty street urchins. There was no place in Valascaa for ascended nobles or the sons of a "mongrel bride," as many of the noble's quarter often referred to their mother. The three, however, were inseparable in their youth and always looked out for one another. They had been involved in many scuffles, even after they moved to the noble's quarter. Talic, in particular, had developed quite a wild streak in his youth and had started many of their brawls. Yet the brothers, even after multiple imprisonments, always managed to pull through for one another.

The group contemplated what Marec told them. "The Lion was a ruffian back when he was a boy?" At least they understood where Eliza's wild streak came from, and Alec could not help but relate to being poor and on his own within the commoner's district. He had always been looked down upon. The group all listened in as Marec continued his story.

Most of the brawls they engaged in, involved some condescending noble lashing out with a fiery tongue, bringing with it insults and disdain towards their family. Talic had always had the worst temper, when it came to those who looked down upon us. In fact, I think that he took some great pleasure in "disciplining" those ignorant enough to think that the son of a beast master would lie idly by when his own were attacked. They lived this way for some time, though always made sure to be on their best behavior when their world weary father would come back to them and tell them stories of the outside world.

He sat with them one night and told them stories of his youth and how he had become an ambassador of Valascaana. He told them that it was his job to keep the peace within and outside of the country to ensure that his sons could have the luxuries of a peaceful, war free world that he was denied. They admired their father so very much and it was him that I tried to emulate once everything we knew came to an end.

Relations with the beastmen tribes to the north broke down after a time. Our father did his absolute best to keep negotiations open but wise words are oft wasted on closed ears. Tensions on both sides of the conflict added fuel to the fire. The Valascaans had their prejudice and their sense of superiority over the "savages" of the northern mountains, though the beastmen had their own beliefs of the Valascaans and their need to consume and destroy their environment. After a time, negotiations became impossible and instead of peace talks, several ambassadors, launched a surprise attack on the beastmen tribes.

When the trio learned that their father had died in battle, their relationship became completely redefined. Marec embraced religion along with Talic and together with their youngest brother joined the knight's college. The three working together formed their own squad along with two great friends, Raven and Kristiana.

Over the years serving together, Kristiana and Talic grew very close and everyone here knows the eventual result.

During their time serving as knights, a great deal happened. There was an attack on Valascaa by the beastmen tribes of the northern isles, relations between them and the council having deteriorated shortly following their father's death. The war was delayed for some time though everyone knew that it had been inevitable as the council had deemed it necessary to eliminate any "undesirables" that could not be contained or controlled. This is where Talic earned his status defending the walls while I was first approached by the paladin Zerendil, who noticed my talents during battle. However, it was during this campaign that we lost our brother Talos.

He died in battle defending the northern wall alongside Talic. It was this event that forever redefined our lives. Talic rose to the call and reclaimed the northern wall as I led the defense to the west, but it was the loss of our brother that eventually drove Talic and I apart. I have always loved my brother and will always be his man should he call, yet, when Talos died, I was unable to cope. After watching for my brothers for all of those years, I was unable to deal with the pain of losing one of them. I needed a way out, a way to repent for my failure as a brother and possibly the only father figure either of them had ever known.

I found Zerendil, once the battle was won, and enlisted with the paladins as an initiate without so much as consulting my brother. I believe that Talic felt betrayed and abandoned, because after everything that we had been through, I could not be by his side during this time. My training was difficult, and I pressed myself to the brink of death on a near daily basis. I was stationed in Highmoore and after my first year, I was initiated as a paladin, and after ending an impossible romance, returned home to Valascaa for my brother's wedding to Kristiana.

I returned home and found that things had grown drastically different from the way that I had left them. The council had taken over everything and the commoners were now deprived more so than ever. The noble's quarter was now enveloped within a massive wall segregating the people further. Poverty ran amuck. My brother, now referred to as the Lion, was a knight commander and his beautiful wife Kristiana was a well-respected council advisor after a successful career as an assassin.

I also learned, upon my arrival, that my dear friend Raven had been branded a traitor and was executed. I found my brother and our reunion was not one of happiness. It seems that it was Kristiana that had bid my return against her future husband's wishes. Your mother had tried for years during my absence to repair the rift that formed between my brother and I, yet she had proven unable to, Talic still harboring the pain of my abandonment. We did our best however and I attended their union and it was a beautiful service, filled to the brim with love and happiness.

Your mother, Eliza, radiated beauty. She looked magnificent and for a time it seemed as though everything had returned to the path it was always meant to follow. Though with the absence of Talos there was little we could say. I stayed near *a week and then it was time for me to return home to continue my training. It was not long after that I heard that your mother was with child yet it took me several years to return home to visit my newborn niece as I was usually out on assignment as a bodyguard to an important official.*

After a few years, I was able to visit and, though things with my brother were not as they once were, they were much better than they had been during my last visit. You were so small and resembled your mother so much. Already, I could see that you had your father's wild streak and your mother's fiery determination. I stayed with you for nearly a year until I was appointed to be the protector of Miss Talia as it had been recently discovered that she was a divine.

The next time I saw my brother was several years later during the fall of Highmoore. The attack came suddenly and from within, the true signs of a traitor. We should have seen it coming however. It had only been a matter of days since we had discovered a number of our lion hawk eggs missing.

The gates to the egg keep were made to look as though they had been broken into, yet it was obvious that the lock had not been broken from the hinge. When the attack came, I had just been reprimanded for a certain indiscretion and I was left alone within the keep, with the order of guarding Lady Angelica and Mistress Talia. The Forsaken, having the advantage of surprise, quickly overwhelmed the guards that had been stationed at the keep and High priestess Angelica charged me with the protection of Miss Talia and the rest of the Aneiran high order. I barricaded us in the uppermost levels fighting off the Forsaken for days. It was towards the end, when we had nearly run out of provisions that your father arrived with his band of knights. His men broke the Forsaken lines and drove them from the tower long enough for us to get out.

We managed to escape but, on our way out, we ran into the Daemon knight Belias. He attacked with a ferocity that had been unheard of before. I tried to fight him and his demon bear long enough for my charges to escape with a band of your father's knights. I was greatly outmatched however and was mercilessly defeated. My brother barely managed to drag me away before returning to the fight to repel the invasion. Unfortunately, our home was lost that night and so for a time, I returned to Valascaa to recover. Then, until I was called to the grand shrine, where I remained until the near present when Miss Talia and I began the journey we are on now.

At the conclusion of Marec's story, the group grew silent. Only Alec and Talia fully understood the pain behind Marec's words. They rode in silence for several minutes. Alec near to Talia, who he knew must bear the same pain as he and Marec. In an attempt to abate the silence, Zelus spoke up.

"Well at least now we know why Eliza is so beastly. It must come from the blood running on her father's side." Zelus smiled, obviously amused with himself until Eliza slugged him in the shoulder. Zelus rubbed his shoulder and spoke no more of the matter. After a few more, awkwardly tense moments, Eliza spoke up.

"Thank you uncle, I did not know much about my family other than what little I knew of my mother and father. I do appreciate you sharing this with us."

"It was my pleasure Eliza. I only hope that I may repair my relationships in the near future. There are many regrets I have and a great many unbearable sorrows, which I have endured. After Miss Talia and I have returned to the grand shrine, perhaps I will have the opportunity to start over." Marec suddenly looked to his saddle as if something severe has begun troubling him. Alec looked around him and saw that everyone save he, Tear and Oz also stared down with an extreme expression of despair.

"Will you be staying in Valascaa long enough for us to celebrate Talia's birthday?" Alec looked around and the general consensus he gathered left him to believe that he had somehow made a most grave error. It was Talia who answered.

"I am afraid that my duties as a priestess require that I return home at my earliest convenience." She paused for a long while as if trying to find the words to say. "I must make ready to help bring about the revitalization of Valoria."

"Talia, it sounds as though you are extremely important. Maybe there is some way I could come visit you and assist you?" Talia shook her head looking for an answer.

"No, I am afraid that this is a task that must be completed by myself." Alec was confused yet still so ignorant.

"Well then, perhaps once you have finished, I can come down and visit you. I know Oz will want to see you as well." Talia had no other answers for Alec.

"Yes, that would be nice, I would like that should it be possible." She turned her attention elsewhere as Zelus came to her rescue.

"Hey, come on Alec, let us not focus too much on the future. We will need to set up camp before long then, tomorrow, I am going to show everyone back home how much stronger than you I have gotten." Alec looked at Zelus with his usual challenging stare.

"You are ready to go home tomorrow just so I can show everyone how disillusioned you still are?" Zelus bantered with Alec as they usually did, except this time glad that his distraction worked out. They rode on for several more hours before they came upon their camping ground. Everyone unloaded their horses and began making camp while Marec readied the fire. Alec had just finished his tent when Oz perked up suddenly.

"What is it Oz?" Alec asked. Oz jerked his head to the side as Eliza came up.

"Did you hear that?"

"Hear what?" Both Oz and Eliza lurched again.

"There it is again, please tell me you heard it." Alec shrugged his shoulders and shook his head. He focused on Oz's thoughts for a moment.

"Oz thinks someone is crying."

"Yeah, that is what I heard." Eliza began searching around as Alec still strained to hear what it was that they were going on about.

"Which way are they Oz?" Eliza asked and Oz began running off toward the tree line, Eliza and Alec raced to follow him. As they neared the tree line Alec began to hear the sound of whimpering, a puppy was crying.

"Now I can hear it Eliza, it sounds like a pup."

"Well, of course you can hear it now. They are right ahead of us." They stopped and Eliza knelt down and stared into the bushes.

"Oh my, Alec look what they have done to her." She pointed forward. Alec slowly approached and looked to where Eliza was pointing. Alec looked at the grisly sight and saw that, apparently, some of the Forsaken had grown restless and wandered off towards the woods, where a momma wolf and her pups were. Alec could only assume that the mother was defending her pups and by the look of the mutilated tufts of fur, she had put up a remarkable struggle. He continued to stare with pity at the sight before him as Eliza cried and pointed.

"Look Alec, the little tufts over there. They went for the pups as well." Alec looked and confirmed what Eliza saw. He looked over to Oz and then down to the two remaining puppies, fur grey, white and black, debating his next move. The pups prodded their mother hoping to rouse her but to no avail. She had been long gone and by the looks of the two puppies, they had gone hungry for at least a few days. Alec turned his head to Oz and rested his forehead against the sympathetic griffin.

"Oz, could you please go and fetch them some food?" Oz chirped and quickly trotted off into the trees. Alec knelt down in front of the puppies and examined them. One was mostly white save for black splotches that formed around its extremely bright blue eyes and had a grey swish for one of its three tails. Alec gasped as he realized that both of the puppies had three tails, each tucked beneath their bodies in fear. Alec pointed at the discovery and Eliza simply nodded her head.

"These are baby dire wolves. They are extremely rare and sacred to the Valorian knights." Alec placed his hands on his knees as he eyed the other pup. Again, mostly white, but with a grey underbelly, and like its sibling, the bluest eyes Alec had ever seen. The puppies looked at Alec and scampered behind their mother. Eliza slowly walked forward with her hands out in front of her.

"What are you doing?" Alec whispered to her.

"I am going to take them with us." Alec looked at her again but could see the raw determination on her face.

"What is your father going to say?" Eliza looked at him as if annoyed.

"Do you for one instant believe that my father is going to tell "his little princess" no", she spoke being sure to use a heavy amount of emphasis on the princess part. Alec shook his head and smiled.

"No, I suppose not, but first you're going to have to catch them." Eliza looked from Alec back to the pups, which were still shying away behind their morbid defense. Eliza approached them and continued to reach out her hands.

"Come here babies. I am not going to hurt you. I am going to look after you now." The pups whimpered some more for their mother, but to Alec's surprise they came out from behind their shield and stopped in front of Eliza. "Good boys!" Eliza cheered to them as she scooped them into her arms and held them.

"How do you know that they are boys?" Eliza again looked to Alec with her annoyed stare and Alec was forced to remember the incident with Oz.

"Yeah, you are probably right." Eliza mouthed the word, "yeah," as she rapidly nodded her head at him. The two pups in her arms Eliza turned and began to head for camp as Oz came barreling out of the woods, with three rabbits in his beak.

"Thank you Oz." Alec spoke as he pet the lion hawk. They walked back towards the camp, and it was Tear who noticed them first.

"PUPPIES!" She cried out and ran up to them. Eliza held out her hands as the pups began to squirm in her grasp.

"Calm down Tear, you are scaring them. You need to come at them slowly to pet them." Tear's eyes grew large and she slowly capered at a snail's pace and carefully reached out her small hand towards the pups and felt their soft fur.

"They are so soft!" Tear grew more excited as Talia and Zelus approached them.

"Are those dire wolves?" Zelus was the first to notice the extra tails. Upon his mention, Talia turned her head to the side as she and Tear examined the additional tails. Eliza nodded her head as she marched towards the camp.

"Where did you find them?" Talia asked. Eliza sat down and pulling out her skinning knife, began cleaning the rabbits and fed strips of them to the pups.

"We found them over by the tree line." Eliza seemed keen to leave it at that though Alec felt the need to relay the whole story. By the time he was finished,

Zelus was snickering, while Tear and Talia looked to Eliza in amazement.

"Tis, quite an impressive feat, to be able to perceive such an acute sound, from so far off. You are most remarkable Eliza." Eliza thanked her as Zelus continued to snicker to himself. Finally, Eliza turned on him with her annoyed fiery tone in her voice.

"What is it, Zelus!?" Zelus looked up at Eliza as he scooted back a few paces.

"So, you found the pups, hearing a noise that only you and Oz could pick up. Then, you adopted two WILD DIREWOLF puppies as if you were their puppy mama." He snickered again. "You actually are a beast girl, are you not?" Eliza glared at Zelus as he mocked her by making howling noises up at the sky. Finally, Marec came up to the camp and saw the pups.

"You realize Zelus that were Eliza truly a beast master, with only a word she could command those pups to devour you." The collaborative looked up at Marec with astonishment.

"But, they are so little. What could they possibly do?" Marec smiled as he petted the pups, which were growling to protect their food all the while.

"They may be small now Zelus, but, once they are grown, they will be near the size of an ox." Again, everyone gasped and stared at the puppies as they began tearing into the second of the rabbits.

"Marec, will they grow that large?" Marec nodded his head.

"Indeed, the Beastmen, before they were wiped out, use to use them as war mounts. If they are lightly burdened they will travel as fast as a horse and be agile upon all terrains."

"It sounds as though you have found yourself quite a find then, congratulations Eliza." Eliza nodded her head to Alec and continued to feed her puppies until the three rabbits were gone. Eliza walked to the river, the two following her and washed her hands. She marched back toward the camp and opened up the flap on her tent.

"In you go," she spoke and the pups bounded in and began to play, wrestling and tackling one another.

"What shall you name them?" Talia asked of her. Eliza thought hard for a moment before answering.

"Baldur and Aurick." She said softly. Talia thought for a moment.

"Brave and valor, they are fine names."

"Thank you, good night everyone." Eliza spoke as she closed the flap of her tent and presumably went to sleep. Alec looked around the campsite and patted Oz on the flank.

"Well, I think that I am going to turn in as well, good night everyone." The party returned the gesture. Alec closed his tent and quickly fell asleep.

Talia searched around the room that she was in. It was made of marble and the sun was shining down upon her. She attempted to move, but her arms and legs would not heed her commands. She looked down and found herself bound by iron shackles to the floor. She tilted her head back skyward and could see an elaborately designed oculus that opened part way to allow the sunlight to enter. Beyond that, she could see a large moon hovering overhead, threatening to blot out the sun. Talia knew full well what it was that she was bearing witness to and it terrified her that Aneira's sight had brought her even this.

She heard a man calling to her, screaming in fact. She turned her gaze down from the raised platform that she was chained to and saw Alec, kneeling on the ground, severely wounded. Talia's vision changed, and now she looked upon herself as she called for Alec to stay down, but Alec refused to stop fighting for her. Talia could feel the strange sensation in her heart overflowing yet again as she realized that Alec would be willing to die for her when this day finally came to pass.

She watched as her dream state self's body jerked violently backwards and began radiating light, which poured into the now eclipsed sun. Talia could not help but imagine that she herself were crying as she watched Alec cry out for her to stop, then, after a moment, the light left her other self and she lay on the platform talking to Alec, who had crawled over to her and was reaching out for her. Her vision began to fade in front of her eyes and Talia desperately willed for herself to remain asleep. She saw Alec burst into a violent red light, which consumed him, and, the last thing that she saw was the boy from her dreams collapsing to the ground, his eyes wide open, blank, lifeless, dead.

Talia jolted upright as she awoke from the terrible vision. Quickly, she pulled herself out of her bedroll and ran to Alec's tent. Oz bolted up to his feet, startled by Talia's sudden appearance but was quickly eased as Talia held out her hand and brushed the top of his strong beak.

"I just need to see Alec." She whispered to the noble griffin and Oz lowered his head, which Talia took as a sign that he would allow it. Talia reached out carefully and folded back the flap of Alec's tent only enough to peek within.

She had to admit to herself a small amount of guilt, this having not been the first time that she had done such a thing, but normally she could not help but stare upon the beautiful man who accompanied her. Now, she found herself truly fearful of him, not that she felt threatened by him, but because she knew of what he was capable of, and what he would do to ensure he remain by her side, forever. This made her feel selfish. She knew deep within her heart she could not forgive herself, should her fate, determine his.

Assured that Alec's health was not at stake this night, Talia sighed with relief as she walked away from the tent and quietly crept back to her own where she lay down her head and attempted to go back to sleep, terrified by what the sandman might bring her next.

They awoke early that morning and started to ride out before first light. Now, several hours later, they could see the walls of Valascaa. Talia's vision still haunted her and, after a long talk with Marec, they determined that the best course of action would be for Alec to remain in Valascaa, whilst they completed their business at the Grand Shrine.

Chapter 34 – Not As It Seems

"We are finally home. I left a knight and returned a paladin." Alec felt overwhelmed with the sight of his home. The gates swung open to greet them, as did the gate to the lower district of town. Alec could smell the salt in the air from the nearby ocean but, as they walked inside, Alec's eyes were filled of reminders of what it was like to live outside the grace of the council.

Everywhere he looked the people seemed happy. The market stands were filled, trade was being made abundantly yet, as he looked around, he could not help but see the mass number of people congregated that wore ragged clothing.

"I look forward to the changes you make, Talia. This world needs change now more than ever." Talia nodded her head in answer to him. Alec continued his search around the town and noticed as people began to stare at Oz. Oz bounded about happily as he ran in the direction of Alec's old house.

"No no, Oz, we do not live there anymore. Come on now, you are going to scare whoever lives there now." Talia looked at the quaint little house and turned back to Alec.

"Tis a fine home Alec. How long have you lived there?"

"Ever since I first came to Valascaa. When Highmoore was destroyed, Eliza and her family adopted me, and placed me into a small home that they owned. I am very grateful to them for that. It kept me from becoming homeless like many of the survivors from that night. Marec inspected the house and smiled to himself.

"This was the home that we lived in as children until we moved up to the noble's quarter. It seems oddly sentimental of my brother to have purchased the place after so much time had passed."

"Sir Marec, this was once your home?"

"Aye, back when it was just my brothers and my father. It has been some time since I last looked upon it."

"I am sure, if you wished, we could stop for a quick visit?"

"That is unnecessary Alec. We have much to do and so little time in which to complete it." They marched through town until they entered the noble's quarter. Marec halted and turned to face the group.

"Here is where we must part for now, my friends. Perhaps later, before Talia and I leave to return home, we shall take some time to say goodbye. Eliza, Zelus, I think the two of you should return home. Eliza will want to find a place for Baldur and Aurick to rest. Alec, I suggest you head for the shrine and prepare for your final trial. Do not worry, Talia, I shall wait for you." Alec smiled as he dismounted his horse and, leaving it in the stables, left to head for the shrine. As Eliza, Zelus, and the others unsaddled their horses and shouldered their belongings, Zelus turned to Eliza.

"Hey Eliza, why do you not head on home? I will go meet with Dominick and Nilus and we can meet up again tonight?" Eliza nodded to Zelus.

"Alright Zelus, I will see you tonight." Eliza turned without further ado and ran off in the direction of her house, her pups quick on her heels. Zelus smiled as he shouldered his own belongings and headed out into the direction of the knight's college. Zelus' walk across town was rather short, as he spent no small amount of effort attempting to find any sort of distraction to free his mind.

He walked up the stone stairs and carefully pressed open the solid oak double doors. He looked around inside and took relief in the sight that nothing had changed since he had been gone. Everything was just as he remembered it. He knew exactly where he needed to go in order to find Dominic and Nilus.

"Zelus, when did you get back?" Nilus was the first one he came across.

"Just now, I thought that it would be wise for me to start on my report. Eliza has already gone home to speak with the commander."

"Alright, great! Well, I was just on my way to the tavern to meet with Dominic. Why do you not come with me? We can always help you with the report." Zelus thought about it for a moment and then agreed.

"Yes, sounds great, I can tell you guys what happened and you can help me to fill out the report as I tell you our story." Nilus clapped Zelus on the back and led him towards the tavern. They exited the college and headed straight for the tavern that lay just on the outside of the noble's quarter.

"Zelus, how have you been?" Dominic greeted them as Zelus entered the tavern. They spoke together for quite some time as Zelus began to relay the story of their travels.

"So it seems Alec is a paladin now, that is amazing. It also looks as though you have grown stronger yourself."

"I have learned much and seen more, I do like to think that I have grown since I departed." Zelus' attention was pulled away for a moment as a commotion broke out amongst some of the other patrons. Zelus turned his head to see the source of the commotion and he saw a man in black armor pull a knife from his side and sink it into a table. The two men continued to argue but Zelus' attentions were otherwise detained as he looked at the knife. He studied it carefully, watching its curved edge and hand carved ivory handle and realized where he had once seen the blade. Zelus lifted his eyes up towards the face of the man who had plunged the dagger into the table.

"Are you sure that you want to cause problems for one of Aneira's grand temple knights?" Zelus was struck with a sudden panic and he turned to his friends.

"I am sorry, but I must go and find Marec." Zelus rose from the table and ran as Dominic and Nilus approached the temple knight in order to calm the disturbance.

Meanwhile across town, Eliza sat in front of her parents relaying their various adventures. She explained to her mother about Belias and the wounds she had received that Talia had healed. She told them about the incident at the church in Remora and obviously about Baldur and Aurick. Kristian sat playing with the three-tailed dire wolves as the Lion still sat in the back of the room. Krisitana was quite intent to hear of her daughter's tales of glory while the lion stared at her as if afraid that at any moment she were going to up and vanish. As Eliza continued to relay her story, Kristiana could not help but notice her husband's reactions.

"Oh, honestly dear, your daughter has just undergone the thrill of a lifetime. Be happy for her." She prodded at the lion who grumbled at his wife. After several more awkward moments a knock came from the front door and Kristiana went to answer.

"Oh my, Marec, how good to see you." She gasped as she opened the door to see her brother-in-law standing before her. Marec hugged Kristiana but bore a grave expression.

"It is wonderful to see you as well, sister, but, if I may be so prudent, might I borrow my brother for a moment. I have a matter of the utmost urgency to inform him of." Kristiana looked back to her husband and daughter, the latter of which bore a grave expression to match her uncle's.

"Of course Marec, Eliza was just telling me of your travels together. We shall have to catch up later as Eliza and I continue our conversation outside. Come Eliza, please walk with me and leave these two to their discussion. Dear, are you going to be alright if we leave our grandchildren here?" She joked and the both Eliza and the Lion looked at her oddly. Kristiana laughed as she allowed Marec to pass and then walked outside. Eliza followed Kristiana outside as Marec approached his brother. Marec cleared his throat before he spoke.

"I am sorry to ask you this brother, but I need a favor."

"I am listening."

"It is about Alec. I need for you to take care of him a little while longer. I am afraid that he will need everyone he cares about for some time to come. I am afraid that the unforgivable has happened and I have allowed him to fall in love with my ward. I lacked the courage to tell him on our travels of that and the other matter and I just need for you to help me a small while longer." The two men continued their discussion as Eliza made a revelation of her own.

Eliza had been retelling her story when she stopped dead in the middle of the street, frozen by fear of what she saw. As Kristiana and she had neared the marketplace, Eliza's eyes caught sight of an armored man who walked with a heavy limp, as if his right leg had recently been injured. The man eyed Eliza for a moment and smiled as he realized who she was.

"Are you ready for round two? You should have known that a knight on his holy mission would not be kept in a prison."

Across town, Alec had reached the steps of the cathedral. He looked up at the massive building in front of him and climbed the stone steps. He gazed around at the large collection of parishioners marching in and out of the enormous doors. Alec then looked toward his right and saw a massive covered carriage surrounded by men in black armor. Alec thought to himself for a moment in an attempt to remember where he had seen similar armor before.

After a few moments, he remembered the flames of Remora and he snapped his head back toward the church and hurriedly marched inside, being sure to blend in with the people already headed there. Alec made it within and began to scan his surroundings. Several more armored men waited within, all seeming to be guarding one important looking woman clad in long flowing robes of white, silver and gold adorned with several insignias of the high order proving that she was from the grand shrine. She had long blonde hair and smooth milky skin, an attractive woman by all accounts. She spoke at the head of the church as the regular priests and priestesses all paid her much respect and adoration. Yet, even though she was obviously a very important person to the Aneiran order, Alec could not help but sense the presence of hatred and malice before him.

Alec quietly marched toward a row of pews and sat down listening in while remaining inconspicuous to the others around him. He knelt down as if in prayer as he eavesdropped in on a group of temple knights who were questioning some of the other people in prayer.

"We are looking for a young priestess. It is of the utmost importance to the Aneiran order that we find her. We know that she arrived here in Valascaa just this morning. She is of average height, long flowing amber hair, green eyes, goes by the name of Talia Degracia." Alec did his best not to jump in surprise as he slowly finished his prayers and quietly exited the cathedral. He burst out into the sunlight and began to think frantically of where he might find his friends. Considering his options he dashed off towards town square.

"Oh, by Aneira, thank goodness I found you Zelus." Eliza panted as she nearly tackled Zelus. "The ones that attacked us in Remora."

"I know Eliza they are from the grand shrine and they are here to take Talia into custody."

"What do we do?"

"We need to find Alec and the others. What about Tear?"

"My mother went to find her. She is going to hide her at my house. Uncle Marec has already left to find Talia at the cathedral."

"Alright, good." The two looked around and saw Alec off in the distance, bolting through town like a panicked rabbit.

"ALEC!" Eliza and Zelus screamed. Alec heard the call and came running to them. They could tell that he had activated his regeneration rune as he showed no signs of fatigue, nor did he breathe deeply when he stopped.

"Where is Talia? She is danger."

"We know Alec, Marec went to find her. My mother left to find Tear. We are out looking ourselves right now." Alec nodded his head and quickly tried to form a plan.

"We split up. If we find her, we go to my old house and wait for everyone else to arrive. I already asked Oz to look for her as well. He is trying to…" Alec paused for a moment lifting his head into the sky as if searching for a sign.

"Alec what is it?" Zelus shook his shoulder.

"Oz just found Marec and Talia, Oz is in the town square let us hurry, Oz feels frightened." The three of them took off in a feat of frenzied flight, Alec's speed, having increased due to his intense training, had him leaving Zelus and Eliza far behind. Finally, they caught up to him and gasped at what they saw.

"I am high priestess Angelica, leader of the Valascaan high order of Aneira. Before me are priestess Talia Degracia and paladin defender Marec Kaldur of Valascaa. We are taking Talia back into our custody by holy rite where she will fulfill her sacred duty to the people of Valoria. We shall be leaving the traitor Marec to you as he is of your blood. His crime is not severe enough to warrant death, though he is to be incarcerated until such a time as the leaders of the high order can meet in council and determine what his fate shall be." Alec looked at Talia who looked terrified and sullen. Alec pushed his way to the front of the crowd and quickly pressed back the soldiers. As he ran through, he ordered for Oz to stay back since he did not want the lion hawk to be spotted or harmed by what he was about to do.

"TALIA!" He screamed as he was forced to his knees by two of the temple guards.

"ALEC!" Talia cried back as the men forced Alec's head down and drew their blades.

Alec retaliated and, with a quick succession of combat maneuvers and well placed strikes, freed himself and continued forward.

"I am the Paladin, Alec Dante of Highmoore and I wish to know the reason for this." Angelica turned her cold gaze upon Alec and he felt the embrace of the devil behind her eyes.

"Becoming a paladin does not give you the right to question my authority. Kneel before me naive or I shall have you executed." The high priestess spoke as more armored guards appeared and struck Alec down.

"ALEC!" Talia screamed as Eliza and Zelus attempted to press their own way through the blockade. Alec looked up to Angelica defiantly. Two guards drew out their swords and pressed them on either side of Alec's neck as the others continued to beat him. Angelica looked down at Alec and nearly smiled.

"Kill him." She spoke as if the thought of execution bored her.

"Go ahead you demented bitch and show everyone what you truly are." Angelica shrugged her shoulders and snapped her fingers. Several of her armed guards desisted their brutal assault on Alec and prepared to execute him.

"NO WAIT!" Talia cried as she turned to Angelica. "Please high priestess spare him. He has been my protector during my journey and it is also thanks to him that I have survived. Please do not kill him and I will go quietly with you."

"Very well." Angelica snapped her fingers and the guards sheathed their weapons and dropped Alec's bleeding body to the ground.

"May I at least say goodbye?" Angelica looked around at the angry mob that was beginning to form.

"Very well, say goodbye to your friend." Talia ran to Alec's side and quickly mended him. She knelt down next to him and cradled his head in her arms.

"Alec, you must promise not to come after me. Please swear to me that you will not. Even if we never see each other again. I have seen it in my visions. If you do, they will kill you and I…" She paused as if trying to find the words. "I could not bear to have you killed trying to save me. Alec I…I love you Alec." She kissed him passionately. Their lips locked in an embrace so intense that Alec almost forgot what it was that he was doing.

"Alright, that is quite enough of that." Angelica yelled as one of her guards grabbed Talia and began to drag her away.

"I will come for you Talia, I swear it, I will."

"Doubtful," Angelica yelled back as she motioned towards her guards. "Kill him!"

"Noooo!" Talia screamed as another man grabbed her body and carried her away, binding and gagging her. Seven drew their swords surrounding Alec and several more drew their weapons on Eliza and Zelus.

"SHEATH YOUR WEAPONS THIS INSTANT!!!!" A booming female voice sounded off from beyond town square. Everyone turned their attention to see Kristiana and the Lion marching, weapons drawn a legion of knights behind them.

"We shall take these men into our custody. The Aneiran order has no authority over life and death." Angelica turned and after ordering her men to continue out the gates faced Kristiana.

"How dare you oppose the high priestess of Aneira? What impudence, what incompetence the filth of Valascaa have resorted to." She did not have the opportunity to speak another word as Kristiana quickly cleared the distance between the two of them, taking two guards to the ground with rapid movements that even Alec had trouble following.

"If we are choosing to resort to lawlessness than you shall find that my power lies further beyond my words." Kristiana threatened, her blades pinning the high priestess's neck. "Now, you are to leave this place, without Marec, the paladin Alec, and priestess." Angelica cautiously pressed one blade from her throat.

"We shall leave. You are right. I have no claim to the men but the priestess has sworn sacred oaths to me and I shall see to it that she fulfills them. Let us go." Angelica turned her back on Kristiana and her men rose and followed. Kristiana sheathed her weapons and turned toward Alec and the others.

"That was not smart, Kristiana." Marec moaned to her, having been beaten severely by the guards. "But I admire you for it." He groaned some more as he was aided by Eliza and the Lion. Zelus approached Alec who rose to his feet, threw Zelus' hand from his arm, and turned towards the temple and began to walk.

"Alec, where are you going?"

"To finish what I came here to start and, after that, I am going after Talia."

Chapter 35 – The Final Trial

"Ah, welcome back young Alec. I had not expected you back so soon, yet it does always seem to fly closer to the end." Alec looked around the memory of Highmoore until his eyes met Seraphina's.

"What seems to fly?"

"Time, young paladin. No matter how old, how much, or how little, time seems irrelevant until we near the end, and by then, we always seem to possess none. I sense that you have returned with a troubled heart and a lack of time young Alec. What is it that troubles you?"

"I must complete my training, so that I may go and rescue the woman I love." Seraphina smiled as she walked with Alec towards the second door.

"Ah yes, love. I have experienced such a thing many a time during my prolonged existence."

"Do you mean before you died?"

"Yes, and yet no. When I was alive, I knew love for my father and my mother. I knew love for my homeland and love for my people, yet, I never knew the love of another as I did until after I died."

"What happened?" Seraphina smiled again with her bright radiant smile.

"Ah, that was many years ago by your recollection. I was giving trial to a young, bold paladin. At first, I was unsure of the feeling I felt, yet, as I continued to spend time with the man, the feeling intensified until I was sure of what it was that I felt."

"What ever happened to the man?"

"Ah well, I have not seen him in over a decade and a half by your calendar. However, our love was an impossibility. It was with a heavy heart that we terminated the connection."

"But what happened to the man?"

"I never saw him again. Now Alec, let us focus instead on the matter at hand, your trial." Alec continued to walk with Seraphina when they reached the second door. "Alec, I sense that you are not yet ready for this trial. How about you spend some time within the library and center yourself? I am sure that Highmoore has made more available to you since your last visit." Alec nodded and, opening the first door, walked within and took the path straight ahead, which led to the library. As he entered, he noticed that more lights were now lit so that he could nearly see to the end of the room on the opposite side.

Alec sat down at the desk where he had studied before and read the writing on the side of the first scroll that sat before him.

"Lady Seraphina, the divine paladin." Alec unrolled the scroll and seeing the concealment seal at the top corner of the page pressed his thumb against it commanding the contents within to reveal themselves. The scroll began to bleed out words and letters before Alec's eyes and he began to read of the story of Seraphina.

"Before the paladin Sidonis rose to the heavens to be with his beloved Goddess, she gifted him with a daughter. It has never been determined that Seraphina was indeed the daughter of Aneira or not though this was the legend that we were told as we began recording the history of the famous founder of Highmoore.

Through all of the myths and legends, what we have confirmed, is that the Lady Seraphina was indeed a Divine and a Paladin, following in her father's footsteps. We do know that she was indeed the daughter of the legendary Sidonis and that she died at the tender age of thirty. She was a priestess of the Aneiran high order and died mysteriously while on holy pilgrimage in Valascaa.

She left behind no kin, though many who knew her and the people she sheltered when Highmoore was erected all referred to her as their beloved queen." Alec read further down and saw that the history continued on with her political contributions detailing Highmooria turning into a republic. Alec quickly skimmed to the bottom of the scroll and resealed its contents. He turned towards another scroll and read its title.

"The final death of the Daemon knights," Alec unraveled the scroll and was surprised to find that, when he touched the rune, the information within made itself available to him.

"The Daemon knights are an order of elite evil knights which exist with the sole purpose of serving Daemon in order to help in his eternal battle against Aneira. It is said that the strength of a Daemon knight surpasses that of any living man and that their bodies are assembled using the souls of their victims, though none have been seen since the death of their leader Abaddon.

Over two hundred years ago, Abaddon commanded a mighty army of Forsaken with which he threatened to seize control of all Valoria. He had at his side five disciples, many of whom fell in battle against the early Sidonian paladins. After Sidonis' death and subsequent ascension to the high heavens, his fight was carried on atop the shoulders of his daughter Seraphina. She led her armies into the Scar, where she plunged her sword deep into the heart of the enemy, killing many of the Daemon knights.

Sometime later, near the end of her life, Seraphina encountered Callisto, one of the last Daemon knights and killed him in battle. It has never been confirmed what happened to their leader Abaddon. Yet, it is the consensus of many historians of the era that he died in battle and his remains were never found." Alec suddenly found himself intrigued by the lady and resealing the scroll rose to his feet and left the library.

Returning to the balcony where Seraphina resided, Alec asked the question which had begun to plague his mind.

"Lady Seraphina, how is it that you died? I know you said that you died in battle, yet you never said how. The scrolls in the library seemed to be even less conclusive." Seraphina drew up a deep breath as she prepared to answer Alec's question.

"As I said, I was killed in battle."

"Yes, but how and by whom?"

"I lost my life in battle while fighting the Daemon knight Abaddon."

"But the scrolls in the library say that Abaddon died long before that." Seraphina shook her head before answering.

"To this day, Abaddon lives on. I was unable to overcome him when he fought. I was betrayed, you see, by the leader of my order. She lured me to the grand cathedral in the guise of performing a sacred ritual during the lunar eclipse. During such an event, Aneira's powers are at their weakest and Daemon's at their greatest. She told me that it was important in warding off the evil of Daemon. It was not until after I arrived that I sensed Abaddon's presence within and, by then, it was too late for me escape."

"Did you not possess the skill to defeat him?" Seraphina smiled.

"The skill yes, though I had not my father's prized sword. The one you bear now as your own. Without the weapon to slay evil, Abaddon proved invincible to me. He came at me with his monstrous steeds, the manticore. Outmatched, betrayed and without the only weapon in known existence that could slay him, I had no choice. I prayed to my benevolent mother Aneira to grant me the strength to seal away his soul away within that very same eclipse. To this day I know not what he intended to do with me during the event, though I suppose that it had something to do with stealing my soul as his powers are strongest during the eclipse." Alec had to think for a moment in an attempt to absorb what Seraphina had just told him.

"I believe we have wasted enough time, Alec. You have come here to complete your next trial, the trial of heart."

"I have Lady Seraphina, what must I do?" Seraphina guided Alec again towards the second door.

"Within, the strength of your heart shall be tested. You shall be faced with a great number of disturbing things that shall test every last ounce of your being. Travel through the room to its opposite door and you will have succeeded. Leave before your trial is complete and you would have failed and will never be allowed to wield the Sidonis sword without risk of losing your life." Alec nodded his head as turned the knob on the door.

"Be warned Alec, things will be presented to you that are both disturbing yet true. You may find answers to your most terrifying questions, which you hoped remained unanswered, yet you must prevail should you hope to become the true heir of Sidonis. Clear your mind of these things Alec and your trial may prove less troublesome." Alec opened the door and walked within. He searched about the room and across from him, hung a portrait. Alec examined the portrait and recognized the blonde woman with the devil's eyes staring back at him.

"Lady Seraphina, what is her picture doing here?" Seraphina sighed aggressively, and for the first time Alec sensed anger seething from the nymph.

"I wish that I could remove her portrait, but alas this room was birthed from my memory and I was unable to tear it down before my death. This is the portrait of the head of my order, Lady Angelica." Alec was too stunned for words. His mind raced with panic as he contemplated the impossibility of the situation.

"What is the matter young paladin? Do you know of this woman?"

"She just took the one I love from me. She is still very much in charge of the Aneiran high order. How is such a thing possible?" Seraphina thought for a moment before answering.

"I am unsure, though it is possible that, if she is indeed working with the Forsaken, it is possible that Daemon has prolonged her life as Aneira has mine." Alec's continued to panic ever more greatly, trying to determine what he would do.

"My Lady Seraphina, I must apologize, but I must be away."

"I am sorry sir Alec, if you leave here now, you will have failed your trial." Alec's heart raced so hard, it threatened to burst from his very chest.

"I have no choice. Talia is in danger and I have to save her." Alec raced past Seraphina and dove head first into the pool. The world around him began to spin away as he heard Seraphina call to him.

"Then, I am afraid you shall never possess the strength needed to fulfill your mission."

Chapter 36 – The Oath

Alec's eyes opened wide and he was back within the cathedral shrine. Quickly, Alec rose to his feet and ran for the exit. As he bolted through the building, he contacted Oz using their link.

"Where are Zelus and Eliza?" He asked Oz. Oz responded with feelings that reminded Alec of home.

"Alright then, are Zelus and Eliza at Eliza's house?" Alec swore he could hear Oz chirp in answer to him.

"Thanks Oz. I am on my way." Alec continued to run at his insane frenzied pace until he reached Eliza's house. Gently rapping on the door, he waited for it to open and he saw a pair of eyes looking at him from the window before they came to answer the door. The door swung open and it was Kristiana who answered.

"Come in quickly, Alec." She ushered Alec inside and after looking around outside closed the door behind him.

"Welcome Alec, I am afraid after that commotion yesterday we have been under high alert as of sorts." Alec thought to himself for a moment and realized what she must be referring to.

"Are you in trouble with the high council?" Kristiana smiled as she walked across the room and took a seat.

"Of sorts, they are most displeased with me as of the moment yet they will not act upon their displeasure as, lawfully, that woman had no claim to you. They merely wish that I had acted less rashly."

"If you had I might be dead right now."

"That is why I am unconcerned. Now, what is it that you need? Eliza and Zelus are in the other room speaking with your young friend Tear."

"I did come here to talk to them. I am sorry that I got you into trouble." Kristiana laughed at Alec as if his response were unreasonably comical.

"Dear, if I had not been in trouble for your sake, I am certain that I would have surely found something. You can go on ahead dear. They are just in the other room." She waved her hand towards the hallway and Alec bowed his head to her as he walked past. He entered the next room where sat Eliza, Zelus and Tear who was sleeping soundly on the couch.

"Hey," Alec whispered to get their attention without waking the little one. At first, they did not respond, but upon a second calling their heads poked up. Alec motioned for them to join him in the hallway and they both rose to their feet to do so.

"Alec, what is it? Are you not supposed to be at your trial?" Eliza asked.

"I went to it, but when I was there I learned something terrible. We need to go and speak with Marec." Eliza and Zelus looked at one another uneasily.

"Alright, fine, he is in the barracks, it isn't too late yet, we should still be able to visit him." The three of them walked back towards the greeting room, where Kristiana still sat waiting.

"Mother, we need to go and speak with Uncle Marec. Would you like for us to tell father anything while we are there?" Her mother shook her head as she rubbed the corners of her eyes.

"No dear, do not worry, just be safe and be watchful of anyone following you."

"We will mother." The three of them exited the house and looked around to make sure that no one was watching them. They did not breathe a word to one another as they hastily moved through the streets towards the barracks. Alec opened the door and they all entered within. As they walked inside, they came across a guard who sat with his back up against wall.

"Ah, why hello Eliza. Are you here to see your father?"

"Not just yet, Keagen I have actually come to speak with my uncle. The man who was moved in here earlier today." Keagen thought for a moment then turned back to them.

"I know just the man, alright come this way. You will not be able to visit for long, we were just getting ready to close up for the night."

"Thank you Keagen." Eliza spoke as the man rattled his keychain and, finding the right one, unlocked the door beside him allowing them entrance. The trio walked down the long corridor passing various cells, some containing prisoners though many were still empty. The three made it to the end of the hall and saw Marec sitting on the bed of his cell waiting.

"Marec!" The three called excitedly, Eliza's being the exception as she started with "uncle." Marec looked up to them and smiled.

"What are you three doing here?"

"Marec, I have to speak with you and I thought I would save time by speaking with Eliza and Zelus at the same time."

"Did you already go to your trial?"

"I did."

"And have you completed Seraphina's final test?" Alec did not answer and quickly deviated the conversation.

"Marec, while I was undergoing my trial, I came across some information, some very old information, and I believe that Talia is in grave danger." Zelus, Eliza and Marec all looked back and forth to one another and then looked back to Alec.

"Alec, we cannot go after Talia. I know that you want to but we mustn't go after her." Eliza was the first to speak. Alec stood in shock as one after the other both Zelus and Marec agreed with Eliza and attempted to convince Alec that he should leave Talia and forget about her.

"Alec, I know this is hard and I know that you love Talia, but what she is doing is for the betterment of all Valoria." Marec spoke his piece. Alec shook his head angrily with his rebuttal.

"No, you do not get it. Talia is in great danger. If I do not go after her she could..."

"Die? Let me guess, you were going to say that she could die. Alec, Talia's mission was and still is to become the vessel of Aneira's restoration. She was born with the sole purpose of dying." Marec spoke, anger growing in his voice. Alec looked at his instructor startled.

"You mean you knew that she was going to die?"

"Of course I did, Alec. When Talia was a small child, it was discovered that she possessed the gift of Aneira's sight. Within the high Aneiran order, it is written that should one who possesses the power of sight return to Aneira and give of herself during the time of the lunar eclipse that Aneira's power shall wash down upon her and revitalize the land. What Talia is doing, she has prepared for her entire life. If you go and try to stop her, you will have destroyed everything that she has worked for her entire life." Alec could feel himself growing angrier, his fists tightened into hard balls.

"You mean to tell me that you knew of this all along? Not only did you do nothing, but you went along with it. What is wrong with you? Do you think it is alright for someone to make Talia live that way?" Eliza tried to calm the situation.

"Alec, this is what Talia wants. She is doing this so that others might live, in a world free of the Forsaken." Alec snapped his head angrily towards Eliza.

"Did you know?" Eliza had not even managed to speak her answer and already the tears began to pour from her eyes. Zelus walked to Eliza's side and placed his hand on her shoulders, comforting her.

"We all did, Alec." Alec could feel the turmoil within him growing to near explosive heights. He wanted to lash out and strike somebody, yet he knew he needed their help in order to accomplish his mission.

"You all lied to me? You all watched me fall in love with her and lied to me, knowing we would have to say goodbye and that she would have to go to her death alone?" He spoke, his tone ripe with the hurt of his friends' betrayal.

"Alec when you say it like that." Zelus started.

"It would not matter how I said it!" Alec raged as he grabbed ahold of Zelus' collar and pinned him to the bars of Marec's cell. "It would still be wrong." Eliza placed her hand on Alec's shoulder and he shrugged her off letting Zelus go in the process. He walked away and began pacing, his heart racing, despair filling his being. His eyes met Marec's, and he could feel the anger swell within him.

"And you, so called Paladin of Aneira. How can you bear that mantle, and feel anything other than shame?"

"Alec, that is uncalled for." Eliza started.

"Are we not the defenders of Aneira's flock? What good are we, if all we can do, is sacrifice others, lay down and die, when we are told. You are a disgrace of a paladin. This is not the way of the savior, as the Lady Seraphina and Sidonis dreamed."

"Alec please try to understand…" Marec attempted to calm Alec.

"It is all of you who do not understand! What I learned today when I was in my trials, your big secret you all kept from me. You have all done nothing but sentence Talia to death by the hands of the Forsaken."

"That is most preposterous Alec! I know that you are upset with us but lying about it will not help matters." Marec was now the one growing angry.

"Me, the liar? Now, you of all people, are the one placing the blame, Marec? You remember your life's mission, the one that you fulfilled to the letter, at the cost of a young woman's life? Angelica, the woman that came here today, she was the same Angelica who two hundred years ago betrayed the Lady Seraphina. I know because I asked her. She told me that Angelica betrayed her to the Daemon knight Abaddon, who attempted to consume her soul, she told me that…" Alec paused for a moment. The other three were growing intrigued by his story.

"She told you what Alec?" Alec had placed the final piece together, he now knew of Angelica's grand deception.

"She is going to use Talia's blood to bring Abaddon back! Do you not see? We have to go stop them!" To Alec it seemed as though the others still needed a final push. Without thinking, Alec took his hunting knife from its sheath and tore it through the flesh on his hand.

"Alec what are you doing?"

"I, Alec Dante of Highmoore, swear upon my life and immortal soul, that as a Paladin of Valoria, I will save the Priestess Talia and bring about an end to her eternal sadness." He finished the ritual before anyone had the chance to stop him. His blood began to glow and a deafening stroke of thunder bellowed outside confirming that his oath, had been accepted by the goddess. Eliza began to cry, though, through the tears, Alec could see nothing but anger beyond her eyes.

"You ass!" She screamed as she punched Alec in his face, knocking him onto the ground. "How can you go about and trap us like this?" She continued to yell various other curses as she stormed away. Alec dabbed his lip and, seeing that it was indeed bleeding, quickly mended the wound and turned to Marec.

"I swear Marec, upon my honor that I am telling you the truth. Lady Seraphina herself confirmed what I am telling you." Marec stroked his beard before gazing upon Zelus.

"Sir Zelus." Zelus snapped to attention as he was called.

"Yes sir!" Alec made an odd expression at Zelus' response.

"Zelus, I need you to run after Eliza and try and convince her and Talic of what Alec has just told us. We will most certainly need their help in rousing a force strong enough to attack the citadel." Zelus acted shocked, yet Alec knew that he too was eager to strike back at them for what they did to Remora and for seizing Talia.

"It shall be done sir Marec." Zelus spoke as he sprinted from the barracks. Alec looked to his instructor.

"What shall you have me do?" Marec continued to stroke his beard in contemplation.

"Have you any friends within the knights that would follow you to the death even if it went against their orders?" Alec thought for a moment and realized that indeed he did.

"Yes, Dominic and Nilus would follow me, to the ends of the earth if they thought the cause was just. Shall I go and speak with them?"

"Not just yet, first there is something that I need you to do for me."

"Name it and it shall be done."

"I need you to prepare for battle and also to gather my things. Have at least two horses ready in case we need to make a quick getaway." Alec leaned in and whispered to Marec.

"Are you suggesting that I may need to break you out of here?" Marec looked down either side of the hallway and nodded his head slowly.

"The high order's influence is quite strong here. You will have a very difficult time convincing the council I am afraid."

"Then why even bother asking the council's permission to begin with? Let's go now and attack, catching them off guard."

"It would be suicide. First off we have just finished traveling across country and back in a relatively quick fashion. We are all exhausted and would not stand a chance against the temple knights, let alone however many Forsaken. No, it would be best that we take a day to rest, gather our strength and forces and ride out tomorrow."

"Talia may not have that long. It will take us nearly an entire day just to get there."

"Be calm Alec, I am sorry and ashamed to admit that I did know of the ritual you speak of. Granted, I thought that it was in the name of Aneira's light returning to Valoria, but, I do know that whatever this ritual is, it must be performed during the lunar eclipse, which will not occur for two days." Alec hated to admit to it, but he knew that Marec was right. They would do Talia no good if they showed up to battle already half dead. Alec punched the wall in anger and then looked again to Marec.

"I will have our things ready. Once I am finished, I shall speak with Dominic and Nilus."

"Very well, I shall see you in the morning." Alec nodded his head and walking back down the hall he had come down, said goodnight to Keagen and went outside. The night air was cool, wet it filled his lungs with a salty calm as he marched with purpose towards the stables. He reached the stables where he had left his things and found that they were not where he left them.

"Looking for something young Paladin?" Alec whipped around to see the Lion staring at him.

"You know exactly what I am doing here." Alec spoke. The Lion nodded his head.

"Aye, and just so you know, it must be the most foolish thing that you have ever attempted. Were you one of my knights, I would order you to stay here."

"Were I one of your knights?" Alec was curious to know where Talic the Lion was heading with this.

"Precisely, were you one of my knights, I would order you to stay behind. I would order you not to check the hay bale near your horse for the keys to Marec's cell and I would further advise you not to send one of my men to speak with the eastern garrison, which is out on patrol in that area. Were you one of my knights, it would be my duty to inform you of your folly and to not assure you that I would lend you my full support were I not bound by the council. I would also strongly advise you do not check the second key on that ring while exploring the armory. You will probably not find yours and Marec's things already prepared for you."

"Thank you, commander."

"I have no idea what you are talking about. I was merely informing you of what I would tell one of my knights. You may sleep at our house tonight. Oz is already waiting for you outside of the gates. I believe that he will meet you at your destination. I have had the blacksmith busy since you arrived yesterday." The Lion walked away and vanished into the night. Alec walked over to the bale of hay near his horse and sifted through it. Sure enough their rested a key ring with two keys on it. Alec carefully slid the keys into his pocket as he strolled over to the tavern where he was sure to run into Dominic and Nilus.

Alec pressed the door open and entered the tavern, where the usual aromatic assault of fine food and drink filled his nostrils. Alec took a few steps inside and saw his friends Dominic and Nilus already seated next to Zelus in the middle of an intense conversation. Zelus noticed Alec and flagged him down to join them. Alec obliged and pulled up a chair next to Zelus.

"Gentlemen," Alec said casually as he sat down and looked to his friends. Dominic was the first to speak his piece.

"So you need us to march into battle, against the high order? I hope you know that is just a little insane." Alec nodded his head and carried on.

"I am sure Zelus has told you what I figured out is going on did he not?" Dominic leaned back as Nilus looked to grow uneasy.

"He did."

"Then you know that we have no choice but to do this."

"It would most certainly seem that way." They sat together for a moment as if trying to find some better way to save Talia. Nilus spoke up.

"Alec, do you love this girl?" Alec smiled as he answered with a nod.

"I do."

"And you would be willing to do anything for this girl."

"I already swore the blood oath to show it." He said as he lifted his left hand, revealing the mark he had made earlier. Everyone else at the table leaned in to examine the mark.

"Well, I suppose that settles it. Alec, tomorrow I ride with you." Dominic however did not look as eager about the trip as Nilus did. Nilus sensed this and began questioning his brother. "Come on Dom, what say you?" Dominic continued to sit in quiet contemplation as everyone's eyes began to bore into him.

"I require some time to think, alright? You leave tomorrow so, if I plan to leave with you then, I will be there when you leave." He rose from the table and walked outside the tavern, disappearing into the night. Nilus looked back at Alec with a furrowed look on his face.

"I will talk to him."

"Let him make this decision for himself. We cannot make him help us. I understand that Dominic is deeply religious and that this is going to be hard on him."

"Well, Alec, Zelus, I want you two to know that I will fight with you."

"Thank you Nilus, we ride out tomorrow morning. The eclipse will not begin until the following night." Nilus nodded his head and rose from his chair to leave. "We will save you priestess, my friend." He spoke clapping Alec on the shoulder as he made his way outside. Alec stood from the table along with Zelus and they both locked their hands as if shaking at eye level.

"Do not go dying on me tomorrow. I still have to kick your butt and prove to everyone that I am the best."

"Likewise Zelus, without you, who else would I beat up?" The two rivals smiled at one another as they left and marched off to get some rest for the morning ride. Alec neared Eliza's house and carefully rapped on the door. Kristiana opened the door and beckoned for Alec to come inside.

Alec arose the following morning before dawn, to two dire wolves nipping at his hands and Eliza shaking him.

"Alec, you need to wake up." Alec sat up and opened his eyes.

"Is it time already?"

"I am afraid plans have changed. The council convened late last night and they have ordered that the gates be sealed. They refuse to send the knights. If we do not go now, we will be trapped inside as well." Alec quickly rose from his bed and gathered his things attempting to navigate around the bounding wolves.

"Alright, go collect Zelus, Dominic and Nilus, I will go and grab Oz and Marec."

"Oz is already waiting for us. Father saw to it that everything we need is with him." Alec looked to his right to see the sleeping Tear lying on a small sofa. She was resting so peacefully that Alec could not find it within himself to wake her. If he did, she would likely insist on joining them anyway and he already doubted that they would all return from this battle.

"She will understand Alec. As long as we bring Talia back, she will forgive us. Baldur, Aurick, will you keep Tear company, while we are gone?" Both pups let out a gentle bark. Alec nodded his head as he finished tying his boots. As he rose to leave, he watched the puppies jump up on the couch next to Tear, curl up and snuggle into her.

"Alright it is time." He and Eliza both made their way outside.

"I am heading for Marec first. If I took both horses, it would rouse too much attention."

"Good idea, I will meet you right at the gate to the noble's quarter." Alec nodded and spirited away toward the barracks. Alec ran through the darkened streets until he reached the barracks. Alec noticed that none of the torches were lit. He turned his back and saw that again none of the torches were lit.

"Thank you." He spoke to no one knowing that, though the Lion could not order a march on the citadel, he did not have to make sure that his knights did their jobs to the letter. Alec opened the door and walked inside. Alec saw that Keagen was still sitting at his post and smiled as he saw Alec enter. He reached out his arms and stretched out his entire body.

"Awww!" He yawned as he continued to stretch and rose from his chair. "I wonder where the other guard is? My watch was over a while ago. Oh well, guess I will just leave these here for whoever takes over. The next watch should be here in five minutes." He walked away towards the other side of the room. Alec hastily reached for the keys and unlocking the first door, threw the keys aside and proceeded into the cellblock. Half way down the row, he saw Marec eagerly awaiting his visit.

"Marec, it is time."

"I know, I was informed only moments ago." Alec began to fumble with the key ring and found the one that he needed. He shoved the key into the lock and turned it. The lock clicked and Alec quickly opened the cell door.

"Hurry Marec, we do not have much time." Marec and Alec bolted for the door. "Thanks." Alec yelled as he flung the keys to Keagen who was sitting by the other side.

"Keep them, you have one more door and I need to go hide in the cell." He laughed as he closed the locked gate behind him and walked towards Marec's cell. Alec turned to the gate to the armory and, using the remaining key on his ring, unlocked it. Alec pressed the cage door open and ran inside where his and Marec's things sat waiting for them.

"Here, Marec." Alec called as he threw Marec's pack to him. Marec likewise threw Alec his pack and called back to him.

"Alec, there is some armor here. You could probably use the upgrade."

Alec turned and saw sets upon sets of battle armor. Alec quickly began to throw off his ragged clothes and pulled a suit of armor from the rack complete with chainmail, gauntlets, greaves, helmet and pauldrons.

"We need to make haste, Alec. You can put all of those things on once we are at a safe distance." Alec nodded and began to run towards the door. As they made it outside, they could see over the castle walls that light was beginning to pour out from the horizon. They had nearly run out of time. Alec and Marec sprinted across town towards the gate leading to the market district. They had nearly made it when they heard someone screaming.

"The prisoner has escaped! Sound the alarm, close the gates!" Alec could see as the watch began to arouse and the gates began to close.

"Too late!" Alec smiled as he and Marec blew through them with plenty of time to spare. Eliza sat there impatiently waiting for the two of them, the reins of two extra horses in her hand.

"Let's go, let's go." She yelled, and quickly they threw their things into the saddlebags and, mounting their horses, were off. They raced towards the gates to the outer wall and ducked their heads in case there was trouble. Alec rolled his head to the side looking up towards the wall and saw a group of archers looming in overhead.

"Everyone look out!" Alec cried as he saw the archers loose their bowstrings. Alec quickly cast his projectile ward, watching as Marec did the same. The arrows bounced off their wards stopping in midair.

The stream of arrows continued to rain upon them as they made it through the last gate, closed behind them. They rode on passed the gates at full speed hoping to be a safe distance from the capital shortly. As they rode out, Alec looked to his ragtag band. There were only three of them and he could sense that Oz was going to meet them ahead to the southeast. Alec diverted course towards the direction, in which he felt him. They rode for hours and it was nearing close to late afternoon before he had a chance to think.

He began to contemplate his method for attack but he knew that the odds of them succeeding were slim to none at best.

"What is the plan?" Eliza rode next to him yelling over the sounds of the horses' hooves.

"Oz is up ahead. We go there first, that should put us a safe distance from the capital. He is on high ground so, if indeed the council sends someone after us, we should see them coming.

"Also, if I know my brother and your mother, the knights will be stalled significantly." Marec added to the battle planning as they continued to ride with blazing intensity. They all agreed that for now the best course of action would be to regroup, count their numbers and then decide what course of action they should take. They continued to ride in the direction which Alec led until they came to the top of a large hill, where sat Oz waiting for them.

"Oz! Talk about a new look!" Eliza exclaimed as Oz ran up to them, wearing a full set of gleaming battle gear.

"This is what the Lion was talking about. He said that he had taken steps." Alec examined his companion carefully. He was adorned in griffin oriented breastplate, helmet and leg guards. His beak had been reinforced by steel, though his claws, which were already exceptionally deadly, had been left alone.

"Are you ready for a fight?" Alec asked as he stroked Oz's back in the places that were not covered. The griffin cooed merrily, and Alec could sense a juvenile eagerness within him. "Are you still going to be able to fly?" He eyed the griffin's armor suspiciously and, as if offended, Oz cooed bitterly before proving with a few practice flaps that he could indeed lift himself off from the ground. Alec threw his hands up in front of himself to declare that he was wrong and Oz snorted in triumph. Eliza turned toward Alec, reminding him of the urgency of the matter.

"What is our next move, Alec?" Alec looked over the top of the hill to the citadel that lay out in the distance. It was rested behind a high wall, defended by several watchtowers, which he imagined would have several guards stationed at each. Beyond the walls toward the north side of the citadel lay a large wooded area that would offer them some cover from archers yet, with only three fighters and a lion hawk, he did not know what chance they stood. He scratched his head and turned towards the three allies he had mustered.

"We wait here for now. We need to know where our allies are, if any. This mission will be suicide with only four." Eliza and Marec both dismounted their horses and began to unload their things.

"Eliza, can you keep a lookout to make sure that no one from the capital has followed us? Everyone on our side will buy as much time as possible, but that does not mean that they will not come." He began to unload his pack, pulling out a block of cheese and throwing chunks of it to Marec, Eliza and Oz. Alec took a piece for himself as Marec approached Eliza.

"Eliza, might I borrow your bow and quiver?" Eliza looked to her bow and quiver lovingly and reluctantly handed them over. Marec, in turn, looked to Alec and handed them to him.

"Alec, I think now would be an excellent time for you to practice your inscriptions." Alec reached into his back pouch and pulled out his focus crystal.

"What would you have me inscribe?" He asked. Marec smiled to Alec as he began to unload various different weapons and pieces of armor.

"We are going to need every advantage we can muster. Alec, I want for you to use your rune magic to level the playing field. If you do this today, by tomorrow's battle your energy will have already recovered. I am afraid mine would take a couple of days. I am still worn from our duel." Alec's head twitched to the side at the thought. The weariness he had felt from their fight had left his body days ago, yet Marec, a master paladin, was still recuperating after nearly a week."

"Is it typical for my energy to recover so rapidly?"

"Not in the least, but then again, you never were what I would classify as a typical student. Being young, yes, your energy should regenerate quickly, yet the only ones I have encountered that recover as quickly as you are Miss Talia and your friend Zelus, though his case is not nearly as extreme."

"Wait, Zelus can use runes?" Marec shook his head as if the question were obvious.

"No, but runes are not the only type of magic that has been granted to the people of Valoria. Perhaps, in a previous life, an ancestor of his possessed one of these other forms. I must admit like you, he is a unique student. Though, I do not suppose that his talents shall lie with the paladin paradigm. I feel that his talents may yet reveal themselves. I fear their nature may be more brutal, primal even."

"How much of his potential have you helped him to unlock?" Marec shrugged his shoulders.

"That is quite the quandary, much the same as with you, I cannot nearly tell how much potential he has to compare to. Tis impossible to compare the size of a droplet of water, against the depths of the ocean, when one does not know how deep the ocean goes." Alec contemplated his teacher's words, imagining the endless potential that he and Zelus possessed. Turning back to the task at hand, Alec sat with his focus crystal and the various objects that Marec was lying before him.

"What would you have me inscribe?" Marec began to relay his ideas to Alec, who began to inscribe the first of many items. The task required hours of work and concentration. Alec could feel sweat pouring from his brow. Oz looked on eagerly as he began to inscribe the griffet's new armor. Alec set aside the last of Oz's pieces of armor and looked up to Marec, exhausted.

"I am afraid that you are not yet quite done. We have company." Alec looked up and, though he knew that his legs would quake beneath should he stand, he could not help but smile at the people marching up the hill, which turned out to be Zelus and Nilus.

"It is about time you all decided to show up." He tried to push himself off the ground and felt his legs give way. He looked down at his helplessly lifeless legs and with a broad drunkard's smile look up to his arriving friends. "Is it going to be alright if I greet you guys later?" He continued to smile up at them as Marec looked upon him.

"I am sorry to ask this Alec, but do you think that you possess the strength for a few more inscriptions?" Alec looked around him. He had inscribed a full quiver of arrows, Eliza's bow, Oz's armor, his long sword, halberd and a handful of small gems that he found in his pack, which he inscribed with healing runes.

"Sure, why not, what do you need done now?" He spoke awkwardly as if intoxicated. Marec smiled as he placed his hand on Alec's shoulder.

"Get some rest. We have a Divine to save tomorrow. A proud mission for any paladin, be he a master or initiate." Alec did not need to be told twice he closed his eyes and fell onto his side, sound asleep. Pulling a blanket and bedroll from amongst his things, Eliza covered Alec and placed his head atop the rolled mat. Confident that her friend would rest peacefully, Eliza turned to Marec and Zelus.

"So what are our odds?" She asked. Marec shook his head as he thought.

"Not good but the six of us may still stand a fighting chance, if Aneira wills it." Eliza turned towards Nilus.

"Dominic could not make it?" Nilus smiled.

"He will be late, but he will be here. He rode out first thing yesterday morning to the second garrison out to the north. They will follow him."

"What is the strategy?" Eliza asked. It was Marec, who answered.

"Tomorrow, we split into two teams. Alec, Zelus and I shall slip inside. Once we are in, spread out and wait for the commotion to start. Once that happens, the attention will be drawn inside. Zelus shall have an entrance ready for you. Sneak in back and secure an escape route for us. Alec, Talia and myself, will all be counting on you. When Dominic and the others arrive, have them reinforce us. The shorter this battle, the better."

"Alright then, what do we do now?"

"You all wait for morning, Zelus, you come with me. There is one thing you and I must do first." Zelus walked away with Marec, while the others gathered their things and attempted to get some rest for the battle tomorrow.

Alec awoke abruptly the following morning before dawn with Marec shaking him gently. Alec opened his eyes and stared at the paladin.

"Is it time?"

"Soon, but first we have to move toward the tree line at the bottom of the hill." He pointed slightly further to the north and Alec saw the forest that ran alongside the cathedral. Alec searched about and saw that only he and Marec remained.

"Where is everyone?"

"They are waiting for us. You were so tired that we didn't dare disturb you. Oz stayed here last night watching over you while the rest of us set up camp below and discussed a strategy." Alec was appalled that he missed out on the before battle war council.

"Do not worry. I will fill you in on the way, though I fear that your part and mine are going to be the most dangerous of any." Alec rose and pounded his fist into his opposite hand.

"I would not dream of having it any other way." He spoke confidently as he realized that it felt as though his energy had completely returned to him. "You were right sir Marec, I do feel completely revitalized even after all of those items I inscribed."

"Good, I was counting on such a thing. Now, if you please, rise. We need to make haste so that we can be ready for the soldiers." Alec and Marec made their way downhill where they joined the others who were waiting within the concealment of the trees.

Chapter 37 – The Assault

"Are you familiar with the rune of kindle?" Marec asked his student. Alec nodded his head in response.

"Yes, I happened upon it while I was studying in the library of Highmoore." He knew that Marec longed to return to his home as much Alec. He felt a small amount of guilt for pointing out that he had seen it as it was during its days of glory but now was not the time to hold any information back.

"Alright, good. Last night, Zelus and I dug several deep pits and filled them building a large collection of bonfires, which contain a fair amount of dried kindling. We are going to light the bonfires and fan the flames so that smoke begins to spew over the tops of the trees. Thinking that they have a forest fire on their hands, a small garrison of knights shall be sent out to deal with it. That is when you, Zelus and I assume their identities and return inside with the rest. From there, Zelus will sneak within the temple and arrange a route for the others to join us inside after they are done drawing out the enemy. Is this clear so far?"

Everyone nodded their heads and Alec looked toward the cathedral. Whatever it took, he knew that they needed to move quickly once inside. He looked up to the morning sky and already he could see the moon rising to strike the sun. He estimated they had until early evening to rescue Talia.

"When do we begin?" Marec traced Alec's vision back towards the moon. A desperate light twinkled in Marec's eyes and Alec knew that he was secretly praying for more time.

"Do we have an update on Dominic and his reinforcements?" Nilus shook his head reluctantly.

"He said that he would be here, that is all I know." Alec paced impatiently running his left hand through his hair threatening to tear it out.

"We do not have time to wait! If we do not go in there, Talia will be dead." Alec leaned against a nearby tree and looked toward the citadel. Marec also began to pace impatiently as he made his decision.

"Alec is right. Under normal circumstances, I would advise caution and wait it out. However, in this case, haste is our only option." Marec walked forward and looked at the first bonfire. Marec cut his hand open.

"I, Marec Kaldur, solemnly swear to rescue the priestess Talia Degracia or die trying." A stroke of lightning, followed by a blast of thunder, sounding off, far in the distance. Marec and Alec both looked at the scars on their hands. They knew that if they failed and Talia died then they would die as well.

"I have one more rune to teach you, Alec." Alec looked to his teacher.

"I am ready." Marec held out his finger and drew a four sided diamond body an arm's length in height and a forearm's in width. Next Marec proceeded to draw a picture of a cloak within its center.

"This is the rune of concealment. It is a rune that is best inscribed to a piece of equipment as it takes too long to draw to be of much use in a bind. You will have need of this rune in order for us to sneak up on our enemies." Alec began to trace out the rune. Marec waved both hands in front of him to stop him.

"There will be no need for that. First, you must possess the blueprint. The armor of one of the temple knights. You must envision what you wish to appear as and then channel the rune." Marec reached into his pouch and pulled from it a stone.

"I have not left any energy within it but, once everything begins, channel this rune and you shall be concealed." Alec accepted the gift.

"Thank you Marec."

"Are you ready for battle?" Alec turned around and looked down to the first of the bonfires, which were covered in small branches ripe with greenery.

Alec began to draw out his rune. First, he drew an oval then within its center marked crisscross lines with three upward pointing arrows resting above it. As he finished the rune a blue light resonated from its perfectly traced lines and the tips of Alec's fingers lit with up with little flames.

"Are you ready to get this started?" Alec's smile showed that the psychosis was indeed sinking in. Marec drew out his own rune and looked back towards everyone else.

"Get into position, things are about to get loud." Alec and Marec both turned in separate directions and began to throw flames into the bonfires. They ran back, their preliminary work completed and hid back in the trees. Everyone stood back and watched as smoke rose high into the air. Alec drew out the force rune propelling the smoke even higher. They waited for several heart-clenching moments when, suddenly, they could hear the sound of the citadel gates opening followed by the sounds of armored men marching. They listened intently to the sounds of the armored men, the smokescreen had grown too thick for the eyes to see.

"Hurry, this way, I can see the smoke funneling out from here." Alec heard one guard yell and by the sounds of the clinking. He guessed that there were three more following. Alec looked over to Marec who nodded his head. Alec waited for the last guard to run by and he struck him mercilessly in the head, Marec striking the one next to him.

"What was that?" The man in the lead yelled from further down the path. Marec and Alec quickly cast their runes of concealment and turned to answer.

"The new kid fell down." Alec quickly took his opportunity to remove the young man's armor and place it to the side for Zelus. Quickly, he tied the body to a rope Eliza dropped from a tree and tugged on it, giving Eliza the signal to pull the body up into the air. Alec began to pick himself off from the ground as if he had fallen. Marec tied off his guard and they watched as he was sucked away through the cloud of smoke.

"I am sorry sir, it will not happen again." Alec brushed off his armor as he fell in line behind Marec.

"Never mind that right now, we need to put out these fires!" The lead temple knight began to throw water atop the fire nearest to him as Alec, Marec and everyone else approached and one by one began to systematically knock out the knights, tie them up, and anchor their limp bodies high up in the trees. As Marec and Alec approached the last of the guards, one of them turned and noticed that their numbers had been diminished to but a small few.

"It is an ambush! Quickly, fall back!" The man screamed as Nilus, Eliza, and Zelus tackled them to the ground and with Oz's help, dragged them further into the woods. Next, Marec turned to Zelus as he wrestled to remove his own armor and replace with that of the guard Alec had knocked unconscious. Zelus, having finished equipping himself, turned to Marec.

"What is next?" He asked. Marec turned toward Eliza and walked up to her.

"Alright Eliza, now we are going to need some of the non-enchanted arrows." Eliza pulled five normal arrows from her quiver and handed them over, all the while looking over her uncle very cautiously as he was now wearing the guise of a temple knight to her eyes.

"Are you ready?" Marec asked Alec who nodded his head. Marec first took Alec's arm and wedged an arrow into the shoulder joint. Alec flinched feeling the pinch as the arrowhead was forced through the arm joint. He then found that he could no longer properly lower his right arm as Marec went on to his waist and lodged a second arrow there. Next, Marec turned to Zelus and lodged three separate arrows into his armor, one into the left leg, left armpit and into his back.

"Alright Alec, get on Zelus' right side so that you can use your arm to hold his weight. We will have to make this look convincing. Zelus, you will be playing the role of the body in this act." Zelus nodded his head as he stood and allowed Alec and Marec to begin dragging him behind them. They all looked back to Eliza and Nilus, who nodded their heads, placed their fingers to their lips and saluted, silently wishing each other luck as they went about their separate missions.

"Ahhh! Help, beast men!" Marec yelled as loudly as he could, hoping to attract the attention of more temple knights. To this end he was successful as men began to pour out onto the road, weapons drawn. Alec shouldered Zelus' weight while attempting to make his own wounds seem believable. The leader of the group of temple knights came up to them.

"What happened?" Marec did his best to act frantic as they accidently dropped Zelus.

"There was an ambush. We went to clear the fires and it was a trap. There are beast men in the forest. There were too many of them. We got separated from the others and these two were wounded."

"Get these two inside. Get them medical attention immediately. We will be back shortly." Marec nodded his head as he and Alec picked Zelus' limp body off from the ground and dragged Zelus the rest of the way into the citadel. Once inside they looked around. It appeared as though their plan had succeeded. There was not a single guard in sight. They had all gone out to fight the beast men. Marec and Alec let go of Zelus. Zelus looked up at them as he quickly began to remove the arrows from his armor.

"Alright, get out of here and stay out of sight. There are likely more guards around here somewhere and we do not want you to be caught." Zelus nodded and ran off trying to be cautious. Alec, having removed the arrows in his armor, helped Marec as each grabbed a door and began to push it closed. They grunted and groaned but, between the two abnormally strong men, they managed to press it closed.

"Alright now!" Marec yelled as he and Alec both grabbed and set the massive wooden beam that would serve to keep the guards locked outside. Alec patted his hand on the door.

"Be safe, everyone. You are on your own now." Alec turned to Marec. "Where to next?" Marec turned and pointed to the tallest building Alec had ever seen. Alec traced his eyes up the side of the marble colored building, until the skyline, and the reflection of sunlight cut off his vision.

"Miss Talia will be up there in the Goddess's Spire. That is where the ritual will be performed."

"Are you certain?"

"Aye, that was where it was to be performed before I knew what it was." Marec bore a painfully solemn expression.

"We will have time for blame and regret later, first we have to save Talia."

"You are right. Let us away." The two men ran in the direction of the tower being sure to duck around corners and to stay out of sight of the numerous guards still on patrol within the cathedral's walls. Marec, who had taken the lead, shot his hand up in the air to halt Alec.

"What is it?" Alec whispered.

"There are a large number of Forsaken up ahead."

"Forsaken here?" Alec spoke and then thought for a moment afterward.

"So it is true then, Angelica was from the beginning, working for the Forsaken." Marec shook his head despairingly but instead Alec turned to anger.

"And Aneira's shield shall fall to the hands of the sentinels' betrayer." Alec considered the final line of the fragmented prophecy that Triam had imparted upon him back in Remora.

"Marec...Triam's prophecy. Angelica plans to kill Talia. Talia is Aneira's shield, which means that Angelica is the one who betrayed Highmoore." Marec's head snapped back towards Alec.

"How can you be certain?"

"When I was with the Lady Seraphina, she told me that she had been betrayed by the same Angelica who has betrayed you and Talia. Angelica was working with the Forsaken then and she was there when Highmoore fell. Did you not say that someone from within the tower of Highmoore must have allowed the Forsaken access?" Marec clenched his fist angrily. Alec could hear the bones popping from the strain.

"I believe that you are right Alec, we must end this today. We must claim vengeance for what she has done." Marec turned to face the Forsaken then ducked around the corner as he saw a vision of horror standing over the high balcony. Marec quickly pressed Alec backwards, pinning him to the wall.

"What is it?" Marec placed his finger to his lips signaling Alec to be quiet. Marec stood frozen in fear as he continued holding Alec in place. They heard the sounds of battle emanating from outside the walls. Alec knew that Dominic must have arrived with reinforcements but then he heard the sound a little bit differently a second time, as if closer within the walls.

"Zelus is in trouble!" Alec jerked sideways but Marec pressed against him and shook his head.

"He will have to manage on his own. We must save Talia." Alec nodded his head. He listened some more as he could hear the Forsaken clattering about. He and Marec stayed back in the shadows to remain unseen by the many Forsaken that were beginning to swarm. They sat and waited for them to pass but, instead, Alec heard the one voice that terrified him most.

"DO NOT GO AFTER THE USELESS KNIGHT. HE IS THE DIVERSION. THE PALADINS ARE HERE WITH THE SWORD OF THE ENEMY!" Alec could never forget such a booming powerful voice. He turned back to Marec who nodded, fear and fatigue pouring from his eyes. Alec remembered the power that the Daemon knight's voice carried and gripped the hilt of the Sidonis sword tightly, the final thing that would stand between he and Talia was Belias.

"What do we do?" Alec asked of Marec. The senior paladin scratched at his beard as he watched the sky already nearing evening. He turned and looked again to the lightly clad Forsaken troops then turned confidently to Alec.

"We must not allow Sir Zelus' sacrifice to go to waste. We shall save our priestess."

"I was growing tired of hiding anyway," said Alec. They both rose to their feet and dispelled their runes of concealment. Marec drew his weapons as did Alec.

"Hrraaaaahhh!" They both cried out as they ran to meet their enemy head on and to lash out at them with the fury of rabid beasts. Alec cleaved through a Forsaken adversary and it turned to dust beneath his blade. He and Marec slew several more as they ran into the courtyard where Belias still stood watching.

"ARCHERS! FIRE!!!" The Forsaken bowmen drew back their bowstrings and let fly a massive plague of arrows. Alec focused on his projectile ward as did Marec and they repelled the waves of arrows as they ran for the doorway to the spire. Arrows rained down upon them from all directions and without dropping their shields, they possessed no definitive way of defending themselves.

"Aahh!" He yelled. Alec could see the doors right in front of him. He was only a few steps away from them when two arrows penetrated through his back exiting from his right hip and left shoulder. He stumbled the last few steps but managed to keep himself firm enough to ward off the remaining arrows. More arrows began to strike his shield as Marec forced open the doors and dragged him inside. As Marec slammed the door behind them, Alec snapped both arrows in half and began to brace himself to remove them.

"Hurry Alec, they will soon be at the door." Alec took in a deep breath and wrenched the arrow in his hip free.

"Aahhh!" He hollered as the shaft of the arrow tore free. He reached for the second still in his shoulder. He closed his eyes and, again, took a deep breath.

"Aaahhhh!!!" He cried again as Marec tore the shaft from his shoulder while he prepared. Alec shot back a combination look of aggravation and gratitude as he focused on his shield and accessed the mending rune. He gritted his teeth as he felt the flesh sewing itself together.

Alec then rose to his feet and drew out the force rune, facing the walls. He turned his head towards Marec and smiled a daring smile. Marec turned from the door and looked to the opposite wall and also drew out the rune.

"Hyaaah!" They both cried out as they forced their hands through the center of the runes causing the walls to explode. Alec and Marec ran out of the way, as rubble from the floor above began crashing down around them.

"Are you worried about them getting through the door now?" Marec smiled and looked at Alec.

"The fight ahead shall be the most difficult yet. I think now is the time to prove that you are Sidonis' heir." Marec told Alec and Alec hesitated, realizing that he never told Marec how he had failed his final trial. Alec sheathed his sword and took in a deep breath as he pulled the Sidonis sword from its sheath. The blade hummed in his hand and he could feel the immense amount of power flowing out of him and into the blade. The first wave of Forsaken appeared atop the staircase leading higher into the spire.

"Hyyaaaah!" Alec and Marec cried out as Alec brought down the very power of Aneira upon his foes.

Chapter 38 – The Battle Outside

Across the citadel, Zelus ran for his very life as hordes of Forsaken chased him down. He had snuck across the grounds to the opposite wall and secured a line for Eliza and the others to scale once Dominic and the reinforcements arrived. He had just finished and was beginning to head back towards Alec and Marec when he had been discovered.

Now, droves of Forsaken raced after him to gut him and use him in a stew, or whatever it was, the Forsaken did for kicks. Zelus ran up a stairway, cleaving through a cloth adorned Forsaken guard. He kicked through the creature as it evaporated into dust and continued to fly along the wall. He looked back briefly and found that there were too many for him to count without stopping to ask.

Deciding against trusting their manners, he continued to run until he neared upon a guard tower. He cut through three more Forsaken as he attempted to dash along the outer wall then came to several archers that blocked his path. They each trained their bows on him and without other options, Zelus dove to his right, onto the roof of a nearby structure, and ran across it avoiding the volley of arrows that was unleashed at him. Bounding from one roof to another, Zelus made his way past the archers and back onto the wall, where he reached the tower.

Zelus ran inside and began to climb the stairs, being sure to knock anything within arm's reach down the stairs toward his adversaries. He slew two more Forsaken as he scaled upward and threw the disintegrating bodies down on their comrades without thinking about how useless such an act was. He arrived at the very top of the tower and after closing the double latch doors, flipped a table on top of them.

He could hear the clicking of the Forsaken's voices below as he began to knock over weapon racks, chairs and tables overtop the doors. Zelus hit the end of the line as he stared out over the wall. He had run out of places to go. Zelus turned around and ran toward the side of the room overlooking the doorway, taking up his stance, he prepared to take as many of them as he could with him.

The Forsaken began to tear through the barricade and though he could not understand the clicking and chattering, he got the sense that there was nothing beyond the barrier save malice and hatred. Zelus could see clawed hands reaching up and moving pieces of furniture out of the way.

Lunging out, Zelus began hacking away at their hands as they attempted to enter. He could hear them hiss in agitation as he cleaved their hands away. After the seventh or eighth hand Zelus claimed in this fashion, the Forsaken began to pull away. Zelus ran across the room to the window and looked out over the wall and watched as a force of horsemen could be seen coming over the hilltop. He saw a flash of light from up above, Eliza's signal that all was well and they were ready to begin their assault. Zelus flashed back, capturing the sun's rays on his sword blade, so that Eliza knew he was alright. Turning to face the window frame, Zelus stood triumphantly with his hands on his hips, one foot up on the windowsill and took up his hero's stance.

"BOOOM!" the building around him began to shake and shimmy, as a malevolent force pounded against it. Zelus dipped his head out and saw a massive hole had been blown into the wall and more Forsaken approached. Beyond them, he could see the horror that was Belias, his massive black sword held high commanding them to charge. For a split second Belias' head turned towards Zelus almost causing him to seize up and faint.

"BURN LITTLE VALASCAAN WORM!" Belias boomed holding out one hand in front of his face as if offering up a gift. Zelus' eyes shot open wide, as it appeared Belias blew into his palm, spewing fire forth like the dragon gods of old. Zelus pulled his head up in time to avoid being seared alive. Zelus turned back towards the window and estimated his chances of survival should he have to jump. He looked to the right, the left and straight down and found nothing that he could jump to. He turned back towards the staircase, which was now filled with flames.

"Jump to my death, be burned alive…open casket, king's pyre." He contemplated his options further as if the entire event were some sort of twisted joke.

He listened intently over the cackle of the flames to the sound of Belias' maniacal, evil laugh. Zelus winced in pain as he could feel the inner cochleae of his ears being assaulted mercilessly. He tipped to the the side, afraid that he was about to vomit, and then realized that Belias must be laughing. Laughing, because he had found out Alec and Marec.

"HEAD BELOW. KILL THE ELDER PALADIN AND BRING ME THE YOUNG ONE. THE TIME FOR THE RITUAL HAS COME AT LAST. TONIGHT MY MASTER SHALL BE FREED AND, WITH HIS REBIRTH, SHALL COME THE END OF ALL WHO EMBRACE THE GODDESS. ONCE WE HAVE MASSACRED ALL THAT SHE LOVES, WE SHALL REACH UP INTO THE HEAVENS AND PEEL THAT BENEVOLENT WENCH FROM THE SKY AND RIP OUT HER HEART." Zelus did his best to cover his ears in an attempt to drown out Belias' overpowering voice. He pulled his hands away and saw that they were covered in blood. He dabbed his ears again and found that the sheer power of the Daemon knight's voice was alone enough to kill a man.

Zelus' tower shook as Belias blasted it again, this time causing a hole to appear directly in front of Zelus. He now stared out at Belias and raising up his right hand lowered two fingers, forming a rather rude gesture. Zelus felt for a moment that Belias laughed as he blew his flaming breathe again.

Zelus raised his hands out in front of himself, prepared for the worst. Before he had a chance to realize what had happened, Zelus was engulfed in flames as Belias' blast seared past him, blowing apart the opposite side of the tower. Zelus stared down at his hands and marveled at the miracle that he was still alive. He raised his head up to see Belias walking away, believing him to be dead. Zelus stood and looked about himself at the cataclysmic scene that he stood within.

"How am I still alive?" He spoke aloud, still unsure that he was in fact, living. He pinched himself and flinched from the pain. The tower began to rattle around him as the roof began to cave in. Zelus looked from side to side and quickly thrust his body through the opening. His eyes were filled with the sight of the rapidly nearing ground.

Outside of the citadel, Eliza cupped her mouth and averted her eyes as she witnessed the tower containing her secret love, exploding into a fiery pyre and crumbling to the ground only a short few seconds later. Many of the knights that now sat next to her gasped in unison as they watched the stone wall begin to crumble from the force of the violent eruption. Many of the men turned away as Eliza had done but Oz raised his mane high into the air and screeched out against the sky angrily.

Eliza turned her head towards the brave griffin as did many other men, as he spread his wings to their full length and let out his shrill battle cry. Eliza sat up straight in the saddle of her warhorse, raised her sword into the air and attempted to match Oz's fearless call for battle. Eliza rode to the front of the lines next to Oz and turned to face the troops Dominic had brought with him.

"I am Eliza Kaldur. I am the daughter of Talic the Lion, knight commander of the Aneiran knights. We have all gathered here today because in the absence of justice and truth. A tyrant has arisen. A tyrant who hides under the guise of high priestess of the Aneiran order. She has taken her power and has used it to taint the word of our holy mother and now she holds some of our own, behind an army of Forsaken monsters. I am here today to overthrow this tyrant in the name of the holy mother." Eliza threw her sword arm back into the air as did many of the knights all calling out violently and daring for any to come out and face them.

Eliza turned with her horse and pointed her sword as she called for the charge. Oz spread his wings and with a few powerful flaps took flight. She and her garrison of knights commanded their steeds to ride and their bodies were propelled with surreal animation as the knights rode to save their allies.

They neared ever closer as the gates began to part before them. Eliza could see ahead that, within the gate, marched hundreds of the Forsaken. As she rode to meet them, she cried out to her men.

"Do not fear them, men. Their might is nothing but fable and myth. They are not of this land and possess no true physical form. Strike out at them with the fury of Aneira's wrath and they shall crumble to ash and dust!" Her horsemen continued to charge. Their battle cries shook the ragged garments the Forsaken wrapped their frail bodies with.

Eliza charged into the front lines of the Forsaken and they lashed out at her with an unholy fury. Hers and the numerous blades of the knights around her slew countless numbers, as the air grew foggy from the abundance of Forsaken evaporations. They continued to lash out as one after another disappeared, but for every one they fell, more came to take their place. Eliza looked back as her forces grew encircled by the Forsaken hordes. She turned her horse, cut down another of the wicked beasts and addressed her men.

"Form up!" She called and her knights began to form up around her. She could see Dominic off to her side as he sliced through Forsaken by two and three at a time with the massive swings of his halberd. Dominic looked to her for a second as a great shadow blotted out the sun.

"Shields up!" Eliza called and everyone began to raise their shields as they attempted to fend off the approaching creatures. Eliza waited as she sliced again and again and watched as Oz swooped down time after time shredding more Forsaken than any of the others who fought beside her. Eliza tipped her head to the side after a moment to see that not a single arrow fell. She lowered her shield and looked up to the sky to see that the moon had begun to eclipse the sun.

"We are too late!" She spoke to herself as the Forsaken continued to swarm around them.

Chapter 39 – The Sacrifice

Alec pressed his force rune against the wall and screamed as he willed the cold stone to crumble at his command. The walls collapsed, dropping thousands of pounds of debris atop of the Forsaken charge that had met them a floor below. Alec turned to Marec who was panting heavily and bleeding. Alec took a moment to examine himself.

He, too, was growing weary, the power of his sword still sapping his strength. They had been battling for well over an hour in an attempt to conquer the spire. Alec looked to his shaking hands and to the blood that was rolling down his arm. Reaching into his pocket, Alec pulled the last of his mending stones and tossed one over to Marec.

"Last two." He spoke as they both looked up and saw that they were nearly to the top of the sky piercing monolith. Marec turned back toward Alec and slipped the one stone into his pocket.

"Save them. We will need to be at our best before we are able to face Belias, if need be." Alec nodded his head still terrified of the thought that he may have to face Belias once more. He had barely escaped with his life last time and that had been without Belias revealing his true power to Alec. He only hoped that he had grown strong enough in the past couple of months to defeat him once the time came for the hammer of fate's bell to strike.

Alec looked up and saw that his blast had cleared a path for them to cut through the wall over the rubble that had fallen down. Alec climbed onto the new staircase built of conquered stone and passed through the opening he had created. He turned immediately and, with Marec at his heels, proceeded up the stairway. He turned and peeked around the corner as the Forsaken lay in wait for them to pass through the corridor they had just avoided.

Marec clapped Alec gently on the shoulder as they clamored up the stairs, saving themselves precious time. They neared the top of the stairs and stopped as they came face to face with a force of Forsaken warriors waiting for them. The room opened up into a grand display of stone and marble. The ceiling was opened up as if a massive oculus. Alec could see the moon touching the sun. The ritual had nearly begun. Marec and Alec could see the tip of the Grand Shrine where Talia was bound and gagged, kneeling at its edge.

"TALIA!" Alec yelled as he stepped forward. He saw that Talia was chained down at the top of the stairs. She was shackled at both of her wrists. He turned his head slightly to the side as Angelica walked out barefoot onto the marble dais where Talia was being held.

Angelica wore an elegant long black gown, which flowed behind her as if made from thousands of feathers. Talia screamed from behind her gag and Alec could see the tears rolling out of her eyes. Alec looked to the marks on her flesh and he could feel the rage within ignite. Talia bore several scratches on her flawless face and burns on her arms and in the nape of her neck. Alec could only imagine the horrific tortures they had rendered on her flesh. Alec guessed that Marec noticed as well, because he could feel the swell of energy rising off from Marec's body.

"Welcome!" Angelica spoke as she stopped next to Talia. "You have come at long last, to bear witness to the rebirth of Daemon's progeny. It was on this day, two hundred years ago, that we lured the Lady Seraphina to these very chambers in order to perform a similar ritual. It was our agenda to allow for our Lord Abaddon to consume her soul. He was to rise up, fulfill his destiny and tear Aneira's throne from the heavens. Striking her down, he would rest her at the feet of her father, Daemon, for the final judgment.

We were thwarted however, as Sidonis' cursed spawn caught onto our plan in time. Enough to seal away our lord and master's soul within the very eclipse that would have given him invulnerability along with the sacrilegious weapons he would use for the assault. Now, enough time has passed, and we shall bring our master back to us to lead us to greatness." The oculus continued to open until it had reached its full circumference.

"Well, about that, first my friend and I are going to cut up your little rag dolls," Alec gestured towards the Forsaken. "Then, when I am done with all of them, I am going to come up there and pay you a visit. One which leaves me walking out of here, with the young priestess there, and leaves you in wretched misery, until the end of your days." Angelica began to laugh at Alec's seemingly unlikely threat though neither he, Marec nor the Forsaken returned her laughter.

"You march into my citadel, climb my tower, are hopelessly outnumbered, and yet you honestly believe that you still have a chance of saving the sacrifice? Why bother? Why go through all of this trouble just to throw your life away? To bring about the renewal of Lord Abaddon's power is the sole purpose for her existence. This is the reason she was born!" Angelica was beginning to descend into madness. She was becoming rageful, hateful. Alec remembered his own emotions and began to wrestle for control of them so as not to lose himself within the presence of Daemon.

"Because you are an evil wench!" Alec answered matter-of-factly as if it were obvious. Again, Angelica laughed as if she were laughing at the folly of a young child. She looked up at the moon, which had nearly covered the sun. A dark shadow spread across the room and was coming nearer to Talia, with every second they allowed Angelica to stall them.

"It is because you love her, is it not? Ah yes, I can see it on your face. That is what it is. Well, then tell me lover boy, do you like what we have done to her thus far?" Angelica forced Talia's head from side to side, displaying her many wounds for Alec to see. Alec gripped the hilt of his sword. It's draining effect had gone by unnoticed for some time as Alec could feel his power steadily rising.

"I am going to kill you." He threatened.

"Not before I kill her!" Angelica yelled as she reared on Talia and began to blast her with bursts of energy. Talia screamed in pain as she was struck again and again by the blasts of lightning. Alec watched as the pain eventually caused Talia to enter into her trance state. Her hair blew back into the wind alive and ablaze as if wreathed in fire. Her eyes glowed bright emerald and light shot up from her body and passed through the opening of the oculus penetrating the sky.

"She is using Talia's trance state to bring back Abaddon's soul. If she remains in that state for too long then she will die and Abaddon shall return." Alec yelled.

"Quite right, once the energy of her spirit is expended, the trance will drain her life force, summoning Abaddon back into the world." Angelica confirmed.

"TALIA!" Alec and Marec cried as they charged the Forsaken lines and began to let loose the wrath of heaven upon their adversaries. With the Sidonis sword's power, the first rune emblazoned, Alec's simplest slice cleaved through dozens of Forsaken at a time. Marec too fell many Forsaken one after the other. They slashed, parried and blocked countless attacks in an impossible attempt to dwindle their numbers. Alec looked around to watch as Angelica continued to torture Talia, whose cries of pain pierced Alec's heart. He blocked another attack and watched, as Marec was overtaken by the Forsaken and dragged down to the ground. He was beginning to grow desperate. He had not come all of this way just to watch his love die.

A haunting wind picked up around him, Alec could feel his veins coursing with pure energy. He opened his eyes, which turned blindingly bright and his hair changed to waving gold. The Forsaken backed away from him as the aura surrounding him began to burn away at their flesh. Alec looked around as they moved further away from he and Marec and he plunged his sword into the ground to make use of both of his hands.

His hands, as if reacting instinctively, drew out separate runes of force. His head drooped down as his hands slowly crafted each of the lines necessary. After each hand finished drawing out the body of the runes, he whipped his head up, his face void of fear, anger and despair. Void of everything except for the raw undeniable look of determination, to not let anything stand in his way.

"HYAH!" He cried out as he forced both hands into the center of their runes, causing a massive burst of energy in two separate directions. The Forsaken were propelled backwards as large pieces of wall collapsed, releasing the Forsaken bodies which poured out over top of the citadel. Angelica smiled as the floor on one side began to collapse, falling onto the hordes that waited below. Alec and Marec now stood in the center of the room, held up by the small amount of marble that remained.

"Now I understand why my master has asked for me to spare your life." Alec looked up, still maintaining his trance state as Belias walked out.

Alec examined Belias to see that he was carrying a black suit of armor similar to his own, yet this was far eviler. It was darker, more twisted, it bore horns and spikes as if it were intended for Daemon himself. Yet Belias walked with the armor, lovingly as if in admiration of it. He knelt down next to Talia, placing the armor down as if laying a babe to sleep and performed what Alec could only guess was a prayer. After he was finished, Belias rose to his feet and drew his sword.

"I do not care what your master wants. I am going to stop you here and now." Belias slowly walked down the stairs, Alec could feel his power closing in around him making it difficult for him to breath. Alec stood his ground as Belias unleashed his true power. The temperature of the room increased several times over. Sweat began to pour off from Alec's brow as he and Marec stood side by side ready to take on the knight together. As Alec looked to his side, he could see Marec's knees trembling from the force of Belias' gravity aura.

"Now this is quite a treat, is it not? The Paladin of Highmoore and the boy who narrowly escaped the fall. Do you remember me boy? Do you remember when I killed your sister?" Alec's vision blurred as he remembered that night when his sister was slain.

"Do you wish to know how she died? I will tell you regardless, you see. We Daemon knights thrive on souls and none better than the souls of the Divine. Your sister was a Divine you see, and her soul was oh so delicious." Alec pulled his sword from the ground and raising his shield charged at Belias. Marec followed close behind screaming with rage as Belias tipped his head from side to side as if stretching.

"My souls have grown restless in their time of wait. It will feel exhilarating to let them taste fresh blood." Belias cut his sword horizontally through the air causing a shockwave to lash out at Alec and Marec. Alec dropped to a knee as he had the last time Belias used this attack and placed his body behind his shield. Marec was not as quick and was flung across the flooring, barely catching onto its edge.

Alec rose from his knee and slashed at Belias who parried with his sword. The force of the two weapons colliding, knocked Belias back a step and Alec slashed again. Belias raised his shield this time catching Alec's attack. The force of Alec's attack striking Belias' shield knocked Alec off from his feet where he struck a broken pillar on the opposite side of the room.

"GAH!" Alec groaned as blood sprayed out of his mouth and he fell to his hands and knees.

"It appears as though you are yet unworthy to wield the Sidonis sword. I find this most amusing that you have not been killed by it already." Marec looked over to Alec as he had finally gotten to his feet. Alec looked his teacher in the eye and smiled, blood oozing from his mouth.

"What can I say, Talia was in danger and I have a tendency to be a little bit impulsive."

"Do you have a plan?" Marec shook his head and waited for Alec, to come to his side. Alec looked at Marec with shock on his face.

"You are the senior paladin here. I am just making this up as I go."

"You are the one who can assume trance." Marec rebuttled. Belias stood waiting for them to make their move.

"Ah who cares? Let us just kill this beast. HYAH!" Alec yelled out as he struck out at Belias as did Marec. Belias defended himself against the two attackers with ease as he parried Alec's sword with his own and continued to hold Marec at bay with his shield. They both acted wild and desperate trying desperately to land a blow against Belias. Alec and Marec made eye contact for a brief moment and both feigned an attack. Belias raised his defense to block the blows but instead Alec and Marec changed direction mid swing and raked their blades against the sides of Belias' armor.

"HRAH!" Belias bellowed as their blades sliced across his armored flesh. Alec's sword, left behind a sizeable wound. Marec's enchanted claymore blasted into Belias' opposite side. The blade shattered, though being imbued with the force rune forced Belias to a knee.

Alec's body was forced sideways from the force of Belias' souls leaking out as they had before. His body was thrown to the stairs below Talia. More blood sprayed from Alec's mouth as he could see that Marec was now alone dropping to his knees, covering his ears at what Alec could only imagine were the effects of the banshee's shriek.

"ENOUGH!" Belias boomed with his powerful voice knocking Marec to the ground. Alec looked for his sword, which lay next to Marec. Belias rose and held his side firmly as he limped toward Marec.

"FOOL PALADIN!" Belias continued to boom, continuously blasting Marec with the force of his voice. He walked up to Marec and kicked him in his ribs. Marec's body was launched against the remaining wall. He smacked into it hard and fell back to his knees. Belias walked forward and kicked Marec again and again until Marec could not rise from the ground.

Alec pressed himself up and Belias turned on him, pulling the broken claymore blade from his side. Throwing the blade like a spear, he impaled Alec in the shoulder. Alec fell backwards and began to try to remove the blade. Belias walked up to Marec and lifted him into the air as Alec rose to his knees and wrenched the blade out of his shoulder with a spray of crimson.

"NOW YOU DIE!" Belias called, Alec took off in flight. Marec looked up. Barely conscious, he smiled and, drawing his force rune, knocked the blade over to Alec. Belias stared into the paladin's eyes as he closed his metal hand tightly and pulled back his arm. Marec looked over to Alec and smiled. Belias punched him hard in the stomach. The force behind the blow was enough to tear deep into Marec's body, forcing an explosion of metal, blood and gore to burst from his back.

"NOOOO!" Alec cried as he brought the Sidonis sword down towards Belias' head, who turned just in time.

"GRRRRRRRAAAAAAAAHHHHHHHH!" The Daemon knight screamed with all of his horrific power as his arm was again cleaved from his body and massive cracks appeared within his armor. Alec's was thrown backwards and this time, was certain he felt several of his own bones breaking. He tried to lift his body up, but fell back to the ground. His vision blurred. He wished that he had lost his hearing instead of his vision as he heard Belias' deranged laughter rattle the spire.

"You nearly killed me, though, unfortunately for you, you missed your mark. It will take a long while for my body to repair itself this time. Sheath your sword, Paladin. I do not want you dead and that sword has left you with nothing." He rolled Alec over onto his back and Alec could see Talia above him fall out of her trance and lie on the ground, looking down at him. Angelica ceased her assault on the helpless priestess and turned to look at the sky. Talia looked into Alec's eyes, tears pouring from them, her body ready to give out. Alec could tell that her heart was slowing, she was dying.

"Alec, thank you for trying to save me." Alec used what strength he had left to hold back his own tears. He turned his head from side to side in an attempt to deal with his grief.

"I told you that I would always come for you." She smiled weakly as her eyes began to close.

"TALIA STAY WITH ME!" Her eyes snapped back open and she looked at Alec.

"But, I am so tired." The decibel of her voice was nearly that of a whisper. Belias lifted Alec and sat him up so that he kneeled before Talia.

"Look to your love, Paladin. You shall watch as she dies and your despair shall open your heart to Daemon. My Lord Abaddon shall be reborn and we shall use you to lead our armies to glory." Alec pulled his arm away from Belias the best that he could.

"I will never serve you, I would die before I led your army." He yelled, defiantly. Belias placed Alec's hand under his shirt. "Hold your wound, you are bleeding to death. Your death may yet still arrive should you choose to resist us, though now is not that time." Alec reached within his shirt and he could feel his fingers growing sticky and wet. An idea struck him as he continued to talk to Talia. Alec closed his eyes, breathed deeply and looked to Talia.

"You have to stay awake Talia. You have so much to live for. You have to live on so that I can break your sadness. I still want to walk with you and show you the world just as I promised." Alec dug into his wound some more and began to trace over his heart with one finger.

"Alec, I think we both know that can never happen now."

"I know it cannot, I so wanted to be the one to make you happy again." Alec spoke as he continued to fidget with his wound. With his other hand, he reached into his leather pouch on his belt for the second mending stone Marec had told him to save. He closed his eyes, activating the rune as Talia continued to say her final goodbyes.

"But Alec, you did make me happy again. You taught me what it was to love someone. And, I love you so much." She held out her hand to him as if she were going to attempt to touch him. Alec could feel the mending rune's effect run out. He only hoped that the energy that it gave him would be enough for his final act of courage.

"I love you too, Talia, always have, since the very first time that I saw you. I made you a promise…" Alec reached out for her, and with a quick twist of his wrist, flung her necklace into her outstretched hand, which by now was covered in his own blood.

"I INVOKE THE RITE OF MARTYR!" Alec cried as he ripped away his shirt revealing the rune of Martyr engraved on his chest, which written in his own blood, began to glow.

"WHAT!?" Both Belias and Angelica turned on him as Alec took their surprise as his opportunity. His limbs were weak, but his legs would hold him. His arms were numb, but his fingers could still grasp. Alec with one quick fluid motion slashed his sword upward and struck Belias on his other side. The Daemon knight cried out in pain as his other arm was removed and his body was thrown backwards in a spectacular explosion. Alec was flung hard against the marble. Belias no longer held the strength to fight him, and Alec sheathed his sword before it killed him.

"I told you I was coming for your other arm." A darkness seemed to engulf the room. Alec realized that he had barely managed to strike in time.

"Lord Abaddon! I am sorry. I did not know." Angelica began to speak frantically as she dropped to her knees and began pleading for her life.

"I AM DISAPPOINTED IN YOU NEMESIS. I THOUGHT THAT THE BOY'S PLOY WAS OBVIOUS. HAD I THE STRENGTH, I WOULD CLAIM YOUR SOUL FOR MINE OWN."

"Please, Lord Abaddon. I could not have known. Such a technique should have been destroyed long ago. I ordered for all records of the old paladin order to be turned to ash."

"YET YOU FAILED TO GRASP THAT THE BOY COULD HAVE ACCESSED THE INFORMATION WHILE TRAINING WITH THE LADY SERAPHINA. NOW, YOUR FAILURE HAS COST ME MY VESSEL! I SHOULD HAVE KNOWN NOT TO EXPECT SO MUCH FROM A NYMPH, FALLEN FROM GRACE!" Alec looked up at Angelica and could see now why she looked so familiar to him. Visions of the Lady Seraphina flashed before his eyes and he realized that the two looked as if they could have been sisters. The mad Nymph dropped to her knees for a moment.

"Please my lord, forgive me! Whatever your desire, I shall repent! I shall fulfill your every desire, if only you would embrace me again, in your darkness." She pleaded as the voice began to address Belias.

"BELIAS! YOU HAVE ALSO DISAPPOINTED ME. THOSE CENTURIES I SPENT PREPARING YOU, TEACHING YOU MY ANCIENT SECRETS AND EVEN LEADING YOU TO DEVOURING YOUR OWN DIVINE. THIS IS HOW YOU REPAY ME?" Belias who still could not move spoke from his position on the floor.

"Please forgive me my lord. Once my body recovers, I will be happy to repent for my failure in whatever way you deem necessary."

"THAT I SIMPLY CANNOT DO. YOUR FAILURE WARRANTS NOTHING SHORT OF DEATH!"

"But my lord, it was I who came to your rescue while the others sat in the Scar or half a world away, merely biding their time. Without my efforts, you would not be able to return at all."

"THE OTHERS EACH HAD THEIR OWN MISSIONS TO FULFILL. EVERY PIECE UPON MY BOARD HAS FOUND ITS PROPER PLACE SAVE THIS. THE LANDS TO THE WEST ARE IN CHAOS, THE SOUTHERN CONTINENT IS ON THE VERGE OF CIVIL WAR. SOON WE SHALL BASK IN AN ENDLESS TORRENT OF FRESHLY HARVESTED SOULS AND THE ALL FATHER'S HEART SHALL BEAT AGAIN.

THE HEARTS OF SIN HAVE BEEN LAIN AND NOW GATHER THE ILL INTENT OF THIS WORLD'S DENIZENS. AND WHILE ALL OF THE OTHERS HAVE SUCCEEDED IN THEIR MISSIONS, YOU ARE THE ONLY ONE WHO HAS FAILED ME. AH, BUT IF YOU FEEL THAT YOU SHOULD RECEIVE A SPECIAL REWARD FOR YOUR SERVICES THAN YOU SHALL. YOU SHALL SERVE AS MY VESSEL FOR NOW!"

Belias screamed a horrible metallic cry as his broken body was lifted into the air, and floated over top of the armor on the floor. His cries grew more intense, as his armor began to disintegrate one piece after another into a fine ash, which rained down upon the other armor. Alec could see as the souls began their attempt at escape, even as they were being sucked down into the new body, but to no avail as Alec watched each and every one being pulled down out of sight.

"NEMESIS, KILL THE BOY!" The voice that was emanating from nowhere now came from the armor that was moving about on the floor. It's arms reached out as if flailing limbs tasting their first hour of life. The legs twisted and shifted in unnatural positions as the hips rolled to fall in place for the legs to press the rest of the body upward. Slowly it rose to its full height and began to flex its limbs. Turning away from her master Angelica turned back towards Talia and Alec.

"You see boy, you have stopped nothing. You cannot stop me from completing the ritual." Angelica, or Nemesis as the voice had called her, began to zap Talia with her magic and Alec immediately felt the effects transfer over to him. Alec cried out in agony as he saw Talia rise to her feet, the life's energy from Alec's body flowing into her, revitalizing her.

"ALEC NO!" Talia cried as she realized what it was that he had done. Talia strained against her chains trying to reach Angemesis to stop her, but she lacked the strength. Talia turned back to Alec who bore a triumphant smile on his face while the light in his eyes continued to fade. Talia renewed her attempt to reach out to him.

"Alec, please do not die, I need you."

"I am sorry Talia, this is my sacred duty, I have fulfilled my oath and now you can live. My only regret is that I did not have the chance to take the sadness from your eyes." Alec could no longer support his own weight and he fell to the ground, landing hard on his side, his eyes still watching Talia's. Talia continued to sob as she pulled against her chains desperately, screaming for Alec all the while.

"Do not worry child, as soon as he dies his Martyr rune will dissipate and then you will join him."

"I think not!" Everyone save Alec who no longer had the strength, turned their heads to Eliza, Zelus and Dominic who had just arrived. Eliza pulled back her bowstring and shot an arrow at Angelica, who reached out with one hand and caught the arrow.

"It will take much more than that to kill me." However, when she caught the arrow, she was forced to momentarily cease her attack on Alec via his rune of Martyr. Alec eased for a moment as the pain subsided.

"That is why I used an enchanted arrow."

"What?" Angemesis barely had time to look down at the arrow before it exploded with the power of the force rune. Nemesis and Abaddon were thrown backwards and Talia's chains shattered. Talia, now free, dove off from the side of the dais and grabbed Alec into her arms as the others swarmed the marble stairs leading to the oculus.

"Lord Abaddon, what shall I do?" Nemesis asked as she began to rise. Cracks had appeared upon her face, arms and hands as if she were made of glass. Blackened lines appeared within the cracks as her malevolent energy seeped out. The suit of armor began to rise grasping at a couple of stray pieces that had fallen off from his body.

"I CARE NOT, MY BODY IS INCOMPLETE. I MUST RETREAT FOR THE MOMENT BEING. IF YOU WISH TO REDEEM YOURSELF FOLLOW ME." Nemesis rose and took her master's hand and vanished. Everyone's attention had now turned to Marec, Alec and Talia, who was desperately attempting to heal Alec. Eliza ran up to Alec, as did the others. She knelt down next to him and began speaking with him hoping to keep him conscious.

"I am sorry that we did not bring Oz. He could not fit through the narrow hole we dug to the stairwell and his wings were not strong enough to lift him up this high. I assure you, however, that he is alright." Eliza tried to comfort her friend as she looked over to the mutilated body of her uncle.

"I...am...sorry...Eliza." Alec strained to speak. Talia pulled Alec up to her chest and rocked Alec's head in her arms. Eliza shook her head as she cried, looking at the broken bodies of her uncle and best friend.

"There was nothing you could have done. This was his choice." Eliza spoke as she sniffled and attempted to wipe the tears from her eyes before Alec could see them. "Do not speak, Alec. You need to save your strength." Alec smiled weakly and let out a scoffing exhale, which sounded as though it may have been his last breath and he batted his hand playfully through the air.

"No...worries...I...feel...great." Everyone in the room could not help, but let out a nervous laugh as they looked at Alec's shattered body, Eliza especially.

"You are a lousy liar." Alec smiled again at her response.

"Talia, hurry, can you not heal him!?" Zelus yelled at her. Talia shook her head, screaming hysterically, tears pouring from her eyes.

"I CANNOT! I TRIED TO HEAL HIM, BUT THE RUNE HE USED TO SAVE ME WILL NOT LET ME!" She quaked and trembled as she continued to cry. Her tears continued to pour onto Alec's face, keeping him awake. Alec reached up and placed his hand on Talia's cheek.

"Not..much..for..parties..but..happy birthday." Everyone, including Talia smiled at Alec as each continued to weep.

"Thank you, Sir Alec. Please stay with me?" Talia smiled at him.

"You..are..free..now." Talia's eyes began to burn from the mass number of falling tears.

"But my freedom will not mean as much, if you do not stay beside me." Alec smiled.

"Promise...me...something?" Talia placed her hand over his and nuzzled it lovingly.

"What is it?"

"Li..ve" Everyone huddled closer around Alec as he looked over his friends one last time, smiled triumphantly and then died. Everyone tipped their heads and cried as the light faded from his eyes. Talia leaned her head down and gently kissed Alec's brow as she reached her hand over his face and closed his eyes.

Eliza collapsed to her knees and Zelus, whose eyes were now entirely swollen stepped forward.

"No, Alec!" He walked forward and knelt opposite of Talia. You cannot die, you selfish bastard! Not now!" Zelus continued to break down as everyone gave up on holding back their tears. Talia wrapped her entire body around Alec's lifeless vessel, gripping at his arms and chest as the shock fully sank in. Far down below, they could hear the terrified cries of Oz as he desperately tried to reach his empathy partner.

Everyone passed the time in silence, fates pendulum having frozen those sorrow filled moments eternally, until suddenly a burst of light struck the room, restoring time and blinding everyone.

"I am Aurora, nymph of Aneira and speaker of her holy rite. I come with a message from the Lady Seraphina. You are worthy." Everyone, save Talia, backed away from Alec as Aurora's bare feet touched the ground and she walked to Alec. Talia looked up to Aurora, her eyes swollen with tears.

"Please do not cry young divine, I am not here to reap him." Aurora knelt down and pressed her finger into Alec's chest.

"GAH!" Alec's body shot upright as he took in a deep breath, filling his lungs.

"ALEC!" Everyone cried though no one dared to rush up to them. Talia leaned down to listen to his heartbeat and having felt its gentle rhythm kissed him on the forehead.

"He's alive." Talia assured everyone who cheered in unison. Talia continued to hold Alec as Aurora began to speak again.

"I am afraid that he will have to come with me still." Talia looked up to

Aurora with fear in her eyes.

"I thought you said that you were not here for him?"

"I said that I was not here to reap him. However, his body has been badly damaged and will not recover by normal means. His recovery shall take quite some time, which you do not have. He requires training and so I shall leave his body with you but his spirit must come with me until his body has been repaired."

"What do you require of us? How can we heal him?" Talia asked, her body still quivering from the shock of it all.

"Return to Valascaa. Within the temple at the center of the labyrinth the knights use for their trials, there is a shrine. You must take him to this shrine and lay him upon the altar beneath the Aneiran blossom. The nectar the tree produces is normally poisonous to people, yet, to him, it will help speed his recovery. The tree will produce sap for him once a day. He will need for you to aid him in drinking the sap. Do this, and he shall return to you stronger than he is now."

"How long will his recovery take?"

"It is difficult to say, but it will take several months before he becomes able to awaken. You must endure and be patient young divine and your love shall come back to you." Aurora began to glow brightly, everyone averted their eyes as the light intensified and she vanished. Talia opened her eyes and began to do her best to care for Alec.

"What did she say to you?" Eliza asked as she kneeled down grabbing Talia's shoulder.

"She told me to take him back to Valascaa. Once there, I am to care for him. I can explain on the way but we need to get him back as quickly as possible."

"Of course." Eliza turned back to her deceased uncle. "We shall need to bury our dead as well." Dominic and Nilus covered Marec's body and lifted him up and began to descend the tower as Zelus kneeled down next to Talia holding out his arms.

"May I?" She looked up at him and helping him to remove Alec's armor, allowed for Zelus to lift Alec into his arms and begin to carry him down below. As they exited the spire, they looked up to see that the moon had now passed the sun, which now shone dimly as it began to sink below the horizon. After several minutes, they managed to arrive within the entrance to the spire, which had been widened by several of the knights who had remained below.

"*BREE!*" Oz screeched ferociously as he ran up on the party and began to inspect Alec. Zelus dropped to a knee and lifted up Alec's hand for Oz, who nuzzled it with his beak.

"We got him Oz." Zelus spoke to the griffin softly. Oz turned his eyes toward Zelus and gently rubbed his face alongside his.

"Oz? Are you going to be my friend now?" Zelus reached out to pet the lion hawk's beak.

"*Scree!*" Oz shrieked as he snapped at Zelus' hand as if trying to bite it off.

"Ah, you stupid bird!" Zelus began to yell at Oz who squawked back at him savagely while the others stood around laughing at him weakly, their hearts still thoroughly broken. Finally, Eliza turned towards Oz.

"We need to return home Oz. We have to heal Alec so that he can come back." Oz chirped and trotted off toward the northwest, where Valascaa lay. "Talia, would you do the honors of riding with Alec? We need someone to hold him so that he doesn't fall off from the horse." Talia nodded her head as she reached out for the horse that one of the knights pulled forward for her.

Very carefully, Zelus lifted Alec up onto the horse in front of Talia and began to tie him down. Handing Talia the reins they secured Alec further so that she would more easily manage the burden. Next Eliza turned to Oz.

"Oz, you can reach home much faster than the rest of us. Can you deliver a message to my father?" Oz chirped which they took for yes, so, as Dominic, Nilus and Zelus worked to remove Oz's battle armor, Eliza wrote out her message.

"Thank you, Oz. Please hurry, we will want to come as quietly as possible." Oz took Eliza's message and with a couple of flaps and a running start, flew off towards the northwest. As Oz disappeared from sight, Eliza whipped her hand in a circle around her head, signaling for the knights to mount up and prepare to leave the citadel behind. Dominic and Nilus stayed on the ground as did nearly half of the knights.

"Alright, you all know the plan. We shall return home with our report. Everyone else stay here and hold the citadel until someone returns with further orders. Thank you all for your sacrifice today." The men cheered as Eliza, and all those bound for Valascaa, turned their horses and rode home.

Chapter 40 – The Last Paladin of Highmoore

When they arrived home, a full day had nearly passed and the sun had long since set. The sky was now dark. The ground was lightly luminesced by the light of the full moon. As they approached the gates of Valascaa, they found them to already be opened, with a group of knights waiting for them. Talia held Alec close to her trying to use her body to keep him warm. They passed the guards who followed behind them closing the gates as they came in.

Talia flinched slightly as she heard the gates shut. The anxiety from the past few days had left her quite rattled. She rode her horse in at a slow trot, following Eliza. Talia was having a difficult time keeping her eyes open as they had not stopped to rest once since they left the citadel. They had dared not ride hard due to Alec's condition and Talia was eager to take Alec into the labyrinth. She watched as the Lion walked up to her and, placing his hand on the horse's mane, walked beside her.

"I am glad to see that you are alright?"

"Thank you Sir Talic. I thank thee for your assistance. I fear I would not be here now if it had not been for your aid." Talia said.

"Alec would have come for you either way. He and my brother both." The Lion turned his eyes towards Marec's body, which was draped over the back of his horse, still covered by Dominic's cape.

"I am also very sorry for the loss of your brother. I assure you that he met a most valiant end."

"He would have had it no other way. Out in a blaze of glory, that is the Kaldur way." It seemed to her that, despite the Lion's powerful demeanor and brave face, inside, his soul had been crushed and was burning. The Lion paused for a moment as he looked at the horse bearing the mantle wrapped remains of his elder brother.

"Enough of the fallen. There will be a time to mourn and a time to bury our honorable dead. What is it that must be done with Alec?"

"I must take him to center of the knights' trials. I need to take him to the shrine within where he will be kept safe."

"I see, though I do not understand. I shall guide you there myself." Talia looked around.

"Is Tear safe?"

"Yes, she is in my home. You are welcome to stay with us as well if you like. It would probably make for an easier transition if you also posed as my niece."

"I would agree. I most graciously accept your offer."

"Excellent. Once we have taken Alec within the maze then we shall move you in so that you can get some rest." Talia turned towards Eliza and Zelus.

"Sir Talic and I are going to take Alec within the labyrinth. You two please head on without me. Once I have tended to Alec, I shall return to Eliza's house." Eliza nodded and rode off while Zelus eyed Talia.

"Will you allow me to come with you in the morning?" Zelus asked. Talia nodded her head.

"Of course Sir Zelus, now please go get some rest." She requested. Zelus nodded and then rode further into town. Talia followed the Lion across town, trying desperately to keep her eyes open. Finally, they arrived outside of the trials. The Lion helped her to dismount from her horse, first helping to pull Alec down and then allowing for Talia to brace herself against his shoulders and lower herself.

"I shall carry Alec. Please follow my lead. The maze should not hinder us." The Lion spoke as he carried Alec inside. They walked within and straight forward leading them to the old building.

"Normally it is not as easy to get through here but, seeing as how our mission is not to prove ourselves but to save young Alec, it has made it easy for us to make it through." Talia ran in front of the Lion and opened the door for him.

"Thank you," the Lion spoke as he walked inside and began walking across the temple. They neared the altar where young knights knelt to drink from the fountain, which opened up, allowing for light to pour in during the day. There they found the Aneiran blossom. The Lion walked over to the altar that rested beneath the ancient tree and laid Alec down.

Talia approached Alec and saw that the tree had already begun to leak the precious sap that she needed. She ran over to the fountain and grabbed the cup that sat next to it. She held the cup protectively beneath the tree and watched as the sap flowed and dripped down into the cup. The sap stopped dripping out, leaving Talia with about half a cup.

Taking the golden sap, she lifted Alec's head up from the dais and gently began to pour the sap into his mouth. After allowing him to slowly sip the sap for several moments, she had managed to aid him in drinking all of it. She sat with him for a moment stroking his hair. She stayed there with him for several moments before she kissed him on his lips and turned back toward the Lion.

"We should leave his things with him." Talia nodded her head as she grabbed Alec's swords and shield and laid them next to him, placing the Sidonis sword within his hands.

"I am ready now."

"Alright then, please follow me." The Lion turned and led Talia back through the labyrinth. They exited the maze and walked out into the cool night air. As they walked, Talia thought to herself about what she was to do now that Alec was gone. She knew that from now on she would have to protect Alec. She considered to herself all of the things that she had learned from he and Marec.

"Sir Talic."

"Yes?" He looked at her as they walked.

"I wish to join the knights. I must learn to honor Alec by becoming a defender of the people."

"Very well, I shall see to it that you start at the beginning of next week. I will have Eliza take you under her wing as a private tutor. We will not be able to use your real name while you stay with us I am afraid. Have you given any consideration as to what you wish to go by while you stay here?" Talia thought to herself for a moment considering the nature of her new identity.

"Then I shall be your niece. Just call me Relina Kaldur."

"Agreed." They continued to walk across town until they arrived at the Lion's home.

"Tomorrow, I must convene with the council, to sort out this whole situation. We have more than enough proof that Angelica was plotting an attack against the capital. The problem will be convincing them that what happened will play in their benefit should they take claim of the event. I would not have my niece troubling herself with the politics of the matter. After you have tended to Alec in the morning, how about you have Eliza show you around and begin tutoring you as a knight?" Talia nodded her head as they reached the door and quietly walked inside.

"I would very much like that."

"Glad to hear it, for now, please come this way. I am sorry that we lack extra space. For the time being, we will have to have you share a room with my daughter and Tear." Talia smiled and curtsied gracefully.

"Your hospitality is most gracious, I thank you for your troubles. I would be more than happy to share a space with Eliza and Tear. We have grown quite close over the past few months."

"Very well then. Rest well priestess." Talia curtsied again as she carefully opened the door and, entering the room, laid on the bed and immediately fell asleep.

Alec opened his eyes and rose from the cold stone that supported him. He traced his hands over his body searching for his wounds. Confirming that he was, in fact, whole, Alec threw his legs over the edge of the table and stood. He looked around and began to walk the strange room.

It was a wide space similar to the room he was in when he first arrived in Highmoore though this was not that room. The floor was still the same, the walls were of the same marble like stone yet there was no fountain in this room. Alec looked out and saw that the room he was in was nearly identical to that of the top floor of the goddess spire.

He looked at the floor and saw a long red carpet similar to what he would expect to see in a throne room, he turned following the carpet and found a throne sitting at the end of it. He looked up the walls and saw magnificent curtains hanging from the window ledges, bearing the seal of the lion hawk.

"So, I am in Highmoore." Alec spoke aloud to himself as he walked over to the window ledge and stared out over the massive balcony that wrapped around the tower. Below he could see the town, hidden behind its mighty walls and he imagined what it must have been like to once live there.

Alec left the balcony and, following the red carpet down the stairs, walked towards the massive double doors at the end. Alec pressed the doors open and walked outside into the great marble hallway. He stared around at the cathedral ceilings as he found a stairwell. He descended the stairs and looked to his left, seeing the familiar entrance to the library and, turning to his right, opened the door and walked inside.

As he expected, he entered the room to see the Lady Seraphina on the opposite side of the room awaiting him. She slowly turned and smiled her beautiful smile as her eyes met Alec's.

"Welcome back young paladin, you have made me most proud." Alec looked at her with confusion apparent on his face.

"Why am I here? I thought that I had failed my trial." Seraphina smiled wider before answering Alec's question.

"Please forgive my deception, young paladin. Your trial did not begin until you chose to leave here. I showed you the portrait of Nemesis's human form in order to push you in the right direction. The trial was a test of heart. You fought Belias and won, all the while controlling your rage and not letting it conquer you. Had you failed to do this, Daemon would have claimed your heart and not even Aurora would have been able to save you. You only further proved your worthiness when you chose to cast the Martyr rune in order to save the divine Talia Degracia." Alec stood in shock and awe, for once his impulsive decision making had paid off. He thought about what Seraphina said in regards to Nemesis.

"I have another question if I may Lady Seraphina."

"What do you ask, young one?"

"Who is Angemesis?"

"I am afraid I know not who you refer to." Seraphina's smile vanished. Alec scratched his head as he tried to explain.

"Well, she calls herself Angelica. You and Abaddon call her Nemesis. I decided to go with Angemesis." Seraphina's smile did not return, but she nodded her head indicating that she understood.

"I had never considered that Angelica and Nemesis were one in the same." She began. "That would explain how she had lived for so long and been undetected by any of the other nymphs. She was once a nymph like myself, the nymph of Aneira's wrath. Our holy mother was not always as loving and kind as she is now.

Long ago, during the dark times, when our world was newly created, Aneira was young and as is the case with all youth, she was known to embrace a darker nature from time to time.

It was during her battle with her father that Nemesis was created. She was the youngest of the nymphs before myself and it was her that was chosen to carry Aneira's sword. With Aneira's sword in hand Nemesis struck back at Daemon's legions in the name of her beloved mother and, with her help and the aid of her siblings, Aneira managed to seal Daemon away." Alec had to halt Seraphina.

"What do you mean when you say 'her siblings'?"

"Yes, Aneira has many brothers and sisters and each is given credit for birthing one of the races of Valoria."

"We have never been taught anything about the other races. I suppose I never suspected that there was more than Aneira and Daemon."

"That would be thanks to Nemesis and Daemon."

"Why is it that Nemesis betrayed Aneira?" Alec was curious to learn more of the connection between the two. Again, Seraphina's smile vanished.

"Depending on who you asked, it was Aneira who betrayed Nemesis. Nemesis did just as she had been created to do. She rained Aneira's wrath down upon Daemon's forces and brought ruin to all those who supported him. It was towards the end of the war when Nemesis plunged her weapon into the heart of the country of those who supported Daemon, rendering it of all life. This was the day that the Scar was created.

Aneira was horrified at the atrocities her favorite child had enacted. It was then that the war ended. Aneira went into isolation for a time and it was left to Aurora to decide the fate of Nemesis. When Nemesis returned home, she was enraged that she had been unable to finish wiping out the enemy, citing that they may one day rise to resurrect Daemon. Aurora had no choice but to take from

Nemesis her sword and called for Nemesis to dwell on the cost of her actions. It was not long after that, Nemesis with her rage turned against Aneira who she believed abandoned her." Seraphina stopped and looked out over the balcony.

"Is that all? What happened next?"

"Simple, Nemesis could not be swayed. She grew corrupted gave into those things which Daemon held sacred and for such she fell from grace. After she fell, Abaddon appeared to her and she has been lost to him ever since. After so many years, I had assumed that she had vanished, but it seems now that she is back in the fold." Alec thought to himself about Seraphina's story and considered himself even luckier that he had managed to survive a run in with such an enemy. He looked back to the Lady and asked her.

"So, what is it that I am doing here? I have not died, have I?"

"No, quite the opposite, you are here to grow stronger so that you are ready to face off against the enemy." Alec remembered the final moments of his battle with Belias. He cringed when he thought of the immense power Abaddon possessed if he were able to eradicate Belias with nothing more than a few words.

"What will Abaddon do now that he is freed?" Alec had never seen such a glum look on Seraphina's face.

"I imagine that he will spend some time to recover. Then, he will begin to recreate his army. First, he will start by bringing back the manticore."

"What exactly are the manticore? I have heard of them before though I have never known of one outside of legend."

"They are abominations. Abhorrent creatures that feed on death and despair. They possess the body and head of a lion, the wings of a giant bat, and the tail of a scorpion. To defeat one shall require you to face the deepest of nightmares."

"How do I defeat something like that?"

"You must train. Your body has been rendered to a near catatonic state. Your spirit, however, has been left to me to make stronger until you are able to return. Likewise, one of my messengers will approach your friends, to inform them to train as well. The strength of all Valoria is to be tested in the months to come."

"Where do the manticore come from?" The Lady Seraphina looked down at her own feet with a most distraught expression upon her face.

"They are born, hatched from the eggs of tainted Lion Hawks."

"What!?" Alec jumped back with alarm at the news. Seraphina nodded her head before she spoke again.

"Abaddon, found a way to not only harness the power of the Valorian soul, but to harness the powers of most creatures that live on Valoria. He uses this power to twist the creatures of this land into horrific forms. The manticore is one such creation and they are born from the eggs of the lion hawks." Alec thought to himself for a moment and realized that was the reason that Rayne found Oz's egg that day. Oz was meant to become a manticore. Angelica had merely laid the groundwork for Abaddon's return by allowing the Forsaken to steal them and cripple the only force on Valoria with the knowledge, power and ability to defeat them.

"How long do we have before Abaddon makes his move?"

"In your reality, I estimate that it will take Abaddon six months to recover and then perhaps another month before his army marches."

"How can you know this?"

"The holy mother deeds us with many gifts. Mine was once sight, but with it has come a deal of intuition. This is how I knew what would compel you to begin your trial."

"When do I begin?"

"Now! Rise up and become the true heir of Sidonis!" The wind engulfed Seraphina as she grew in stature, her hair whipping violently through the air, and rose to attack.

Acknowledgments

As I fully step into this new phase of my life, and with my words, determine my new course, I wish to thank a few special people.

My first fan, my mother, who has long told me, to follow my passions, even if people think you are crazy.

My 12th grade Creative Writing Teacher, Mark Sundermann, with whom I may not have rediscovered my love of writing.

My daughter, Ashlynne, for asking me to read you a story, I had never intended to finish.

And to my wife, Kristian, whose stories, I hope to inspire. Thank you for being with me at my lowest, and for accepting my weirdness.

Other works by J.A. Bullen

In the Legends of Valoria;

The Rise of the Divine Knight (Book II)

Coming Soon

The Shield of Aneira (Book III)

Upcoming Series;

Blood in the Rain: Chronicles of the Hunter

Made in the USA
Lexington, KY
08 September 2017